The Naked Light

Also by Bridget Collins

The Betrayals
The Binding
The Silence Factory

YOUNG ADULT
The Traitor Game
A Trick of the Dark
Tyme's End
Gamerunner
The Broken Road
MazeCheat
Love in Revolution

The Naked Light

BRIDGET COLLINS

THE BOROUGH PRESS

The Borough Press
An imprint of HarperCollins*Publishers* Ltd
1 London Bridge Street
London SE1 9GF

www.harpercollins.co.uk

HarperCollins*Publishers*
Macken House, 39/40 Mayor Street Upper
Dublin 1, D01 C9W8, Ireland

First published by HarperCollins*Publishers* 2025

1

Copyright © Bridget Collins 2025

Bridget Collins asserts the moral right to be identified as the author of this work

A catalogue record for this book is available from the British Library

Hardback ISBN: 978-0-00-842408-4
Trade Paperback ISBN: 978-0-00-842407-7

'Peace' by Eleanor Farjeon © Eleanor Farjeon, 1953, published by Oxford University Press, reproduced by kind permission by David Higham Associates

This novel is entirely a work of fiction. The names, characters and incidents portrayed in it are the work of the author's imagination. Any resemblance to actual persons, living or dead, events or localities is entirely coincidental.

Set in Meridien LT Std by HarperCollins*Publishers* India

Printed and bound in the UK using 100% Renewable Electricity by CPI Group (UK) Ltd

All rights reserved. No part of this publication may be reproduced, stored in a retrieval system, or transmitted, in any form or by any means, electronic, mechanical, photocopying, recording or otherwise, without the prior written permission of the publishers.

Without limiting the author's and publisher's exclusive rights, any unauthorised use of this publication to train generative artificial intelligence (AI) technologies is expressly prohibited. HarperCollins also exercise their rights under Article 4(3) of the Digital Single Market Directive 2019/790 and expressly reserve this publication from the text and data mining exception.

This book contains FSC™ certified paper and other controlled sources to ensure responsible forest management.

For more information visit: www.harpercollins.co.uk/green

For Nicole

Peace

I.

I am as awful as my brother War,
I am the sudden silence after clamour.
I am the face that shows the seamy scar
When blood and frenzy has lost its glamour.
Men in my pause shall know the cost at last
That is not to be paid in triumphs or tears,
Men will begin to judge the thing that's past
As men will judge it in a hundred years.

Nations! whose ravenous engines must be fed
Endlessly with the father and the son,
My naked light upon your darkness, dread! -
By which ye shall behold what ye have done:
Whereon, more like a vulture than a dove,
Ye set my seal in hatred, not in love.

II.

Let no man call me good. I am not blest.
My single virtue is the end of crimes,
I only am the period of unrest,
The ceasing of horrors of the times;
My good is but the negative of ill,
Such ill as bends the spirit with despair,
Such ill as makes the nations' soul stand still
And freeze to stone beneath a Gorgon glare.

Be blunt, and say that peace is but a state
Wherein the active soul is free to move,
And nations only show as mean or great
According to the spirit then they prove. -
O which of ye whose battle-cry is Hate
Will first in peace dare shout the name of Love?

Eleanor Farjeon

I

Sketches for A Mask, pencil on paper, 1918

Kit had not expected it to be so beautiful. That was her first impression, as she pushed open the *portière* and set down her suitcase on the paving stones, digging her hand into her aching shoulder: she was taken aback at how beautiful it was. She drew a long breath, looking round. After the hot dust and bare stone of the street, the courtyard was as still and cool as a basin of water. The street she had left was not exactly ugly – Paris could never be that, even after three and a half years of war had left it scarred and grim – but this little garden with its diminutive plane tree and well-swept paths might have been a different world, orderly and serene, the shadows dappled green, the air scented with lavender. There was a cat basking on a window sill, as plump and well-fed as any peacetime pet, and from an open window above she heard the bright strains of a gramophone playing 'Over There'. There was a burst of male laughter, and two sets of footsteps hurried down an unseen staircase, growing louder as they descended; a moment later two young men in uniform emerged from the tall door that stood open to her left. They sauntered past her without an acknowledge-ment of her presence, jaunty and able-bodied, one of them offering a cigarette to the other as he pushed the gate open. As they went into the street they were still laughing.

She stood looking after them for a moment, wondering; but if one of them happened to glance back, and saw her staring . . . No, it would not be a good start. She stooped for her suitcase – she had not brought very much, but the delayed boat-train and the walk from the Gare du Nord had made her wish she had sent a trunk ahead of her instead – and with a grimace carried it into the building and up the stairs. The first floor, Portia had said. Again, the door stood open, the music louder now, and she hesitated, not sure whether to knock. A handwritten paper label pinned to the doorframe said neatly, in English, *Studio For Portrait Masks*. Another hand had scrawled, below that, *By appointment only please*; a third, so cramped it almost went over the bottom edge of the paper, had added, *Uniquement sur rendez-vous!!*

There was no bell that Kit could see. She took a deep breath – suddenly her heart was beating as hard as it had the first morning she walked into the Antiques Room at art school, when she had been almost too nervous to hold a pencil – and stepped over the threshold. '*Bonjour,*' she said, 'hello . . . ?'

The room was empty. Empty, that was, of people. There were long benches running perpendicular to the window, scattered here and there with tools; at the far end of one, a china vessel that looked like a chamber pot was connected with clips and rods to some kind of electrical contraption. Shelves ran across one wall, stacked with boxes and equipment. To her left, above the connecting door, hung the Union Flag, the Tricolore and the Stars and Stripes, all equally faded to pale blue and pink.

She took a curious step towards the bench. But before she could examine the thing with knobs and wires – she guessed it was an electroplating machine – she felt someone's eyes on her, disapproving. She turned, already smiling and holding out her hand, ready to introduce herself; but her smile froze, and her heart gave another uncomfortable thump. The wall she was now looking at, beside the door she had come in, was covered with plaster faces. There were rows of them, white and blank-eyed, so that it was like turning to discover she was on stage, in front of an audience; the gaze she had sensed was not human, but the blind, lifeless stare of a hundred plaster casts.

And they were not . . . not ordinary faces. She drew a breath to steady her heart, and stepped closer. Unpainted, they were more akin to Greek marbles than living men, and she was rather glad. The details that met her eyes were not macabre, as they would have been in life, but melancholy, as if the missing noses and jaws and eyes were the effect not of modern shrapnel but time, and the necessary, unremarkable damage of spades and eager fingers prising up something long buried. Here was one mostly intact, but for a patch of sheared smoothness at the side where an eye should have been; here was one with a mouth that was a ragged hole, as though he had somehow savaged himself with his own teeth; here—

But here her detachment failed. The first test, she thought, and was glad that she had not moved or made a sound.

Here was a face that had been obliterated almost entirely, until it was hardly more than a pattern of craters and mounds. It had one ear, a charming ear, clinging like a fungus on a bole of rough bark; the rest was— not there. Even in plaster, it commanded pity. And when you remembered that it was a model of real flesh, a real man . . . She shut her eyes, as if to catch her breath; then she opened them again and made herself look at the thing carefully, with an artist's gaze, noting the shapes and the way the light fell on it. She had better practise now, on something that could not return her gaze. And after a moment she raised her hand and ran her fingertips over the gnarled valley that might once have been a mouth.

'Kit, darling!'

She spun round. It was Portia, of course: Portia pale and without kohl or lipstick, in a shapeless sculptor's smock, her hair caught back from her face with a makeshift band. She flung out her arms in a dramatic flourish of welcome; and then, without pausing to extinguish her cigarette, gathered Kit into an embrace. She kissed both Kit's cheeks, *à la française*, and for a moment as they drew apart their lips brushed together; but there were more footsteps, and she muttered, 'More later, darling . . .' before she turned, with perfect composure, to announce, 'Eustache, this is Kit. She is *enchantée*, and so are you.'

The man who had followed her into the room was older, grey-haired and weary. He nodded, as if her words had relieved him of the need for pleasantries. 'Portia showed me your sketches,' he said, in nearly unaccented English. 'You have a talent for portraiture. But it is hard work here. I hope you are prepared for it.'

'I hope so too.'

Portia broke in, 'Don't be silly, Eustache, I've given Kit the dope – you know, the low down – oh dear,' she added, to Kit, 'half the soldiers who come to us are American, I'm afraid I've picked up all their slang . . . I mean I've told her what it's like,' she concluded.

'Yes,' Kit said, 'Portia has warned me. About the air raids and the strikes and the *pain national* as well.'

'Not to mention the shorter skirts,' Portia said, 'which are frankly *shocking* . . .'

Kit bit her lip. It would not do to laugh; she could not

tell how much this man Eustache knew about Portia, or indeed about Kit herself.

But Eustache only shrugged. 'It is war,' he said. 'We do what must be done. Today you follow Portia. She will show you everything.'

'I will – and thank you—'

'Two rules,' he said. 'First, this is a cheerful place. These men are not patients, they are honoured guests. We have laughter, we have music, we have cigarettes and playing cards. We are giving them back their lives, you understand? Their manhood.'

'Yes – of course—'

'Second,' he said, as if he had not heard her, 'there is one face above all to which you must pay attention. You comprehend? That is, *yours*. You will wear a mask as complete as any of theirs. If for one instant you show revulsion, horror, pity – then you have failed. It is a paradox, yes? We give them a new face, for they must have one to walk down the boulevards – but we never, never flinch from the one they truly have.'

'Yes,' Kit said. 'I understand.'

'Very well. It is hard, very hard,' he said again, shaking his head as if she could not possibly imagine; then he marched out of the room without another word.

Portia met her eyes, and giggled. 'He's awfully solemn,' she said. 'You should see him try to guffaw when the men crack jokes. He knows he ought to, but he hasn't much natural aptitude.'

Kit smiled; but she said, '*Is* it as hard as he says?'

'Well, darling, you've read my letters. It isn't a picnic, how could it be? But that's not the point. It's worthwhile. And it's a wonderful challenge – *such* good practice for after the war – think how improved your portraits will be.' She offered her hand to Kit, as if she heard the introductory bar of a waltz. 'And we'll be together. *So* much better than mouldering away at home, doing nothing.'

Kit took the hand she was holding out; but when Portia tugged she resisted, not wanting to embrace when anyone might walk in. 'I'm glad to be here,' she said.

'Good. Come this way, then. And later I'll show you our digs. Not Byzantium, I'm afraid, but thank God you're not a sybarite like me.' She led Kit to the door. 'Oh, darling,' she added, throwing a smile over her shoulder, 'I am *so* pleased you came! It will be the making of you, you'll see.'

'Yes,' Kit said, 'I know it will.'

She believed it when she said it. But as she turned to pick up her suitcase she met the gaze of one of the plaster masks, and its wound gave it a crooked sardonic smile, as if it knew better.

Phoebe climbed the hill in long strides. Already her dress was sticking to her. Sweat trickled down her spine. It was so hot that if she closed her eyes she wouldn't have known whether the sun was in the sky or at her feet, buried in the chalk. She came to the end of the glaring path and swung herself over the stile without pausing. She was not hurrying, exactly. She only wanted not to be seen, not to be called home.

When she reached the top field she slowed and glanced over her shoulder. There was no sign of anyone, no face at any of the windows of the vicarage. It sat in its hollow as still as a painting, its flint walls rising over the darker shadows of the garden. Her father was in his study; Mrs Reed was in the kitchen. No one had seen that she had gone. She was invisible, and free.

She wiped her forehead. The movement brought the sour scent of black dye wafting into her face. When Mama had died, long before the war, she had been too little to understand why she had to wear mourning. She had been bewildered by the kind women who measured her with long tapes and then produced, not the pretty things she wanted, but three frocks in plain black. She had only worn them because she had thought, confusedly, that Mama might come back if she did; at least until old Mrs Bone told her plainly that Mama was dead . . . But now there were no new clothes. She smelt of cheap dye, like everyone else, and her nicest summer dress was ruined. She was not even in mourning for a brother or a cousin, like the other girls at school. That would have been something. They huddled in groups, murmured to one another, and swapped poems about pale youth and its sacrifices. Once, sitting down for a lesson, she'd found a crumpled draft caught under the leg of her chair, *And when our country's call rang out, / He gave himself for me*; but a sharp hand had plucked it out of her grasp before she could read more, and a sharp voice hissed, '*You* wouldn't understand, Phoebe Manning.' It was true. She was top of her class in English, but that meant nothing. She was outside that enchanted circle. Mourning for fallen heroes was glamorous, mourning for an old woman was not. She could imagine how they would look at her: as though the death of her grandmother was self-indulgent, in bad taste, when so many young men laid down their lives every day. As though she was a poor relation, claiming kinship with the aristocracy.

She stared over the shoulder of the hill, narrowing her eyes. Could she hear the guns? There was no breeze to carry the sound. She could not even hear the sea. No, it must be the roar of blood in her ears, or the chalk thrumming in the heat. She stood still, listening, until she heard the hooves and wheels of Old Comfort's pony trap. A faint blur of dust rose from where the road ran between the trees, out of sight. In a few moments it would roll to a stop outside the vicarage. If she stayed still, straining her ears, she might hear voices, and the bell, and the unloading of baggage.

She swung round and carried on up the hill. It was steep, now. The grass was tough and thin, the bones of the world very close to the surface. Her blood drummed harder. At last, a few steps away, there was a wide length of bare chalk. She tilted her head up to stare at the rest of the pattern. It was the simplest possible face, a face in four lines: brief horizontal eyes, vertical nose, long impassive mouth. It was so familiar she could not remember ever seeing it for the first time, but from where she was standing some trick of perspective gave it a different expression. She sat down on the grass beside it and leant back. Under her skull the ground seemed to vibrate with a thick wasp-bottle hum. She closed her eyes. It was so hot, so hot . . . The whine in her ears grew. She was as giddy as the time Papa had left his tantalus unlocked and she'd sneaked a glass of brandy.

'You'll get a sunstroke,' a voice said. A shadow fell over her.

She opened her eyes. She didn't know how much time had passed. Even with a man blocking the sun she could tell it sat lower in the sky. She sat up.

The shadow did not move. But in spite of the dazzle she could make out his broad shoulders, his short knotty hair. He smelt peppery with young man's sweat. 'Hullo, George,' she said.

He stepped aside, grunting. Then he bent and picked up a clanking bucket. He set off up the hill. When he had reached the far eye of the Face he knelt down, his back to her, as if he were scrubbing a floor. He must have known that she was watching, but he didn't acknowledge her. After a while he reached for his bucket. He went over the eye again, then the other, and the nose. It was only when he came back down the slope to the mouth that she could see what he was doing. First he cut away the turf, neatening the edge of the line; then he crushed pieces of white stone and mixed them into a paste with water. Then he pounded it into the long line of chalk, painstakingly, shuffling along on his knees. When he reached the end he rolled his shoulders and stood up with a groan. He picked up the glass bottle lying on the grass and took a long drink from it, gulping until water ran down into his open collar. Then, at last, he met her eyes. Wordlessly he held out the bottle to her.

She took it. The mouth of the bottle was rancid from his lips, but she was thirsty. 'Thank you.'

He dropped to the ground beside her, took the empty bottle and slung it towards the bucket. It missed and rolled to rest against a tussock of grass.

'Ma made me come up here,' he said, at last. 'Before I go tomorrow.'

She nodded. A bird of prey was drifting high above them, a fleck in the blue.

'She doesn't want me to go. Not surprising, I s'pose.' He plucked a blade of grass from between his legs and ripped it into pieces. His sleeves were rolled up to above his elbow, and his arms were golden-brown, thick with muscle. 'But I've been waiting long enough, haven't I? And I'll be glad to get away from her. Since Peter copped it she's gone about with a face like a puddle of shit.'

'Aren't you scared?'

'Nah.' He grimaced and flicked the shreds of grass away. A gust of wind caught them and blew them across the nearest patch of newly whitened chalk.

'The Face looks better,' she said, to break the silence. 'I'm glad.'

'Huh.' He snorted. 'Ma's got you believing in it, then?'

She did not answer. She did not mind George – he was better than his brothers had been, they had imitated her accent and made 'stuck-up' faces at her when Mrs Bone was not looking – but when he sensed a weakness he dug his teeth in like a terrier and would not let go.

He smirked, amused by her silence. "Course you do,' he said. 'Always been fey, you. That's why Ma likes you so much.'

Fey. Mrs Bone often said that Phoebe knew things without needing to be told, which was the same thing; so she was not sure why George meant it as an insult.

'I s'pose girls like that sort of thing. Ghoulies and ghosties . . . Pity you're not a Bone, or you could do it for me.' He put on a high voice which was not at all like his mother's and squawked, '"Keep it awake. Keep it working. It's our job to keep it in good nick, us Bones. No one else can do it."'

'Why are you bothering, if you don't believe it?' Phoebe put her hand flat on the ground, as if the earth would feel her touch.

He snorted. 'I'm just keeping her happy. Suppose I should be grateful she doesn't want me to do it the way her granddad did, in the dead of night with the blood of a virgin.'

She felt her cheeks flush a little at the word *virgin*. It was not the word itself – it was in the Bible, wasn't it? – or the fact that she did not entirely know what it meant, except that it was something to do with not being married. It was the way he glanced at her as he said it. If she wanted to know once and for all what it meant, she might ask him now: but somehow she thought she would rather not. Instead she said, 'But—'

'Just another way to keep us in our place, isn't it?' He uprooted more grass, tearing and tearing. 'Bugger that. I'm not staying here for ever. When the war's over I'm going to go to London and be a motorcar mechanic.'

Did you need two hands to work on motorcars? He might not have both his arms, if he came back at all. But they were not supposed to say that kind of thing. When a schoolmistress had mentioned the maimed soldiers a few days ago there had been frowns from the girls, shaking heads, censorious looks. Even after four years of men returning crippled – disfigured, shell-shocked, blind – they pretended that all the sacrifices were glorious. She drew her knees up under her dress and gazed at the saggy, charcoal-coloured fabric. Poor George. He was a young man, not a boy, but suddenly, vertiginously, she felt older than him. She couldn't help glancing sideways. He was staring down the hill at the vicarage as though he were already seeing France.

She reached out and grasped his hand. It was meant to be motherly – elder-sisterly, at least – the way Aunt Florence had taken hold of her own hand at the funeral. But from the way George turned to stare at her, she had misjudged it somehow. Abruptly the word *virgin* rang in her head, striking a warning. He looked her up and down, and there was a sort of surprise in his face, a wondering, amused, gratified sort of expression. Her stomach clenched. She'd meant to console him; not – this.

'How old are you, now?'

'Thirteen,' she said. She tried to draw back her hand, but he was hanging on to it.

He smiled. His eyes slid back and forth, over her dingy black dress, over her knees and waist and chest. She hunched her shoulders, trying to hide the shape of her body. His grip tightened, his smile widened. 'And so pretty already,' he said.

In a polite little voice she said, 'Thank you.' She went

on trying to pull away, but he met her eyes, so obviously pleased by her discomfort that with an effort she let her arm go limp.

'How about a proper goodbye for a departing hero, then, Miss Phoebe?'

'Goodbye,' she said, in the same small voice; then, because he snorted and yanked at her arm, she made herself smile at him.

'Call that a goodbye? I might die out there. What about a kiss?'

He was bending towards her, his lips wet. His collar was gaping, showing the damp curls of hair on his chest. She thought, stupidly, of the girls at school. *He gave himself for me* . . . Would they tell her to kiss him? Wasn't it their job, the girls, to send the men off to war happy?

'Come on, sweetheart. Just a little kiss. Something to keep me warm when I'm in knee-deep in mud.'

She swallowed. Her mouth was drier than it was when she climbed the hill. If she kissed him, would he let go of her?

She tried to lean backwards, imperceptibly; but he leant with her, so that now she was off-balance, and his face was still too close to hers. She drew in her breath. She looked past him at the summer sky, the furthest hills, and put her lips to his cheek. She did not let herself think about what she was doing. Soon he would be gone. She would never have to tell anyone.

There, it was over. His skin was moist; it left a slick of sweat on her mouth. She wanted to wipe it away, but it would have been bad manners. She said, as if it were an etiquette lesson, 'Goodbye, George. I wish you the very best—'

But he did not let her finish. He jerked her into his arms, pressing his lips over hers as if he wanted to consume her.

She recoiled, but he moved with her, his body pinning her to the ground. She couldn't breathe. Panic swept through her: another moment and she would be swallowed whole, trapped—

She rolled frantically from side to side, trying to shake him off. He laughed, his mouth sliding wetly down her chin, and loosened his grasp. 'Don't be like that,' he said, but in the instant it took him to speak the words she had flung herself sideways. She struggled to her feet, but before she could take another step he had got hold of her ankle. He wrenched it and she fell. The ground was like stone, but she did not feel any pain. Only the impossibility of breathing, the impossibility of defending herself. The world shrank to blazing white chalk an inch from her face and the weight of hot hands on her waist, holding her down. She tried to crawl out from under him. She could feel him laughing.

Something thudded into the small of her back. It smashed her flat, her chin bouncing on the chalk. She might have been able to fight him if the rest of his body had not been on her leg, grinding her knee into the hard earth. His other hand slid up under her dress, grabbing for the skin above her stocking-top. He gripped a fistful of her flesh and squeezed, huffed with satisfaction into her ear. His breath was damp. 'You won't forget me while I'm away,' he gasped, hoarse, pleased. His fingers released, only to creep upwards. He chuckled.

She stopped moving. In front of her face the white chalk made an alien landscape: bare as a desert, pale as bones.

George grunted. He pushed himself up on one elbow, so that cool air reached her cheek. He fumbled with something, nudged her buttock with his knuckles. A drop of his sweat fell on to the back of her neck. She saw a hand on the chalk beside her head, and for a moment she did not realise it belonged to her. It was a pale hand, small, with the last softness of childhood. It lay limply, as though it was waiting for someone to take hold of it. But no one did. It was sympathy for that hand, that other child, that forced her to move.

Now. Now, while he was bearing his own weight – while he was tugging at his trousers, hissing through his teeth . . .

She flipped herself over, pushing so hard against the ground that it felt as if it pushed back, helping her. Her head hit something – George's elbow – and for an instant he reared up, caught off-guard. His shirt was untucked, his hand still at his groin. She jerked her knee up with all her strength and then, as he yowled and toppled, scrabbled out from underneath his fall. He curled into a ball, whimpering. She staggered down the hill, the slope steeper than she was expecting, as though the earth had tilted away from its ordinary axis. Now she was far enough away. He would never touch her again. She came to a halt: not because she wanted to linger, but because she had started to shake. She did not trust her legs to hold her up. She crouched before her knees could betray her, and watched George's sobbing breaths slow.

At last he sat up, and bared his teeth at her. 'Bitch,' he said. 'Bloody bitch.'

She had only ever heard the word used by Major Fenlow, about Taffy and her pups. But she understood, at least, George's contempt. She had stolen something from him. Dirtied the floor, soiled a priceless rug . . . But the shame washing over her met something else, something that would not let it in. She slid her hands forward through the short grass. She could feel the hum of the stone under the thin earth, and the prickle of heat under her skin. In her ears the deep chalk-song rose again, that hornet-whine of latent power. He was sitting right across the mouth of the Face, the renewed line beneath him as clear as a wound.

There was a smear of white dust down the side of his head, a vertical half-mask.

'You'll die out there,' she said, with a deep, unexpected certainty.

'What?'

But there was no need to repeat herself. He had heard the words, he could still hear them, he would go on hearing them. He would die hearing them, knowing that at last they had come true. And they *would* come true. She got to her feet. She was completely steady now: the shuddering had gone, poured out into the Sussex ground through her fingertips. She looked at him, and he flinched.

The graze on her chin began to sting. Her dress was streaked with pale dust.

'Goodbye, George,' she said. And somehow it was easy to turn her back on him and walk down the hill towards the gate of the vicarage garden, leaving him glaring after her, nothing but a temporary blemish on the face of the hill.

Florence sat down upon the sagging bed and bowed her head. Her suitcase sat empty upon the threadbare rug at her feet. She had never noticed before how warped and stained it was. Not that it had mattered, while it sat unused in the box room of their old house; not that it mattered now, when she had unpacked it and had no prospect of travelling anywhere else. She flipped it shut with a stockinged foot, kicked it backwards, out of sight under the bed, and looked around the room.

Her things looked even more meagre than they had before she unpacked them. The clothes she had brought with her fitted easily in the chest of drawers and wardrobe; the rest would follow in a few days in her trunk, and be carried up to the attic to await the colder weather. And there was very little else – little enough to show for nearly twenty-six years of existence. Perhaps, if she had begged to be allowed to keep Mother's treasures, Dr Manning would have humoured her, against his better judgement. But what good would it have been? For a moment she saw this small room crammed to its sloping ceiling with dinner services, silk flowers, jelly moulds, bed linen, candlesticks and silly little vases too diminutive for anything but snowdrops. No, it was better to let it be given away or sold, and be left with nearly nothing. She had her work basket, and letter case, and a dozen or so books. And on the mantelpiece, at a cramped, drunken angle, sat Alexandra Euphemia, her old doll, her dress dingy and her ringlets a little lopsided. Florence remembered unwrapping her one birthday – had she been five, or six? – casting aside the bright paper as Imogen suggested foolish names to make her giggle: 'I do think Candelabra is a lovely name – or Encyclopaedia – or Effluent . . .' No, that detail could not be right, she would not have known what *effluent* meant. But the memory was so vivid she could close her eyes now and see Imogen laughing, in a pale lacy gown, her hair up; and Mother and Father, too, smiling. For once she, Florence, had been the centre of attention. That must have been before she became awkward and mulish, overshadowed by Imogen's easy loveliness. And the doll – Effie for short, unless she had been naughty – had slept beside her for years, and then, when Florence was too old for toys, sat beside her mirror, never quite cast aside.

She was quite a big doll, too big for the mean little mantelpiece; she might slide off into the hearth and break. Florence replaced her in the suitcase and slid it back under the bed, out of sight. That was better; although now the shallow mantel looked very bare. Never mind. There was nothing she could do to improve it. She already guessed that any fire in the grate below would be too small to give proper heat, if it drew at all; and no doubt it would be as cold in December as it was oppressively hot now. Yes, it was a shabby, cramped, uncomfortable room, a maid's room. She should not resent that, when she would be living on Dr Manning's charity – but she did, naturally she did, she would not have been human if she didn't. Imogen's bedroom was below, empty and pristine, as if Imogen might return; and even if Imogen had been alive, she would have given Florence the day nursery, instead of making her sleep up here . . . But Dr Manning had not thought of it, or cared.

She strode to the window. For a desperate moment she thought it had been painted shut. Then, at last, it gave, and she staggered as the sash jerked up. The exertion had brought out a sweat on her forehead, but the air outside was so still that even with the window wide there was no breeze to dry it. She leant out over the hot tiles, and at last a sweet soft eddy touched her face and neck. The deep green of the treetops and the garden below calmed her; she drew a long, conscious breath, and caught the scents of dust and jasmine. A woodpigeon was calling in the tree overhanging the road, the notes repeating with an incessant yearning monotony. It brought back a flash of summer childhood afternoons, spent reading or making paper bonnets for Effie in the shade of a chestnut tree; and all of a sudden her eyes were hot and her throat aching. Those afternoons on the lawn of the Eastbourne villa, while Mother cut ribbons beside her, or helped to spell out the hardest words, or rang for lemonade and seedcake . . . In spite of Mother's faults – and a kind daughter would forgive her those without even counting them – she had loved her children. It was only after Father died, leaving her disconsolate and bewildered, that her love took on a sour, possessive note; and only after Imogen escaped that Florence had felt the full force of that love concentrated on herself. Poor Mother. If her sons had lived . . . But if her sons had lived, they might still be dead now; and it must be worse to lose a son in manhood than to give him up early, before he was really a person. Florence had said as much once to Mother, and they had quarrelled terribly over it. But it stood to reason. She did not miss her brothers, never having known them; why should it have been so different for Mother? Dead infants were better than dead boys – a mercy, a silver lining . . .

Suddenly she bent her head, unable to hold back her tears. She was crying for Mother, poor Mother, heartsick and lonely; and for herself, too, bereft, unable to make amends for all the unkind things she'd said, all the times she'd felt Mother's affection pinch like an outgrown shoe, and let it show . . . She cried out of shame for her own thoughts, despairing of her own character, because she was bitter and ungrateful and selfish, and because now she had no one to love. And then, because once she began to cry it was hard to stop, she cried for the world and the last years, when somehow it had become mere pragmatism to be glad that little boys had died early.

At last the church clock struck a lazy three-quarters, and she found that she had run dry. She wiped her face with her palms and took one, two, three steadier breaths. Better. She hoped, belatedly, that Dr Manning had not heard her through his open study window. How loudly had she been sobbing? She should not have let herself go like that. Mother would have— no, if she thought of Mother she would set herself off again. Resolutely she raised her chin and gazed out at the garden. Beyond the trees rose the church tower and a few scattered roofs. On her right was the village; on her left, if she craned sideways, was the thinner, drabber green of the down, rising to meet the flat hot sky. A figure – a young man, one of the farmer boys, she guessed – was making his way down the slope, his head lowered. Above him, cut into the chalk, was a pattern of lines – a pattern so spare and brief that it was astonishing how clearly it was a face.

The Haltington Face, of course. She remembered how proudly Imogen had pointed it out to them when they visited, adding, 'But you must ask Horace. He is the expert on it. It has a whole chapter in his book.' The ten-year-old Florence had tried not to giggle, distracted by the absurdity of Dr Manning's name being Horace; and Mother had swept on past the window, being more concerned with the plumbing and ventilation. But two years later, when Florence was sitting beside Imogen in the day nursery, gazing out into the spring sunshine, Imogen had said in a different tone, 'Are you looking at the Face? It is friendly, isn't it? At first I didn't like it, I thought it was watching me. But now I think it looks after us. When I was waiting for Baby to come, I would lie on the chalk and watch the clouds and dream, and I knew it would keep us both safe . . . And when she did come – well, I won't tell you all about it, darling, it was horrid – but I could see it from the bedroom window, and I was in such a state I almost prayed to it. And then when the nasty bit was over, at dawn, I think it must have been the first face Baby ever saw. Before mine, anyway.' She laughed softly. 'Don't tell Mother or Horace, will you? Horace says it is a leftover of pagan rites, and it would be sinful to let our curiosity cross over into reverence. But I am glad it is there. It keeps us company, Baby and me.' She drew Phoebe closer to her breast, and smiled down at her: a shining gold-and-ivory icon, *Madonna and Child*.

Florence smiled too, but she was glad to have an excuse to turn back to the window, hiding the sting of exclusion. The sparse chalk marks stared back at her. The eyes were flat ovals, the mouth a horizontal line. Was it a friendly face? She would not have said so. Nor was it exactly *un*friendly.

It had no expression at all, really – or every expression at once, like one of those illusions that flickered between contradictory images, reflecting back to you whatever you were looking for. She preferred the White Horse at Hindover: that, at least, you could understand.

'It is marvellous by moonlight,' Imogen had murmured, resting her cheek on Phoebe's downy head, 'when no one else is awake but Baby and me . . .'

'Doesn't the nursemaid get up at night?'

'I don't wake her.' Imogen made an impish moue, as though she were admitting to a peccadillo. 'Baby is so very sweet when she is feeding. We sit here alone, and everything is so silent, and nothing can harm us. I think she will be a lucky child, living here, just under the hill.'

Florence did not answer. She did not especially care for the chalk pattern – *pagan rites* sounded almost as dull as Dr Manning's sermons – but she felt an odd ache in her chest. What was it like to be Imogen, watching the darkness with the weight of her baby in her arms, happy in spite of her pallor and violet-touched eyes? She opened her mouth to ask if she might hold Phoebe, and shut it again. Phoebe was not hers. It would not be the same.

'Dear old Florrie,' Imogen said, absently kissing Phoebe's tiny fist. 'I am sorry, you know, that you're stuck with Mother all on your own. But it won't be for long. And when you're married – when you have your own baby . . .'

'Suppose I never do?' In sudden panic Florence thought of Miss Parks, who gave her piano lessons: poor Miss Parks, to whom Mother said one must be kind. 'Suppose no one wants me— ?'

'Don't be silly.' Imogen began to stretch out a hand, but the movement woke Phoebe, who began to wail. 'Ah, darling, is the naughty sun in your eyes? Shall I draw the curtain, then? Hush, sweet one, hush, diddle-dumpling . . .'

And just like that, Florence knew herself forgotten, relegated without malice to the second rank of Imogen's affections.

But after all she had not been silly. If Imogen had foreseen the future, she could never have spoken so easily, with that Victorian, unthinking certainty that all would continue as it should. But Imogen had never admitted defeat, or even disappointment. She had been gallant to the end. As her health failed she clung more and more to her hopes for the future. A few days before she died, too weak to sit up, she had propped herself on an elbow to dictate a menu for the picnic she had promised Phoebe when the fine weather came; and when Mother left the room she whispered to Florence that she hoped the next children might be boys, so that she could name them after their little lost brothers. Florence had believed that it was not so very serious after all, and Mother was only fussing. Then, the next week, the telegram came. That was before the War, when it was still unusual to see the telegraph boy on his bicycle; Florence had taken the envelope from the maid with curiosity instead of dread, turning it over in her hands as she ran upstairs to Mother.

She took a long breath. She would not start to cry again. Hadn't they all learnt, in the last four years, that the only thing was to carry on with as much dignity as possible? She was not the only woman who was left alone in the world, without prospects. She was lucky to have a brother-in-law who was prepared to take her in. And it could be worse: the smallest room in the vicarage must be better than digs in Eastbourne or Seaford. Here there were fields and space, trees, the chime of the church clock. She stared at the empty sweep of the down and the lines of the Face, brighter than she remembered, and told herself that it was beautiful.

Time to bathe her eyes, and . . . and then? Should she enquire of Mrs Reed if there was anything she might do to help her? Or should she sit in the drawing room with a book, ready to leap up as soon as Dr Manning looked in? She quailed, suddenly, at the thought of all the days ahead of her, which she would have to fill. But there were men in France being shot at – shot to bits; she had no right to fear anything, let alone too much time, too long a life. Yes, she must go downstairs - since the jug on the washstand held nothing but a fine layer of dust - and wash her face. That was the first thing. And then, minute by minute, she would learn how to live.

She stepped out onto the landing, and down the stairs. Footsteps crossed the hall, echoing on the tiles, and came up the stairs towards her. A moment later she rounded the corner and came face to face with Phoebe.

She had been thinking so vividly of Phoebe as a babe in arms that it was a shock to see her now: slender, with the look of fragility that marked the beginning of adolescence, her gaze almost on a level with Florence's own. She did not have Imogen's classic prettiness; instead she was plain, her face too wide at the temples and too narrow at the chin. Her hair was so pale it was almost white, although her eyes were hazel and her eyebrows strongly marked. Her expression was stony. She stopped, but she did not move aside to let Florence pass.

'Phoebe,' Florence said, and then did not know what else to say. They had not seen each other since Mother's funeral. She had taken the child's hand as the coffin was carried forward; she hadn't known whether she hoped to comfort or be comforted, but Phoebe's fingers had twitched and lain limply in hers, and after a second she had let go. Now it would hardly be appropriate to offer condolences, as though they were strangers. If only Phoebe had been here for her arrival, when Dr Manning had rung for tea and they had murmured about the weather, smoothing over the awkwardness! She told herself it was thoughtlessness, not contempt; but it was hard to believe, when Phoebe stared at her like that. 'Where have you been?' she said. She had not meant to speak so sharply.

'I went for a walk.'

'It's very hot. You must be careful not to be ill.'

'I won't be.'

'Good.' Now was the moment for Phoebe to say that she was glad to see her – to call her Aunt Florence – or to smile, at least. Nothing came. Florence hesitated; but instead of stepping back to let Phoebe past, she said, persevering, 'Where did you go? Did you stay in the shade?'

'I went up to the Face.'

'Oh! I was just looking at it from my window,' she said, too cheerfully, as though they had discovered a mutual friend. 'It is picturesque, isn't it? I must ask your father about it at dinner.' She paused, still hoping for some sign of friendliness. Phoebe was only a child, and her grandmother had just died. Did she feel it more deeply, after losing her mother so young? Perhaps what seemed like stoniness was grief – so much grief that she was dazed by it, hardly knowing what to say or do. Florence exhaled slowly. 'I suppose you wanted to be alone,' she said, 'I understand . . .' But as she spoke she remembered the young man she had seen striding down the slope below the Face, and she broke off.

Phoebe turned her head towards the window, as though she had heard something: but there had been no sound except the soft calling of the pigeons. Now Florence saw that there was a red raw patch over her chin, and a hank of hair had come out of her plait. White dust streaked her dress. What on earth had she been doing?

'Was there someone else up there?' Florence said, and now she did not care whether she spoke sharply or not.

Phoebe looked at her, and then back to the window. 'I

saw George Bone,' she said, in a cool, distant voice. 'He is going away tomorrow. His mother told him to make sure the Face was working before he went.'

'Working?'

'He cut the grass away and whitened the chalk. It's the Bones's job to look after it.'

Florence stared at her. Phoebe had seemed quite self-possessed; but under Florence's gaze a flush began to spread up over her cheeks, and she pressed her lips together.

Florence said, levelly, 'Did you help him?'

'No.'

'Then how did you end up in that state?'

Phoebe met her eyes. There was a strange stillness in her gaze, as though she were thinking very quickly and trying to hide it. It was wrong for a child to look like that. Florence felt her own face change in response, although she could not have described her expression.

'I fell over,' Phoebe said.

Florence would have known it wasn't true, even if she had not seen Phoebe decide to lie. And Phoebe knew that she knew. Which meant, she thought, with a cold clarity, that the real answer was worse than a lie. What was worse than being a liar? 'I'm sorry to hear that,' she said. 'You must have fallen more than once, to get chalk on the back as well as the front of your dress.'

Phoebe turned her head again to the window. 'Yes,' she said, in the same bloodless voice. She did not even bother to defend herself.

Florence clenched her fists. Was it possible that Phoebe – a child, this child, Imogen's child! – had been in the arms of a young man, rolling over and over on the chalk, letting him kiss her face raw? No – it was mad, impossible, it could not be – but there she stood, shameless and silent, as if it was not worth trying to convince Florence otherwise . . .

A wave of anger went through her, so strong she began to tremble. Mother was dead, and Imogen, and the whole world was wrong, and Phoebe had been lying in the sun with a man – it was obscene—

'Can I go now?' Phoebe said. Her face was still stony. How foolish Florence had been, to imagine that it was grief.

Florence stepped aside, drawing her skirt in as though the stains on Phoebe's dress would brush off on her. She could not help it; she felt sick.

Phoebe saw it. For a split second she paused, and something passed over her face – something that might, after all, have been childish, and hurt. But it was too brief to be sure. Then she was gone, her feet pattering away down the passage, leaving Florence alone.

She put her hands over her eyes. Already the anger had died, extinguished by regret. Should she turn and call Phoebe back? What would Imogen have done? But she was not Imogen. Mother would have said something worse – something that would have festered like a splinter; at least she had not done that. But it was small comfort, remembering Phoebe's expression as she pushed past.

Her skin was hot and tight around the temples, and when she blinked she felt crusts of salt clinging to her eyelashes. It seemed like hours ago that she had decided to wash her face. She drew in her breath, rather shakily, and let her hands fall. If she paused, she knew she would feel so lonely that she might drown; so she would simply not pause. She hurried down the stairs, straightening her shoulders and raising her chin, and as she rounded the corner she fixed a smile on her face in case she ran into Dr Manning.

II

'Midwinter': *Study in Black*,
charcoal over pencil on paper, 1919

Aggie heard the door open and the creep of quiet feet, so bloody tactful that you'd know you were dying just from the sound. The vicar's sister-in-law, again. Aggie said, without turning round, 'Oh, it's you.'

A sigh. 'Mrs Bone—'

'I don't want you. Go home.'

Silence. Aggie knew the girl wanted to obey; of course she did, it was late and freezing cold and this was the last of today's errands, the last and least important. No doubt she'd been scuttling about all day from sickbed to sickbed, the Levett boy and the Sharrard brothers and the vicar himself – although they said that he, at least, was on the mend. No doubt after all that she resented the prospect of sitting by an old woman's side through the longest, darkest night of the year. But you had to give her credit: she came steadily into the room and set the basket down on the table as if the only thing on her mind was Aggie.

'The range has gone out. Shall I— ?'

'No.'

'Then you must go back to bed. I'll bring you up some hot— some warm soup.'

'No need.'

The girl – oh, if only her mind were better at hanging on to names! Frances, was it, or – no, Florence, that was it, Florence, a name ill at ease in an English winter – surveyed her through the treacherous lamplight, biting her lip. 'Mrs Bone,' she said, not ungently, 'you cannot sit here all night in the cold. If you go upstairs I can light a fire in your bedroom—'

'Light a fire if you want. Then go home. I'll go upstairs when I'm ready.'

Florence sighed. She had the long-suffering, insufferable look of a ministering angel. Aggie could have slapped her. If only the younger one had come instead, the sprite-slip of a moon-girl that Georgie had had his eye on. Phoebe. *She* knew what she was doing; she would be good company at your deathbed, curious, pitiless. You could tell her what you really wanted, and she would help you. Not like this one.

'Why are you in your coat, Mrs Bone?'

'I'm going out.'

'Now? Where on earth— ?' She hesitated. Then she drew out a chair and sat down opposite Aggie, leaning into the circle of light. 'Mrs Bone,' she repeated, very softly, 'you're at home. You're safe. You've been ill, and perhaps you are confused—'

Aggie cackled. She didn't mean to, but there was a certain satisfaction in seeing Florence flinch. 'Oho,' she said, 'I'm not mad yet, girlie. I know where I am, and all my sons are dead and gone, and it's the middle of winter, and I'm dying. Have I missed anything?'

Florence said, 'Not that I can think of.'

'But I've got something to do first. So go along home, and let me get on with it.'

'I told Dr Manning that I would see you to bed. He was worried about you.'

'The parson? Ha! Us Bones are a thorn in his side.' She said it with too much venom, and began to cough. At least Florence did not leap up to help her. But when she regained her breath her head was spinning. She did not have enough air, enough time left to waste. 'If you want to be helpful,' she managed to say, at last, 'go and get the other girl. Phoebe.'

'Phoebe? What for?'

'She can walk me up the hill. She knows what's what.' She added, 'Brought her into the world myself, when the doctor didn't get there in time.' Yes, that had been a good day's work – a good night's work, rather – and at the end of it she'd held up the baby to the Face, showing the young one to the old one, before she put it on its mother's breast.

'She's with her father, Mrs Bone, you know he is only just recovering—'

Aggie coughed again, and spat a wad of phlegm into the sink. Florence flinched. 'Then leave me alone. This is my house. Get out.'

A pause. Another breath, gone.

'Mrs Bone—'

'Leave me alone, stupid girl.'

'I'm twenty-seven. I'm not a girl.'

'Never be a wife,' Aggie spat, 'never be a mother. What are you, then? Not a woman. Not in my book. Don't care how old you are. You're a girl.'

Florence lowered her eyes. For the first time Aggie felt something other than contempt for her: the girl had a kind of strength, after all, even if she only used it to quell her own impulses. At last she stood up. 'If you insist, then. Good night. I'll come and see you in the morning.'

Aggie shrugged. If she was still alive in the morning she might welcome someone to light the range, and make her a hot cup of tea. She stared straight ahead as Florence moved past her and to the door. She did not move until she heard the door close.

Now there was no one to interfere, no one to raise the alarm, no one to follow her. She felt the familiar pulse of loneliness that came from being the one in charge. She was too tired for this. It should have been Peter, or Tommy, or George . . . No use crying about that. Spilt milk. Think about tonight.

With an effort she got up. Her joints ached, her skin was raw and tender. Her head swam. She must not fall. She clung to the chair, reached out for the table, navigated her way to the corner of the room hand over hand like an infant, bent for the bucket and lifted it with a groan. It was already heavy, empty. Now the knife.

Five steps – ten – and she was at the door. The night outside was fierce and clear, the stars still and wild overhead. A waning sliver of moon hung over the dark mass of the hill. The thin, pale lines of the Face were just visible, as if they were suspended in space. She shuffled to the pump and drew a splash of water into the bucket.

It was so heavy. Her hands were so cold. Midwinter. Last year had not been so bad: mild and wet, miserable but only something to be numbly endured; and midsummer had been easy. It had never occurred to her that she could be too old to carry a bucket of water up the hill, or too ill to move without shaking. This was her task. It must be done, it must be.

She took up the bucket, and set off towards the gate in the wall. It seemed so far away that she thought she had got lost somewhere on the short garden path. Surely it could not take so many steps, so many burning breaths? An eternity of stumbling. Now – ah, here. The freezing metal latch, the squeak of hinges. Then the short down-grass underfoot, the hard chalk. Don't think. Foot after foot. The earth rising under her.

Next time, or the time after that, she would be dead. Who would do it then? It was all wrong, with the young ones gone. No Bones left. There was no order now. All the old ways were broken. Someone had to do it.

She looked up. She was nowhere near the Face. She would never get there, not before dawn. But she must. If she did not . . .

She was so small. She could feel the hum, the power of it, the wintry song calling in notes too deep for human ears. What would she hear, if she were not human? If she were made of darkness, hungry and thirsty . . . ? Whatever passed between the Face and its prey, she could not hear it, it was not meant for her; but it filled her skull, drew her closer.

Foot after foot. The ground seemed to move under her, arching and flexing. There was nothing to hold on to. The bucket clanked in her shaking hand. Keep going. She must. The Face must be served, must be renewed. If not—

Surely she was nearly there. She had all night to cut away the turf and re-mark the lines. It did not matter, as long as it was done by dawn. If she only kept breathing, kept moving . . .

The world swayed one way and then the other. The ground came up to meet her knees. The bucket tipped out of her hand and rolled into the darkness.

Damn it. She was too old for this, too sick. This was George's job. Why wasn't George here? And Peter, where was Peter? Or Tommy? Why were none of them here? How could they leave her like this, alone on a freezing hillside? Why didn't they come to help? She knew, distantly, that there was a reason; but she could not remember exactly what it was.

She found that the sky and the ground had reversed. Now she was looking down into infinite light-filled depths, while she hung weightless above the void. The stars were dancing. She watched them unravel, trailing streamers of white fire, and dissolve into black.

III

Deletions, pencil, ink and paint on paper, ragged margins, absent pages, 1920

Phoebe lay upon the bed in what had been her mother's room, her stockinged feet neatly together, her hands by her sides. There was a particular stillness in this room, a stillness that was not explained by its position at the back of the house, or the green shelter of the down rising outside the window. Neither was it entirely explained by the fact that it had remained untouched and unchanged for years, with Mama's jewellery box upon the dressing table, her sketchbook and pens neatly stashed in the writing desk, her sunhat hanging upon the back of the door, trailing its faded ribbons. It was as though the air itself, through not being breathed, had thickened and settled on the dustless surfaces and the soft drapes, muffling everything. It was like a Sunday afternoon; and the stifling, somnolent silence of a Sunday afternoon was only slightly less absolute, she thought, than the silence of death.

In fact she did not know whether Mama had died here, in this bed. All she remembered from that time were fragments: the crowd of murmuring, sombre grown-ups, a white lily she stole from a vase, her new clothes all black,

Papa telling her there would be no picnic. In her memory Mama was a golden shimmer, a bee-sting followed by a kiss, the taste of barley sugar that she must not tell Papa about. Phoebe could not conjure her face or her voice; she could not quite comprehend that Mama had existed at all. It was not that she did not believe that she, her actual flesh, had come from Mama's – and that *had* been here, in this bed; but she could not make the knowledge fit with that lovely mirage. Lying on the counterpane, staring at the cracks in the ceiling, she tried to imagine a real person who looked like Mama, a person who had really, truly carried her, Phoebe, herself, inside her real body. It was impossible. She might as well have been in Haltington Church, staring up at the plain east window, trying to imagine God.

She yawned, giving up the effort. There were faint footsteps overhead: Aunt Florence crossing the landing, then descending the stairs. Then there was a very quiet click of heels along the tiled passage below, to the drawing room. Finally there was silence again, inscrutable. What did Aunt Florence *do*, for hours, days on end? What was there to do? Nothing, Phoebe thought, nothing but read or sew or think, nothing but scream. If only Aunt Florence would scream! Phoebe felt her own throat tighten. *That* would break the silence, at least. She breathed slowly, playing with the temptation, pretending to herself that she would give in to it.

But she did not, and eventually the desire passed – or lessened, anyway, dying to a simmer that was easy to ignore. She followed the cracks in the ceiling as though they were a map of a river and its tributaries, a route into *terra incognita*. This place – this room, the vicarage, all of Haltington . . . it was even worse, this year, since the end of the War. At least the war had been interesting. Then there had been the bitter punchline of the Spanish flu. And the last few deaths, the wounded who took so long to succumb that surely their families were relieved to see them go. At least, while that went on, there was still an end to look forward to. But now there was only the miserable aimless trudge of peace, peace that was nothing more than a kind of absence.

But that was not it. She sat up, and drew her knees to her chest, frowning. No, it was not only the peace, there was . . . something else. Something deeper and older that had slipped out of true, taking the whole world with it. She could not be sure when it had slipped – only that it was wrong now, and had been wrong for months. She stared through the window at the green sweep of the down without seeing it, searching for the thought as though it were a scrap stuck in her back teeth. Then it came to her and she leant forward, clutching the eiderdown with her fingers. The Face . . .

It was gone. Or rather, it was there, visible, but only because she knew where to look and what to look for. The grass had grown over it, leaving faint shallow lines in the green; only the subtle play of light and shadow showed where the chalk lay closer to the surface. Was it still a Face? Yes, just, she thought, but then she was not sure. For a strange moment she felt as if it might dissolve entirely as she watched, the whole hillside changing shape, breaking and dying like a wave. If the Face disappeared . . . she did not know exactly what would happen. But Mrs Bone had made George go over the lines before he went away, and after he was killed she had done it herself, struggling up the slope in spite of her rheumatism; and she had died trying to get to it, on Midwinter's Eve. What was there left to be afraid of, when all your sons had been killed?

No one had touched it since then. No one cared – or no one dared. George had said, *it's our job, us Bones. No one else can do it.*

Phoebe jumped off the bed, and paused. The almost-blankness on the green slope drew her eye, like a storm cloud or a crawling hornet, but there was no use staring at it, wondering, when there was nothing she could do . . . She resisted the temptation to twitch the curtain across. The trick was not to touch anything, so no one knew she had been here. She smoothed the crumples out of the bedspread, erasing the shape of her own body, and slipped out into the corridor.

Mrs Reed and Aunt Florence were talking downstairs, both their voices taut with repressed weariness, as if the other were a child to be humoured. The Sunday afternoon feeling closed over her again. She swallowed, feeling the tightness in her lungs and diaphragm, as if she were under glass and running out of air. What would happen if she screamed? But after the fierce exhilaration of release there would be nothing but a fuss, a scolding or a visit to Dr Boulter in Eastbourne to discuss growing pains and hysteria. It was not worth it.

She could not have said what drew her to the stairs that led up to the top landing, or prompted her to climb them. Perhaps it was the sound of Aunt Florence's raised voice, as impatient and unapologetic now as if she were the mistress of the house, exclaiming, 'Well, perhaps you should ask *him*, then!' before the parlour door shut with a thump and Mrs Reed stalked back to the kitchen; or nothing at all, neither curiosity nor malice, not even anything as strong as a whim. She pushed open Aunt Florence's bedroom door and stepped inside.

She had not been in here for a month or so. The last time had been brief, a quick creep to Aunt Florence's bedside table to slip her bookmark back a few pages before replacing the book at exactly the same angle; but today she had nothing particular to revenge, and no inclination to snap a hook and eye off Aunt Florence's stays or drive her thumbnail into the seam of a stocking till it split. Instead she stood with narrowed eyes, wondering what she *had* come for. The dingy little room was stale and close, waiting. It was directly above Mama's room; she knew without looking that from where she was standing she would be able to see the grassy slope of the down through the window, and the disappearing Face.

She dropped to her knees and peered under the bed. That was where Aunt Florence kept her suitcase, as if she might leave at a moment's notice – although so far she had not, worse luck. Phoebe dragged it out, wrinkling her nose at the rolls of dust that clung to her hands, undid the catches and flipped up the lid.

A space opened in her head as though a clock had stopped ticking. But there was no clock in this room, and nothing had been ticking. If anything had paused for an instant, it must have been her heart.

She was looking down at Aunt Florence's old doll. That was all. She had seen it before, blank-faced, a little repulsive with its bird's nest of hair and faded frills; it had been lying in the suitcase the last time she looked, exactly like this. Nothing had changed. But the glass eyes . . . She stared down at that fixed gaze, feeling her tongue stick to the roof of her mouth. She had a horrible, sickening conviction that the doll would blink.

It did not. Of course it did not. And when she forced herself to stretch out a fingertip and touch the nearest eye, it was smooth and hard – not wet and yielding, as she had, for a second, thought it might be. It was an old doll, that was all, an embarrassing object for someone as ancient as Aunt Florence to keep, but not sinister, not— not alive, not *hungry* . . .

The word shocked her, as though someone else had said

it. It hummed like a plucked string, refusing to die away. She watched the doll. The doll watched the empty air.

She dug her fingers into her thighs, through her dress. Then, without letting herself think, she took hold of the doll's body, got to her feet and brought its head down hard on the edge of the iron mantelpiece. There was a crack as loud as a gunshot. But she did not stop; she went on swinging, over and over, until splinters and sharp-edged petals of porcelain dropped into the hearth, and the head was only a concave hemisphere, a few shards of cheek and temple gleaming, uncannily bloodless, through the mess of dull hair. Then she let her arm drop, conscious of the trickle of sweat down her spine and the smell of her own exertion.

She had made too much noise. She held her breath to listen. But by some magic, no one was mounting the stairs or calling her name. Swiftly she crouched down and gathered all the pieces of china into her lap. The rosebud mouth still smiled, broken in two; one eye was still intact, surrounded by its painted lashes, pretty as a bead. Then she scooped up the last splinters with the flat of her hand, careful not to cut herself. She laid the headless – almost headless – doll on top of the remains of its face, and picked up her skirt by its corners, as if she was a little girl bringing home blackberries. She nudged the door open with her elbow and ran lightly down the stairs, along the passageway and out into the garden. No one looked out of the parlour window or opened the back door to ask what she was doing. She tipped the mess of frills and hair and porcelain into the overgrown shadows behind the compost bin, covered it with dock leaves and pushed it down, hard, into the earth. Later she could find a trowel and bury it properly.

She stood up, unconsciously wiping her hands on her dress. She spun slowly in a circle, feeling a cool breeze on her cheeks, and as she turned she glanced up, briefly, at the hill beyond the garden wall. But her gaze did not linger; and a moment later she shrugged a little and went back into the house, with the sense of a necessary chore well done.

The Bone house had stood empty for months, so long that Florence began to forget that it had ever been occupied. Sometimes, walking back from the railway station that spring or summer, she would pause and look past the cottage to the slope beyond, where the grass grew inexorably over the shallow lines of the Face; but she stopped noticing the rising tide of the patch of garden behind the low flint wall, or the broken window-panes. As the seasons changed it hunched deeper and deeper into the hollow, surrounded by green growth, and after a while it seemed destined to go to ruin, and she hardly thought of it as a house at all.

So when she came around the bend in the road one morning she thought, at first, that there were seagulls circling around something in the bushes, rising and falling on the wind. It was only when she passed the oak tree at the corner that she saw what was really there, and stopped dead. A line stretched between the lowest branch of the tree and one of the window catches. On it were pegged three shirts, men's shirts, flapping.

She stood still. The white material billowed in the overgrown garden, and reflections danced in the dim windows. She did not know why it was so beautiful. It was September, but the feeling that flooded through her was like the onset of spring. The colours, she thought, the white and green and brown, like snowdrops . . . but it was not that, not really. It was the sight of a man's shirt, open-collared, flying like a flag outside a house that had been abandoned. Now that she looked, the broken window had been reglazed, the gutter cleared of leaves, and the worst of the brambles cut back. The front door was still peeling, but the encroaching ivy had been torn away, and the path to it cleared. Someone was living here. A man – a man alone, since no other garments hung beside his on the line.

She felt herself smiling. How absurd, to feel so happy! She had seen Dr Manning's clothes drying many times, and hardly gone into raptures then. But she wanted to laugh aloud. It was only the thought that the occupant, whoever he was, might see her staring that made her wrench herself away and continue down the road.

Mrs Reed shrugged when Florence asked, casually, whether the Bone cottage had been sold; she carried on mixing the pastry and rolled it out before she sniffed and said, 'I heard it was an artist, down from London. It's not right, an outsider taking the Bones's house.'

'I suppose,' Florence said, from the kitchen doorway – it was not her place to venture any further, while Mrs Reed was working – 'I suppose that there was no one left to inherit it.'

'No, well. Better it stood empty, then.'

'You don't know his name?'

'I expect we'll find out soon enough.' She laid the pastry in a flaccid sheet over the pie-case, and pressed it down. 'Tourists don't stay long here, anyway. Don't get your hopes up.'

Florence felt her cheeks burn. 'I don't know what you mean,' she said, and stepped out into the passage, shutting the door on Mrs Reed's *hmph*. She had wondered, that was all – she had felt the joy of possibility, when she had thought there was none. It was unjust to stare like that, insinuating, as though she were some callow girl practising a new signature in the margins of her French prep. Or, she thought, as she trudged upstairs to her room, as though in her situation any flicker of happiness must be self-delusion.

After that, she carefully did not mention the Bone house or its tenant. She did not want anyone else to regard her as though she were cheap and calculating; she did not want to tarnish her memory of the windy autumn morning, and the shirts on the line. It was an image of hope, and God knew that was scarce enough, these days. But she turned the words over and over, as if they might reveal another hidden meaning, longing to know more. An artist. An artist from London . . . But if Dr Manning had heard of a stranger moving to Haltington, he did not think it was important enough to communicate it to her; and Phoebe, who sometimes picked up gossip from the other girls in the village, would deliberately have withheld the information if she thought Florence cared to learn it. She herself began to be afraid that she had imagined the whole thing – that it was only some neurotic fantasy, worthy of the romance books she borrowed sheepishly from the lending library; she had just enough self-respect not to go out of her way to walk past the house, to check.

And gradually, after a few days, the image of the shirts bellying in the breeze lost some of its joyous potency. She had almost forgotten it – at least, she was not consciously thinking about it – when the postman came up the path one morning and she leant over the garden gate to take the letters from him. As usual he turned away without acknowledging her thanks, and – as usual – she felt a flash of guilty resentment as he limped back to his bicycle. She missed the girl who had done the rounds so cheerfully during the War, humming sea shanties as she struggled through the worst weather, never departing without a grin and a wink. Of course it was right that the men should have had jobs to come back to – but what about all the women who had done them so well, and been cast aside? And it was not Florence's fault that the postman had been wounded – she had not asked for the War – he had no need to treat her as though she would never be able to thank him enough. She watched him pedal painfully round the corner. Then she leant against the gatepost and riffled through the post to see if there was anything for her. At the bottom was a letter, addressed to *Kit Clayton, The Cottage in the Hollow, on the Litlington Road, Haltington. (Please deliver if you can, I do not know the exact address. The cottage has a green door and an oak tree at the corner of the garden at the front.)*

She hesitated: but she knew without looking that the postman had ridden out of sight and out of earshot. There was no point calling him back, even if she wanted to. Kit Clayton, she thought, and liked the neat competent syllables, their matter-of-fact earthiness. Perhaps he was a sculptor—

Oh, for goodness' sake! She tucked the other letters into the pocket of her apron, rolling her eyes at herself. But there was a warm, ticklish sensation in her insides. She had been in the middle of cutting a bunch of dahlias; she picked up her secateurs from the garden bench and cut the last few stems before she allowed herself to go into the house. Then she filled a vase and put the flowers in the drawing room, took off her apron, laid Dr Manning's post on the sideboard in the hall, and called out, to nobody, 'I'm just going down the road.'

The morning was clear, with the deceptive balminess of autumn. She left her coat unbuttoned and strode out, her heart beating harder than was justified by the pace of her walk. Leaves spun down from the trees, turning from gold to brown paper as they landed by her feet. It seemed a shorter distance than usual to the bend in the road and the Bones's house – although it wasn't the Bones's house any more, it was Kit Clayton's . . . She stopped at the sagging gate, touching the letter in her pocket. There were no shirts drying today. The house looked smaller, more private, its windows reflecting blank sky.

There was no bell, only an old-fashioned iron ring knocker that made the whole door shake when she used it. She waited. No one answered. She might perfectly well slip it under the door and go back to the vicarage, none the wiser. After a moment she stepped off the doorstep, and picked her way through tall tufts of grass to stand in front of the window. But the curtain was drawn and she could not see anything but her own pale reflection. She raised her hand to tap on the pane.

There was a crack and a thud. She jumped, but the sound had come from behind the house, not inside it. It came again. She trod carefully through the long grass and peered around the corner of the wall.

He was there, his back to her, chopping wood. He was in his shirtsleeves, the cuffs rolled to his elbows; the fabric clung to his back, a long damp patch running down his spine. He was slighter than she had expected, almost boyish. But she could see from the way he moved that he was not lame, or blind, or gasping for breath. His hair was chestnut coloured, a little long, curling over his collar – but then, he was an artist, she thought. And it had not a trace of grey in it. He was young – the word rang in her head like a bell – young and healthy, raising his axe and letting it fall with a precise rhythm that was not quite aggressive.

She would have watched him for ever, forgetting everything but the pleasure of seeing him move, if he had not paused and wiped his hand across his forehead. As soon as he bent to collect the split wedges of wood he would see her; and although part of her wanted to creep away, secret and unseen, she knew it was too late. She dug for the letter in her pocket, and said, 'Forgive me – are you Mr Clayton?'

He spun round, and Florence felt her stomach clench.

It was a woman. A woman with short hair, and wearing men's clothes – wearing one of the shirts that had danced so splendidly in the wind, so promising, so male! – a woman with an axe still swinging in one hand. She stared at Florence, her eyes narrowed, as if it was Florence who held a weapon.

'Who are you?'

'I – I am looking for Mr Clayton. I live,' she stammered, 'I live at the vicarage. The postman gave me a letter by mistake – a letter for Kit Clayton – so I thought I would come here myself, to give it to him . . .'

The woman held her gaze for a moment. Then she hung the axe carefully on a nail, crouched down to gather the pieces of wood, threw them into a basket that stood by the back door, and carried it into the house. Florence stood still, her heart thudding; but almost immediately the woman returned, wiping her hands on her trousers. 'Thank you,' she said coolly, and held out her hand for the envelope.

'Are you . . . ?'

'I'm Kit Clayton.'

'I thought . . .' But she had just enough sense to shut her mouth before she spilt out a mortifying admission.

The woman gave a crooked mouth-twitch of a smile. 'Yes,' she said, 'lots of people do.' She gave the letter a swift glance and put it in her pocket. 'Thank you. If I see the postman I'll ask him not to put you to the trouble again.'

'I didn't mind. I was curious to meet you.' It was true; so why did the woman give a slight tilt of her head, as if to signal that she was not deceived? 'Are you living here alone?'

'I'm afraid so.' Again, that irony in her voice.

'Well,' Florence said, 'welcome to Haltington. The vicarage is just down the road, before the church, if you need anything.'

'Thank you.' It was now that the woman might have invited her inside. Florence had no inclination to step into that narrow little kitchen, or sip tea from what would very probably be dirty cups; but she felt the snub of not being wanted. The woman stood quite still, self-possessed, waiting for her to leave.

Florence said, 'Goodbye, then.'

'Goodbye – Miss . . . ?'

'My name is Florence Stock.'

'Miss Stock.' She did not say it with any particular emphasis, but Florence's name sang with the loaded ambiguity of a pun: solid, culinary, fecund. With the *miss* it was one vowel away from *mistake*.

Florence gave the woman a taut, unfriendly smile – the sort of smile Mother would have given an overfamiliar shopgirl – and turned away. She thought she heard a soft exhalation, a bitten-back word, but she did not look back. She walked neatly down the side of the house and down the garden path, lifted the gate with exaggerated care so that it did not scrape on the stones, and stepped out onto the road. The sun had gone in, and the wind picked up. A gust caught her unpinned hat, threatening to lift it off her head, and blew her coat between her legs as if to trip her. A branch had come off the oak that stood at the corner of the garden. It lay across the roadway like a giant bony arm. A handful of dingy leaves still clung to it, shivering in the wind.

It might catch in the wheels of Old Comfort's trap, or make a bicyclist swerve dangerously towards the ditch. Dutifully she stooped and picked it up.

But she did not cast it aside. Her hand tightened around it. Was this what her life had come to? Delivering a stranger's post, then picking up sticks, unnoticed, unthanked, before she trudged home? And a wave of anger swept through her, catching her off guard, so strong she could hardly see. She raised the branch above her head, then swung it down and sideways, breaking it into pieces against the garden wall. She did not stop until the piece she was holding was hardly as long as her hand. The ground was littered with leaves and fragments of twig. She was panting. Slowly she uncurled her fingers and dropped the last sad length of stick in the road.

A gust of wind buffeted her. There was a movement in the corner of her eye, and she spun round – no, it was only a reflection in the window – no—

It was not a reflection. The woman – Miss Clayton – was standing in front of the house, her hands in her pockets, watching.

Florence felt a scalding blush spread across her cheeks. She had a horrible feeling that she had been shouting wordlessly. At least, she hoped it had been wordless. If not . . . For a furious, desperate second she wondered if she might bend and pick up the pieces of branch, pretending she had simply wanted it for kindling; but the thought of crouching and scrabbling in the road while the other woman looked made new sweat break out in all the creases of her body. How supercilious, how damnably *rude*, that cool gaze – and how idiotic she herself had been! If she had only waited until she had turned the corner before she lost her temper – out of sight, and (oh God) out of earshot . . .

Miss Clayton said, 'Your hat, Miss Stock.' She inclined her head towards where it lay at Florence's feet like a collapsed pudding in dingy felt.

That was the last straw. Florence ducked for it and broke into a foolish trot, her hair coming loose on her neck, her coat flapping, her shoes kicking up dust. The seagulls called derision, their shrieks criss-crossing over her head. She raced along the road, without looking back. She did not stop until she had reached the front garden of the vicarage, her throat tight and her face still burning.

There was an apple on a plate. It was afternoon now, there was pale constant light from a clouded sky. It fell sleekly on the apple, wetly on the enamelled plate, grittily on the grimy wooden table beneath. The plate was perfectly round, but the apple was not. It leaned to one side, listing away from the swell of its redder cheek, its stem askew. It was a very real apple, precise in its imperfections.

Once, Kit thought, she would have taken great pleasure in paying attention to the form of this apple, just as it was. She would have yearned for colour – for cadmium yellow and alizarin red, burnt sienna and raw umber for the speckles, Payne's grey for the shadows – but she would have shrugged that away, bending her head and her mind to the discipline of pencil on paper as if she were back in the Antiques Room. She would not have thought about how her gaze turned the simple apple on a plate into *Apple and Plate* – from reality to composition, from random things to still life; she would not have thought about how it changed her, either. Only when she came back to herself would she wonder where she'd been while her eyes looked and her hand drew, and marvel. How could a feeling so negative, so purely absent, be so sweet?

She would have given a great deal for that absence now. But now that she wanted it, it proved elusive. She stared at the apple, and did not lift her pencil. She did not want to draw it; she wanted to *want* to draw it.

Begin, she said to herself, as though she were her own teacher, standing behind her chair: begin, and the rest will come. She drew a curved line on her paper. There. Now the rest should be easy, or easier.

But the line did not look like the apple. It did not look

like anything at all. And the apple itself . . . it was untranslatable, closed, impossible. Without thinking she reached out and picked it up, and unexpectedly her fingers found a soft spot and a drop of clear liquid oozed from a break in its skin. A bruise, brown under the red, the sunken place clear-edged as the bones of a face, where the plane of cheek met the jaw . . .

She thought, all at once, of a mouthful bitten out of white-green flesh; of the slow wither of rot, with its overripe stench; and of men who were whole, sometimes even beautiful, until they turned to look back at you. She stumbled to her feet, and the chair fell backwards with a thudding smash. An apple was not a face – was not a man – but her head was swimming, her hands clammy.

Oh God. She tried to hold on to the present with all her strength. She was here, not in Paris – not in the studio . . . but her mind's eye was full of the pale plaster heads that had haunted her dreams ever since she first saw them hanging on the wall. She felt the breath catch in her throat: there they were, hanging in front of her, baleful as the reproachful dead themselves. Christ, those nightmares! It was stupid, that her mind should have fixed on the masks: when she was awake, they had been nothing but a tool, a surface on which to sculpt new eyes or ears, and even the trickier ones were only a kind of puzzle to be solved. She never spoke to them, as Portia did. *Pass me Henri, will you?* Portia would say. Then she would hold it up to the light, and add, *There you are, darling, how do you like your new nose?* Kit reserved her friendliness for the men themselves: the masks were objects, the men were not. But at night . . .

She had not told anyone about the nightmares, although Portia had known, of course. As the months went by, and she slept less and less, she learnt to look away from the mirror over the grimy washbasin, ignoring her swollen eyes and sharp cheekbones; and if anyone asked whether she was ill, she said she was hungry, and tired, and missed home – and anyway none of that was a lie, and no one was exactly happy. What good would it do, to tell anyone? Even if she had wanted to, she could not have put the nightmares into words. *They come to life*, she could have said, *the masks come to life* . . . But that would not have expressed the depth of her horror, the terror and shame – shame almost most of all, because in her dreams she knew that it had been her decision to lift each mask down from the wall, and her fault it had become conscious. Somehow she had summoned it into being. And what could a man do, without a body, without even the back of his head? No breath or throat to speak, no tongue, only the mute white craterous landscape of the face, and the eyes that watched her . . . Sometimes, in the last gasp of sleep, she overheard herself thinking: *I suppose he will have to live in a drawer*. Then she would wake rigid and tingling, choking. But they were only nightmares. She had never shrunk away from the men, or from the work she had to do – not, that was, until the last day . . .

She did not want to think about that. She took a deep breath, and another, and another: refusing to let herself pay attention to anything but the surface of the world, the light on the table, the touch of the air on her lips. With a shaking hand she lifted the chair back onto its feet. Then she sat down on it, pressed her palms into her thighs, and stared down at the dusty floorboards. After a while she lifted her head and looked at the wall: and all she saw, of course, was peeling whitewash, cracked and damp-stained, but blessedly bare. There were no masks, no flags, no smells of cigarette smoke or electroplating solution. She was in England, alone.

The apple had fallen to the floor. She bent and retrieved it, picking it up by the stem. It was shiny with juice where the skin had split over the bruise. Below the fresh notes of honey and leaves was a faint fermented scent of decay. She breathed in, testing, until she was sure that all she could smell was what was here, now. Then she set the apple back on the plate, in the light from the window.

Pick up the pencil. Make another line. Any line. It did not have to be a good line. Today a bad drawing, tomorrow a better one. That was why she had come here, wasn't it?

She drew a hand over her forehead. Oh, but what was the point? Even a better drawing was still only a drawing. She was too tired for this. It was hard enough to live – to keep the range alight, to chop wood and cook and wash her clothes. Why on earth did she care if she would never be able to work again? She snatched up the apple, threw open the window and flung it with all her might into the road. It broke apart with a wet thud.

Oh, how childish! It reminded her of the woman who had surprised her this morning. Miss Stock – Miss Florence Stock. She had looked so demure, at first; but when she thought herself unobserved she had burst into that absurd spree of fury, bashing a dead branch into smithereens. How mortified she had been to see Kit watching; and how guiltily she had stooped for that soggy pie-crust of a hat, and scurried away without a backward glance! Would she have been comforted, to see Kit's apple thump down from the window in an identical fit of temper? Perhaps not; perhaps she would have been insulted by the comparison. The back of her neck had been pink, like a blancmange – no, like a rose petal. A curly, corn-coloured tress of her hair had escaped from its pins, and clung glittering to her coat as she ran. A modern nymph, caught *in flagrante* . . . But the image had a bitter aftertaste. She had been so utterly transparent: her hope as she asked for Mr Clayton, and her confusion and disappointment as it dawned on her that Kit was, after all, a woman. Kit had received her fair share of contempt; but it still stung to be relegated, in the blink of an eye, from an object of desire to – well, the opposite.

Damn her. A Sussex vicar's wife – no, she was Miss Stock; a spinster, then. In any case, not worth bothering about. Kit had no reason to let the memory of those clear blue eyes get under her skin like a thorn. What had she said? *A letter for Mr Clayton – I hoped to meet him . . .*

Kit slid her hand into her pocket, and felt the edges of the envelope. She had forgotten about it, until now. She hesitated – it had always been her habit to leave her correspondence for the evening, after she stopped work – but the apple was scattered in the road, and the best of the light was gone. Tomorrow she would start earlier, and stick at it. Now she might as well admit defeat.

It was Portia's handwriting, of course. She had seen that before Miss Stock put the letter into her hand, in the first glimpse of curled 'S's and Greek 'e's. It was familiar, almost as familiar as her own, and infinitely more beautiful. Now it sent a little shiver down her spine, which she told herself firmly was curiosity and nothing else. *I do not know the exact address.* No, Kit thought, and that should have told you how little I cared to hear from you. But she slid her thumb under the flap with the same wry self-knowledge with which she had first slipped the letter into her pocket: she had always submitted to Portia's will, in the end. Always, except for once, when she left Paris – but she swerved around that thought, and unfolded the paper. *My dearest, darling Kit*, she read.

The first thing you will ask yourself – or the second, if you admit that you are inordinately eager to know whether I still want you as much as ever – is how I tracked you down. (Here Kit winced, because Portia's moments of acuity always took her off-guard.) *Well, it was quite by chance, as I ran into old Muckle at* the Café Royal and he told me that you had sent him a letter. I told him that he must rank very high in your affections to receive even that crumb of consideration, but poor Muckle was very crestfallen that you had gone without saying goodbye to his face. Anyway he was so keen to talk of you even in the most indirect terms that he waxed quite lyrical on the bucolic details of your cottage, and from that I was able (call me Sherlock my dear!) to make a stab at addressing a letter to you. I take it I have succeeded, since you are reading this. You should know by now that I am not to be shaken off easily – I am a burr my darling, and I will stick.

But do not worry. I can see you now, with that deep scowl you have, horrified at the prospect of my company, and I must leap to reassure you that I have no intention of descending upon you until you ask – no, beg! – me to. I will wait like Patience on a monument. Speaking of which, did you know that Septimus has won the commission for the Lawnbridge War Memorial? He maintained for the duration of several glasses of sherry that it was to be the figure of a boy face down in the mud, like Nevinson's *Paths of Glory*, and almost carried off the bluff. As for your own work my dear, you know you MUST begin again, and quickly. Not only because there is no time to lose (although which of us has enough remaining?) but because what I saw in your face when you left Paris frightened me. It is so strange to think that was the last time I saw you. I hope by now you have lost that wary, blank, watery expression – that look that made me fear that you would never touch a pencil again – but what I hear about you and your life now does not reassure me. Muckle says that you have produced nothing, nothing! since you came back to England, and that your letter was full of high-minded sentiments about Art but no plans for any actual pictures. (Damn him, Kit thought: it was true, but he had no business saying so to Portia, of all people.) *You MUST work my darling you MUST. You must not let your whole life's purpose be spoilt by a silly war. Put it all behind you and move onwards. That is what everyone else is doing. It is not as if you and I had a bad time, really. Think of the men we saw! Which reminds me, did you hear that Julien was in London? He is another one who is keen to have your address – and as I know you were fond of him, I would have obliged him if I could. Oh darling, think of the GOOD we did him, and all of them! That is something to keep us going, isn't it, that our art HELPED rather than HURT people? So you must NOT give up—*

Kit crumpled the letter sharply into a ball. She had been wrong to open the envelope; she should have thrown it straight into the range – or, better still, pushed it back into Florence Stock's hands and feigned ignorance of the mysterious Mr Clayton. If only Muckle had held his tongue about her whereabouts, as she'd asked him to! But it was too late now. She squeezed the ball of paper more tightly. It was stupid to feel so invaded, as if Portia had pushed through the front door unannounced, in a Parisian waft of Gauloises and garlic. Portia was not here, would not come, had no hold over her – and neither did Julien, clever quiet Julien, whose mask she had been so proud of – or any of the others, the men who had lined up to present their terrible faces, wordlessly demanding her attention and her skill, daring her to flinch. She did not have to go back, ever. She was free.

She found she was staring at the plate on the table. It was difficult to wrench her eyes away from it, as if it were not empty but held something invisible and malign.

IV

A Bottle of Light, oil on wood panel, 1920

The journey home from Paris had sickened Kit, with its seas of people, and London had been even worse. The War was over, but it had left its stained fingerprints on every part of life: the men with empty trouser legs and sleeves, the rationing, the women who laughed too loudly, their skin still yellow-tinged from working on munitions. She hated it all. She could hardly remember how to smile, or speak. She spent hours watching the damp stain on the wall above her piled-up luggage, and only went downstairs to get her post from the landlady. The letters from the agent in Eastbourne were the only glimmer in those long dark days: she opened the envelopes as eagerly – more eagerly – as she had ever opened Portia's. And when at last he wrote, *I believe there may be a property which answers your requirements*, she had dreamed of the promised idyll: the wide skies, the rolling downs, the sea, the solitude.

Whenever she had wanted anything this much it had proved – sooner or later – a mistake. She did not care. She arrived with her suitcases, never having seen the cottage, knowing hardly anything of Haltington except what the agent had said: and in spite of the peeling paint, rotting front door and cracked window-panes, she had felt her insides give a kind of lurch like steel encountering a magnet. She was quite certain she had never been here before, but something – the low, hunched cottage itself, or its setting at the foot of the down – seemed familiar, ringing an elusive note of nostalgia in her head. Did it remind her of a painting, or an illustration in a beloved book? But she could not put her finger on what it was, and after all it did not matter. She was here now. It had been hard work to unpack, to get the range going and cook a meal and to find a lamp to light the way to bed. But it was thoughtless, childish, absorbing work, like playing at houses. It had been good to go to bed tired and aching, while the wind blew salt-scented mizzle against the window.

And as for being alone . . . Muckle had written to her before she left London, warning her. *Dear Kitten*, he had said, in his neat public-school handwriting, *you know men go mad when they are deprived of company for very long.* Naturally, when he said 'men' he meant everyone. He meant that she should have asked him to go with her, to hold her hands when she had night terrors, or murmur soothingly when she sobbed in his arms. But to hell with that, she thought, and wrote back, *maybe at Christmas?* safe in the knowledge that there was plenty of time to withdraw the invitation. She had no intention of needing his comfort. She was better, not worse, away from other people. When Mrs Smith, the washerwoman, ventured to ask one morning if she was a widow too – poor Mrs Smith, who had the dazed, imbecilic look of a grieving child – she answered in a discouraging monosyllable, taking the parcel of sheets and shutting the door as soon as she decently could; and she resolved not to answer the door at all if Miss Stock came back. Her peace was too precious to be broken. Day by day, like an essence condensing in infinitesimal drips, she felt her self returning.

And today, at last, she had begun to paint.

It had been a kind of miracle. She had left an empty bottle on the table in the kitchen where the midmorning sun fell sideways on to it, casting its bright unshadow on the scrubbed wood. When the weather was fine – which was less often now, as October gave way to November – she stood in the doorway to drink her first cup of tea, listening to the birdsong and the blessed, blessed absence of human voices. Today she had slept late, and the sun had risen over the dew-glittering down, throwing the garden into deep contrasts of emerald-gold and dark. For the first time since she could remember, the turning leaves had whispered to her of paints, of cadmium yellow and aureolin and Brunswick green. And then she had turned, smiling, to put her empty mug into the sink, and seen—

Oh, it was nothing, really. Only a bottle on a table. It might have been an exercise of draughtsmanship, the sort of task she would have rolled her eyes at when she was studying. Then she would have resented it for not being a face. But today, now, it could not have been more beautiful. The light, the shape, the precise brush-sweep of reflections on the bleached grain of the table, the emptiness that surrounded the glass, leaving every line untouched by anything but air . . . Very slowly she moved towards it, as though its loveliness were a wild thing that might be frightened away. Nothing changed. She felt a wild rush of covetous ambition – the excitement that finally, at last, she could make a picture that would express what she wanted, a perfect picture – knew with a sardonic, self-aware part of herself that she always felt like this, and always failed – and rejoiced.

'Don't move,' she said, aloud. She turned and ran up

the steep little staircase, spots of sun-dazzle blinding her in the darkness so that she almost tripped on the last step. She dragged her suitcase out from the corner where she had pushed it, and threw the lid open.

A day ago, she would have winced at the neat order of it all, the clean brushes and palette, the notebooks tied together in brown paper, a couple of old paintings and an envelope full of sketches from a holiday in Oxfordshire, labelled *Misc, Mill House, August 1914*. It was all so perfectly, optimistically ready for her to go back to it: so that when her important war work was over, she could resume her brilliant career without missing a note. How young she had been when she wrapped and packed it all, how stupid.

But today she did not care. She lifted the largest sketchbook out of the way. Yes. Laid flat against the bottom of the suitcase was a primed square of wooden board. She turned it over, loaded it like a tray with everything else she would need, and carefully descended the stairs. She might have been a maid, she thought, taking tea to her mistress . . . Then she was back in the kitchen, and the bottle shone even more brightly than she had remembered, and she could not think about anything else.

She worked until the light had swung – in the blink of an eye – from the east over the garden wall and then behind the Downs, until the quiet glory did at last fade. She was left with nothing but the dim kitchen, her painting – hardly blocked, in solid dull shapes, only a beginning, but a beginning – and an exhaustion so deep it was like water. She pillowed her head on her arms, and let it close over her.

When she woke she was ravenous. She took the heel of bread and a cup of milk into the garden, and sat on the woodpile, her face turned up to the sky. It was the depthless, medieval blue of a book of hours. If she reached up she could touch it, and it would come off on her fingers like wet egg tempera. To the east a final band of sunlight still clung to the ridge, outlining it in gilt.

When she had finished her makeshift meal she balanced the mug on the nearest log and strode out of the garden gate, taking the path that led up the hill. If she climbed to the top she would see the sun dipping over the sea and the serpentine estuary. She went as fast as she could, not quite running, until she felt the sweat break out on her forehead. When she reached the top the Haven was spread out at her feet, a winding gold-platinum ribbon of water leading to the gap between the cliffs. The sun was low and blazing in the unblemished sky. Another painting she might do – *would* do, soon, as soon as she had finished the one she had begun today . . . She stood there until the cool breeze dried the moisture on her face and her damp shirt, and she began to shiver. It came to her with a sudden shock – a foolish shock, for God's sake, it was schoolgirl geography – that she was looking towards France. Towards Dieppe, and beyond that, Paris.

It didn't matter. It could not touch her, it would not tarnish the day. But all the same she turned away, feeling the chill intensify, and began to pick her slow way down the slope. She did not want to go back to the cottage yet. Perhaps today was the day she would go into the public house – the Half Moon – and brave the looks of the Sussex farmers who drank there. Look the publican in the eye, and dare him not to serve her . . . But she shook her head, grimacing as though someone else had suggested it. No, not today. Maybe never. That was something Portia would do, not her. Portia would enjoy the stares, the muttering hostility, she would slip her arm into Kit's with a flaunt of her head as if her men's clothes, her lipstick, her sapphism were a performance especially for them. And Kit would play along, half exhilarated, half ashamed. She did not have to do that now. She was free.

Under her feet the grass met the flat bare path. Now she could walk without concentrating on keeping her footing. She put her hands in her pockets and slowed down, enjoying the view of the church tower and the scattered roofs. It was an old flint church, with a hillocky graveyard full of leaning tombstones, and on a whim she swerved away from the path and took the little unmade track that led between two houses to the lychgate. She stepped through it into the churchyard. The cold air smelt of woodsmoke and something sweeter; she glanced up and saw an old apple tree leaning over the wall, gnarled and heavy with fruit. The shadow of the down had almost swallowed the village now: only the top of the tower still glowed with low reddish light. Below it, everything was soft and tinged with blue-grey, as though seen through a veil. She could paint this too, she thought. She *would* paint it. She could start tomorrow . . .

She pushed her way through the unkempt grass towards the west door. It was very quiet, as if the walls were higher than they really were. As she passed by a long carved tomb under a leaning oak tree she caught her foot in the grass and stumbled, catching herself on the stone edge; then, with a sickening fluidity, the prone figure on the top sat up and looked at her.

She managed not to scream. A second later, when the figure swung its legs over the side of the tomb and jumped down into the grass, she realised that it was flesh and blood: a girl, pale and spectral in the dusk. The top of the tomb itself, she saw now, was flat and plain. 'Christ!' Kit said, and then tried to laugh. 'Sorry – you gave me a shock . . .' She stopped speaking, conscious that her voice held not the steady note of amusement she had aimed for, but a quavering admission of weakness.

'Hullo,' the girl said; if she had been as startled as Kit, she did better at concealing it. She looked Kit up and down, rather appraisingly, as if she were the elder of the two, although she could not have been more than fifteen. 'Are you all right?'

'Yes. Yes, perfectly, thank you.' Now that her vision had cleared, she saw that the girl was – what? Not beautiful, not exactly. But she had an extraordinary face, the eyes set too widely apart, the mouth full but the jaw narrow. The eyebrows were straight and dark, the eyes hazel, but the girl's skin was white and fine and her hair was so fair it might have been peroxided. She did not have Florence Stock's solid gold-and-pink handsomeness; instead she looked as though she were in the wrong place or time, an illustration from a medieval romance clad in a muddy pre-war frock. Kit said, glad that at last her voice was level, 'I wasn't expecting— I thought I was on my own, that's all. I thought you were an effigy.'

'There aren't any effigies here.'

'No, well, I can see that now.'

'Or any pictures in the windows. Not of people, anyway. Not in Haltington.' She said it with a strange emphasis, as if the absence were significant.

'Oh. I see.'

'My father will tell you about it, if you ask. He has written a book about Sussex folklore.' She added, after a moment, 'He's the vicar.'

'How fascinating. But I don't – I'm not much of a churchgoer.' She felt, absurdly, that the girl would see through the words to the deeper truth they implied: but the girl's expression did not change, and after a moment she held out her hand.

'I'm Phoebe Manning,' she said. 'I suppose you are Kit Clayton.'

'I— yes.' She clenched her jaw, the feeling of exposure deepening under the girl's level gaze. But it was a small Sussex village, not London: of course they already knew who she was.

'You're an artist, aren't you? And you're living at the Bone house.'

'The . . . ?' It summoned the image of a charnel – or worse, the stories Septimus had told of the trenches, the corpse propped in a doorway, the empty eye sockets and fixed rotten smile.

'The house where the Bones lived. Bone is an old Sussex name, Papa says.'

'Oh. Yes.'

'Mrs Bone was a witch.'

There was a silence. She had said it so matter-of-factly that for a second Kit wondered if she had misheard; but it was followed by a sly sideways glance that told her she had not. For a disconcerting moment she thought of Portia, but could not imagine why.

'Was she,' Kit said. 'Well, I'm not sure I really believe in that sort of—'

'She knew things. I know things too, you know.'

'Do you,' Kit said, with the same noncommittal inflection. Her first instinct had been to laugh, but the girl's – Phoebe's – gaze was too challenging, too shrewd. 'I see.'

'I've always wanted to live there. Mrs Bone let me visit whenever I fancied. Especially after her sons were killed. But she died, trying to get to the Face.'

'The— ?'

'The Haltington Face,' Phoebe said, with a sudden frown. 'Don't you know— ?'

'Never heard of it,' Kit said. 'Well, you can't come to visit me. I don't want any visitors.'

Phoebe regarded her, tilting her head to one side. Kit had the sense that she was considering something, weighing up whether to say it – and abruptly, from a different part of her brain, she realised why she had thought of Portia, whose eyes were always sharpest before she leant in for a kiss. Although this child was not at all like Portia, of course, and there would certainly be no question of a kiss.

At last Phoebe said, coolly, 'That wasn't what I meant.'

Kit pushed her hands into her pockets. 'Why,' she said, casting about for a new subject, 'why were you lying on that tomb?'

But Phoebe only shrugged. They stared at each other until Kit blinked; then Phoebe bent to pick up a book and two apple cores that had been nestling in the long grass at the base of the tomb. There was something reassuring about the objects, as if they confirmed that she was an ordinary child after all. Kit imagined the afternoon she must have spent, reading until the light failed, turning the pages with fingers that were sticky with apple juice – and as for lying on the tomb, well, it was the sort of thing Kit might have done herself when she was little, when death was make-believe, when Juliet and the Lady of Shalott could be woken by a kiss . . . Long may it last, she thought, long may this girl go on thinking that death is a kind of game, it is charming. But a moment later she was not so sure.

'I have to go,' Phoebe said, flinging the apple cores over the wall into the brambles. 'Goodbye, Kit Clayton.'

'Goodbye.'

But Phoebe hesitated. Then, with a slight narrowing of her eyes, as if she were saying it against her better judgement, she added, 'You had better stay inside after it gets dark.' She did not wait for Kit's response, but spun away, walked across the grass and slipped through a concealed gap in the wall, lifting a curtain of thorns and leaves carefully and letting it fall again behind her.

Kit stared after her. Then she let out a huff of exasperation and amusement — oh, that warning, delivered with such condescension! Not to mention impeccable timing. It was a relief, really, that Phoebe had not been able to resist that final touch of melodrama. Now that she had made her exit, it was easy to see what sort of child she was: the sort who had learnt to discomfit adults, and revel in it.

A breeze swept across the back of Kit's neck, ruffling her hair. The shadows had crept upwards, swallowing the church; the final blaze of sunlight on the tower had died, leaving the whole world murky and cold. The grass whispered around her feet.

She did not take Phoebe's shortcut, but strode swiftly along the path and out onto the road. Something was nagging at her, small but uncomfortable like a stone in her shoe; a thought that had almost risen to the surface, and then sunk again, just out of reach. When Phoebe had risen up from the tomb like that . . . There was a scene in a novel, wasn't there, something from the last century . . . ? But she could not get hold of it.

It was not until she got back to the house — the Bone house, somehow the name had stuck in her head — and was fumbling in her pocket for the key to the kitchen door that it came to her: but the answer was not the title of the book she had been searching for. It was Phoebe's narrowed eyes, as she said, *The Haltington Face — don't you know—* ? And Kit felt the distant twitch of a memory, from long ago, before the War. She *had* heard of the Haltington Face. She might actually have bought a postcard of it, on the seafront in Eastbourne. Yes, she was sure now. She remembered her mother saying, 'How lovely, darling – it is awfully arresting, isn't it?' It had been a simple photograph, showing a dark slope against a sky with layers of cloud, behind a seam of wintry trees; and on the slope, a white face, made of nothing but a few lines – the sort of thing they might have argued about at art school, analysing the power of a well-placed mark. And at the bottom of the landscape, almost incidental, had been a low flint house, beside a curve in the road, with a single oak tree.

She craned backwards, staring over the garden wall. It must be overgrown now, or she would have noticed it before, and it was too dark to see ripples in the grass. But the Face was there, or had been there.

For God's sake, she thought. No wonder she had felt that spark of recognition when she arrived. If she had known, when the agent recommended the property . . . She had left Paris to get away from faces, refused to paint them, look at them ever again. And now this! It was like a divine joke at her expense: *think you can run away, do you?* She found the key in her pocket, unlocked the back door and slammed it behind her with a thud.

At least, she thought, at least it's grown over. It was there once, but it's gone. That's something to be grateful for.

V

Dahlias, oil on board, 1920

Florence saw Phoebe emerge from the churchyard, ducking under the brambles and pausing on the path to pick a few lingering tendrils from her skirt. But after she had stepped away from the trailing hedge she did not start walking again immediately; instead she stood for what seemed a long time, looking up at the grassy slope where the Face had been, although in the twilight there was nothing to see but shadows. Then, with a little twitch that might have been a shrug, she took the path down to the garden gate of the vicarage. Florence did not watch her lift the latch and come up the path to the back door; it was too like spying, and anyway the angle was awkward, she would have had to lean out over the sloping roof. But as she drew back from the window she saw something move in the deeper shade of the church, and caught a glimpse of a mannish figure – a pale face and cropped hair, white collar and cuffs – before it disappeared behind the yew tree beside the road. Kit Clayton, in the churchyard . . . Had she seen Phoebe there? Had they spoken? She felt an irrational prick of jealousy. It was not as if a woman like Kit would ever be friends with Phoebe, who was a child and a difficult one at that; but all the same . . .

She turned back into the room. She was restless today; she had moved from place to place, looked out from every window in every direction before she ended up here, as always, in her own stuffy narrow bedroom. What did it matter what Kit Clayton thought, or who she spoke to? She should try to drive Kit Clayton out of her mind, and along with Kit Clayton this drifting, beguiling sense of— of what? But that didn't matter either. Tomorrow she would go for a walk, a long, long walk – the sort of walk that they advised in ladies' magazines to chase away the 'bachelor-girl blues'. Yes, that would be the ticket. Fresh air and exercise. A strenuous walk, a new book from the lending library, a very small glass of brandy before she went to bed. Small pleasures, and no more self-pity. Unless . . .

Unless what? It was not as if she had any choice. Well, about the self-pity, perhaps, she thought wryly – but the loneliness, the sense that somewhere, tantalising, lurked the possibility of a different life, no, that was simply what was to be expected. It was the War, always the War! And the years which had followed it had almost been worse. She winced at the word, because it was contemptible even to think such a thing when men had died every day in the trenches, but it was true. She would give her here and now for any there and then at all.

She dropped to her knees, dragged her suitcase out from under the bed, flung it open and jumped to her feet again without pausing for breath, reaching out to open her chest of drawers. It was ridiculous, she knew that – a childish impulse, as if she were six years old and stamping her foot: 'Well, in that case I shall *run away*!' But she pulled a handful of underthings from the drawer and dropped them on the bed in a jumble, swinging back immediately to jerk open the next drawer. It stuck, as it always did. She wrestled with it, tugging until the whole chest shuddered forward and back, thumping against the wall; but it took so long that her arms started to ache, and she grew conscious of her resolve crumbling, if it had ever been real. Even if she did want to leave, where on earth was she planning to go? And what would she do once she got there? How would she pay for it? At last, with a jolt, the drawer burst loose and she stumbled back, dropping it with a crash. Her blouses lay with their empty arms entangled, all shades of grey in the dusk.

No. Of course she was not going to run away. The spark of defiance died to ash. She could imagine Mother, her lips pursed, regarding her as she stooped to gather up her sad, threadbare clothes. *Poor dear Florence*, she would say, *I suppose your monthlies are on their way.*

Perhaps they were. It was not as if Florence could hope that this time they would not come. They would come again and again, her monthlies, regular as a tolling bell, until at last Florence's body shrivelled inside and gave up. She put the heels of her hands over her eyes. When she was sure she was not going to cry, she scooped up her blouses and underclothes. She forced herself to fold them before she put them back in the drawers. After she had tidied them all away she bent to close her suitcase, and stopped.

There was nothing in it except a short length of slender fraying ribbon that might once have been pink. The lining paper was peeling, and feathers of dust clung to the inside corners.

Her doll, Effie . . .

She looked round, frowning. She had lain the doll carefully in the case when she had arrived here and unpacked. 'Effie?' she said, stupidly, as if she might get an answer.

Might she be misremembering? She got to her feet, turning on the spot as if she were playing hide and seek. But the room was small and mean, and there were so few places to put anything. She went to the wardrobe, and peered inside.

There was nothing on the shelf but a few sad hats, and nothing on the floor but her shoes. She closed the wardrobe again and glanced round at the window, the mantel, and the little table beside the bed where her book sat, with its bookmark sticking out like an impudent tongue. Actually, Florence turned down the bottom corner of a page to mark her place; she had done that for years, advancing the bookmark at random, ever since she realised that Phoebe liked to play tricks . . .

Phoebe. Of course. And just at that moment the front door closed, and Phoebe's shoes clicked on the tiled floor of the hall. Florence strode to the door, and hurried down the top flight of stairs to the middle landing. Phoebe was just rounding the corner, trailing a dirty hand along the banister as she passed. She looked round with wide, guileless eyes. 'Aunt Florence,' she said. 'Have you had a pleasant afternoon?'

Florence curled her fingers into her palms. 'Where is Alexandra Euphemia?' she said, trying to keep her voice level.

Phoebe frowned. She had Imogen's frown, a single mild line between her brows that made her look elegant and quizzical. Imogen had used it when she was trying to be particularly aggravating. 'Who is Alexandra Euphemia?'

'Alexandra Euphe— my doll! I brought her with me, when I— never mind. Where is she?'

'I don't know.'

'She was in my room, in a suitcase under my bed. Have you moved her?'

'Why would I move it?'

'To play with, I suppose. I don't care why. She was there, and now she isn't.'

'I'm much too old for dolls, Aunt Florence.'

'Much too old for fibs, as well.' She should not have said

it. She saw Phoebe register the insult, and knew it would be revenged over and over again in wide-eyed questions over dinner, clean stockings plucked from the line and trodden in the mud, mysterious tacks pressed into the tyres of Florence's bicycle. 'Perhaps you borrowed her,' she said, trying to be fair, 'and then forgot to put her back.'

'No.'

'Where has she gone, then? I can't imagine that Mrs Reed took her, or your father.' Phoebe shrugged, and began to walk past. It was all Florence could do not to grip her arms and shake her. How difficult could it be, simply to admit you had taken something? Something that you cared nothing about, which you knew was important to someone else . . . 'Please,' she said, despising herself, 'please, Phoebe, I won't say anything to anyone – I only want to know where she is.'

'Why?'

'Because she was – because . . .' She bit her lip. If only she could explain; if only Phoebe would understand, or care to understand.

'Perhaps we've been burgled,' Phoebe said. 'Is anything else missing? Have you counted your handkerchiefs?'

'Of course not, I'm not talking about—'

'Do you still play with dolls, Aunt Florence?' A tilt of her head. 'I expect you could order another one from London.'

'Don't be impertinent.'

'I wasn't trying to be.' Another lie, of course; another lie that she delivered with angelic composure, and a faint air of bewilderment. 'I only meant . . . what would you do with it, if you found it?'

'Nothing! But I want to know she is safe. She was very precious to me, when I was little—'

'But you're not little any more.'

Florence took a long breath, hearing her stays creak,

and held it for a moment until the blood rang in her ears. 'That isn't the point. I suppose you can't understand – I don't imagine anything is precious to you, you don't have a loving bone in your body—'

'Oh,' Phoebe said, with a curious, flat surprise. 'Oh, I see! Were you hoping to give it to your own daughter?'

There was a silence. Phoebe smiled.

Without the smile, Florence might have believed – might have told herself, at least – that it had been said thoughtlessly, without malice. But the pause went on, and Phoebe's gaze did not even flicker. It was not exactly mocking: but it left no doubt that Florence would never have a husband or a child, and that any hope of either was an absurd delusion.

When you're married, Imogen had said, *when you have your own baby . . .*

It took all of Florence's strength not to reply. She must not. She must not. But she could not move, either, she could not turn her back and walk away. If she could have raised her hand, finally, after years of goading and dislike and sly vicious hostility, just once—

Heavy footsteps ascended the stairs, and the shape of Dr Manning loomed behind her. 'Hallo, Phoebe – and Florence . . . Let me pass, my dears.' He chuckled, looking from one to the other. 'My goodness, how serious you both look. What's this, a mothers' meeting?'

Phoebe laughed.

Florence could not bear it. She pushed blindly forwards, not caring if she struck against either of them, and stumbled up the stairs. Dr Manning said, in a different tone, 'Florence? Are you ill, my dear?' but she did not look back. Phoebe could explain, if she wanted to.

She flung open her bedroom door and dropped to her knees beside the bed, burying her face in the counterpane. It was foolish to weep, but she wept anyway, thinking of

Effie taken out of the suitcase and thrown away – abandoned, mistreated, broken.

At last, when the wave of loneliness and fury had passed, she raised her head and looked down at her upturned supplicant hands. Imogen had said that her life was written in those lines. A long life, three children, a journey overseas. The palms gleamed with moisture. She curled her fingers over, making fists.

Then, with an impulse she deliberately, carefully did not think about, she went to the wardrobe and looked at herself in the full-length mirror. In the dim evening she could have been as young as Phoebe. She stared at her tear-streaked face in furious concentration, trying to see herself as someone else might see her, trying to believe that she might be beautiful.

The painting of the bottle was finished. Kit could not put her finger on where it had gone wrong. It was awry, that was all: some mistake of shade or perspective, something that made the bottle sit badly against its background, spilling light instead of containing it. It was skewed, as though there were a kink in her eyes, or hand, or brain.

She had finished it the previous day, in a rush, as the sun set. It was only this morning that she had been able to hold it up to the daylight in her makeshift studio, really looking; and then she had seen the wrongness of it. It was, she thought suddenly, the same strangeness as the girl Phoebe had: you had to keep looking in case there was something you'd missed. She sat down slowly and laid it flat on the table. It was a relief not to see it any more, and yet she found herself reaching for it, tilting it up again, staring. A bottle of light – overbrimming, burning . . .

It was not the kind of work she had done before. Before the War, she had done exact, elegant portraits, almost like photographs: she had enjoyed the discipline, and the challenge of sneaking in a mood or a thought through the tiniest details of light or angle, so subtly the sitters were not quite sure she had done it. At the long drunken parties at Septimus's flat, when they all gave stumbling speeches about Art and Life and Meaning, she had sometimes tried to explain how hard it was to find the balance between face-as-truth and face-as-mask, the dance of concealment and revelation in someone's features and expression . . . She thought no one had ever listened, but later, in Paris, Portia had quoted Kit's words back to her: 'It's the magic of masks, my darling! Isn't that what you always say? How no one can live without a mask?' And Kit had rolled her eyes and retorted, 'I didn't mean it literally.'

That must have been early on, only a little while after she arrived. Later, Portia had stopped teasing her. She had known then that it was only a matter of time: once Portia, of all people, began to be kind . . . ! It was like being wounded, and seeing the nurse beside you hover and hesitate, her fingers already twitching, ready to close your eyes. But she had held on, determined to stick it out, until—

It had been so trivial, really. That was the worst thing. It was nothing she had not done before a hundred times, quite cheerfully. She had been tired, that was all – the nightmares came every night by then, even though she drank as much wine as she could, in the hope of oblivion – and her head was aching, and the light had hurt her eyes. None of that was an excuse. She had not felt particularly worse than usual . . . She remembered passing her hand over her forehead as she arranged her brushes, trying not to look at the man sitting in the chair, ready to have his mask painted; as she mixed the first colour she could hear Portia and Eustache discussing money in the next room, and Marianne on the stairs, exclaiming, 'Oh! *Quelle drôlerie!*'

Then with an effort she had smiled, and said, '*Il fait beau, aujourd'hui, n'est-ce pas?*' and picked up a brush loaded with the shade she had been mixing. She touched it to his mask, and saw that it was muddy and too dark. 'Damn,' she said. The man – she could not even remember his name, for God's sake! – had moved a little under her hand, with a sympathetic huff of breath. Until then she had been looking at the mask; now, for the first time, she met his gaze.

He had steady eyes, the same blue-grey as Parisian roofs. Beneath them, the thin metal line of the mask followed his cheeks like a visor. He would not be able to smile, or speak distinctly, or eat without taking it off. For the rest of his life—

She stepped backwards. She heard him make a strange high sound, like the beginning of someone calling across a wide distance; then, to her horror, she realised it came from her own throat. Her paintbrush dropped to the floor and rolled away. Her vision blurred.

She said, 'Excuse me – *excusez-moi*—'

He said something that she did not understand. But she dared not pause to reply, or ask him to repeat it; she was afraid she would start to cry. She flung herself towards the door, shaking, and heard Eustache exclaim, '*Tiens!*' as she barged between him and Portia. She had to get outside. She could not breathe. She must not let anyone see . . .

Now she stared at the Sussex daylight falling on the paint-flecked table, trying not to remember. She had collapsed, that was all. The details were not important. It had been the end. She had caught the next available train for London, and she had never seen the studio again. There was no use dwelling on it now—

The door opened. The sound jerked her back to the present: she was on her feet, whirling round, before she had time to think. Florence Stock was standing in the doorway;

at the sight of Kit she stumbled backwards, her hand on her heart, as if she did not know which of them was the intruder. She gasped, 'I'm sorry – I'm so sorry – the door was open, the kitchen door – so I thought – I startled you, Miss Clayton—'

She caught her breath. 'Not Miss,' she said shortly.

'I'm so sorry— I beg your pardon?'

'Clayton. Or Kit will do.'

'Kit, then – honestly, I didn't mean to . . .' She reached out in wary reassurance, as if to quiet a growling animal.

Kit was holding a paintbrush, pointed at Miss Stock's throat. She did not remember picking it up. She laid it down on the table beside her painting. 'What do you want, Miss Stock?'

Miss Stock hesitated; then she said, with a tentative step forward, 'Perhaps if you are Kit, then shouldn't I be Florence? There are so few people who call me by my first name.' She added, in a rush, 'I should be so pleased . . .'

'Florence, then.' Kit regretted it instantly; it made it harder to repeat, 'What do you want?'

'I – I interrupted you,' she said, biting her lip. 'Did you paint that? It's lovely.'

'No, it isn't.'

Florence blinked. Then she walked round Kit, and stood looking down at the painting. She said, in a quieter voice, 'No, you're right. It isn't. It's all – funny. Did you mean it to be like that?'

What a bloody cheek she had! But somehow Kit's anger had lost its edge. Some people would have thought she was looking for compliments, and insisted with false brightness that it *was* lovely. She shrugged. 'I'm not sure.'

'It doesn't like being trapped. It wants to be alive.'

Kit started to repeat, 'I'm not sure . . .' and stopped. It was true: the bottle seemed to lean towards the surface of the painting, pulling free of its surroundings. Florence met her eyes, smiling.

'I must get back to work,' Kit said. She plucked the painting away from Florence and stood it against the wall, facing the crumbling plaster.

'Yes. Yes, of course. I'm sorry. I didn't mean . . .' Florence took a step back. 'I only came to apologise, anyway. I'm afraid I was awfully rude to you when we met.'

'Were you? I didn't notice.'

'Yes – at least, I thought—'

'There's no need to apologise.'

'Oh, I'm so glad! Thank you.'

Kit had not meant that, exactly: but she could not quite bring herself to quench the light in Florence's face. What did it cost, to let her think it had been meant kindly? She pushed her hands into her pockets and shrugged.

'I hope you won't think I was taking liberties, but I thought – that is, if you're here on your own . . . I brought you a few things to eat.'

'I'm perfectly happy on my own.'

'Of course – but without anyone to cook for you, I mean—'

'I can cook.' She added, in spite of herself, 'Eggs, mainly.' As soon as she'd said it she wished she hadn't: Florence laughed, and she found herself cracking a reluctant smile at her own expense.

'Well, that's good, because I brought you some more. And a pat of butter. And some apples from the tree in the garden, and some rowan jelly – that's from before the war, no one at home likes it – and some bacon. I wish I could have brought a cake, but the sugar ration—'

'My God. Do I look hungry?'

There was a silence; perhaps she *did* look hungry. She did not want to be the object of charity – still less did she want to be anyone's friend – but it would be churlish to refuse. And butter, and bacon . . . She swallowed, hoping it wasn't obvious that her mouth was watering.

Florence gestured towards the stairs. 'I put it on the table in the kitchen. The door was open.'

'Thank you.' There: it had not been so painful to say it, after all.

Florence's cheeks pinkened, and she clasped her hands in front of her as though she were a singer at a recital. 'You're welcome, Miss— Kit.' She hesitated. 'Is it short for something? Catherine? Or Kitty?'

Kit had an odd sense that the stammered *Miss* and hurried correction had been deliberate. 'Just Kit.'

Florence nodded. 'And . . . ?' She hesitated. 'I thought you were a man, at first.'

'Yes,' Kit said, 'I know.'

'I suppose,' Florence said, raising her shoulders a little, 'your clothes are very practical. For painting, and chopping wood, and cooking— eggs.'

'Yes.'

'And it doesn't bother you, if people think . . . ?' She stopped.

'That I'm a man? No. Why should it? Besides, as soon as they see my face, or hear my voice, they know I'm not.'

'Some people might think, in that case – when they realise – they might . . .'

'Disapprove? Bugger them, then.'

'Oh!' Her hand flew to her mouth; but she was laughing. There was an impish delight in her eyes, as though she had never heard anyone swear before. Maybe she hadn't. Kit imagined living at the vicarage with no one but the vicar and that disconcerting child, and felt a sudden inconvenient flash of sympathy. 'And if they gossip . . . ?'

'I'm used to it,' she said, unable to resist bravado. 'It's

no business of theirs, anyway, what I wear or who I—' She caught herself just on the edge of indiscretion, and bit her tongue. A split second later she knew she should not have stopped: if she had carried on blithely, it would have been all right. It was the silence that betrayed what she had meant, the silence that brought a new look into Florence's face. 'Who I am friends with,' she stammered, belatedly, but it was too late. Oh, fuck it, she thought, and imagined saying *that* in front of this wide-eyed spinster. It was out now, anyway. 'I keep strange company,' she said, 'or rather, I did, before I came here. If you don't like that, you had better not bring me any more Red Cross parcels.'

A flush spread along the tops of Florence's cheekbones, and down the inch of skin visible above her collar. 'It isn't a Red Cross parcel,' she said, and her voice trembled.

Kit stared at her. Had she, in fact, not understood? Florence stared back, her mouth pressed together like a child who had been caught in a misdemeanour. 'Yes,' Kit said, at last. 'I know. It was kind of you.' She gave a cowardly, awkward smile.

'I'm sorry.'

'No. I mean it. Butter and bacon – you're an angel.'

'Now you're making fun of me.'

'Are you hungry?' The words were out before she could stop them. She did not want a guest. She wanted her blessed solitude; she wanted time to think about her picture, and its skewed compelling wrongness.

To her relief Florence shook her head. 'I must go home, I told Mrs Reed I would be back for lunch. Otherwise I would have loved . . . Thank you.'

'Oh,' Kit said, trying to sound sorry, 'well, never mind. It's probably a lucky escape for you, really. Just because I can cook eggs doesn't mean I should.'

This time Florence's laugh had a deep, throaty note that took Kit by surprise. Her flush had faded, leaving only a pink, half-translucent glow. 'Another time, then,' she said. 'I'll leave you to work.'

'All right.' She walked to the door, and held it open – gallantly, she hoped. 'Thank you for coming, Florence.'

Florence nodded. She had a lightness in her step as she crossed the creaking floorboards, tapping a finger on the corner of the table as if to say that she would see it again soon. She paused in front of Kit, smiling. Their eyes were almost on a level – in fact, Kit noticed with a shock, Florence was taller by an inch.

Florence opened her lips to speak. But she didn't. Instead she leant forwards and pressed her mouth against Kit's.

Kit could not remember ever having been kissed so inexpertly. She felt Florence's teeth, and a slight roughness where her lips were chapped and dry. There was a scent of violet *eau de toilette*, and the faint warm fragrance of female skin. A wisp of curly hair tickled her cheek.

She had enough time to notice how little physical pleasure she found in it – and how, in spite of that, her heart leapt, full of heat and electricity as it had not been for months, years . . . Then her better nature won, and she recoiled, thrusting Florence away with both hands so that they ended six feet apart, staring at each other, breathless. 'What the hell are you doing?'

Florence gaped at her, slack-jawed, as though it had been Kit who had leapt upon her. Another blush – red, this time, not a charming rose-blossom tint but true scarlet – swept up and over her face, staining every inch of skin the colour of garish window-box geraniums. 'I don't know,' she said, her voice strangled, 'I didn't – I wasn't . . .'

'You didn't mean to, I suppose?'

Florence held her gaze for a few more seconds, her face unmoving, her eyes wide with shock. Then she dipped her head as if she were cramming herself through a low doorway and stumbled away, into the narrow passage and out of sight. Her feet thumped so quickly down the stairs that Kit braced herself for the cry and crash of a body falling: but the footsteps raced to the bottom, through the kitchen and away. A door slammed.

If Kit had turned her head to look out of the window, she might have seen her running out of the garden gate and round the corner. But resolutely she did not move until she was sure that the road outside would be empty. Then she walked – slowly, calmly, as if to show that she at least was in control of herself – down the stairs into the kitchen. On the table were a couple of waxed-paper packages, a box of eggs, a wooden trug of apples and a jar of clear ruby jelly, arranged like a Dutch still life in the light that slanted through the window. Beside them was a bunch of dahlias, the stems wrapped in damp newspaper. They were beautiful: knots of autumn fire, the veined translucence of the petals like flames where the sunlight caught them.

Kit clenched her jaw. That kiss, that schoolgirl embarrassment of a kiss, that humiliating, lacklustre, chapped-lips kiss – what on earth . . . ? They had said hardly ten words to each other – had only met twice! Surely she had not invited, not given any suggestion that she would welcome . . . ? Damn it, what had Florence expected? That Kit would be grateful? That Kit would pull her closer, tighten the embrace, fasten on her mouth like— oh, it was unbearable even to think about it! She would never have done it to a man. Was *that* what stung the most? Perhaps. Not because Kit wanted to be a man – she had heard that old accusation enough, and knew it wasn't true – but because she did not count as much as a man. She did not matter. She was not – dangerous.

Or was it something else? The memory of the split second before her pride took over, when in spite of the awkward flatness of Florence's lips she had felt—

And the dahlias, for God's sake! Dahlias from the vicarage garden, no doubt, wrapped elaborately in wet newspaper so that they would not wilt in the five minutes between being cut and being put into an old jam jar. Dahlias the colours of bronze and copper and gold, burning so bright you could hardly look away. The rest could be ascribed to charity: the flowers were something else.

God rot Florence's dahlias. And her kiss. And her.

She swept up the bunch of flowers and dropped them into the dustbin. They lay on top of the ash-covered rubbish, their blaze refusing to fade or gutter.

VI

Untitled ('Nightmare'), pencil on paper, 1920

When Julien was finished he went to the grimy little sink and washed up his brushes and glue pot. He set it neatly upside down on the side, watching the water pool underneath. Then he washed his hands, very thoroughly, until he had removed every trace of dirt and paint from under his nails. He stood there for a long time, looking down at his long, perfect, clever fingers. If he stared long enough he would start to believe that they were not his; but today he had enough strength to turn away before they began to horrify him.

By now the brief light had slid past the window, and the room was almost dark. Sometimes he thought the murk had its own smell, mixing with the staleness of grime and old food, and the musty sick-man stench that came from his body. But if he opened the window the noise of the street drifted up, making him cringe and jump at every shout and bang. Better to sit in stinking quiet. And better not to open the window, than to open the window and discover that the stench was in his imagination, and could not be chased away.

He wiped his hands. He hung the thin towel back on its hook.

This was his favourite moment. It was finished. He took his seat at the table where he had been working, and waited. If he concentrated, the room seemed to grow even dimmer, the distant noises softer; and the scene in front of him grew larger, looming. He had learnt this trick when he was a child, with his first toy theatre that Grand-maman had bought from Pollock's. He had taught himself to sit in front of it, his eyes narrowed, his breath quickening, until he was almost sure that the little characters would break out of their frozen positions and speak. He would lose track of time, absorbed in an ecstasy of almost-belief. Amélie laughed at him, but it was only the same thing that she did, on her knees in front of the altar of Sainte Quitterie: he chose to pray for something else, that was all.

She would laugh even more to see him like this, a grown man still playing with toy theatres. She would laugh, that is, until she looked more closely at what he had made, and then she would recoil, disgusted. He would want her to.

At first glance, it looked like his best one from when he was a boy, or at least how he remembered it looking. It was not the largest he had made, but it was the most ornate, decorated in black and dark red and gold leaf. The proscenium arch was curved and gilded, and he had hung real cloth curtains from it – curtains he had made from one of his own shirts, painted deep carmine, because he did not want to go out to buy velvet. The curtains could be drawn across on tiny wires, although now they were pulled aside to allow the scene to begin.

Amélie would have glanced at it, then peered, stiffening, and drawn back with an indrawn breath. He smiled, in his own painful way, at the thought. He would have liked to take hold of the back of her neck and hold her there, forcing her to stare. Her, and every woman in the world – they were so keen to stare, if they wanted to stare at something here it was. Yes, he would keep her there while she protested and kicked, making sure she had time to notice all the details he had spent so much time on. The deformed men, with their monstrous limbs and gaping wounds, the toothed, clawed weapons striding through the landscape with skewered bodies dangling from their jaws, the shit-coloured morass in the background that had swallowed children, leaving nothing but drowned hands and feet. Here, he would say, this is what it is like. War? No. Not just war. The world. This is what the world is like.

He would let her go, then, and let her sink to the floor, aghast and tearful. He would like that; that was the response he wanted. That would be real. That would mean that she saw the truth. What he could say, not what he was – the artist, not the monster. But Amélie was dead, or as good as, buried in some provincial village – probably widowed, or as good as . . .

He settled back in his chair. He let his good eye almost close, so that the darkness grew soft. Now was the time for the landscape between the curtains to take on the tense, liminal quality of a real stage; for the grotesque figures to be only momentarily paused in their horrible pursuits, ready to resume at any moment. He wished they would. *That would be art, if you liked.* If his orgy of truth and hate could come alive . . . That would show them – all the women who stared, all the men who repressed grimaces, all the unmutilated men, all the old men who had promised glory, all the women who did *not* stare, the women, the whores, the damned women . . .

He sat, waiting, on the edge of a climax that never came. After a long time the room was too dark to make out any of the details, and the theatre was only a shadowy box on a shadowy table. His eye was stinging from the effort of staring. He bent his head, and laid a perfect hand very gently against the unfamiliar no-man's-land of flesh where his other eye and cheek had been.

Then he got up and fumbled through the dark to the cabinet beside his bed. He slid out the drawer and looked down at the missing half of his own face. It stared up at him, pale in the murk, unblinking. He hated it; hated it because it was beautiful, because it had been made to look like him, and he had been beautiful. He had always pitied his friends when they could not simply smile at a young lady and see her long to melt into their arms; he had preened in his uniform in front of the mirror before he went to war. He had been handsome – he had been so handsome it had almost had a capital 'H', as though it were his name.

He had been so handsome. He would settle now for not being a monster.

He picked up his mask. It was lighter than you expected, although it grew heavy when you wore it for a long time. It was thin enamelled copper, painstakingly painted to the colours of flesh; or rather, some colours of flesh, the colours of flesh on a hazy, unchanging day – and there were so few hazy, unchanging days . . . It was lifelike, until it hung upon his head, and then it was – something else. He remembered sitting in the corner of the clinic in Paris, while Portia Forbes-Lascelles squinted at him thoughtfully. It had made him dig his nails into his thighs, through his trousers: that was the way men looked at women. Or worse, that was the way men looked at objects: engines that had to be repaired, walls that had to be shored up, corpses that had to be buried.

It had had to be borne. Even though he simmered with rage. He submitted, he thanked, he sat with the others, playing cards, smoking cigarettes, forcing his new blurred, horrible laugh when someone made a joke. At least the others were as bad as he was. But Christ, why did there have to be women there at all? Surely they could see how it added to the humiliation . . . And Portia enjoyed it. He was almost certain. Not that she ever showed it, the bitch. Only, one time . . . He had passed an open doorway and seen her laughing in the studio, leaning against the counter, lighting a cigarette while Kit mixed colours. 'I just think,' she had said, in that cut-glass English that he so despised, 'that a little discreet monogram, on the inside – honestly, what's different from a portrait?'

'We're not God,' Kit had said, quietly.

'Oh, don't be so self-righteous, darling. We make their faces, we should be allowed to sign them. "Paul Tanguy, by Portia Forbes-Lascelles." Or if you insist, "by Portia Forbes-Lascelles – a copy, after God".' She drew on her cigarette with a smack of her lips, tossing back her hair. When Kit did not look over her shoulder she laughed again, and slid a hand through the other woman's hair, caressing her neck. 'Silly old Kit,' she said, 'you know we can't always be solemn. The men make jokes—'

'They're allowed to. They make the jokes, we laugh.'

'Because they're men?'

'Because they're *mutilated*,' Kit said, swinging round. 'Because—' Then her gaze met Julien's, and she stopped.

He had forced himself to go on walking down the corridor, as if he had not heard. He had not cared very much about Portia – had told himself he did not care, anyway, because he had hated her already. But try as he might he could not forget the way Kit had repressed a grimace. Not ashamed on Portia's behalf; no, ashamed on her own account, because she had said aloud that he was no longer a man but a *mutilé*, and she knew that he had overheard. And that it was true.

Kit. He had – *liked* her. Even after that, even though she had never apologised, or spoken of it again. Even though she let Portia maul her about like a whore. She had been calm, and steady, and she had not stared too long or looked away too quickly. Her men's clothes had seemed . . . tactful. As if she did not want to upset him by reminding him that she was female. When at last they began work on sculpting his face, and he gave her the photograph Amélie had dutifully sent back, he had felt a tiny, tiny trace of his old pride: because look, he had been handsome. Even in dog-eared black and white, in two dimensions. Kit had bent over the photo with a magnifying glass, lowering her head with such respectful attention that, in that moment, he had almost felt handsome again.

And she liked him, too. She had cadged cigarettes from him, and asked him where he learnt his good English, and never forgotten to put a paper straw into his cup before she passed it over. She had lent him a book on Hieronymus Bosch that she had picked up from a *bouquiniste* beside the Seine; he still had it somewhere. He had trusted her. He had let himself *hope*. He had believed that it would all be worthwhile. He saw the others with their new faces – Gérard with his new jaw, François with his new nose – and the way they sauntered down the street shoulder to shoulder, and returned laughing as if every observer had been deceived and the whole thing an excellent practical joke. The mask Kit made for him would be even better, because he had been handsome to start with – and yes, the first glance in the mirror (how his heart had thundered in his ears!) had been astounding, marvellous, a miracle. Praise God, praise Sainte Quitterie, his face had come back! He had swung round to embrace Kit, pulling her into his arms, pressing his half-flesh, half-mask lips first to one cheek then to the other; but then . . .

She had recoiled. Not very much, but enough.

Had he realised at that moment? No. He had ignored that tiny qualm, and held on tightly to his hopes. Perhaps it was later, when he wrote to tell her he had moved to London, and she did not bother to reply. Or even later, months later, after the slow attrition of stares and gasps, the women who ducked their heads hurriedly and turned away if he looked back at them? Or seeing himself in the mirror as he lost weight – his fucking *teeth*, if only he could chew properly! – and the mask began to gape at the edges, no longer fitting his skull but hanging like a pale hat on a hook, starkly perfect, its eye serene and uncaring . . .?

Or last night, when the whore he'd picked up in Leicester Square had shrieked and scrambled up from the bed, catching him by the arm and pushing him out into the street again, and shouted through the slammed door, 'Ugh, I won't do a bloody—' She used a word he didn't know, but whatever it was he guessed it meant a *gueule cassée*. Was that when he had understood, really understood, that he would never be whole again? If he had been his old self, she would have swooned into his arms, and been grateful – but now, just because he looked the way he did . . . They were all the same, women, they expected you to defend them, fight for them: but when you did, it turned out that you weren't a glorious hero after all, you were nothing but shit to be wiped off their shoes. Monstrous shit. Mutilated shit. He would have beaten down the door if he could, and then beaten her – but there was a burly man, maybe her *maquereau*, lurking on the landing, and it was no good anyway, he could not make the bitch want him. Even a whore, even a street whore, even for double the price.

A sentence from that book about Bosch came suddenly into his mind. *The people wanted to see Hell: and his art showed it as it must be.* Would Bosch himself ever have imagined that centuries later, men could look at his paintings and recognise a country they had visited? When Julien was in hospital he would have liked to send the *Visio Tondali* to

Amélie, instead of the field postcard: *I am getting on well / expecting to be discharged soon, I have received your letter / telegram / parcel, I am having my guts drawn out like threads / being sodomised by a devil / hanging from a gargantuan key.*

He gave a bark of laughter, and heard the gargle of his soft palate and the flat note where there were no bones to resonate. An ugly noise. It was the last irony, that he did not even sound like himself any more. Even a blind woman would know.

He carried his mask to the table, and wrapped it in brown paper. Then he dragged open the drawer in the cheap reproduction writing desk, laid out a pen, paper, envelopes, and blotting paper. There was no need for stamps, since someone else would deliver the letters he was going to write.

VII

Litlington Church (unfinished), oil on board, 1920

Phoebe spotted the parcel on the hall table when she was halfway down the stairs, and her heart lifted. She hurried down the last few stairs to pounce on it. It was no one's birthday, and not Christmas yet, and Great-aunt Josie, who had sent presents and records from America, had died before the War – but perhaps the Philadelphia cousins had suddenly remembered Phoebe's existence and decided to make up for lost time, or read about the bare shelves in the toyshops and felt a sudden access of guilt. Or perhaps Papa had wanted to surprise her – although that would be very unlike Papa – or even Aunt Florence . . . But as soon as she turned the package over the small pang of excitement died. *Kit Clayton, The Cottage with the Oak Tree, Litlington Road, Haltington.*

Of course it was not for her. When would anything be for her, ever?

She leant her head through the doorway into the drawing room, where Aunt Florence sat embroidering a handkerchief, her hand rising and falling like a machine. 'Aunt Florence, why is there a parcel for Miss Clayton here?'

She did not pause in her stitching. 'I suppose the postman delivered it by mistake.'

Phoebe stared at her rigid profile. 'What shall I do with it?'

'I daresay the postman will take it to the right place tomorrow, if I leave it out for him.'

Phoebe nudged the architrave of the door with her foot, not quite kicking it. Aunt Florence did not sit stolidly, sewing and sewing, as though she were quite content to be still; and yet now she was doing exactly that. 'Maybe I should take it to her,' Phoebe said.

A shrug. 'If you like.'

Phoebe opened her mouth, and shut it again. Aunt Florence disapproved of Kit Clayton – well, naturally; but if, for some reason, she refused to admit it . . . it was no fun. And if Aunt Florence did not care where Phoebe went, or whom she visited, then who did? Papa could hardly be relied on to notice. 'Very well, then,' she said, like a prefect volunteering for prep duty, 'it is the neighbourly thing to do. Poor Miss Clayton must be rather lonely, on her own.'

Aunt Florence did not answer. She picked up her scissors, cut the end of her thread with a precise snip, and held up the handkerchief to examine her handiwork. Phoebe tossed her head, snatched up the parcel, and went out of the front door, closing it behind her with pointed dignity.

She had hoped, of course, that Kit Clayton – not Miss, that Miss would not sit properly in her head, it was absurd to think of the possessor of that androgynous glamour as a prissy, spinster Miss – would be at home. But she had always had an unerring instinct for the presence of other people, and as she walked up the garden path and around the corner to the back door she knew with utter certainty that no one was in.

It was the first time she had come to the house since Mrs

Bone died. At first glance it had not changed very much, except for the slow deterioration of the paintwork and the creeping ivy. There was still a hagstone beside the doorstep, and – she reached up to check, standing on her tiptoes – a long nail slid into the gap between the lintel and the flint wall above. It was funny to find the back door locked, but the spare key – yes – the spare key was still under the rock by the garden gate. Roots had grown over it, so that she had to prise and tear it from the earth. She put all her strength into turning it in the lock. At last, with stiff reluctance, it gave. She stepped into the kitchen.

Most of the girls at school would have come this far by pretending all they wanted was to put the parcel where it would be safe and sheltered, in case it rained. Phoebe did not need to tell herself that. She put it down on the table by the window, and stared round, taking in the mess – just, but only just, the right side of squalor – and the other things that were new: the smell of garlic, the brightly coloured tin of shop-bought biscuits, the black-and-white pottery jar of stilton from Fortnum and Mason's, a half-empty bottle of wine. Then she wandered soft-footed through the door to the stairs, and up; not creeping, because she was not ashamed, but nonetheless silent.

The front bedroom, the larger one that the boys had used, was no longer a bedroom. It smelt of paint and turpentine, so that she guessed before she got to the top of the stairs that it was being used as a studio. The table was covered with drawings, some in pencil, some coloured; sketches were tacked to the walls, their corners lifting a little in the draught. There was an easel, although it had nothing on it. Propped against the fireplace – she saw, when she stepped further into the room – were two paintings, both strange and skewed. One was a bottle throwing a bright shadow; the other was a bunch of dahlias in gold and orange and scarlet. Her dahlias, she thought with an inward jolt, dahlias from the vicarage garden. No one else in the village grew dahlias like that. She was oddly pleased. So Kit Clayton was a thief. Kit Clayton had stolen from her. And they looked stolen, too. They were pulsing with light, bright as forbidden fruit. If she had been a child she would have wanted to lick the canvas.

She went back into the passage and opened the door of the small bedroom, the one where Mrs Bone had slept. There was a single bed, unmade, and a battered suitcase in the corner. She knelt and opened the suitcase: but after rifling carefully through the contents she sat back, frowning. The neatly packed piles of sketches and materials were impersonal, functional, only artists' things. She shut the lid and looked around. There must be a trunk somewhere, with clothes and books and – well, whatever you took with you when you began a new life. Things that would reveal who Kit Clayton was, or who she had been. Letters, photographs, a diary.

But she knew that she would not find them. Instead she drew back the rumpled sheets and put her face into the hollow on the bed where Kit Clayton's body must have lain.

Nothing moved, no one gasped at her audacity, no one dragged her to her feet and slapped her face. Slowly her heart slowed again. She breathed in, trying to distinguish the scent of sweat, the scent of sleep, the scent of skin.

It was sunset when Kit packed up her things and got to her feet, chilled and aching. Until today she had not noticed how thin the autumn air was, or how little heat it held once the sunlight had disappeared. She had been quite warm enough, sitting on a boulder sketching the church from the other side of the field, but now, fumbling her sketchbook and watercolours into her knapsack, her fingers and feet were numb. She shook the circulation back into her limbs, and set off down the gulley – which was a path, really, although the past days' rain had lifted the stones and carved tributaries into the mud between them. It had been a good day's work. From this distance the church was an abstract composition of triangle, square and parallelogram, half submerged in tattered lace; the layered colours behind, in fading, subtle shades of silvery brown and grey, made it seem as though a silken veil had been dropped between the viewer and the world, an obscurity that was part warning and part enticement. Yes, if she could recreate those colours in oils – to make it as elusive, as softly lucent as the reality . . .

She thought about her painting all the way to the back door, and stepped through with a pleasant jolt, returning to reality. The kitchen was warm, thank God; before she even took her knapsack off her shoulders she fed the range with logs, letting the heat blaze on her face until her eyes stung. In a moment she would light the lamp, and get herself some bread and cheese and wine; but first she shut the door of the range, slung her knapsack on to the floor, and dropped into a chair. There was a package on the table, addressed to her in Portia's handwriting.

How had it got there? The door had been locked. But as her stomach turned over she caught sight of a muddy footprint on the floor, the mark of a small, corporeal sole. Hannah Smith had a key. Perhaps she had come on the wrong day to pick up the washing, and found Kit gone and no dirty sheets waiting, and brought the parcel inside in case it rained. No doubt she had meant well – but damn it, what a liberty! Next time Kit would have a word with her, and ask for the key back. And as for Portia, who had sent the parcel . . . She rolled her eyes: but Portia was so distant now, so much part of another life, that she did not really mind. She drew the parcel towards herself, picked the knot apart and unfolded the brown paper.

The air in her mouth seemed to turn to clay, solid, unbreathable. She could not move her eyes from the thing on the table, the thing that shone through the dusk as though it were sucking every particle of light into itself.

It was a face – half a face. Julien's face. His open eye stared at the ceiling, the fine lashes glinting, his cheek smooth . . . No, not his face – Christ, not an actual face! She forced herself to think, to breathe. Julien's mask. The mask she had made, helped make – the mask she had drawn studies for, sculpted, grown in an electrolysis tank, painted . . . the mask that Portia had suggested, jokingly, that she put her signature to.

She stood up and went to the kitchen drawer for matches. Then she lit the lamp and brought it with her back to the table. The circle of light made the darkness in the corners of the room darker; but the thought of extinguishing it again was even worse. If that eye blinked . . . There had been a letter in the parcel. Now she drew it into the lamplight and read it, again and again, until at last she had understood what it was saying.

Julien was dead. He had killed himself in his room in Soho.

Thank goodness he did it with a gun, so the man below heard the shot. Otherwise no one would have known for days. Oh dear I am being macabre, but it is too too sad, really, to think that he was so utterly unhappy and alone. And after we worked so hard! I know you will be heartbroken my darling, would you like me to come down and keep you company for a while? He loved you I think. And you were so kind to him, what a shame you did not keep in touch, but you must not reproach yourself. I hope his letter is not too upsetting . . .

His letter. She had not seen that there was another letter.

She slid it out from underneath the mask. A sealed envelope: at least that meant Portia had not pored over it with avid curiosity. *Chère Kit.*

You can have this back. It wasn't enough.

She knew she would not be able to eat or sleep, so she did not try. She sat in front of the feeble fire in the tiny parlour, wrapped in blankets that did not keep her warm. She drank scalding tea, and that did not keep her warm either.

Julien was dead. She did not know why she minded so much. She had not known him very well; and what did one single death matter, now, in the scheme of things? *He loved you I think.* No, that was only Portia's melodramatic gloss on it – but he had seemed to like her, and she had liked him, too. She stared into the fire that was more smoke than light, remembering. He had been one of the first she had seen at the clinic, when she was still eager. And he had been – different. Striking – horribly striking – because his wound had been so dramatic, as though a surgeon had deliberately erased one exact half of his face, and because even so you could see how handsome he had been. And his voice had not been so bad, really, he managed most consonants one way or another, although sometimes when they were drunk Portia imitated it with sickening accuracy. Once you grew accustomed to it you could understand pretty well. And when he did speak it was mostly about books or art. He had not tried to flirt, like some of the other men. Instead he sat quietly and did drawings, cunning little drawings that were stomach-turning and enviable – so that when she first saw them she said, with genuine pleasure, 'Oh, how horrible!' delighted for once that she could say something that was both true and flattering. After he said he hoped to move to London one day she had given him a card for Septimus's friend's gallery that she found in her pocket. Why shouldn't he be an artist? God knew he had earnt it. She had cherished hopes on his behalf – she had felt, oh, she remembered now, she had felt like his mother! That was foolish; he was five years younger than her, no more. But it had been hard not to feel that she was helping to bring him back to life. If he could leave the clinic, whole . . . not whole, no, she was not crazy. But if they could give him back – enough . . . She had made Julien's mask beautiful. She had spent far too long on it, so that Portia rolled her eyes and told her pointedly how many men were waiting, because she had been determined to get it exactly right. She had been proud of it. After he left for London, she had liked to think of him there. While she and Portia cursed Paris and the air raids, and grew short with each other from exhaustion and misery, and the nightmares got worse and the colours drained out of everything until she held brushes up to the light, struggling to believe that they held anything but grey . . . She had sometimes paused to imagine him safe, walking down the street without attracting any second glances. It was not so far-fetched, really – if it were a rainy day, or at twilight, or if he bent his head and pulled his hat down as low as it would go. The thought of him had been a tiny comfort: one man, at least, who had a new life, who could make great art and forget about the war – one man, she had thought, for whom she had done something good.

But now he was dead. *It wasn't enough.*

The mask was on the kitchen table, behind a closed door. But she could see it in her mind's eye as clearly as if the wall had turned to glass. It lay motionless on its brown paper. The open eye stared at the soot-stained ceiling, its grey-green iris like an agate: beautiful, pitiless, mocking all the effort she had put into it. A piece of enamelled copper, when a man's head had been blown apart. Of course it hadn't been enough! Nothing anyone could do would ever be enough.

She got to her feet, went into the passage, opened the kitchen door, and put the lamp down on the table. The light was soft, blurring the edges of the mask, lending a fleshy warmth to the skin and a shine to the eye. She forced herself to reach out and touch the cheek. It was rigid under her fingers, metal and enamel and paint. But it was so like him, so like Julien . . .

Her throat ached. She swallowed, hard. If she wept for Julien, she would have to weep for all the others too, and then when would she stop? And that was before she wept for herself, and everything she had given and lost, for the futility of it. *It wasn't enough.*

She gathered the corners of the paper in one swift movement, bringing them together so that the mask was a mere brown package. Then she stumbled to the back door and out into the garden. The moon was up, and there was enough light to see by. She had meant to throw the mask on the midden – anything, to stop herself thinking about it! – but as the cold air met her face she knew that was impossible. It was not an ordinary piece of rubbish, to be disposed of easily. Why had he sent it to her, for God's sake? What was she supposed to do with it? As if he had sent her a part of his body . . .

Maybe she should dig a hole and bury it. But the idea of scratching about in the dark was distasteful – not to mention that she would have a grave in her garden for ever afterwards. No. Not earth, but fire. A warrior's end. The tin of the mask would melt, wouldn't it? Or at least the colours would burn away, leaving it only a warped, charred bit of metal that she could decently treat without reverence. She laid the mask down in the tussocky grass near the wall, and began to gather the dead branches which clogged the ground underneath the trees behind the outhouse. Twigs scratched at her arms and face, and dead roots caught between her legs as she walked, but after a few trips back and forth she had piled up enough wood to set alight. She stooped for the mask, but when she went to lay it in the middle of the makeshift pyre she hesitated, and after a moment's thought hung it in the crook of a tall branch instead, at the same level as her own eyes. He hadn't met death lying down.

Somehow, once she had hung it there, she did not like to turn her back on it; but she did, scrabbling against the back wall of the outhouse for the rusting can of fuel she had seen there. It sloshed in her grip, icy cold and heavy. She got the lid off and poured the liquid over the skeletal pile of wood in great splashing gouts. The stink of petrol rose, as heady as alcohol. In the moonlight the face had a deathly tinge. But when she stepped back, wiping her hands on her trousers, the single eye gleamed, watching her. It was so lifelike, with its wet shine, its fine wire eyelashes, that she expected it to blink.

She dug her nails into her palms. Stop it. She had left the matches inside the house. She ducked into the kitchen and rummaged for them in the drawer. Her hands were shaking. She did not let herself think, because if she did she knew she would lose her nerve and slam the door, leaving Julien's mask hanging there like a remnant of flesh in no man's land. There. She grabbed the box and hurried out again into the moonlight.

It was so cold. She told herself it was the beginnings of frost in the air. She tried to strike a match, and felt it snap. She tried again. Her hands were too unsteady. She lowered the box, taking a deep breath; she had to calm down, or she would run out of matches.

But the pause did not help. Instead the chill swept

around her like a tide, running up her backbone, tightening her throat; and with it came the conviction that—

That *what*? That the world was on the edge of something – something monstrous, something *wrong* . . . Septimus had told her once about the pre-dawn grey in the trenches, the waiting before they went over the top. It was not like that, not at all, but the dread, perhaps, yes . . . She turned her head, listening. The little ordinary noises of the evening had stopped, the way birds quietened when a predator approached. There was no sound but the hammering of her heart.

Julien's mask seemed to gather the moonlight into itself. She stared at it as though it were a vessel, slowly filling. The eye looked back at her, knowing.

A match. Strike a match, for God's sake! She raised the box again, and fumbled with numb, clammy fingers. There was a scrape, a spark, a flame leaping in her shaking hand. She lunged forward and threw it. The nub of light dwindled as it fell; then with a joyous gasp the fire leapt up like a row of tongues, unfurling red and gold. She saw them flap raggedly among the branches and lick at the curved edge of Julien's cheek. The firelight danced in his eye; smoke billowed and eddied where the other one should have been. It was too soon, surely, for the metal to soften in the heat: and yet his features seemed to move, his half-mouth drawing breath . . .

The swirling column of smoke thickened, whirled, dissolving and reforming. For an instant a dark figure hung in the middle of the fire, flickering, blurring, going in and out of focus like a motion picture. The mask jerked on its branch like a piece of flotsam caught by a current. No, it was impossible – it was only the wind, or the hot air rising—

Then there was a spitting, crackling burst of flame, and the pale metal shimmered and slipped, falling into the heart of the fire; the smoke billowed outwards in a rush of blackness like a wasps' nest bursting. For an instant she felt the blast of it on her lips, like stinging fog: then it was gone, and she was alone.

She stared round wildly, letting her gaze slide past the ragged flames to the darkness behind: the empty moonlit garden, the oak tree with its last ragged leaves, the hill rising on the other side of the valley. The wide intact sky with its salting of stars. Nothing. No one.

The fire was sinking, the fuel-fed flames dying into ash. The mask had gone, melted or charred to invisibility, and the smoke curled and drifted, acrid and ordinary, pulled this way and that by the breeze. There was not much heat coming from the subsiding embers, but she felt faint warmth on her face and hands, thawing the deep chill in her bones. An owl called from the other side of the road.

Nothing. She had seen nothing. There had been nothing to see.

For an instant, as she opened the back door and went inside, she thought she caught a glimpse of something moving beyond the garden wall: a dark bird swooping, or a cloud blown across the moon. But when she paused to look, there was only the massive uneven shadow of the down, and the pale thread of the path that led upwards; and everything was perfectly still, and only the owl called and called again, as if it was repeating someone's name.

VIII

Sisters (I), diptych, oil on board, 1920–21

Florence had stayed in Eastbourne longer than she had intended, and when she disembarked from the train at Haltington Halt the sun was very low on the horizon and the air was chilly. She shivered as she unlocked her bicycle and clambered onto it, adjusting her skirt; she would have liked to wear trousers, but she could imagine Mrs Reed's smile and Phoebe's raised eyebrow, judging her for trying to be something she wasn't. Already her hands were cold in spite of her lumpy knitted gloves. She swung her satchel into the basket and set off down the road. She had borrowed more books from the library than usual, and the extra weight made the bicycle veer heavily to the side.

It was a long, mostly flat road, crossing streams and waterlogged fields. The sunset sky reflected in flashes from the still water. She slowed down, filled with a sudden yearning that was as compelling and visceral as pain. She did not want to think – it was dangerous to think. But surely she could let herself feel, as long as she did not put a name to what she felt? Oh, if she were somewhere else – somewhere where her heart could break open and let all of this in . . .

She paused at a junction, then picked up speed again, coasted over a stone bridge and round a corner, down a lane where the trees met overhead for a short way before the Downs spread out again like wings on either side. Haltington was not far now. She would be home in time to wash and change for dinner. She grimaced, baring her teeth into the wind, refusing to think about the long dull evening that awaited her. No, stay here, in the freezing, flaming present moment . . .

She was nearly home now. She passed the Bone cottage (carefully, carefully not thinking) and let her gaze drift away from the road ahead, seduced by the colours in the western sky, the perfect gradations from apricot to primrose to *eau de Nil* to azure. Then she caught sight of something in the grass, glanced once – twisted further to see – and suddenly the handlebars tilted and her wheel slid sideways with a crunch. She wobbled, righted herself, and skidded, gasping, to an undignified halt, her bicycle perpendicular to the road.

Oh God. If she had realised . . .

But it was too late now to pretend. All she could do was clear her throat and say, as levelly as she could, 'Hullo.'

It was Kit Clayton, of course. She was crouching on the verge, so that in her long brown coat she might have been some kind of animal.

She did not move. She looked up at Florence, and her face was white, her eyes staring. Florence felt with a jolt that, whatever Kit was seeing, it was not the Litlington Road on a November afternoon, and it was not Florence. 'Miss Clayton – Kit?' she said, forgetting to be cool and distant. 'Are you ill?'

Kit blinked. She moved backwards, stumbling to her feet; then, as if she could not speak, she pointed.

There was a squirrel on the edge of the road.

It should have been dead. Its back legs had been crushed into a sickening smear. But through some horrible force of nature, it was still moving, its mouth open, its sides pumping with rapid breaths, its front legs scrabbling as if refuge were only a paw's-length away. Florence saw from the blood on the road that it had dragged itself a yard or so. It was still trying to reach safety; it would go on trying, hopelessly and agonisingly, until it died.

She said, sickly, 'What happened?' But it did not matter, really. It might have been a predator, or the wheel of a pony trap, or even an automobile: the end result was the same.

Kit shook her head, without moving her eyes from the wretched animal.

Florence looked back and forth between Kit and the squirrel. She should turn her bicycle round and pedal home. If she didn't hurry she wouldn't have time to change before dinner, and she could imagine Phoebe's sidelong disdain at her wind-ruffled hair and mud-spattered hem. She said, 'You can't do anything. It isn't your fault.'

Kit made a wordless, resistant noise as though Florence had pushed her.

'Come on,' Florence said, 'it's getting cold. Leave it. It will die soon enough.' She bit her tongue, because it could not die soon enough, it had already gone on too long. She glanced at Kit, hoping not to see contempt in her eyes, but it was almost worse that she seemed not to have heard. 'Please. You can't . . .' But Kit *could* stay here until it died; obviously she could, it was not as if Florence could stop her.

Florence said, with an authority she did not feel, 'All right.' She looked around. Every cottage in the village had a collection of flints on the doorstep, each one with a sea-bored hole through its heart. She got off her bicycle, cast one brief look at Kit to check that she was still rooted to the spot, and hurried back along the road to the Bone house. She banged open the garden gate, ran up the path and snatched a heavy lump of stone from where it lay half hidden by an overgrown shrub. Her fingers, as if by instinct, found the hole in it, and held it tightly. Her heart was battering in her fingertips. She forced herself to walk, not run, back to where Kit stood like a statue.

She had never killed anything. As she looked down at the struggling squirrel she felt her gorge rise. It was too late to drop the stone and run. But the poor thing – the poor, poor thing! Her own body ached in absurd empathy. Those tiny paws, scrabbling . . . that horrible wound, a bloody messy absence, an obscenity . . . She told herself that a swift ending was the kindest thing; but how could anyone see something suffering so much, and deliberately make it worse? She could not do it. She simply could not. Let nature take its course. At least then she would not have been part of it – she could walk away, cowardly and clean . . .

But then it would suffer more. And – she glanced again at Kit – and Kit too, Kit would stand there staring with glazed eyes, as if she were the one in agony, no more able to walk away than the squirrel itself. Florence was the only one who could help her; the only one who could make it stop. She drew a long, preparatory breath, as if she were about to step over a precipice: and then she did not give herself any more time to think.

She had always thought that killing something would be terrible. She had never realised that if you were sure that you had no choice, it might be both terrible and easy. Once you conquered the first faltering of your hand, and simply let gravity and rock work together: yes, it was terrible, but it was simple, too. A necessary task. A crunch of bone – a sour taste in the back of your mouth – the horrible dying of something with its own mind, its own everything – oddly easy, oddly something to be proud of, when at last you stood up and threw the bloody stone into the ditch.

At first she had to blink at the horizon, to hold back a mounting sob. Then, when at last she steadied herself and looked round, the same shaky reflex resurfaced, this time – shamefully, guiltily – as laughter. Was it the way Kit had finally met her eyes, with a strange wondering expression, like a sleeper waking? Or, mixed with the horror and pity of it, the unexpected exhilaration of having discovered that she was stronger than she thought?

She wiped her hands on her skirt, although they were not dirty. Then she took hold of Kit's arm. 'You're cold,' she said. 'Let me take you home.'

'Thank you.' She meant: for what Florence had just done.

'Come on.' She piloted Kit down the road. It was like walking with a child; Kit let herself be led, dazed and docile, although the colour was beginning to return to her cheeks. Neither of them spoke until Florence had manoeuvred them both through the garden gate and around the side of the house to the back door. It was locked – old Mrs Bone had never locked it – but the sound of the latch rattling as Florence tried it made Kit shake herself and dig in her pocket for the key. She stepped past, unlocked it and turned. 'Thank you,' she said, 'I am quite well now—'

'Let me come in.' Florence had not meant to say it, but the words as they came out still held some of that mysterious authority, earned in blood. And Kit blinked and stood aside, submitting with the same childlike lack of protest.

Florence went in ahead. She did not recognise herself as she checked the range and set the kettle on to boil: she would never have behaved like this at the vicarage. But here, in this cramped little kitchen, she could play at being in charge, she could enjoy seeing Kit draw back a chair and sit down while she bustled about. Anything but think about the squirrel, the poor thing, her hand coming down— no, stop it. She made tea in a teapot that was so dark inside it was almost black, and fetched a jug of milk from the tiny pantry. She found bread and butter and cheese, and put them on a plate with the last wrinkled apple. By the time she set it all on the table Kit's eyes had cleared. She looked up at Florence, and smiled a quiet, constrained smile. 'Thank you,' she said. 'Again. I am getting repetitive, aren't I?'

'I don't mind.'

'I'm sorry. You shouldn't have to look after me – you shouldn't have had to do – *that*. I'm ashamed of myself. I don't know what happened—'

'Don't be silly,' Florence said, settling opposite her. 'It was horrid. Poor thing.'

'Yes.'

Silence. Kit pushed the plate across the table. 'You eat. I'm not hungry.'

'Try,' Florence said. 'You need something. You were as white as a sheet.'

'Not because I was hungry.'

'No. No, I know.'

Another, longer silence. She should have lit a lamp; she did not want to get up now, but the kitchen was getting dark, and in a few minutes she would not be able to see Kit's face. The sweet certainty which had taken hold of her drained away. What was she doing here? What a liberty, to treat Kit as a guest in her own kitchen! And suddenly, bursting through the wall which she had built in her mind, came the memory of the moment weeks ago – oh God, the moment when she had let that stupid – that *mad* impulse—

'I'm so sorry,' she blurted out, cursing herself, but she could not stop. 'I made a fool of myself – I don't know what came over me. Last time I came here, when I – kissed . . .'

Her voice cracked. She cleared her throat, but it would be too humiliating now to recover herself and go on, even if she knew what she wanted to say.

But Kit did not rescue her. She leant back in her chair, crossing her legs at the ankles.

'I kissed you,' Florence went on, after all, forcing through the consonants as though they were obstacles in her path. 'I didn't mean to. It was only – your picture, and you standing there, and your clothes and – oh, *please*,' she said, half laughing, 'please won't you put me out of my misery?'

'Like the squirrel?'

'Oh! No. I meant—'

'I know,' Kit said, and at last she smiled. 'Let's forget it, shall we? Least said, soonest mended. And the squirrel too, Christ knows I don't want to think about that. Is it a bargain?'

'Yes. Thank you.' She had to look away to hide her relief. Her gaze fell on the teapot. 'Shall I be mother?'

'If you like.'

She poured two cups and passed one across the table. It was almost dark now, and everything was soft and powdery with shadows. A bubble of happiness rose inside her, expanding until she could hardly breathe. If she had known, this morning, that she would be sitting here with Kit, how eagerly she would have leapt out of bed, how easy it would have been to shake off Phoebe's sidelong glance at her hat, how joyfully she would have boarded the train back from Eastbourne! It was a lesson in optimism.

Kit met her eyes through the murk and raised her teacup in a wry little toast. Then, as if a new thought had struck her, she asked, 'What happened to your bicycle?'

Florence sprang to her feet, one hand flying to her mouth. Her bicycle! She had left it lying in the middle of the road. What was she thinking, how had she forgotten, how could she sit here in such complete oblivious contentment? She glanced at the window and saw a deep blue sky, and the evening star blazing in the bare branches of the oak. 'I must go back. I must get home,' she said. 'Heavens, I didn't realise how late it was.'

'Goodbye, then.'

'Goodbye.' She hesitated.

'I shall be quite all right. I promise.'

That was not exactly why she had not wanted to go; but she said, 'Yes, of course,' and made herself smile.

'Come back another time,' Kit said, 'if you'd like.'

'Oh! May I?'

'You might as well.' Then, with a sudden disarming grimace, she added, 'I don't know what I should have done if you hadn't come along. I'd still be there. I wouldn't have had the strength to do what you did.'

'It had to be done, that's all.'

'Yes,' she said, with a glint of mockery, 'but I couldn't do it. Go on, you'd better go. I daresay there's a better dinner waiting for you than bread and cheese.'

'I'll come back,' Florence said. 'Thank you.' It was all right, all of it was all right: the squirrel, that stupid kiss, her whole clumsy self. And she would come back soon, and it would be more than all right. But it would be embarrassing to linger any longer. She raised her hand in an awkward wave, and blundered through the darkness to the door.

The air outside was keen and cold, almost scentless; the moon had not risen but the stars were as bright as – as stars, she thought, and wanted to laugh, she had never seen stars that filled her with such wordless, inarticulate exaltation. She did not care that she would surely be late, and Phoebe would ask her pointedly where she had been. She would lie. Why shouldn't she lie? She had a right to her own secrets.

She strode down the road towards her abandoned

bicycle with her hands in the pockets of her coat, refusing to let herself dance.

Something had changed, Phoebe thought. Something was wrong. It was more than the tilted-off-axis drift that had been growing inexorably for months: no, this was something else, a sharper, newer sensation that made her want to scratch irritably at the furniture like a cat. It was Aunt Florence. Aunt Florence was . . . different.

For a start, she had replaced her horrible collapsed pudding of a hat, and bought a new winter coat too. As she rode home from school Phoebe had wobbled on her bicycle and almost gone into the hedge when she realised that the lady in green velvet with a fur collar was Aunt Florence. The girls in her form would have swooned over that ensemble. It did not suit Aunt Florence to be fashionable: she had the wrong kind of face to go under a turban, which was chic and daring and utterly inappropriate for someone like her. And how had she afforded it? But when Phoebe asked as much – treading the line between faux naivety and impertinence like a high-wire artiste – Aunt Florence only replied calmly that she had had a little inheritance from Phoebe's grandmother, as if she had not noticed the malice behind the question. Then she had smiled, stroking her fur collar with languid fingers. That gesture had infuriated Phoebe more than anything. It was indecent, somehow.

It was not just her clothes, either. Her face was brighter, her skin clearer. Not that she used rouge – no, Phoebe might have understood that, and pitied it as her aunt's doomed attempt to cling to youth. Whatever the glamour was, it was deeper than her skin. She smiled more, and her eyes slid away to the middle distance, as if her attention were constantly elsewhere: as if Phoebe were a midge, a mote, nothing at all. Even her hair seemed brighter, as if she were brushing it for hours, and washing it with egg yolks and vinegar. Perhaps she was. But then – why?

She went out more – for walks, she said, and to run errands, volunteering to go to the general store in Alfriston when Mrs Reed ran out of anything, and to Eastbourne every week, even when Phoebe was sure she had not finished her library books. And when she came home she was light-hearted and kind. Kind! The cheek of it, Phoebe thought, hopelessly resentful. It was not fair. She was the one who dreamed of escape – and now Aunt Florence was behaving as if she had already escaped, as if her soul was somewhere else, soaring above the Downs on languorous wings. She was slipping away, as Mama had done—

No. That was not it. It was nothing to do with Mama. It was only that it was all wrong. Phoebe watched her: watched her leave, watched her return. Watched her smile to herself as she embroidered in the drawing room after dinner, when a month ago she would have frowned over the same task. Watched her sit for whole minutes over a single page of a book. Wherever she went then, it was infuriating not to be able to pursue her. Even at school, the thought of Aunt Florence was like a piece of grit in Phoebe's shoe. She could not concentrate on her lessons for wondering. What was she doing now? Why did it make her so happy?

Then, one day, she saw Aunt Florence coming out of the Bone house. It was Founder's Day, and an annual half-holiday, so Phoebe was coming along the road hours earlier than was usual. She slowed down, not wanting to be seen: she was sure, somehow, that Aunt Florence would not have stepped out so blithely if she had known Phoebe was there. She was dressed in her new green get-up, and had an empty basket over her arm like the heroine in a fairy tale; and she was humming quietly, her voice dying on the higher notes so that the melody was full of holes.

Phoebe watched her go round the corner, until she was lost to sight behind the lacework of winter hedgerow. Then she leant her bicycle against the front wall of the cottage, and went up the garden path to the back door. It stood slightly ajar: Kit Clayton was in the kitchen, washing cups. Her sleeves were rolled up, like a man's, but her shirt clung to the shape of her breasts and showed a V of skin where her collar was unbuttoned.

Phoebe knocked on the open door. Kit Clayton called, 'Come in,' and at the same moment pivoted on her heel, smiling. When she saw Phoebe her smile changed a little; so that Phoebe knew immediately that she had thought it was Aunt Florence, returning for something she had forgotten. It made her stomach clench to see that spark of intimacy flare and die in the same instant. Was that why Aunt Florence looked so happy?

'Oh,' Kit said, 'I thought . . . Phoebe, isn't it? Your – Florence has just left. You might catch her up if you hurry.'

Phoebe said, 'Are you and my aunt friends, now?'

'I – yes, I suppose we are. She brought me some jam.' There was a pause. Kit swilled out a teapot with water and set it upside down on the side to drain. She said, 'Did you – er – want something?'

'Are you painting her?' That would explain the new hat and the shining hair.

'No. No, I – no.' Kit wiped her hands and leant back against the sideboard. 'Shouldn't you be at school?'

'It's a half-holiday today.'

'And you came to see me?' There was an ironic note in her voice, as if she suspected Phoebe of some ulterior motive. 'How flattering.'

Phoebe hesitated. She should leave; but it would mean admitting defeat, admitting that she had no business here. Admitting, too, that Aunt Florence had every right to be friends with someone who wore men's clothes and no stays – someone who amazingly, gorgeously did not seem to care, as long as she was free . . . She said, grasping for anything, 'You've moved the hagstone on the doorstep.'

'The what?'

'There was a stone with a hole in it on the doorstep. Someone's taken it away.'

'Oh, was there? Well, if it was in the garden, I imagine it was included with the lease of the house—'

'You should put it back. It's bad luck to move it.'

'Really? How quaint. I mean . . .' Kit raised her eyebrows. 'That's very interesting. I didn't realise. If I find it I'll be sure to replace it.'

'Mrs Bone told me that the stones had to stay where they were. A stone at every doorway, and a nail over the lintel, and salt—'

'Mrs Bone – was she the one who was a witch?' There was no doubt now that Kit was laughing at her.

Phoebe curled her toes in her shoes. 'She lived here all her life,' she said. 'She knew. It isn't a joke. You can ask anyone in the village. They'll tell you. Not Papa, I mean, or Aunt Florence, but anyone else. She said that so close to the Face, you had to protect the house.'

'The Face . . . ? Oh yes.'

'The Face calls things to it,' Phoebe said, 'and this house is in their path. You have to be careful.'

Kit rolled her eyes, pushing herself away from the sideboard. 'Aren't you a bit old for this sort of thing?'

'It's true.'

'Well,' Kit said, 'the Face has gone now, anyway. I looked for it the other day, and you can't see it at all. So I won't worry too much about it.'

'It hasn't gone. Not completely. If it stopped working . . .' She stared at Kit, wondering if there were any words that would convince her. It was not fair for Kit to look at her like that, as if she was silly and stupid. She remembered Mrs Bone, after George had been killed, when weariness and grief had worn away at her reserve: once she had said, *they come looking, the dead ones, they want to feed* . . . 'Mrs Bone said the Face—'

'Oh, for God's sake!' Suddenly Kit caught her arm and swung her round, shoving her towards the door. 'That's enough,' she said. 'Shoo. Go on. Run away home.'

'But I—'

'That's *enough*. Florence has told me about you. Go on. And don't come back.'

Kit whirled back into the kitchen and slammed the door. The bolt shot across.

The breeze lifted a few dead leaves and sent them skittering round her feet. Everything else was still and quiet. Phoebe wanted to scream at the injustice of it; she wanted to stoop for a stone and bang the door until it splintered. But she did not move. It would not do any good. It would only make Kit even more certain that she was a malicious, spoilt little girl. No doubt that was what Aunt Florence had said about her. She would not win by fighting now.

She looked up at the blank, blind hillside. She could not see the Face, either; but it was there, still working, only fainter, less visible . . . it had to be. Otherwise . . . But she did not let herself follow that *otherwise*. She picked her way down the overgrown path, to the garden gate. She did not know how she knew, but something inside her was certain that Kit was standing just behind the kitchen door, listening to her retreat.

A few days later Florence woke early, with a delicious tingle in her stomach and a tension in her limbs that made her stretch all the way to her toes and fingers. It was like being a little girl again; like her birthday or Christmas, or the day of the Sunday-school picnic. The sun had not yet risen, and her room was dim with the winter pre-dawn; but in spite of the chill she threw off her blankets and dressed without flinching. She wanted to sing aloud. It was today, today . . .

Mother would have said that she should not get her hopes up; she would have wagged her finger and warned that there was many a slip 'twixt cup and lip. But Florence could not quell her buoyant heart. Today, it was today!

She crept down the stairs in stockinged feet, carrying her shoes. It was like playing truant – indeed, it *was* playing truant, Dr Manning would be perturbed at her absence from the morning service – and it was thrilling. She had been such a dutiful child, hoping that she might make up with compliance for what she lacked in beauty or charm: and even though she had known, of course, that she would never be as beloved as Imogen the habit of obedience had never really left her. Not, she thought, until now – and then smiled, because it was hardly the rebellion of the century to miss church on one single Sunday. Nor was it a terrible crime to make thick doorstep sandwiches from yesterday's joint of meat, or to cut a thick quarter of the cake Mrs Reed had made to celebrate the end of sugar rationing. She wrapped everything in waxed paper and packed it carefully in an ancient but sturdy haversack that she had discovered in the box room. She added a canister of tea, and – oh, *this* was a rebellion! – a small flask of brandy, filled from the bottle that Mrs Reed kept in the high cupboard for medicinal purposes.

It was heavy, but not too heavy. She shut the kitchen door and tiptoed across the passage into the drawing room. No one stirred: no one had heard. She wrote, *Have gone for a walk, will be back this afternoon*, blotted the note and left it on the hall table.

She leant her bicycle against the garden wall, and then went back for Phoebe's. No one would notice it was gone, least of all Phoebe, who only used it to get to school. When she had dragged the second bicycle through the gate she set off, walking between both bicycles and steering them with outstretched arms, trying not to get her skirt caught in the pedals. But she did not care how absurd she looked: she was free, setting off on an adventure like the hero of a picaresque novel. For a moment she could not help but remember the boys in Eastbourne, marching off to war – but that was different. Today was special, she would not let today be tainted by anything.

There was a light in the kitchen of the Bone cottage. She paused in the road, savouring the sight of Kit moving back and forth in front of the lamp; how glorious that someone – and not just anyone, Kit – was waiting for her! Before she was tired of watching, the lamp was extinguished. The back door opened and closed, and Kit came striding down the path, raising a hand that was only just visible in the paling darkness. 'Am I late? Brrr, it's cold. Have you been waiting long?'

'Only a minute,' she lied, and thrust her own bicycle towards Kit. 'Here. I'll have Phoebe's, that way you needn't worry if you scratch the paint.'

'Splendid. Come on, I must get my legs moving or I'll freeze.'

In fact it was colder, at first: there was not much need to pedal along the flat road, and icy air rushed past Florence and made her gasp. But it was like flying, she thought, wanting to stretch her arms out; like being a gull, lifting and falling on the wind. And as they came through Litlington the sun rose, flooding the road with light and then slow, subtle warmth. Kit was riding ahead; she looked round and called out, 'Shall we stop?' and they drew in, panting, to sit on a low flint wall and drink black tea out of Florence's canister. By the time they set off again, Florence was warm all the way through; although she could not have said whether it was because of the sun, or the tea, or the closeness of Kit's shoulder brushing against hers, and the brief touch of their fingers as she passed the cup.

As they rode south, the bells of the different churches rang across the valley in random music. Florence thought of the congregation huddling in Haltington Church and rejoiced that she was not with them. At last they came to the final junction, and ahead of them the river lay smooth and serpentine, curving back and forth across the estuary until it reached the sea. It blazed like fire – halfway between silver and gold – the sky and the water both so bright that a veil of light seemed to lie over the whole world. She swerved and stopped on the verge, wiping water from her eyes, and Kit came to an ungainly halt next to her, laughing. 'My goodness,' she said, 'isn't it lovely?'

'Yes.'

A pause. Kit's face was in shadow, against the astonishing sky.

'Shall we go on?'

'Yes. Yes, I only wanted to get my breath back.'

They went on. Now they were riding along chalk paths, and the bicycles jolted and bucked and kicked up stones. After a while they both dismounted and pushed them. Florence glanced over her shoulder, afraid that after all it had been a bad idea; but Kit smiled at her, and said, 'I'm getting hungry,' and it was all right.

The path ended. They dragged the bicycles a little way up onto the pebbles, and then left them behind as they walked towards the sea. There was not much wind, and the water was glassy, a wintry, opalescent blue. In the sun it was warm enough to sit still, without a hat or gloves; Kit lay down, cradled by a dip in the shingle, and smiled with her eyes closed.

Florence unpacked the food she had brought and pushed a sandwich into Kit's hand, who sat up and grinned. 'Thanks. I brought lunch too,' she said. 'We'll have enough to feed a multitude.'

'I'm not sure about that. I'm ravenous.' And she was: now that she had stopped moving, her stomach felt like an empty bag, flapping against her backbone. She tore into her sandwich, and heard Kit laugh softly. She did not mind. The meat was good, the bread, the butter – she had used too much butter, more than her fair share, and it was rich and slippery and delicious in her mouth – and she crammed mouthfuls in as though she had been starving. She *had* been starving, she thought, although not only for food. She had been starving for Kit's laughter, too, and the space and the sea and the wide sky. For this, all of this. She ate until she was full and lay back on the pebbles.

When Kit had finished too she gathered the waxed paper, folded it neatly and tucked it into her own knapsack. 'Chocolate?'

Florence said, 'Yes, please,' even though it was indulgent to eat more. She dropped the chocolate into her mouth without raising her head, and as it dissolved on her tongue she felt another part of herself dissolve in the same tide of sweetness.

Kit propped herself up on her elbows. After a while she said idly, 'Do you mind missing church?'

'No. I used to find it comforting, but now . . .' She pushed herself up too, so that her face was on a level with Kit's. How extraordinary it was to be the object of such attention, as if her answer really mattered! 'It seems so – meagre. As if it's asking so much of me – asking me to be content with so little – and all it gives back is . . .' She hesitated.

'Yes? What does it give back?'

'I used to think,' she said slowly, 'that it gave me the strength to endure.'

'And now?'

'Now I think . . .' She looked into Kit's steady eyes, and drew a deep breath. 'Now,' she said, in a rush, 'I think it doesn't give me anything.'

It was a shocking thing to say, but Kit did not show any sign of being shocked. 'I understand, I think,' she said. 'I suppose it was different for me. I never believed it, really. I couldn't be good, no matter how hard I tried, so I didn't bother trying.'

Florence said, smiling, 'Were you a naughty child?'

'Not exactly.' Kit smiled too; but then she dropped her eyes to a pebble she had picked up, turning it over in her fingers. 'I didn't go to school. I lived with my mother, and she adored me – so for a long time it never occurred to me that I was anything but perfect. But then . . .' She lifted the pebble, scrutinising it like a goldsmith examining a diamond. 'I realised I was – different. That I'd never want to marry a man. That I . . .' She slid a glance at Florence's face. 'Well – you know what I mean, don't you?'

Florence said, carefully, trying to sound as if she had said the word many times before, 'Do you mean that you are a – a lesbian?'

Kit grinned, and dropped the pebble. 'Yes,' she said, 'that's exactly what I was trying to say. But I wasn't sure whether you knew . . . I mean, I know you kissed – no, sorry, I promised not to mention that,' she added, as Florence winced. 'Don't worry. Honestly. I know you didn't mean it. It's different for you. Go on, what were you going to say?'

'So when you understood that you were a lesbian –' it was easier, the second time, although Florence still stuttered a little '– you felt that God didn't want you, and so you decided not to believe in Him?'

'God? I don't know. The Church, yes.'

Florence nodded. She picked up her own pebble and rolled it in her hand, looking for something that marked it out from the others. 'I suppose it *is* frowned on,' she said, trying to sound worldly, 'to prefer the – the clitoris.'

Kit jerked upright, making a sound like a soda siphon. '*What* did you say?'

'The—' But the sound died in her throat at Kit's expression; then, as Kit first sputtered and then cried with laughter, a dizzying wave of heat swept over her, so strong she could hardly see. At last she said, in a small stiff voice, 'Excuse me. I was under the impression that it was the appropriate term.'

Kit wiped her eyes. 'I'm sorry,' she said. 'No – truly, Florence, forgive me. It was only – I wasn't expecting . . . Where on earth did you hear that word?'

'In the newspapers,' Florence said. 'I had to look it up, to see how to pronounce it.'

'The – ? Oh God, yes, the Pemberton Billing trial.' Kit grimaced. 'Sodomites and lesbians. Disgusting immorality. The treasonous forty-seven thousand in thrall to the enemy. I suppose you never thought you would meet one of them.'

'I didn't think they were people like you. He said that they were dancing girls and actresses. Or judges and MPs.'

'For the record, I am not a traitor,' Kit said, with an ironic edge. Then she raised an eyebrow. 'Why did you need to know how to pronounce it?'

'I was reading aloud to my mother.'

Kit stared at her, her expression serious but her eyes dancing. 'Your mother? And what did she make of it?'

Florence looked away. 'She didn't – make anything of

it. She was dying. I don't imagine she heard.' She could remember it as if it were yesterday: the dim, stuffy room, the rattle of Mother's breathing, the smell of stale flesh and unclean sheets. The nurse had told her that Mother was unconscious, and there was no point speaking; but she had not been able to bear the silence. So she had read the newspapers, carefully, every page. Later she wished she'd chosen something else – Dickens, Eliot, Tennyson – but at the time she had been so numb and exhausted that she had picked up the papers without thinking. She had hardly taken in what she had read; it was only now that she wondered if the last thing Mother heard had been about diseased morals and perversion and sadism. Would it have been worse than the other news, the Germans gaining ground towards Paris, the battles of the Oise and the Marne?

Kit reached out and took her hand. 'I'm sorry,' she said. 'I wasn't laughing at you.'

She did not look round. She held on to Kit's warm fingers until she was sure she would not cry; then, with a rueful sniff, she drew her sleeve across her face and got to her feet. 'I'm going to walk along the beach a bit,' she said. 'Coming?'

'Do you mind if I stay here and draw?'

'Of course not.' She did, a bit; but when she had gone a few yards she looked back and felt a pang of tenderness and pleasure to see Kit already frowning over her sketchpad, her hair whipped by the wind into a crest like a cockatoo. To leave, striding over the shingle, knowing that she was leaving someone behind, someone who would wait for her and be there when she turned back . . . it was another thing she was grateful for, laughable and miraculous. She set off with renewed energy, swinging her arms like a hockey captain.

She walked along the beach until she was standing in the

shadow of the cliffs. There she stopped, digging her hands into her pockets to warm them, and looked out to sea. For a moment she caught herself listening for the sound of the guns. But that low grinding was only the waves, or perhaps her blood. She bent down to search for flat stones, then crouched and sent them skimming over the water.

She could have done this before, she thought. She could have ridden here on her bicycle, and brought a picnic, and played ducks and drakes. She could have been as happy as she was now. But she knew it was not true: she was happy because of Kit, yards away on the beach, oblivious to her presence. She smiled and waved, but there was no response. It didn't matter.

She wandered slowly back to where Kit was sitting. As she crossed in front, Kit looked up and smiled. Florence sat down and poured herself some tea. The heat and bitter tannin made her mouth tingle.

'Do you mind if I carry on?' Kit said, without pausing.

'I don't mind anything if you don't,' Florence said. As soon as she'd said it she was afraid it was stupid, the sort of thing a schoolgirl might have said; but Kit only gave a distracted flash of a grin and tore the page from her sketchbook to start again.

She should have brought a book. But as time passed, and the sun slid round and a haze of cloud built up, she found that it grew easier to sit still, her hands linked around her knees; and that her thoughts quietened until she was hardly thinking at all. It was too cold to fall asleep, but she felt emptier and stiller with every moment: as though her awareness were seeping out of her body into the air, joining the rising breeze and the tide, leaving her body behind.

She had closed her eyes; when she opened them, Kit was sketching again. 'It's all right,' Kit said, her eyes dipping back to the page, 'you can relax.'

But she wanted to sit still, to be a good subject. She felt a twitch building in the corner of her mouth, but she kept it at bay. She stared at the sea without seeing it. She could hear the scratch of the pencil lead, and the flapping of the paper in the wind. Her hair blew across her eyes. Were her cheeks bright red? And her lips were chapped. Would Kit put that in the drawing? She listened, keeping her eyes front, trying to identify curves and angles, lines and shading from the different sounds the pencil made. That rasping might be the shadow next to her nose, that long sweep the bones of her jaw . . . Finally Kit leant back, kneading her neck with her free hand. 'There,' she said, carefully ripping the page from the book and holding it out. 'I haven't got it properly. But you can see if you like.'

'Please, I'd love to.' She took it, already ready to tell Kit how beautiful it was. And it was. But it was not her. She had not realised that Kit was sitting at that angle, looking past her, at the broad sweep of sea and sky and cliffs; there was nothing in the picture to hint at Florence's presence there at all. She said, 'It's beautiful,' with a chirpy emphasis that made her want to bite her tongue, then added, 'Thank you for letting me see,' with a stiff politeness that was almost worse. Then she gave it back. At least, she held it out, but as she did the wind rose in a sudden gust, whipping the paper into wings. For a split second it flapped frantically against her fingers; then suddenly it was gone, whirled into the air and away.

'Oh – damn it,' Kit said, struggling to her feet in a rattle of stones. 'Damn it, I thought you had hold of it.'

'I'm sorry,' Florence said, 'I'm awfully sorry, I didn't mean . . .' Or had she? Perhaps she *had* meant to let it go. She got up too, and took a few helpless steps. The paper danced further and further away, over the waves.

'Never mind,' Kit said. She bent and collected her

sketchbook, lifting it carefully to keep the loose pages between the covers.

'But your lovely drawing . . .' Florence said, to her back. 'I'm sorry.'

Kit shrugged. 'We'd better be getting back,' she said. 'Look how low the sun is. If we don't hurry it'll be dark before we get home.'

Florence nodded. She crouched and packed the tea canister into her bag. They had not eaten the cake, nor drunk the brandy. Her throat was aching, her eyes stinging. Stop it, she thought. You don't deserve pity. How stupid, to spoil the whole day like this. Kit was right to be angry with her. She had had no right to be disappointed. If she had really let it go on purpose— ! No, surely she was not that childish, it had been an accident, definitely an accident. But she should have been more careful. She should have handled the drawing with proper respect. And then to stand there, lumpenly staring, as it blew away! She should have dived into the icy sea and swum for it . . .

The pebbles in front of her eyes blurred and wavered.

'Florence?'

She blinked, without looking up. She must not let Kit see that she was crying.

'Florence, what is it?'

'I'm perfectly all right,' she said. 'The wind is making my eyes sting a bit.'

There was a silence. Please let that have convinced her, she thought. Please let's go home now, without having to look at each other. Then Kit dropped to the ground beside her, into her field of vision, and it was no good pretending.

She squinted up into Florence's face. 'What is it? Not the drawing? You mustn't worry about it – I'll do another. It was only an *aide-mémoire*.'

'I didn't mean to let go of it – honestly—'

'I know. Of course I know. But you mustn't *cry* over it! It's just a drawing.'

'But it was lovely – and then you were angry with me –'

Kit wrinkled her nose. 'I was being beastly. It was my fault it blew away.' She took hold of Florence's arm and shook it gently. 'Now stop it. There's nothing to be sad about. One sketch, flying away in the wind! We've weathered tougher things, haven't we?'

Florence laughed, and sniffed. 'Yes.'

'Good.' She seemed to notice her grip on Florence's sleeve, and let go. 'But you need to grow a thicker skin,' she added, more briskly, 'or you'll die of a broken heart before you're thirty.'

'Mother always said I had a heart of stone.'

'And was she always right?'

Florence laughed again and shook her head. She fumbled in her sleeve for her handkerchief and blew her nose. Then, before she had time to regret it, she said, 'Why didn't you draw me?'

There was a silence. She looked up to see that Kit had turned to stare at the sea. 'I'm sorry,' she said, quickly, 'of course you can draw whatever you want – I mean, I don't know anything about it – you're an artist, my goodness, how impertinent of me – and why *should* you draw me, it's not as if I'm anything very special—'

Kit held up her hand. 'Stop it.'

'Yes – I'm sorry—'

'Florence, *stop.*' Kit shook her head, but she was smiling now. 'It isn't you. It isn't what you think.' A shadow crossed her face, and she seemed about to add something else; but she hesitated, and decided against whatever she had been going to say. Instead she pulled her knapsack on to her back, scrambled up the ridge of shingle and held out her hand. 'Come on,' she said. 'Here, do you need a tug?'

Florence slung her haversack over her shoulder and let Kit haul her upwards. They picked their way over the pebbles to the place where their bicycles lay, pedals entangled. As she mounted her bicycle, she looked back at the sea, breathing in: as if she could capture the day she had had, draw it into her lungs and never let it go. Now the haze almost covered the sky, tinged with gold and rose where the sun was hanging low over the sea. In the east the rippling chalk cliffs faded into bluish grey.

'I want to paint that,' Kit said softly. 'Look at the light.'

The breeze ruffled her hair, blowing it across her mouth, tickling her cheek. 'Yes. The Sisters,' she said, marvelling, 'look at the Sisters.'

'The sisters?'

'The cliffs. The Seven Sisters. That's Haven Brow, nearest to us. I can't remember the others.'

'Ah.' Kit nodded. They stayed where they were, shoulder to shoulder, until a sharp gust of wind battered them and Florence shivered. Then Kit said, 'Come on,' piloted her bicycle round in a tight circle, lifted herself onto the saddle and swerved away down the path.

Phoebe and her father ate their dinner in silence, both trying not to glance too much at the empty chair on the other side of the circle of lamplight. She was not hungry; the cold cuts were tough, and the reheated suet pudding so heavy she could have sworn the table creaked under its weight. She pushed her food about her plate, while her father chewed and swallowed.

She had not known she was listening for the back door until she heard it. Then there were soft footsteps along the tiled passage; they halted outside the dining room and then went on towards the stairs. She sprang to her feet and flung open the door. Aunt Florence had one foot on the bottom step, and her hand on the banister: she looked round and froze, like a burglar. 'Oh,' she said, smiling, 'Phoebe, you gave me a shock.'

'Where have you been?'

'Didn't you get my note? I went for a bicycle ride, to the sea.'

'It said you were going for a walk.'

'Well – a walk, a ride, does it matter? Good evening, Horace,' she called, raising her voice, 'I'm sorry I'm so late. I thought I should go upstairs and change, before I disturbed your dinner.'

'We were worried, my dear,' Phoebe's father said, from his seat at the table.

'I had a puncture just past Litlington.' She laughed. It was a light, delicious hiccup of a laugh, as if *puncture* were a word for something rather marvellous. 'There was no hope of mending it, of course. We had to walk the rest of the way.'

'When it got dark, and there was no sign of you . . .'

'It's wonderful outside,' she said, 'freezing but the sky is so clear and black, and the stars . . . What is that quotation? "They shall make the face of heaven so fine that all the world shall be in love with night." You should go out and look before you go to bed.'

'The cold does not agree with my rheumatism, my dear,' Papa said.

'No. No, of course. Well – I must go and wash, I'm an awful mess. Please don't wait to go back to your dinner.'

'Who is *we*?' Phoebe asked. 'You said, *we* had to walk the rest of the way.' She knew, of course: but she wanted to see Aunt Florence admit it in front of Papa.

'Miss Clayton,' Florence said. But there was no shame in her voice, nor even defiance; and Papa did not even blink.

'Perhaps you have seen her, Horace, she has been living in the Bone house for several months now.'

'Oh? No, I'm not sure I have. She has never been to church, that I recall.'

Aunt Florence hesitated; then she said, 'I would call her a nonconformist.'

'Ah. Well, I have some sympathy, the Quakers did some excellent work in the War.' He raised his fork as if it were an aspergillum. 'You must invite her for dinner. I daresay she does not celebrate Christmas, but we can offer her some hospitality nonetheless.'

'That – that would be very kind.'

'Good, good. Well, tell Mrs Reed when to expect her. I must say, Florence, I am glad that you have found a friend. I know that for women that kind of thing is important –'

'Thank you, Horace.'

'But please do make an effort not to let it disrupt the household,' he went on, with a kindly wave of his fork. 'You must not forget your domestic duties, and your sense of decorum. No more straggling home in the dark like a maid on her day off.'

'Yes. You're quite right, Horace.' But the inscrutable light in her eyes did not waver, as though she were watching a comic play in which she played no part. 'Good night, then.'

Phoebe said, 'Aren't you going to have some dinner?'

'Oh, actually – on second thoughts, I'm not very hungry. We had more sandwiches than we needed.' She gave them a final, unseeing smile and ascended the stairs. She trailed her hand over the banister, Phoebe noticed, wafting and gliding as if she were a lady from a soap wrapper – all flowers and drapery – instead of an ageing spinster in a muddy skirt and dusty shoes.

Phoebe shut the door and sat down in her chair. Papa began to eat again.

There was a silence. A snatch of hummed melody drifted down from the landing at the top of the stairs.

'Well,' Papa said, 'it does me good to see her happy, for once.'

Phoebe did not answer. She put her knife and fork neatly together on her plate, and smiled a sweet, demure smile.

IX

Christmas Card, pen and ink on card, 1920

The door swung open almost as soon as Kit had knocked to reveal Florence standing in the hallway, beaming at her. 'Oh,' she said, 'you wore a dress!'

'I didn't want to embarrass you.'

'Don't be silly,' she said, although Kit had seen a tell-tale flicker of pleased relief in her eyes. 'Anyway, you look wonderful.'

'Not as wonderful as you,' Kit said. She grinned, suddenly a little mortified to have slipped so easily into the sort of gallantry she would have used on Portia: but in fact it was true. Florence was wearing a dress of dusky-blue satin with a square collar and a wide waistband, but no other adornment. It clung to her breasts and hips in a way that Kit suspected was unintentional, and the colour brought out her eyes; most of all, though, its simplicity hinted at an unexpected assurance, an invitation to the observer to pay attention to the beauty of her face and form. And both, Kit thought, *were* beautiful. She had not realised how beautiful, until now. Was she really so shallow – she, an artist! – not to have looked past the unkempt clothes and sagging hair? Or was it something else, the fact that now she felt allowed – indeed, encouraged – to look and judge? As if Florence's satin dress, her perfectly smooth chignon and silk stockings, high-heeled shoes and glittering bracelet, were all for her benefit, hers alone . . .

'Don't stand there in the cold,' Florence said, and tugged her over the threshold. She was wearing scent, and its bluebell sweetness lent her an incongruous aura of spring.

Kit had never been inside the vicarage. Now, as Florence divested her of her wrap – a beaded velvet thing that she had bought especially, too flimsy for any longer journey than the brief walk from the Bone cottage – she looked round, taking in the shabby antique furniture and prim fly-spotted etchings. It would be a perfect interior to paint, she thought, if you wanted to capture a certain detached melancholy: you would stand in front of it and hear – and yes, she *did* hear – the slow ticking of a grandfather clock. She smiled, and Florence smiled too, as if she perfectly understood Kit's amusement.

'Come into the drawing room,' Florence said, and taking her hand again led her down the passage. As they went through the open doorway, Kit found herself adjusting her impression of the house: here, the room was warm and gracious, shimmering with gold candle flames and glossy dark-green holly. There was a fire in the grate, and a garland of gold and scarlet ribbons threaded through the ornaments on the mantelpiece. Dr Manning started forward from his chair, his hand outstretched.

'How do you do, Miss Clayton?'

She shook his hand: it felt thin and papery, an old man's grasp. 'How do you do, Dr Manning?'

'And I believe you have met my daughter Phoebe.'

She smiled dutifully at Phoebe, who was curled with feline grace in the wing chair, all but the side of her face in shadow. 'Good evening, Phoebe.'

'Good evening, Miss Clayton.'

'Sit down,' Florence said, 'here, near the fire. May I get you a glass of sherry?'

'Thank you.' She sat down. It was strange to be wearing a dress; she was very conscious of her ankles, and the heels on her new shoes. She had bought everything at the same time, and had been so weary and resentful by the end of her shopping trip that she had considered giving up and feigning illness. But tonight there was an unfamiliar pleasure in seeing her own body like this: she had transformed herself from watcher to watched, from subject to object. She adjusted the folds of her dress around her legs, looked up and saw genial masculine approval in Dr Manning's eyes. Ordinarily she would simply have stared back until he looked away, but now, for Florence's sake, she gave him an impersonal smile. 'It was kind of you to invite me, Dr Manning. Your flock must make great demands on you at this time of year.'

But as Dr Manning began to answer Florence put a glass of sherry into her hand, and – did she wink? Yes, surely – there was a glint of delightful mischief in her face – and then turned away in a swirl of dusty-blue satin, and Kit was left floundering, trying to compose herself as she nodded at Dr Manning and pretended she had heard what he had said.

'. . . since the War,' Dr Manning went on.

'Yes,' Kit said, 'yes, I see.'

Florence sat down opposite her on a tapestry ottoman. On the table by her elbow a garland of ivy trailed around a silver candelabra; candlelight played on one side of her face, firelight on the other. It was hard, once Kit had glanced at her, not to stare and go on staring. She forced her eyes back to Dr Manning.

'I think it's awfully interesting,' Phoebe said. 'Don't you

agree, Miss Clayton?' She unfolded herself with languorous grace, smiling at Kit.

'I certainly do.' She took a sip of her sherry; but everyone was still looking at her, Dr Manning with benign attention, Phoebe with wide-eyed innocence, Florence with a glint of amusement. 'In fact, Dr Manning,' she said, 'what you said . . . Actually, I've always been fascinated by the life a man like you must lead. Florence mentioned that you're a scholar. It must take great strength and self-denial, to put your congregation first.'

Dr Manning blinked. Then he sat back in his chair, steepling his fingers and looking at her over them. 'My goodness,' he said, chuckling. 'Well, since you ask, I suppose – yes, it has required sacrifices – but I have never wanted to burden anyone with – ah, never mind that. It is rare that anyone is perceptive enough to imagine – to look past what must be a very humdrum exterior, to the spiritual struggles between man and priest – if I may take the liberty of putting it like that. Yes, Phoebe, I daresay you have never heard me admit that I am so human!' He reached for his glass and raised it to Kit before he drank. 'I was indeed – I venture to say I still am – a scholar. But even as a small boy I was sensitive to the promptings of the divine. I remember wandering the hills alone – as Wordsworth did, I believe – and listening, opening my very soul to the voice of the Paraclete . . .'

Kit kept her eyes on his face, feigning reverent attention. She could feel Florence repressing a smile. The air between them sang like a taut thread. It was almost a game, not looking anywhere but at Dr Manning.

'Dinner is ready, sir,' a voice said from the doorway.

'Ah, hmm. Thank you, Mrs Reed.' Dr Manning stood up, and gestured widely. 'Ladies, let us proceed into the dining room.' As they moved into the passage, he continued over his shoulder: 'Then, you see, I began to come back to the religious feelings of my childhood, but having gained the understanding of a man – as St Paul says, of course . . .'

Kit followed, not trusting herself to meet Florence's eyes. She sat down decorously at the table, nodding, murmuring assent when Dr Manning paused, and all the time she was on the brink of laughter, like an iridescent bubble that she must swallow over and over again. She was very glad when the food was served, and she could concentrate on manipulating her knife and fork. The meat and dumplings were bland but solid; they had a comforting weight, and after a while she found that she was able to look up and around without wanting to giggle.

'More wine, my dear?' Dr Manning said to Florence, and then, 'Miss Clayton?'

'Thank you.'

'May I, Papa?'

'Certainly not. But you may have some raspberry shrub instead, to celebrate the winter solstice, if that is not too pagan . . .' He smiled indulgently at Florence as he reached across the table to pour it into Phoebe's glass, as if she were Phoebe's mother.

'Oh,' Florence said, 'the shortest day, that's today, I hadn't realised.'

'Indeed,' Dr Manning said, 'ah, Mrs Reed, yes, we have finished, thank you.' He leant sideways to allow Mrs Reed to take his plate. 'Of course, the rituals of the winter solstice and Christmas have much in common. One must acknowledge the tendency of the Christian calendar to assimilate other beliefs and customs – think of the holly and the mistletoe, for example, whose significance derives from Norse mythology . . .'

Kit drank her wine – which was surprisingly good – and sat back in her chair, oddly content to keep half an ear on Dr Manning's pedantic drone while the rest of her mind wandered. Florence looked beautiful, she thought, as the pudding arrived and they took up their cutlery again. Florence was beautiful, had always been beautiful . . . Not like Phoebe – no, Phoebe's beauty was otherworldly and disconcerting – but like herself, splendidly like herself. Beautiful . . . Kit remembered, with an irrational shock, that Florence had kissed her. It seemed so long ago, as if it had been someone else. It was hard to believe that Florence's mouth – the soft, mobile, full mouth that Kit could not help staring at – was the same awkward, chapped mouth that had pressed against hers. It had been humiliating at the time; she could not understand why she wished, now, that she could recall it more clearly. But she did.

'Like the Face, Papa,' Phoebe said, her clear voice cutting through Dr Manning's monody.

'Hmm – yes,' Dr Manning said, and paused. 'Yes, of course. Although that is not exactly what I was . . . You must be familiar with the Haltington Face by now, Miss Clayton. I am something of an expert on it.'

'I . . .' Kit reached too suddenly for her wineglass, and had to snatch at the stem to right it as it tilted. If they knew what she had been thinking . . . Thank God they didn't. 'The Face,' she repeated, dragging her thoughts away from Florence's kiss, 'yes, I bought a postcard of it once. But there isn't much to see now, is there?'

'It is very overgrown, although the lines are cut into the chalk. It's a terrible shame,' Dr Manning said, 'I must suggest to the parish council that they recut it. Although I am not sure . . .' He chuckled. 'I daresay they think me very eccentric, as a Christian minister, to care about it. But it has historical significance. We must not let the past slip out of sight, must we? We, the living, have a duty to our ancestors . . .'

Phoebe sipped her raspberry shrub, watching her father. Her expression was distant, a little sceptical, like a professor gauging the quality of an undergraduate essay.

Kit shivered. The violence of it took her by surprise; her spoon rattled in her bowl, and the others turned to look at her. She forced a laugh, rubbing her goose-pimpled forearms with her hands. 'Excuse me,' she said. 'Someone walked over my grave, I suppose.'

'Shall we move into the drawing room? I expect it is warmer in there.'

'Yes, please,' Kit said, getting to her feet before she had finished the words. It was rude, but she did not care; she was cold, and the atmosphere in the room had changed. The shadows were darker and the light less golden. She swept up her wineglass and drained it before she strode into the passage, almost going over on one high heel. Damn these shoes. Damn the dress that clung to her legs, hobbling her.

She sat down near the fire. By the time the others entered the room, she had composed herself. She smiled at Dr Manning, said, 'Yes, thank you,' when he offered her brandy, and took it from him with a steady hand. She sipped it, caught Florence watching her, and gave her a private, reassuring smile. She sat back into her chair's embrace, conscious of the air that puffed from the upholstery as she moved. The clock on the mantelpiece showed that it was later than she had thought. She searched for some anodyne topic of conversation, but her mind was sluggish and she could not coax anything onto her tongue.

'So, yes,' Dr Manning said, settling into his own chair. 'What attracted you to Haltington, Miss Clayton?' Before she had time to answer, he went on, 'There isn't much written about it, of course. I venture to suspect that my own work, when it is published, will stand alone as a serious study of this particular part of Sussex. It is surprisingly fertile ground for scholarship. All sorts of history, although my particular interest,' he said, leaning forward as if to share a confidence, 'is in the mythology and folklore. There was a White Horse on Hindover Hill, of course – also disappeared, sadly – but that was very recent indeed, probably cut for the coronation of Queen Victoria. Whereas the Face is verifiably ancient.'

Kit drew a slow breath. 'To be honest, it was simply that the house was cheap, and the agent recommended—'

'Oh, Horace,' Florence said, at the same time, 'you should tell Miss Clayton more about the Face. My sister – Imogen – loved it,' she said, turning to Kit with a smile. 'She used to say it kept her safe.'

'It's late,' Kit said, setting down her glass, 'perhaps another time—'

'Certainly,' Dr Manning said. 'No doubt you think we are absurd to be so proud of our little landmark, Miss Clayton. And to the uneducated eye, it looks – well, looked – unassuming. Rudimentary, indeed. How does the human intellect know, to recognise four simple lines as a face? And yet it is a universal response to see two eyes, a nose, a mouth . . .' He drank his own brandy, drawing in the air with his other hand. 'We put such significance in the human physiognomy, do we not? And that instinct links us to the oldest humans, the settlers who lived here before there were trains, before roads, before houses and farms . . . Before Christianity, of course. The Face was first carved when lives were ruled by superstition and stories – the fear of the unknown, of the dark, of death and the dead.'

There was a silence. Kit wished, helplessly, that she had been quick enough to start a different conversation. They might have been talking about the League of Nations, or hemlines, or Irish Home Rule.

'I have often thought,' Dr Manning said, 'that the austerity of the Downs might have played peculiar tricks upon the ancient mind. Where bare land meets the sky, sky meets sea, sea meets land . . . a place of boundaries, stark lines that nonetheless cannot be entirely trusted – constantly blurred by weather, and light, and time. There is a touch of the uncanny in this landscape. Chalk, of course – as you will know from your geography lessons, my dear,' he added to Phoebe, 'is the only rock that was once alive, being made of innumerable skeletons, metamorphosed by enormous geological pressures. One might make something of that, if one were superstitiously inclined – a village built on stone made of bones . . .' He smiled. 'Not that they would have known that, but its mysterious beauty does not require modern understanding. Who could blame those who came before us if they saw its wild mystery and trembled?'

Kit slid her eyes to Florence. She was rapt, her eyes shining, as if she were a child being told a bedtime story.

'They, naturally, would not have seen it in such psychological terms. They might have attributed particular characteristics to the place itself – a liminality, if you like, a kind of threshold-ness . . . Who are we to judge, when we ourselves acknowledge that there is such a thing as sacred ground? But whatever the cause, they believed that this valley attracted certain – let us say forces, forces of which they were afraid.'

Suddenly Kit had the overwhelming conviction that Dr Manning was quoting verbatim from his own work: but somehow, even so, his words made her scalp crawl. The room was very quiet now. A candle flame flapped briefly in a draught, and subsided back to a steady glow.

'Do you know the Saxon word *thurlian*?'

'No,' she said, 'no, I don't think I do.'

'It means to pierce, or to hollow out. And from it comes

another word, *thurlath*. Do you know what a thurlath is, Miss Clayton?'

'I expect you can guess I do not.'

'It is an old word. A Sussex word, I believe, I have not found it anywhere else. A thurlath is a little like a wraith, or a fetch – a wandering, hungry thing that resembles a man but is not a man. They are hollow, in the sense that they have no soul, and hollow in the sense that they are hungry. They crave life, and they are incapable of it. At first they are insubstantial, shapeless – a little like what is called an "elemental" – but they wander, searching for a way to become more like us. And do you know what they must find?'

This time she did not answer. He nodded, pleased with her silence.

'A *face*, Miss Clayton.'

She must have started, for he gave a small huff of satisfaction, and took a mouthful of his brandy. 'Yes,' he said. 'They must begin by stealing the appearance of a person. Only then does their power increase. But at first they are not strong enough to drive out a human soul. What they are drawn to are those things which look human, but are not: pictures, reflections, statues. You will have noticed that there are no effigies in Haltington Church . . .'

Kit could not help glancing at Phoebe. She was staring at the fire; but she seemed to sense Kit's gaze, and looked up to meet it. 'Dolls . . .' she said, in an absent, thoughtful voice, and out of the corner of her eye Kit saw Florence shift in her chair.

'Certainly,' Dr Manning said, with schoolmasterly approval. 'Any kind of manmade likeness, in fact. They look for faces without life, without consciousness.'

'And so,' Florence said, 'so the Haltington Face—'

'The Haltington Face was cut into the hillside, to draw them.'

Kit drank from her glass, but she would not have known if it was brandy or water. She said with an effort, 'But how could it protect the village, if it drew the – the things towards it? Surely the idea should have been to ward them off?'

'An excellent question, Miss Clayton. But you see, it was a trap. It sucked them in, and down, deep into itself. No thurlath would ever be strong enough to wear the Haltington Face as its own. Once it held them, it would not let them go. They were imprisoned forever in the very bones of the earth.'

'Like a wasp bottle,' Phoebe said. 'Or flypaper.'

'Well – yes,' Dr Manning said, although this time he did not smile. 'Yes, I suppose that is another way of putting it.'

Florence gave an appreciative little shiver. 'Hmmmmmm,' she said. 'How creepy.'

Phoebe drew her knees up to her chest and linked her hands around them. The shadows played on her face, making her eyes larger, her chin even more pointed. 'The Bones were meant to guard it,' she said. 'Mrs Bone said no one else could do it.'

'Oh, that mad old crone,' Dr Manning said, draining the last of his brandy. 'Not to speak ill of the dead, but . . . Last scion of an ancient Sussex family,' he added, to Kit. 'Not much education, and pagan tendencies. Benighted, even. Although it was sad, what happened to her. And her boys, of course.' He stood up, strode to the door, and disappeared into the passage. A moment later he was back, brandishing a handsome leather-bound book. 'The fruits of my labour,' he said, with a modest smile. He gave it to Phoebe. 'I am delighted that you wanted to see it, my dear. It is a trifle, really, but I am proud of it.'

Phoebe glanced at it and smiled up at her father; she might have been an adult, praising a child's scribble. 'Yes, Papa,' she said. 'How impressive.'

He plucked it out of her hands and turned to Kit. 'Perhaps you would like to see, Miss Clayton. No, no, keep it,' he said, as Kit offered it back. 'I have several copies. I had them printed and bound for my own reference. Once it is published, I will have less need of them.'

She did not know what to do with it. It was heavy and ornate, black calfskin tooled in gold, the top edge gilded. 'Thank you,' she said, laying it on the arm of her chair and meaning the opposite.

'Of course,' Dr Manning said, leaning one elbow on the mantelpiece, 'the thurlath, like all ghost stories, are a metaphor for the psychological and spiritual dramas of the human psyche. We are afraid of anything which does not remain in its rightful place, and the power that animates it, whether that is memory, or desire, or grief . . . When the past will not stay in the past – when the dead seem to clamour for our attention – when the certainties of space and time suddenly dissolve under the onslaught of emotion . . . all that is disorientating, terrifying, in fact – and was even more so, I imagine, before we had the great truths of Christianity on which to rely. They imagined themselves to be haunted by real beings, faceless, malevolent. But of course we know that the thurlath, the faceless ones, are only a childish parable – a way for our forefathers to understand the less palatable truth of their own fragility.' He looked round, with the air of a man concluding a lecture. Phoebe was watching him with feline impassivity; Florence was frowning into the fire. 'We must thank God,' he said, heavily, 'that we are more enlightened now. Modern times have freed us from superstition, and left us better able to face life as it is.'

As Kit stood up her dress caught on the chair, and she staggered. She got her balance back, but did not stoop to disentangle herself. 'But we are not,' she said. 'More enlightened. Are we?'

'Well,' Dr Manning said, 'that is . . . Personally, I would suggest that it is indisputably the case that—'

'They kept themselves safe from the faceless ones. They warded them off. Whereas *now* . . .' She tried to step forward, and heard the creak of a seam threatening to split. 'Now,' she went on, 'now the faceless ones are not a metaphor at all. Now they are real. Real men, whose faces have been shot or torn or burnt away, by other men – by us, by the supposedly more enlightened people that we are now. Have you seen a man without a face, Dr Manning? Because I have. Many, many of them.'

'I – ah – I was not referring to—'

'No, you were not. But tell me, which is worse? To make up a story about faceless men, or to make them a reality?'

'Naturally we all regret the horrors of trench warfare—'

'"Regret"? How enlightened.'

'Kit,' Florence said, stretching out a hand.

'During the War I worked at a studio for making masks, in Paris. We saw hundreds of men there, men who had lost eyes and noses and jaws and . . . Once we were sent a photograph of a man who had lost everything. The front of his head was concave. There was nothing left. His doctor asked what we could do, to make him look – human, again. We pored over the photographs for hours, wondering what on earth we could possibly do, how we could even make a mask stay on his head. In the end he died in hospital, and when we heard we were glad.'

There was a silence. Florence's hand was still outstretched, the fingers taut. Kit wished she could take hold of it, but she could not move.

'Faceless men are not a picturesque metaphor. They are not a nightmare, springing from the theories of Dr Freud. They are real. We have created them. And you *dare* to say that we are more enlightened than our forefathers?'

Again she lurched forward, and again she stumbled, held back by the hateful dress. She bent and wrenched at it with ferocious hands. At last it tore and came free.

'My dear Miss Clayton, I did not mean to upset you.'

'I must go,' she said. 'I must go to bed.'

'I'll see you to the door,' Florence said, getting to her feet. 'Oh – your frock, what a shame – give it to me tomorrow, I'll mend it—'

'You needn't worry,' she said, turning away. 'I shan't have an occasion to wear it again. Thank you for your hospitality, Dr Manning. I'm afraid I have not been as exemplary a guest.'

'On the contrary, it has been a pleasure,' he said, but she had already gone through the doorway into the passage, leaving his voice behind. She hurried to the door, grabbing her wrap from the hook beside the door. Florence came after her, but she did not look back. What a way to end the evening! She had disgraced herself. He was only a fool; and she was a fool too, to let his foolishness anger her so much. *Faceless ones . . .*

'Kit,' Florence said, and touched her gently on the shoulder. 'Won't you say goodnight?'

She turned. Florence searched her face with her eyes, uncertainly; and Kit noticed, in spite of herself, the length of her eyelashes, the soft line of her eyelids, the lovely faint shadow of a vein over her temple. 'Goodnight, Florence.'

'I'm so sorry.'

'You? Sorry for what?'

Florence glanced around, and said in an undertone, 'For – my brother-in-law. He bored you senseless all evening, didn't he? No wonder you lost patience. Forgive me.'

'Don't be silly. It wasn't your fault.' If only it had been that simple: driven to rudeness by sheer boredom! Looking into Florence's face, she almost believed it had been.

A lapse of manners, that was all, understandable, almost reasonable. She could forgive herself for that.

'We're very provincial – very dull, here – and you're an artist, you must be used to fashionable parties and scintillating conversation.'

Kit laughed. It felt as though it dislodged some blockage in her chest, making it easier to breathe. 'Oh, Florence,' she said, 'I wish I were as glamorous as you think I am.'

'I wish you knew how glamorous you are.'

Kit looked down ruefully at her torn dress. 'You're very kind,' she said. 'I shall be glad to get back into my real clothes, actually.'

'You're even more glamorous in your real clothes.' Florence lowered her eyes and tugged the folds of Kit's wrap into place. 'Won't you be cold?'

'I walked here, didn't I?'

Florence wavered backwards and forwards, without moving her feet, still staring at Kit's collarbone. Then, with a kind of lunge, she threw her arms round her neck. 'Thank you for coming,' she said. Before Kit could respond – almost before she had realised that Florence was embracing her – she let go, whirled round and hurried up the stairs.

'Goodnight,' Kit said again, although Florence had already disappeared along the landing. Everything was quiet, apart from the ticking of the clock. A shadow moved at the doorway of the drawing room: a slender, girlish, ruffled silhouette.

She did not acknowledge Phoebe's presence. Instead she flung open the door onto the black and star-bright freezing night and launched herself into it.

She went down the path, brushing against the dry stems of the roses and hearing the crackle of their thorns catching her dress. She swerved away, and nearly stumbled into the flowerbed on the other side. When at last she had wrestled the gate open and was standing in the roadway, she looked up and saw the stars inching slowly round, like the face of a clock – no, the hands of a clock – no, the face, if her hands stayed where they were, her hands – and she realised that she was drunk. It must have been that last glass of brandy. Before that, she had been fine. She should have left earlier. She should have . . . but it did not matter, she did not care, being drunk was undignified but it was hardly the worst thing that had happened to her. Nothing that had happened tonight was the worst thing that had happened to her: not Dr Manning's absurd horror stories, or Phoebe's clear-eyed malice, or her disgracing herself. At the end of it, there had been Florence – that moment of brief warmth, too brief, leaving Kit feeling more alone than before. That was not the worst, either. No, the worst had been in Paris – the nightmares, the masks – but never mind the worst, she was not going to think about the worst, worse things happened at sea, in war, all was fair in— oh for God's sake, she thought, and set off down the road.

She left the vicarage behind, deviating slightly from a straight line. These fucking shoes, if only it were not too cold to take them off! Those summer nights, with Portia, in Cornwall, when they had walked home barefoot, through air that was as sweet and warm as bathwater . . . Those summer midnights, when they had made love in the moonlight, and afterwards she would lift herself up from the damp sheets to glimpse, through the uncurtained window, the shimmer of the distant sea . . . She was not much further from the sea at this moment: but there was no warmth, no Portia, no lovemaking. Not even any moon among the stars. She thought of Florence's brief, chaste embrace, and the narrow, grubby bed in the Bone cottage.

She was not tired. If she went back now she would lie there with her eyes open, watching the mottled darkness of the wall slide sideways and reset itself, endlessly. Thinking, perhaps, about the worst . . .

She could not bear it. She had not yet come to the bend where the Bone cottage was visible, but she swerved sideways, off the road. Her feet met uneven ground, frozen into ruts, and she held out her arms like a tightrope walker. Another step took her into a ditch full of brambles: she pushed through them, exacting a deliberate revenge on her dress for encumbering her, and found herself on the edge of a field. One of her shoes had come off in the undergrowth, and now every step was a lopsided lurch. She slipped her foot out of the other and kicked it aside. There was the vicarage on her right, still with a light in the window; on the other side were a few trees and hedges that gave way, further up, to the blank slope of the down. She could just make out the path, a pale thread that led to nowhere. Where was she going? Uphill towards the sea? To see the stars reflected, the abyss of infinity turned upside down?

She pushed upwards. Suddenly the path was underfoot, and then again the stiff crackle of grass. She stopped. She stood in a cloud of her own breath, panting.

It was here. She knew it. The Face. She could not see it, but something told her that she was close to it: as though the calcium in her bones called to the chalk in a language too old for her to understand. She had been heading for it all along. To see it for herself, although there was nothing to see . . .

It was nonsense, of course. All Dr Manning's carefully researched folklore about powerful patterns, cut into the earth, and the – the whatever the word was. She pretended to herself that she did not remember, but her brain knew better. *Thurlath*. It was like a guttural whisper, a breath on the back of her neck.

She crouched down, and put her palm flat on the ground. It was cold. She touched the brittle softness of winter grass, and underneath that the frozen earth. It felt as if the warmth of her body was pouring down her arm into the chalk. She began to shiver, but she did not move her hand. Was there something there, something ancient and aware?

No. There wasn't. It had been like this when Mama took her to foreign churches when she was small: she had sat straining her ears, listening with all her attention, thinking, *come on then, I'm waiting*. And nothing answered. Like now. What a stupid drunken impulse to come up here. What a stupid drunken fool she was. What a stupid drunken . . .

Then she felt it.

It was not a sound, or a movement, not exactly – there was nothing to see, nothing to hear, nothing at all except the hairs standing up on her arms and her heart hammering. She had the sudden conviction that the ground underneath her was as thin as an eggshell, and below it were seething shadows and endless depth . . . *A wasp bottle*, Phoebe had said: and for a moment she believed it, feeling the awful fragility, the humming menace kept back by something man-made and brittle. The world might shatter at any moment, and then—

Then— what? But she had no answer. The darkness writhed in the deep, unseen. It was everything that was appalling and wrong; the moment in *J'accuse* when the dead, prone under a black and smoking sky, began to stagger to their feet . . . It was the moment in Paris when she had stopped, in the middle of dabbing colour onto a man's enamel face, knowing quite simply that she could not go on, that she had come to the end of what she could endure.

It was her heart wallowing, flabby and cowardly, against the natural flow of blood; and her chest burning, her throat closing, as if to refuse any more oxygen, as if her very flesh was rebelling against what it was being required to do. It was bigger than anything she had ever experienced, the universe threatening to peel away like a scab, and leave a haemorrhaging, open wound . . .

She tried to catch her breath. Surely she was imagining it. It was the power of suggestion: the others talking about the Face as if it had real power – Dr Manning saying, *a little like what is called an 'elemental'* . . . A hallucination, like a child's night terror – or shell shock; Septimus had seen corpses on the platform at King's Cross, hadn't he? Maybe this was like that—

But now she *did* see something: a distortion of the air, as if a warped piece of glass passed over her field of vision, expanding. Her horror rose, drowning her. Something was coming. The things, the thurlath. A name, small, two laughable syllables, for— what? Dr Manning could not have imagined— this . . . *Hollow*, she thought, *hollow in the sense that they are hungry* . . . She could not move. She could not tell where she ended and the chalk began. She smelt something rot-sweet in the air, something horrifying. For a moment she felt her skin ache, as if there was a vacuum in the air, passing within arm's reach; if it were any stronger, or any closer, it would suck the meat from her bones. She heard the breath catch in her throat and was afraid she would never be able to inhale again. The horizon was a gaping mouth, the stars guttered, the darkness between them bulged and ran like ink. The Face, she thought, and ran out of words. The Face is alive, it is old, it is – *aware*—

For a second the world hung in the balance, like a ball at the top of a parabola, and she was afraid the earth itself would shatter into a thousand pieces and take her with it. Then, with an unbearable ringing note like an awful bell, she felt reality slide back into place.

A spasm of shivering went through her, so violent she heard her pearls clatter one against another. But slowly she mastered herself, and when she had she was not sure what she had seen, or felt. She was dazed with cold. She took a step and nearly tripped, her numb feet treacherous on the icy ground. Her shoes, where had she left her shoes? But it was too dark to see, and she was perishing, she would freeze to death if she wasted time looking for them.

What had happened? A hallucination, a nightmare . . .

She was drunk. That fact was indisputable: the stars still wandered when she looked up at them, winking as they went, as she trembled. Christ, it was cold. What had possessed her to come up here? Nothing. Some drunken impulse. Drunken scorn towards Dr Manning and his improbably pretty daughter, and their tall tales of Sussex ghosts. And now she was standing here, gibbering with fear, honestly wondering if she might actually have seen a – a thurlath. Oh, for God's sake! Of course she had not. It had been a drunken hallucination. A drunken nightmare, a waking nightmare, the after-echo of Paris . . . not real. Or rather, only as real as her mind.

Painfully she picked her way down the hill. She wished now she had bothered to find her shoes. Fuck, the ditch, the brambles . . . She gritted her teeth and pushed through them. At last she found herself on the road again. As she rounded the corner she fumbled at her hip for her key before she remembered that she had left it under the bucket on her back step because her dress had no pockets. Here at last was the gate. Here was the place to stoop, to fumble with clumsy fingers, and yes, here was the key. It felt good to shut the door of the Bone cottage behind her. She marched up the stairs on bruised, nerveless feet, dragged her blankets around her shoulders and folded herself into a ball on the bed. Then she shut her eyes and let the darkness rock her gently.

But in spite of her efforts she could not submerge herself in the blessed emptiness of sleep; when she tried, there was an inexorable ringing in her ears, just on the edge of audibility, like a high malevolent buzz behind the thinnest of glass.

X

Victory to Love, oil on board, 1914
(artist's dedication added 1920)

Muckle was woken by someone crying out, and he hated them for jolting him back into wakefulness, his leg flaring with pain. The unfamiliar air around him was cold. He was in hospital, he thought. Yes, that was it. Another operation, another long month in bed . . . But when he moved, the ache in his leg was old, without the sickening rawness of an open wound, and there were no rushing orderlies, no other men groaning at being disturbed. And the smell . . . Woodsmoke, old stone, a hint of turpentine. He pushed himself upright, and looked round. There was a slice of moonlight shining through the gap in the curtains, falling on a small, sparsely furnished parlour. He was alone. He was on a sofa.

In a rush he remembered where he was and how he had got there. It had been a long journey yesterday – no wonder his leg was aching! – and after the long walk from Berwick he had been weary and chilled to the bone; and when he arrived, he had almost wished he hadn't come. He winced at the memory of Kit's blank face as she opened the door. He had spread his arms wide, like a magician at the climax of the trick, ready to greet her with a *ta-dah!* and see her laugh; but instead he felt his expression wilt as she stared at him. He had said, stupidly, 'You *said* I should come for Christmas . . .'

'I – did I? Oh! Yes, I suppose—'

'I wrote to ask if today was all right,' he said, 'and telling you which train . . .' He *had* written, although in fact he had only posted the letter that morning. Perhaps, he conceded inwardly, it had been a little dishonest; but he could not have borne it if she had retracted the invitation. If he wanted to be sure of seeing her, it was better to present her with a *fait accompli*.

'Damn,' she said. 'I didn't get it. The postman . . .' There was a fractional silence. He wondered, incredulous, if she was actually considering turning him away. But at last she smiled, and with an unexpected, childish warmth she threw her arms round him. He felt her hair brush his cheek and closed his eyes, warning himself not to hold her too tightly or too long. 'Dear old Muckle,' she said. 'I'm sorry – I *am* glad to see you. Come in.'

He had known then it had been worth coming. He would rather be here with her than anywhere in the world, even if he had to sleep on this horrible lumpy settee, in this freezing cottage—

The voice rose again, the muffled shriek of a nightmare, as universal as the sound of orgasm; and finally his mind caught up. Kit, he thought, it must be Kit shouting. He swung his legs down to the ground, wincing as he put his weight on his left foot.

The staircase was narrow and dark; he leant his hand against the wall and climbed the steps one by one, grunting a little every time he had to bend his bad knee. He was hurrying now, he could not let it go on, he had to get to her, to rescue her, drag her out of whatever fearful vision—

The scream stopped with a gasp. There was a moment

of silence, while he stood stock still, afraid that she had choked on her own fear. Then footsteps, and the door was flung open. It was dark – no moonlight on that side of the house – and he could hardly see her; but he could hear her shaky breath, the sound of her trying to master herself. He knew what that was like, the moment when you tried to remember what reality was, when the tide of your nightmare ebbed away and left you wet and shivering, not trusting the ground underfoot. With a final effort he mounted the last few stairs and reached out for her. 'Kit,' he said, 'it's all right, I'm here—'

She cried out and twisted away, raising her hands as if to ward off a blow. He recoiled, his heart hammering. For a moment all he could think about was keeping his balance at the top of the steep staircase, and the agony in his knee; then, slowly, the fiery haze in front of his eyes cleared. 'It's all right,' he said again, although his own voice cracked.

'Jesus Christ, Muckle,' she said, at last, with a shuddering sort of laugh. 'I thought you – never mind. What on earth are you doing, sneaking around up here in the middle of the night?'

'I thought you – I wanted . . .' He stopped. 'Oh, you know,' he went on, with a laboured lightness, 'I thought I might come and ravish you while you were asleep.'

'Huh,' she said, without amusement. 'It wouldn't be worth the trouble of getting up the stairs.'

He tried to laugh, unsure which of them was the butt of the joke. 'Well,' he said, 'I suppose – if everything is all right –'

'Do you want a drink? A proper drink, I mean, not cocoa.'

'God, yes.' He turned around and carefully made his way downwards. He was not sure, but he would have put money on Kit's hand being outstretched behind him, ready to grab the collar of his pyjamas if he tripped. It made his neck itch.

When they got to the bottom of the stairs, she pushed him gently towards the parlour. 'Go on,' she said, 'sit down, I'll get the drinks.' He did not resist; those stairs had done for his leg. Served him right. He should have known that she wouldn't be grateful to him for seeing her like that. He should have stayed here, listening, trying not to care . . .

Kit came back with a lamp. In the other hand she had two glasses half full of brandy held between her fingers. She set down the lamp, passed him a drink and knelt to make up the fire. Her face was pale, and her hair damp and clinging at her temples and neck. Last night she had built a fire with thoughtless expertise, but now she could not get it to catch. In the end he levered himself out of his chair – suppressing a hiss of pain – and took the matchbox out of her hands. 'Here.' He struck a flame and put it carefully on to the crumpled newspaper. They watched silently as it dipped and finally took hold.

'Thanks.'

He did not have the energy to go back to his chair. He sat down on the floor, his leg straight in front of him. She leant towards the fire, not meeting his eyes.

'Is it every night?' he said.

She shook her head.

He made himself stare into the fire, instead of at her. The longer the silence went on, the harder it was not to break it. He told himself it was a game.

She sipped her drink. 'It wasn't a nightmare, really,' she said, finally, with a gesture that was meant to be casual. 'Just a dream.'

'No,' he said, 'you hardly sounded scared at all. Apart from the screaming.'

'I wasn't screaming.'

'Enough to wake me up, anyway.'

'I'm sorry.'

'Don't be stupid, Kit.'

She sighed and jabbed at the fire with the poker. 'I've had worse,' she said. 'In Paris.'

'Worse must've been pretty bad.'

There was another long pause. Christ, he wanted to put his arms around her. He wouldn't, of course. She would shake him off at once if he tried. Beloved, solitary, untouchable Kit. He felt a surge of the old ambivalence: gratitude that she was near, and resentment that she was not nearer.

'What's the time?'

He looked at his watch. 'Ten past three,' he said.

'In that case, Merry Christmas.'

'Merry Christmas.' He raised his glass to her, and they both drank. The fire rustled and murmured. Maybe, he thought, leaning back against the wall, feeling the warmth of the fire sweep over his skin and the warmth of the brandy sweep through his bloodstream, maybe this was enough to make up for everything else. To be here, with Kit, on Christmas Day. He sneaked a look at her: she was staring into the flames, her face serious and distant.

'Aren't you going to get your sketchpad?' he said.

She glanced at him, with a faint, sudden frown. 'No.'

'Oh.' It was perverse to be disappointed. He had always been irritated by her habit of reaching for her pencil, assuming she had the right to anyone's face, if she chose. It had always rubbed him up the wrong way – he wanted her to look at him, yes, but not like that, not dispassionately . . . ! Because it was not interest in *him*, it was simply the arrogance of the artist, thinking everything in the world was fair game. He shifted a little, kneading the muscles above his kneecap. How she had infuriated him, before the war, endlessly looking at him through that objective lens, refusing to let him look back! And Portia was the same – worse, in fact – but then, he did not give a damn about Portia, except to want to throttle her, sometimes, for the way she talked about Kit. He never wanted to think about the two of them together; it was better to pretend that he did not understand why she felt entitled to that proprietorial air. He had always glanced away when they kissed. He had never let himself imagine what they got up to, those summer nights in Cornwall after they walked home together, Kit raising her hand in a casual masculine wave without looking back. Once Septimus, seeing him stare after them, had passed him a handkerchief, murmuring, 'I say, old man, you're dribbling.' But if he let himself imagine—

He imagined, instead, saying, *I love you*. He could say, *Come back to London with me*.

He could say, *Marry me*.

'Are you all right?' she said.

'Just my leg.'

She nodded and he felt another flash of chagrin: he did not want her pity or concern, but he resented its absence.

He shut his eyes. After a long time he heard her say, very softly, 'Muckle?'

He did not answer. He heard her get to her feet and pause, looking down at him. She crossed the room – he thought for a moment that she was leaving – and then returned, light on her feet. She put a blanket over him, tucking it gently round his shoulders. He felt her hand brush the side of his neck, above his collar.

Now, he thought. He might not even need to speak; he could simply catch hold of her hand, and bring it to his lips.

Then he thought of how she had warded him off, when he had reached out for her in the dark; and he stayed still, feigning sleep, until she moved away and the door closed on the sound of her footsteps.

*

When he woke, it was proper morning, grey and overcast and chilly. The bones in his leg seemed to have fused: it felt like breaking glass to bend his knee. He was glad Kit was not there to hear him grunt through his clenched teeth as he clambered to his feet and dressed. It was like climbing, he thought, remembering cold hours spent clinging to the sandstone face of the rocks near where he had grown up, fighting the numbness that crept into his icy fingers. Back in the days when it was good sport to pit himself against reality . . . Now, if he wanted to challenge himself all he had to do was stand up.

The kitchen was empty. He stumped over to the table and found that the teapot was still hot, and the tea, when he poured it, was dark but not undrinkable. He drank it black, standing with his weight on his good leg, trying to ease the flexibility back into his other knee.

There were footsteps in the room above – not Kit's bedroom, but the room she was using as a studio. He tilted his head up, listening. Was she coming down? Had she heard him? But they passed back and forth, and stopped.

He drank his tea. When he'd arrived yesterday, she had told him to help himself to anything he wanted – she'd meant food and drink, of course, he added to himself, with a fierce amusement – but he was not hungry, or not hungry enough for stale bread and butter. For a moment he remembered the Edwardian Christmases of his childhood, with candle-laden trees and ribboned presents, church in the morning and then, later, a table groaning with food. He had loved Christmas, then. But now he thanked God – or would have done, if he believed in God – that he was here. Better stale bread and butter here, than goose and roast apples at home. He could not have borne another Christmas like that. The smell of meat, which was the same smell as burnt flesh. The children being given popguns and lead soldiers.

The smiles on the faces of the congregation, which showed that they were blind or stupid. Yes, he was glad to be here. If anyone could make Christmas bearable, it was Kit.

When he had finished his tea, he rinsed the cup. Then he bent over and splashed his face until he straightened up again, spluttering. Icy water ran down his neck and soaked into his shirt collar. He needed a shave, but he could not face the fuss of heating water and trying to find a mirror.

He climbed the stairs, very slowly, one by one. He paused at the top to compose himself – it was foolish to climb the stairs again, so soon – and then knocked.

At first there was no answer. It was only when he repeated his knock that he heard Kit say, 'Yes?' politely, as if she had expected him to have left by now.

He pushed the door open. 'Merry Christmas,' he said.

'Merry Christmas, Muckle.' She had been working, but now she turned to look at him, a paintbrush in one hand, a rag in the other. She looked tired, a smudge of pale colour over her cheek as if the bone was breaking the skin.

'Do you want a cup of tea?'

'Y— no,' she said, too quickly, so that he knew she was thinking about the steep staircase and how long it would take him to get to the kitchen and back again. 'No. I'll make another pot in a minute. Did you have breakfast?'

'Yes,' he said, because if she was going to lie then he was too. She smiled, wryly undeceived, and he looked away; he was deliberately not imagining how it would be now, if he had said what he wanted to say last night. If she had let him kiss her – if they had spent the rest of the night together, entwined—

'Do you like it?' she said, her voice suddenly softer.

He jumped. He started to say, 'What . . . ?' and then realised he had been staring, unseeing, at her painting. He blinked and focused on it with an effort.

He did not like it. He was not sure why he did not like it. He said, 'I didn't know you painted landscapes.'

'I don't. I mean I haven't, much. It's a place near here. The Seven Sisters. We could go—' She broke off, then went on, too swiftly, 'I can't get the colours quite right. It's too creamy, somehow.'

He peered at it more closely. It should have been perfectly acceptable, the sort of thing you saw on the walls of seaside teashops: greys and blues, sea and sky, inspiring nostalgic memories of day trips with Nanny and a picnic hamper. 'Lovely,' he said, and glanced round, feigning expertise. There were two paintings leaning against the wall – one still life of a bottle, another of a bunch of flowers – and some scribbled abstract drawings pinned to the crumbling plaster. All, he thought, had the same vivid unlikeability, a prickly dislocated quality that made you want to look twice. But there were no portraits. He said, 'I suppose it's hard to find models, here.'

She didn't answer.

'I could sit for you, if you want.'

'No, thanks.'

'Fair enough,' he said lightly, or as lightly as he could, 'I suppose I'm not the best-looking—'

'I'm not painting portraits, Muckle. Any portraits. That's over.'

'But some of the ones you did before the War were jolly good—'

'*No.*' She had turned away, her head bowed; she looked the way he had felt when his wound had begun to heal and he had realised how crippled he was. Unexpected pity surged through him, so simple it took him aback: for once he forgot how much he wanted her.

'Perhaps,' he said, lamely, 'one day you'll feel differently . . .'

He should not have said it; she flicked her shoulder as if a fly had landed on it. For a moment they stood in silence – both, he thought bitterly, face to face with their own inadequacies; then she took a deep breath, and spun around with a smile. 'Well,' she said, striding to the door, leaving him behind, 'I suppose it's time for Christmas breakfast, do you?'

It was not like any Christmas he'd had before; but it was rather peaceful watching Kit move about the little kitchen – like a woman should, he thought, and refused to feel ashamed of the pleasure it gave him – and then sitting in front of the fire, reading and drinking tea, hearing sporadic showers blow against the windows. In other years he would have insisted on a walk, but he was glad that Kit seemed content to stay inside, only moving now and then to fetch more food, sweetmeats and bread and cheese, small things that they ate like a picnic from plates on their knees. Once, after she returned with a box of candied figs – 'Thank God Portia sent me that hamper, or I'd be feeding you on bread and eggs,' she said, laughing – she settled on the floor by his chair, with her head at the level of his thigh. He looked down and wished he could run his fingers through her hair. Maybe, he thought, maybe one day . . . Instead he took a handful of figs and filled his mouth with sweetness.

The day passed, endless and too short. They had cocktails before dinner, and a game pie; then, with a grin, Kit uncovered a pot that had been bubbling on the stove to reveal a linen-wrapped plum pudding. He doused it with brandy and set light to it, and Kit laughed and called him the Prometheus of puddings. She had made hard sauce to go with it, and although he was full he had seconds, gorging himself. Afterwards they sat back in their chairs, grinning at each other, and he thought that if they married, every day could be like this and he would never want anything more, ever.

Kit yawned. 'How funny,' she said, 'I've done nothing all day, and now I'm tired.'

It wasn't nothing, he wanted to say; but instead he shrugged and said, 'Me too,' although he wasn't.

'Well,' she said, 'I suppose . . .'

No. It was too soon for the day to be over. He stood up, and the sudden movement made him catch his breath and grab the back of the chair, blinking until his vision cleared. Had he done it on purpose, to make her pity him? No, of course not. But all the same he did not shake her off when she took his elbow to steady him. He said, 'It's all right, Kit, I'm all right. Too much brandy.'

'No doubt.'

'Bedtime, then,' he said, and heard it sound like a question.

'Probably sensible, my dear.'

The endearment should have pleased him; instead, it rang in his ears with an easy not-giving-a-damn, as though she were a man and he a woman.

'Wait,' he said, rocking backwards so suddenly it made his knee twinge. 'I forgot. I have something for you.'

'Oh. I didn't think—'

'It wouldn't be Christmas without presents,' he said, and reached into his pocket as if he had really only just remembered the little package that had been there ever since he got dressed, waiting for the right moment. 'I couldn't come empty-handed, could I?' That was a mistake, since the answer sat in the air like smoke, visible to them both: naturally he could, and clearly she would rather he had done. But it was too late to take it back.

She took the package and unwrapped it with unceremonious swiftness. 'Thank you,' she said, 'it's very pretty.'

It was not an *it*, but a *them*: a pair of inlaid cufflinks, masculine and glamorous, the result of a long afternoon raking through trays of trinkets in a West End shop. He had been determined to keep on until he found the perfect thing, even though he had been on his feet for so long that the next day he couldn't leave his flat.

'Don't mention it,' he said.

She folded the tissue paper back over the glinting gold. 'You're very sweet . . .' she said, as if she had not said it once already. 'I'm afraid I didn't get you a present.'

'No, no,' he said, 'no, there was no need, it was a pleasure. I wasn't expecting anything.'

'Oh dear,' she said, as if he had said the opposite. 'How thoughtless of me.'

'Don't be silly.' He laughed. 'Honestly, it's a trifle. A token of my regard. Anyway, we know each other too well to insist on *quid pro quo*, don't we? I wanted to give you something, that's all.'

She bit her lip; then, as she regarded him, her frown cleared. She spun away, towards the doorway. 'Wait,' she said over her shoulder, pounding up the stairs, 'wait there.'

He could not follow her in any case, not at that pace; by the time he would have been halfway up, she was back in the kitchen, holding out a flat rectangle, hastily wrapped in brown paper. 'Here,' she said. 'You can have this. Merry Christmas, Muckle.' She smiled at him, with the triumph of a debtor paying the final bill.

He took it. The paper was not tied or stuck down, and it gaped, showing a patch of painted white and green, and the pale rose and gold of sunlit skin. He guessed then what it was; but carefully – controlling his face as well as his hands – he lifted the picture out of its wrapping, and held it to the light.

'Do you like it? It's an old one – from before the War – but of course you know that. Do you remember that day? How happy we were.'

'It's Septimus,' he said, and clenched his jaw before he could say any more. It was, by any standard, a fine picture. It was not as precise as her studio work had been, but the freer brushwork gave it a vigour that more than made up for the lack of finish— oh, for God's sake, as if he cared a damn about her technique, or how *good* a painting it was! It was Septimus, playing tennis – or rather, between bouts of tennis, lying on the grass with his hand flung up by his head, the dappled shade of the apple tree just falling over his bright hair. Handsome Septimus, his white shirt translucent with sweat, after winning a set to love . . .

'You sat next to me as I painted it,' Kit said. 'Don't you remember?'

Yes. Of course he had been beside her, and not in the picture; why would she have painted him, when the others were there? He turned it over. On the back she had written, *To Muckle with love, Christmas 1920. Kit Clayton.*

There was a pause. Kit said, more uncertainly, 'There's an ancient one of Portia if you'd rather—'

'Christ, no!' He had almost shouted it. Now he forced himself to laugh, and met her eyes, bitterly conscious that he was attempting the same expression of pleased gratitude that she had given him a moment ago. 'It's wonderful,' he said. 'I shall frame it. It will remind me of Mill House, and being there with you.'

'It's nothing,' Kit said, 'but I'm glad you like it.' Her voice belied her: clearly she thought that he had done rather well out of the exchange. 'Now, I must get to bed.'

'Tomorrow,' he said, quickly, before she could put a foot on the bottom stair, 'would you – perhaps I should buy you lunch in the pub, before I go?'

'That's very kind—'

'I insist.'

'Well, if it doesn't make you late for your train.'

'No, it won't. I'm sure it won't.' He swallowed, girding himself: it was not the right moment, but if he did not say it now he never would. 'But, Kit . . . You're alone here, all the time – it can't be healthy for you, don't you ever wish . . . ?'

'I'm working, Muckle.'

'Yes. I know. Of course.'

'And I'm not always alone. The vicar's sister-in-law comes to see me sometimes.' She smiled, as if she knew how ridiculous it was for her, proud distant Kit, to be the object of some old spinster's charity.

'Well,' he said, 'good. But shouldn't I – that is, why don't I stay . . . ?'

There was a silence. She looked at him for a long time. 'Muckle,' she said, at last, 'I'm glad you came. But I need to be alone. Now I'm going to bed. Sleep well.'

He could not believe that she would leave so curtly, as if he were in the wrong. Even as she mounted the stairs, fluent and youthful as a slap in the face, he expected her to pause and look back: to apologise, to soften what she had said, to say that of course she understood that he only wanted the best for her. Or even to remember the small package on the table and take it with her, instead of leaving it where it was among the dirty plates and glasses . . . But she said nothing else, and she did not pause, and there was nothing in the way she moved to suggest that her behaviour had been anything but irreproachable.

The next day, the Half Moon was dingy and cold, in spite of the fire in the hearth. The old men who sat about seemed to seethe with disapproval at Kit's clothes, their expressions as bitter as the ale; Muckle was sure that it was only his age and limp that kept them at bay, so that no one actually muttered or asked them to leave. But all the same, he ate as slowly as he could, searching for witty things to say between bites.

At last there was nothing left on his plate, or in his glass. Outside it was already starting to get dark. Kit heaved a sigh and looked at her watch.

He struggled to his feet and shouldered his knapsack. 'Well,' he said, and hated himself for his disappointment when she glanced at him with a barely concealed flash of relief. 'I've had a lovely time. Thank you.'

'Thank you for coming. Honestly.' It was only a crumb but at least he believed that she meant it. She picked up the wrapped painting from beside his feet and handed it to him. 'I'll invite you back soon. If you'd like that.'

'I'll be holding my breath.' They both laughed. 'Darling Kit,' he added, lightly, 'you're very kind to me. I know I'm an awful lame duck.'

She kissed him on the cheek. 'Goodbye, then.'

No offer to walk with him to the station; he knew it was tact, but it stung. 'Goodbye.' There was so much he wanted to say. He imagined her face if he went down on one knee like a Victorian suitor, and then her face when he couldn't get up again. Ha.

He gave her one last smile, and strode out of the pub with a brisk marching step that would not have disgraced a parade ground. The force of his misery carried him through the village, past the vicarage and the bend in the road; it was only when he had passed Kit's house and was out of sight of its unseeing windows that he gave in, and his gait returned to its usual halting asymmetry.

He became conscious that his bladder was uncomfortably full. There was no one about – apparently he was the only one foolish enough to be out in the freezing December smirr – so he had no qualms about dumping the painting on the verge and urinating against the nearest tree. In fact it was satisfying: here, he thought, watching the stream of piss steam in the twilight, this was what he thought of Haltington, and Sussex, and everything Kit had chosen instead of him and London and marriage . . . He shook off the last few drops, and did up his flies. Then he took up the picture again and swung back briskly towards the road, as if he were a boy again—

He caught his foot in a tree root, and pain flashed down his leg, dazzling and deafening him. He reeled, trying to steady himself, and the breath came out of him in a sobbing squeal. When his vision cleared he saw, in a warm, humiliating rush, that a young woman, an actual, beskirted and behatted young woman, was walking down the road; and – oh, Christ, no, please – she had swerved towards him, and was reaching out, already calling out, 'Is something wrong? Are you hurt?'

'No – thank you – I am quite well – I only,' he stammered, 'only turned my ankle . . .' Thank God he had put his cock away before he tripped – but what a bloody fool he was, to draw her attention to his leg! Now she was tilting her head to look, biting her lip as if she were calculating how many yards of bandage she would need to render him whole again. 'It's all right,' he said, 'it's passing now. Just a bit of a sprain.'

'This road is very bad,' she said. 'My brother-in-law says it's the salt in the air.'

She was, he saw now, not unattractive: when she was older she would be ruddy, but now she had a youthful rosiness, dewy-eyed and blooming. Under her hat – he knew very little about millinery, but suspected it was fashionable – a pinned-up crown of golden hair was jewelled with tiny beads of moisture. He shifted his weight from one foot to the other, pretending to test his ankle. 'It's fine,' he said. 'Honestly, no need to fuss.'

The painting had fallen to the ground, and she picked it up and gave it to him, smiling. 'Here, this was yours, wasn't it?' she said. 'You look much better now. I thought you were going to faint, at first.'

He laughed. The pain had faded and he did feel better; so much better that he did not want to shake off her solicitude. 'It was nothing. A bit of a jolt, that's all. I've had worse.'

'How brave,' she said, seriously. She stepped back, and he wondered if he could fake a sudden relapse. 'Do you know your way?'

'I'm going to the station.' He glanced past her, at the long road disappearing into the greying twilight. Yes, he knew the way. He had no need of help, or even company; and she had been walking in the opposite direction, with a brisk purposeful step. It would be unfair to ask her to come with him – and for what? His vanity, that was all. Or his cowardice. 'I just follow this road, don't I? Don't worry about me. I'll take it easy.'

'Goodbye, then.'

He nodded and strode away. But with the painting under one arm he was clumsy and unbalanced, and the road surface was uneven. A fierce blaze of heat leapt up through his knee, so that he swayed and hissed an automatic obscenity. She was still close enough to have heard, and he gasped, 'Sorry – sorry—'

'Oh,' she said, 'you're not all right at all, are you? Oh, *men* . . . !' She had hurried after him as soon as he stumbled, and now she took the painting from him and held his arm with her other hand, taking more of his weight than he meant her to. 'Let me carry that,' she said. 'Lean on me if you need to. We'll get you to the station one way or another. Unless you'd rather turn back—'

'You're very kind, but you needn't—'

'Oh, dry up,' she said, 'anyone would do the same. It's a war wound, isn't it? You don't fool me.'

He did not answer. He had not twisted his leg on purpose; he had no need to feel guilty for accepting her help, or for letting her think he was a hero. He did not even feel guilty for limping more than he needed to, now that the brief agony had passed. She was being kind; no doubt she enjoyed being kind, and it hurt no one if he – for once – did not resent being the object of kindness . . . As they hobbled along the road, dropping gradually into an easier rhythm, she slipped her arm into his. He thought how they must look: a young couple, pink-cheeked and bright-eyed, smiling. They might be an advertisement for soap, or biscuits, or cigarettes.

'Forgive me, I should have – my name is Florence Stock,' she said.

'How do you do, Miss Stock – or should that be Mrs . . . ?' he said, and was pleased when she shook her head. 'Michael McTrackle, at your service.'

They looked at each other, smiling. She was so eager to please him, so unlike Kit. She did not think he was a poor limping cripple, she thought he was brave, stoical, a man who had suffered but still soldiered on. For an instant he wondered if he was projecting too much into that sweet expression – but no, she was looking up at him with such pleasure, such delight in being useful to him.

All the frustrated yearning of the last days rose up inside him, until he thought it would smother him. Damn it all, he thought, damn behaving well, damn accepting my fate . . . ! On a sudden, reckless impulse, he kissed her cheek.

She dipped her head away from him. But the sound she made – a cut-off giggle, like a schoolgirl – was not discouraging. Quite the opposite; it made him feel absurdly manly and grown-up, and a heady rush of euphoria went through him. *She* would not look at him the way Kit had, regretful and pitying. He lifted her chin with his knuckle. She was blushing a hot, deep red. 'Don't worry, my dear,' he said, and wanted to laugh at the easy assurance of his own voice, like a Victorian gentleman. 'I couldn't resist, that's all. It was a compliment.'

'Oh. Well then,' she said, 'I . . . Thank you.' Her gaze slid up to meet his. Then her eyelashes fluttered as she lowered her eyes again.

It was an unmistakable invitation. For a split second he savoured the anticipation; then he pressed his lips to hers. He felt her respond, with unpractised, touching awkwardness: her mouth puckered, pecked like a child's, and withdrew. 'Mr McTrackle –'

'Michael,' he said, and there was a kind of victory in that, in being free from the nickname that had clung to him since he was at school. 'Say it. Michael. Please.'

'Mr – I mean, Michael –'

'Good girl,' he said, and took hold of her shoulders. 'Yes?'

'Your train,' she said, 'shouldn't we . . . ?'

'No hurry,' he said, 'I expect there'll be another one. You're beautiful, has anyone ever told you that?'

'No,' she said, as though it were only dawning on her now, 'no, no one ever has.'

'They should have done. Everyone should have done. You should have men queuing up, just to get a glimpse of you.' He was not exactly teasing her.

'You're awfully kind. I – don't know what to say.'

'Nothing,' he said, 'you needn't say anything at all.' He kissed her again, and felt her try to speak against his lips. He kissed her harder. She put her free hand flat on his chest, but she was not pushing him away. 'Hush,' he said, and put his lips to the curve of her jaw, sliding his mouth down to the sweet fog-damp hollow where it met her neck. How long had it been, since he had touched a woman like this? Not since that French peasant girl – Françoise? Thérèse? – in the ruins of a church somewhere near the Somme . . . He had forgotten how it felt. He did not need Kit, after all.

'Please – Mr McTra— Michael – we can't – I can't –'

His hand found her breast. It was under her coat – and no doubt her cardigan, and blouse, and stays – but even the vague curve of it was enough to make heat pulse in his groin. He grunted, burrowing his face harder into her smooth skin. Under the chilly slick of moisture it was hot, hotter than his lips, fragrant with toilet water and wet wool. She squirmed and protested, weakly; he murmured something in brief acknowledgement, and held her tighter. Wasn't he due this, after everything he had sacrificed? After the days of being shunned by Kit, and putting up with it, like a dog that still fawned after it had been kicked? Wasn't he *owed*— ?

She said, 'Let go of me. Please let go of me.'

'It's all right,' he said, and his hand found the gap between the buttons of her coat. 'It's all right, Florence,' he said, as if she were an animal he were trying to tame, 'hush, it's all right . . .'

Suddenly she wrenched away so violently he staggered, and a splintery fire swept up from his knee. He gasped, 'Hey – damn it – my leg—'

'Let me *go*,' she said, in a high strident voice, even though he was no longer touching her. 'I never said – I never meant . . .'

'Of course you did,' he said, and for a moment, impossibly, he heard the distant thunder of guns. 'You kissed me back, didn't you? And now you turn round and say – no,' he interrupted himself, 'don't apologise. I'd hate to touch anyone who didn't want me to. Most girls would be grateful. Especially girls – women – like you, who're almost over the hill. Think you'll get a better offer, do you? I wouldn't be so sure.'

She stared at him, tears welling, as if he had struck her. Christ, he had *kissed* her! Why wasn't she flattered, at least? It was true, she must have been easily twenty-five, she would probably never be kissed again. She opened her mouth, and he thought she was going to sob. But she only bent slowly, set down the picture at his feet, and, with a sudden gulp of breath, flung herself past him and away.

She ran quickly, even encumbered by her long skirt and flapping coat. Childishly he willed her to trip and go flying. It was nearly dark now. Her figure grew harder to make out, until at last it disappeared in the fog beneath the trees where he had stopped to piss.

His own coat was undone, too. He buttoned it slowly, with cold fingers, and stooped to pick up his kitbag. Beside it, on the ground, lay the picture, its wrapping crumpled, a long rip running down the centre as if caught by the heel of a woman's shoe. He pulled the paper away to see if the painting underneath was damaged: but Kit painted on board, not canvas, and Septimus's smile was as sunlit and charming as ever, the leaf-dappled shade and green-shadowed shirt entirely perfect and untouched. How like Septimus, to come through unscathed.

For a moment he felt such envy and resentment he felt sick – although mixed with it was his desperate yearning knowledge that he *had* been happy that day, Kit had been quite right, it had been a day of heady delight, as if summer and youth and joy in being alive would endure for ever . . . But oh God, what wouldn't he give to be like Septimus, lying triumphant and languid in the grass, always the victor! Septimus had always won, at everything. And now, for the first time, he wondered if Septimus might have vanquished Kit too – if the power in the painting was not only Kit's talent but her desire, if in spite of her protestations she might have made an exception for some men, just not— not *him* . . . The thought made the picture blur into a merciless blaze of colour, out of place in the winter dusk.

He turned on his heel, and walked away. It was childish, but he did not care; he was damned if he'd carry Septimus all the way home, and put him up on the wall like an icon to be adored. But after ten paces he slowed down, and after twenty he found he had come to a halt. It was very quiet; there was not a breath of wind, or a note of birdsong. The light was fading quickly now, draining the colours out of the landscape around him. Unease stole over him, an irrational conviction that it was not the dusk but the world that was turning grey. If only he had not kissed Florence, he thought, they would be walking to the station now, arm in arm . . .

But it was too late. He had been an idiot. And now something itched in the pit of his stomach. He knew that sensation: he had felt it in the trenches, waiting to go over the top. Not unease: fear. But in the trenches he had never needed to wonder what he was afraid of. He had never dwelt on the feeling. He'd known that the more he thought about it, the worse it would get. Now . . .

The road was empty. He saw bare trees, the tufted wintry verge, the curve of the road, the faraway glint of flat floodwater in a field. Nothing was out of the ordinary, except the slow draining of everything vivid and real, the flattening and blurring of every line. Could he be dying? Oh God, and he had frightened away the only person who might have called for a doctor! But he was not in pain, and his heart thundered on, his guts churned, his breath rasped in his throat. Whatever was wrong was outside his body; or inside his mind. Shell shock. Delayed shell shock. Was that possible?

He glanced wildly around, up to the sky and down. Then, staggering a little, he swung round to look in the direction he had come. In the distance was the tree where he had pissed, and the distant Half Moon with its smoking chimney and windows lit from within; but they were colourless and dim compared to the painting that lay a few yards away. It seemed to glow like marsh gas, the only vivid thing in the twilight. He could not drag his eyes away from it.

It was made of oil and pigment and wood, nothing more; but now the surface of it seemed to ripple, as if the paint were deep and liquid, and something was rising far beneath. Septimus's face held steady, its smile unwavering: but behind it, something shifted, dragged by a slow sly current into an entirely new shape.

He stared down at it, and his heartbeat accelerated until it was no longer a rhythm but a weltering roar in his ears. Life, he thought. It was coming to life.

Only it was not life. It was the opposite of life. It was some – appalling – terrible – parody—

Was it possible that he could long for the clean horrors of the Front? He would not have thought so, before. But he would have done anything to be back there now, in the noise and mud. Anything rather than this, to be alone on this country road, with the— the thing that was gathering in that unearthly blaze of colour, nearly existing . . . The pressure built until he thought his ears and eyes would burst. Then he felt the world open, splitting like flesh under a knife, and something came out of the wound.

There was sudden stillness. He had cowered back, his arm coming up automatically to cover his face; so he could not have told what exactly had happened, or how. But when at last he mustered the courage to lower his hand, the painting was not a painting any more. There was a figure standing beside the verge, as tall as he was, in glimmering, sickly-shadowed tennis whites; it was not quite three-dimensional, but it was as vivid and rough-edged as if it carried Kit's brushstrokes on its skin. It was impossible. It was *wrong*, he thought, helpless with repulsion, it was inhuman, hungry . . . But it was there. He thought he could smell something that was not turpentine or oils, but something darker, more rotten, worse than the trenches. It turned its borrowed face on him, and met his eyes.

There was no more room for fear, then. Only amazement, and revulsion, and a last flash of thought: a detached, ironic sense that it was bloody typical, that of all the people in the world, the thing that came for him should look like Septimus.

XI

Sisters (II), diptych, oil on board, 1920–21

The sound of knocking jerked Kit out of a doze. For a moment she looked around and did not know who or where she was. The knocking went on, louder and louder. Instinctively she struggled to her feet. Somewhere there was a door, and someone needing to come in – oh Lord, Muckle, she thought, and in a flash she was herself again. Had he missed his train? She could not send him away, not on a freezing December evening when his leg was giving him so much trouble, but she was already weary at the thought of having to usher him back inside. She would have to pretend to be thrilled. How like Muckle, to outstay his welcome! You loved him for a day or so, and then you began to get tired of him – while he looked at you more and more pathetically, as if he were a spaniel begging for a treat . . . And you got brisker and brisker in response, and he got whinier and whinier until if he had been a spaniel you would have longed to kick him, and then you began to despise yourself even more than you despised him, because he was a sweetheart as well as a bit of a damp dishcloth. Poor Muckle, poor infuriating Muckle – and he was pounding on the door now, as if he was going to break it down.

'All right,' she called, 'all right, I'm coming,' and stumbled past the kitchen table and the chairs, wishing she had brought the lamp with her.

But it was not Muckle; it was Florence.

She had been in the middle of knocking, and her hand was still raised. She lowered it stiffly. 'I'm sorry,' she said. 'I saw the light in your window, and . . .' She stopped. Then, with a kind of hiccup, she burst into tears.

'Come inside,' Kit said.

Florence let herself be steered past the table and chairs and through the door to the sitting room. She was shaking, catching her breath in little squeaky jerks that suggested she was trying, not very successfully, to stop crying; but when Kit pushed her on to the sofa she gasped out, 'I'm so sorry – what must you think—'

'Shut up,' Kit said, 'there's nothing to be sorry for. Sit there. Do you want a cup of tea?'

Florence shook her head. 'You're being so kind – so awfully kind,' she said, and gave in to a storm of sobs. Kit stood beside her, aching a little at her own helplessness. But the worst thing would be to ask too many questions too soon, so she bit her tongue and waited. After a while she noticed that she had kept hold of Florence's hand, and was gripping it so hard the bones shone white; but although she forced herself to loosen her grasp she could not bear to let go entirely.

At last Florence grew calmer. She fumbled in her pocket for a handkerchief and blew her nose, loudly. Then she looked up at Kit. 'I really am sorry,' she said. Her voice cracked as if she were about to start crying again, but she inhaled slowly, mastering herself. Her eyes were startlingly blue in her blotchy face.

Kit sat down beside her. Now she saw that Florence's hat was askew, her hair falling out of its plaited crown, and her coat was smeared with mud. 'Are you all right?' she said. 'What happened?'

'I fell over. I was running, and I tripped on a stone.'

'Why were you running?'

Florence took a little shallow breath, as if to top up her lungs, and said, 'There was a – a man . . .'

Very carefully, Kit relaxed her fingers, afraid she had clenched Florence's hand in a sudden, involuntary spasm. A man. Two syllables that said everything. 'Did he hurt you?' she said, deliberately not glancing at Florence's mud-stained coat or swollen face.

'No,' Florence said, 'it was nothing, a little kiss, that's all, I was silly to mind. But I . . . I ran away, and that was when I fell over.' When Kit – unable, now, not to look – met her eyes, she smiled; but she could not keep her mouth from trembling, and new tears rose and spilt down her cheeks. 'Oh! Honestly, Kit, you mustn't think – it was nothing, honestly.'

If Florence had not said *honestly* more than once, Kit thought, she might have believed her.

'It was my fault,' Florence said. 'I wanted to be kind, and he thought – I think he honestly thought—'

'*Honestly?*' Kit echoed, shocked by the acid in her own voice. 'There's nothing *honest* about it.'

'I mean – he didn't realise, he thought – I led him on, I suppose – honestly, Kit—'

'Stop saying *honestly*! Is it honest to steal a pound from someone who's offered you a farthing? Even if you think they can afford it? Even if they've given away guineas and guineas? Even if—'

'I'm sorry. You're right, I'm stupid. I didn't mean to say it.'

Kit got to her feet and paced from the wall to the window and back. 'No, *I'm* stupid. Shouting at you, when . . . Forgive me.' Oh, but it was intolerable, to be so angry on Florence's behalf and not to be able to express it! 'They ought to be gelded,' she said. 'Like horses.'

Florence snorted with tremulous laughter, although Kit had not been joking. 'It was only a kiss,' she said, 'and I – I should have stopped him. But I didn't know what to do, and I didn't want to hurt his feelings – so he did, he probably thought that I – was one of *those* girls, you know, and – I should have, I should . . .' Her voice had been steady at first, but it had risen word by word; now she buried her face in her hands. Kit clenched her fists in her pockets, looking down at Florence's bowed head.

'I'm so sorry,' Florence said, at last, scrubbing at her cheeks with her handkerchief. 'It's only because I fell over – it knocked all the breath out of me, the shock, you know. If I'd been more sensible I wouldn't be in this state. And look at me! I'm a perfect scarecrow.'

'If you give me your coat I'll try and get the worst of the dirt off it.'

'Would you? That's awfully nice of you.' She stood up, unpinned her hat, unbuttoned her coat and gave them to Kit. 'I expect Mrs Reed can do something, if it won't come out.'

'Wait,' Kit said, laying the coat on the sofa and catching Florence's wrist. 'Your hand – you're bleeding.'

'Oh, so I am. It's only a graze. I forgot my gloves on the train,' she added, as if Kit would disapprove of her having left home without them.

'It needs a good wash and some iodine. Let me boil some water.'

'You're so sweet,' Florence said, 'looking after me like this, but I – I mustn't presume on your kindness –'

'Don't be an idiot. Are you hurt anywhere else?'

'My knees, I think,' she said, lifting up her skirt. 'But just bruises – there's no need to . . . Oh, look at my stockings – *damn* it,' she said, her voice wavering, as she stared at the rip just below her kneecap, and the bloodied flesh that showed through the hole. 'I am *not* going to cry any more.'

'Good-o,' Kit said, and was glad that Florence laughed. She ducked through the door, put a pan of water on to boil and rummaged in a drawer for some clean rags. When she came back, balancing a brimming basin of hot water, Florence had taken off her shoes and stockings and was unbuttoning her blouse. Kit stopped in the doorway, and soap suds sloshed over the rim of the bowl. With an effort she set it down without spilling any more.

'Oh – I'm sorry,' Florence said, letting her blouse drop to the floor, 'I hope you don't mind – only I – he . . .' She ran her hands over her collarbone, as if to get off some sticky residue. 'I can smell him. His mouth. On me. It's foolish – as though somehow he got under my clothes . . .' She wrung out a rag and scrubbed her decolletage until it gleamed scarlet. Water ran down into her chemise so that it clung transparently to the curves of her breasts where they emerged from her stays. She crouched to rinse out the rag; but instead of turning her attention to her grazed knees she scoured her face and neck again, until Kit was afraid her skin would be raw.

'Do you need me to clean your knees?' Kit said. 'Or would you rather do it yourself?'

'What? Oh.' She looked up, blinking water out of her eyes. 'No, I'll be all right.' She sat down on the floor and drew her skirt up. The down on her legs glinted in the lamplight, and her feet were plump and rosy. A thread of blood had trickled down to her ankle. She rubbed it away with more force than was necessary.

'You're shivering,' Kit said. 'Don't get cold.'

'I'm all right,' she said again, but as she prodded her bloody knee with the rag the spasms grew more violent, and her bare arms grew lumpy with gooseflesh. Kit heard her teeth rattling.

Kit threw another log on the fire and jabbed it with the poker until it showered sparks. If only she had not tidied away the blankets after Muckle left! Then – like a chivalrous schoolboy, she thought, mocking herself – she drew off her woollen jumper and wrapped it round Florence's shoulders. 'Here,' she said, as Florence clutched it closer, 'leave your knee for a moment, while you warm up.'

'I'm all right really,' she said, through still-chattering teeth.

'Have a bath when you get home, I would. That'll thaw you out properly.'

'I wish I could. But Horace . . .' She stopped.

'What?'

'Horace will think it's extravagant. I had a bath yesterday, and . . . He worries about the cost of coal,' she added, with a look that pleaded with Kit not to laugh.

But Kit had no desire to laugh. 'Well,' she said, fighting the impulse to say what she thought of Dr Manning and the cost of coal, 'then stay and have a bath here.'

'Oh – Kit, I couldn't—'

'Why not? The range burns wood, and I've got mountains of it. I won't send you a bill afterwards.' She won her struggle not to emphasise the word *I*.

Florence buried her face in the knitted sleeves of Kit's pullover. 'Thank you, then,' she said, her voice a little muffled. 'If it's not an awful liberty.'

'Of course not,' Kit said. She hurried into the kitchen to take the hip bath off its hook and put on more water to heat. Soap – that was in the sitting room already – a scrubbing brush, a clean towel. Thank God, she thought, as she climbed the stairs two at a time, she had got Hannah Smith to launder all her towels before Muckle came to visit. She took a clean one from the press at the top of the stairs, then hesitated in the doorway of her bedroom. Without allowing herself to think, she took a camisole and shirt out of the rickety chest of drawers, and carried them downstairs as well. She set everything out in the sitting room, suddenly very self-conscious, as though the process were a relic of some folk tradition she did not really believe in. She felt Florence watching her, and did not meet her eyes. 'There,' she said, 'now let me see if the water is hot yet.'

She had to go back and forth several times, and she was sweaty and aching with exertion before the bath was full enough. When she herself bathed she was more spartan, but Florence deserved six inches at least of hot water. At last she set down the jug, pushed a sticky clump of hair off her forehead, and sat back on her haunches. 'It's ready, my lady,' she said. She had meant to make a joke of it, but somehow her voice emerged low and intimate, as if she were not Florence's maid but her gallant. She was glad her cheeks were already flushed from the rising steam.

Florence took off her chemise and began to undo her stays. Kit stood up. 'Well,' she said, too loudly, 'if you've got everything you need . . .'

'Will you stay with me?'

'I – yes, if you want me to – if you're sure—'

'Please. I don't want to be on my own.'

Kit sat on the sofa, her hands between her knees. She imagined drawing what she could see – parallel thumbs and palms in the shadowed valley between her trouser-legs – while Florence's clothes rustled to the floor. Then there was the bell-like note of the hip bath and the ripple of water. Florence sighed. 'That's better,' she said. 'Will you pass me the soap, please?'

Kit got to her feet. She concentrated very hard on picking up the soap and putting it into Florence's outstretched hand.

'Thank you.' Florence caught her breath as she washed her bleeding knee, but then, when she had rinsed herself, she sat back in the tub and let her head loll to one side. Strands of her hair clung in damp loops to her wet shoulders. Kit saw, in spite of herself, that Florence's breasts were full, with large, dark nipples, and she had a mole just over her heart.

'Are you warmer now?'

'Much.' A pause. She let drips roll down her fingers and splash into the still water between her knees. 'I feel safe here. With you.'

Kit said, glancing away, 'Will you tell the police what happened?'

'I don't know. I don't know what I should say, if I did. A man kissed me, that's all. And if he thought I wanted him to . . .'

'Did he tell you his name?'

'Yes,' she said, in surprise, 'yes, I'd forgotten. Michael something. McDougall, McDonald . . . McTrackle.'

'*Muckle?*' Kit said. 'Michael McTrackle?'

'Yes.'

'A man with a limp? Brown hair, clean-shaven? A— ?' A *nice* man, she wanted to say. Like a spaniel. The sort of dog who would never bite. 'Michael McTrackle. You're certain?'

'You know him,' Florence said. 'Is he a friend of yours?'

'Well – yes – I suppose so. In a way.' She felt like Judas, although she was not sure which of them she was betraying. 'He was staying here. He turned up on Christmas Eve. I wasn't expecting him – I mean, I sort of invited him only I forgot . . .'

'You don't believe me.'

'Naturally I do. Only – could you be mistaken – some misunderstanding— ?'

Florence bowed her head. 'Yes,' she said, 'yes, I expect it was a mistake.'

Kit stared at her. Then, with a kind of inward jolt, she said, 'I'm sorry – of course you know best. I'm surprised, that's all, I thought Muckle— never mind.' Oh, for God's sake! 'I'm sorry, Florence,' she said, and dropped to her knees beside the bathtub. 'Truly. I believe you. It wasn't your fault. He was in the wrong.'

'I didn't realise he was your friend.'

'I don't care whose friend he is,' she said fiercely, 'he was a bastard to hurt you.' But Florence covered her face with her hands and – oh God – began to sob again. 'Please,' Kit said, 'please don't cry . . .'

Florence gave a thick mucous sniff. 'Here I go again,' she said, with a shake in her voice. 'Why can't I just forget about it? But I'm so – so ashamed.'

'Yes,' Kit said, 'I see.' If Florence had not been naked she might have patted her shoulder, or taken her hand. With an effort, she said, 'It's foolish to be ashamed of something you didn't do.'

There was a silence. At last, quietly, Florence said, 'It isn't that simple, though. I . . .' She hesitated. Kit watched her. People had always said she was good at reading expressions – *such clever portraits, darling, such insight into what they're feeling!* – but now she felt like an infant, staring uncomprehendingly at the bobbing moon of its mother's face. Florence linked her hands around her knees, in a slosh of water. 'No one has ever kissed me before,' she said. 'Once a boy held my hand after a dancing class, but that was all. He was called Andrew. I knew I wanted to get married – I don't mean to him – but Mother always said there was plenty of time for that. Then the War came, and then . . .' She hunched her shoulders, and a droplet of water slid down her breastbone. 'After he kissed me – your friend –'

Kit bit her lip, and did not interrupt.

'– he said I should have been grateful. And part of me thinks he was right, because who is ever going to kiss me again?' She reached out and took hold of the rim of the bathtub, as if she wanted to bend the metal with her bare hands. 'I'd do it, you know. Put up with it. All the kissing, and the – the other things – if it meant I could have a child, and love someone – *be* someone.'

Kit began to say, 'But you *are*—'

'Endure it,' she said. 'Endure his hands and his smell – his mouth . . .' She made a wry, disgusted moue; then she crossed her arms on her knees and buried her face. Kit thought she was fighting back another wave of tears; but her voice, when it came, was surprisingly steady. 'But do you know,' she said, 'the worst thing of all? The most humiliating part of it?'

Kit did not know if she was supposed to answer. She said, 'No.'

'The most humiliating thing of all,' Florence said, her head still bowed, 'is that now I know how you felt, when *I* kissed *you*.'

There was a silence. Kit had pretended to herself that she had forgotten that kiss: so long ago, so brief, so embarrassing for both of them. Clumsy, inappropriate, childish. Better that it had never happened . . . But now, as if something had given way, it flooded back to her, the memory as vivid as a dream: the hardness of Florence's teeth behind her chapped lips, Florence's open eyes staring into her own, Florence's body rocking forwards, lurching into hers as if the kiss were an accident, a mere stumble. There had been no pleasure in it for either of them, she was sure of that. So why, remembering now, did heat bloom between her legs, curling up into her abdomen like the petals of a flower? She said, a little thickly, 'That was different.'

'Why? Because I'm a woman?'
'Yes. Partly.'
'You weren't afraid I would – assault you.'
'I wasn't afraid at all. And . . .' She took a long breath. 'I knew you didn't mean it. You thought it didn't count. If I had kissed you back . . .'
'Yes? What then?'
'Then . . .' She bit her lip. It was unfair to ask her to imagine it: especially now, while Florence, damp-faced and naked, stared at her with serious eyes. She got to her feet. It helped, a bit, to be looking down, with her hands in her pockets. 'Then,' she said, with wry patience, 'you would have been horrified. You would have felt even worse than you do now. But of course you knew I wouldn't.'
'Did I?'
'Oh, I don't know!' She spun on her heel, and strode to the curtained windows. 'How should I know? You were there, *you* tell *me*. All I'm saying is that . . . that it wasn't the same. You didn't really want me at all. You only did it because you thought there was no danger of – of anything. Anything real.'

She had not meant to sound angry – she had not thought she *was* angry – but Florence shifted in her bath, and said, 'You make it sound worse.'
'Do I? I didn't mean to.'
'What I wanted,' Florence said slowly, 'was – not to know what would happen. It was like throwing myself off a cliff.'
'My goodness. Thanks.'
'I didn't . . .' She looked up, and caught Kit's eye; then, together, they started to laugh. 'I'm sorry,' she said, through her giggles, 'not like that, I didn't mean like that.'
'I've been called a few names in my time, but—'
'Oh, stop. You know perfectly well I didn't mean—'

'– but comparing a single kiss to actual self-destruction is definitely—'

'You're being unkind, you *know* I—'

'Never mind,' Kit said, not laughing any more. 'I understand. You had a moment of vertigo – madness – you thought you were risking your whole life. And then when you stepped forward you found that it wasn't a cliff at all, only a cliff-edge painted on the pavement, and the world was the same flat old place it had always been.'

'Yes,' Florence said. 'That's it. Only it wasn't fair to you, anyway, to use you as a place to jump.'

'No,' Kit said, 'it wasn't. Better than raping me, though.'

Florence glanced at her. Then she scooped up water in her hands and splashed her face and shoulders, busying herself with the soap as if she did not know she was blushing. And not only blushing but blushing all over, Kit thought, fascinated: she had never seen a naked woman blush. It was beautiful.

For a while – maybe half a minute – there was only the sound of splathering water as Florence washed, as assiduously as if she were demonstrating how it should be done, paying unnatural attention to the backs of her knees and the spaces between her toes. At last she leant over the side of the bath to lay the soap carefully on the newspaper Kit had spread out to stop the floor getting wet. Then she rinsed her hands, letting the water trickle through her fingers. She said, 'What if you're wrong?'

'About what?'

'What if I did want you to kiss me back?'

Kit swallowed. She thought: don't. Don't, don't. 'Then I would have missed an opportunity, I suppose,' she said, lightly.

Florence met her eyes. 'I did,' she said. 'I do.'

Don't.

Kit turned away, feigning a sudden interest in – what? The wall, for God's sake? Behind her there was the sound of Florence standing up, the last musical drips of water, and the whisper of the towel against her skin. 'You think I'm joking,' she said.

'I was just—' Kit said, as she turned; and stopped, because Florence let the towel fall to the ground.

She was lovely. Instinctively Kit brought her hand up to shield her eyes, as if she were dazzled; but even in that split second some prodigious part of her brain had taken in every inch of rosy skin, every line of flesh and freckle and hair, every graceful proportion. The heavy breasts, the heavier hips, the wet mass of curls at the join of her thighs . . . Christ, she was beautiful.

'You can look at me,' Florence said. 'I don't mind. Look at me.'

'Florence . . .'

'What's the matter? Don't you want to?'

'You'd better get dressed,' Kit said, in a level, reasonable, kindly tone – ha, as if she felt any of those things. 'Come on, you'll get cold—'

'You think I'm hysterical?'

'I think you've had a very upsetting experience, and you— you're not thinking straight.'

Florence stepped out of the bath, over the towel, and towards Kit. 'Let me kiss you,' she said, 'and this time you can kiss me back, and see what happens.'

Kit dug her hands into her pockets. To be standing here, fully dressed, while Florence was entirely nude, vulnerable, inviting . . . 'You're trusting me to be gentlemanly,' she said. 'Stop it.'

'No.'

'You think I'll be scrupulous with you. You think I'll protect you from yourself. I won't.'

'No.'

'I won't be polite, Florence. If you let me – touch you—'

'It's all right.' She took Kit's hand and put it on her breast, so that the solid nub of her nipple met the centre of Kit's palm. 'I understand,' she said, as the breath caught in Kit's throat. 'You're a cliff-edge. I want to fall.'

Kit was asleep. Florence looked down at her face, closed and trusting as a child's, and did not know what she felt. She eased herself away, lifting Kit's arm gently to extricate herself, and shivered. The log on the fire had burnt through, and the room was cold. She dressed as quickly and quietly as she could, wincing at the cold fabric as it slid over her bare skin. Her chemise was still damp, and its clammy touch made her squirm.

It was late. Would Dr Manning have noticed her absence? Or would he simply think she had stayed at Barbara's later than she had intended? Yes, she would say that. *The children had so looked forward to having dinner with us – it would have been churlish to leave – and then the train did not stop at Haltington, I had to walk* . . . Dr Manning would never know. Unless . . .

Did it show? Would anyone, looking into her face, see . . . ? She resisted the urge to look over her shoulder at Kit, asleep on the floor. Her cheeks grew warm; she laid her hands against them, feeling the cold of her palms, the heat of her face. She had never imagined . . . No, what she had imagined was a wedding night, a young man – moustached, probably, but youthful – and a grand bed in a seaside hotel. She would have lain still, not unresponsive exactly but demure, knowing that her role was to be passive, to be virgin territory, welcoming the intrepid explorer . . . She would have bled, a small red flower on the clean linen; afterwards she would have pulled on her lacy nightgown, wondering if already there was a baby inside her, taking root. Probably he – her phantom husband – would have yawned and gone to sleep, snoring a little with the satisfaction of a job well done. Was *that* the only thing that was the same, here and now – that Kit had fallen asleep?

Everything else . . . The embrace on a hard floor, skin and sweat, the unfamiliarity and hunger of it, the fear that if she did not play her part Kit might grow impatient . . . She had not dared to give herself time to pause or to think: she had wanted it, she was sure she had wanted it, and that had had to be enough. But there was a blurred line between the desire she had felt, and the desire she had feigned: she had flung herself into the dance like a child, because she did not know the steps. And now . . . A woman, she thought, marvelling, horrified: a woman's hand, bringing her to that – that agonising pitch of pleasure, that long note before her body choked and spasmed. A woman's gaze, watching her; a woman's mouth on hers, afterwards, and a woman's fingers on her cheek, not letting her turn away. Even the words made her tingle: *lips, hands, breasts.*

Clitoris. She remembered how Kit had laughed, that day on the beach, wiping tears away while she sat stiffly, utterly humiliated. *Where on earth did you hear that word?* But she had not considered that it might apply to her, to her own body; she had not connected it with the urgent warmth that spread through her sometimes, when she read certain passages or looked at certain pictures, or with the dreamy idling of her fingers on the long dull afternoons when Mother had insisted she should lie down after lunch . . . And how extraordinary that Kit – Kit, down *there* – was the same and not the same, familiar and unfamiliar, so that she, Florence, could guess at what to do and fumble more or less successfully at the same small button of flesh. She had not brought Kit to any – oh God, what word was there? to any kind of— of conclusion; but Kit had been slippery under her fingertips, as wet as a mouth, and she had not actually winced or told Florence to stop. It had only been that Florence's hand had dropped away, as her mind grew blank and her breath quickened. Perhaps, she thought now, it would have been polite to begin again, after her vision cleared and she remembered where she was – or to offer, at least. If only they had taught such things at school, instead of which corner of a visiting card should be turned down, or how to introduce two matrons without suggesting that one was younger than the other! Would Kit forgive her for not knowing? Next time—

Next time. Would there be a next time? What if Kit had not really wanted – if she had only been sorry for Florence, and kind? Would anyone do – *that*, out of kindness? Surely not . . . But then she remembered the man in the road – Muckle – who had expected her to do that, yes, exactly *that*, out of kindness.

Kit stirred, curling into a ball, with a faint grunt of complaint. Florence picked up the woollen jumper that lay abandoned on the floor and, crouching, put it gently over Kit's shoulders. She looked young, smooth-faced, girlish; without her masculine clothes and narrowed eyes she might almost have been ordinary. Florence paused, suddenly filled with an immense longing to put her lips to Kit's forehead, to put her arms around her and cradle her. But if she woke . . . She didn't know why she didn't want Kit to wake, but it was enough to make her creep backwards and get to her feet again, holding her breath.

She must go home. Oh, it was late! She must go home, and hope that Dr Manning had already retired to bed, or his study, so that she could tiptoe upstairs unobserved. Tomorrow, whatever was written on her face would have faded; tomorrow, no one would look at her and guess that she was – that she had . . . She bit her lip. *Was* she a virgin, still? Did it count, if it was not a – a man, and his – his thing? Was it the pleasure that meant something, or only the rip of a membrane, the conquest of a cavity? She could not believe that she was still the same woman, in the eyes of society, or the law, or the Church – Mother would have said—

Mother. Without warning a wave of shame swept over her, so strong she clutched herself, wrapping her arms round her torso as if she could crush herself out of existence. If Mother knew . . . But Mother was dead, Mother would never know. For a second that thought was comforting; then it was worse. What sort of daughter was she? What sort of woman . . . ? Depraved, perverted, unnatural. Disgusting. How the other girls at school would have whispered and hissed; how Dr Manning would gape and recoil; how any young man at all would deride her! And it was done, now, it was like a scent on her skin that could never be washed off. She could not even claim that she was the innocent party, drawn unknowing into sin: *she* had been the one who stood there, naked and dripping, demanding that Kit look at her – the one who had asked to be kissed, who had taken hold of Kit's hesitant hand and placed it full on her breast. A treacherous thrill ran through her at the memory, a taut wire that sent a bolt of electricity from her nipple to her belly. Then she put her hands over her mouth, to quell a groan. How *could* she? To have thought it, yes, to have wanted it, even, but to have done it . . .

No one must ever know. She must pretend even to herself that it had not happened. She shut her eyes and imagined the evening she might have – *must* have spent with Barbara, the two children scrubbed and fidgeting at the dinner table, the train conductor who had told her that her train did not stop at the Halt and she must walk from Berwick. And – and she had tripped, yes, that part of the story was true, she had been hurrying home because it was so late, and she had fallen and got mud on her clothes.

She put on her shoes and coat. Kit had not, after all, got any of the dirt out. It would be easier tomorrow, when it had dried. She bundled her hair up and hid it under her hat.

Kit stirred again, murmuring, her sleepy hands finding the jumper around her shoulders and drawing it closer. Her eyes opened and lit on Florence's face, and she smiled. It was a friendly, pleased, comfortable sort of smile: as though seeing Florence simply made her happy. Then she yawned, stretched, and rolled over, her head pillowed easily on her arm.

Florence said, 'I must go home.'

'Mm-hm,' Kit said, drowsily, without turning her head.

'Good night, then.' There was no answer. Florence felt a sting of – something, not quite resentment, not quite hurt – as she strode to the door, resolving to put every ounce of willpower into forgetting that she had ever come here tonight.

But just as the door opened, she heard Kit sit up and say her name. 'Yes?' she said, swinging round.

'It's all right,' Kit said, holding out a paint-stained hand. Those colour-flecked fingers, with the fingernails cut short, the slender hard bones . . . Florence felt her body tingle, as though they had left traces everywhere they touched. 'Don't worry, will you, Florence?'

'No,' she said, 'no, I won't worry.' She had only said the words automatically; but she found that somehow, in spite of everything, they loosened the knot that had tightened around her heart.

Kit stood in front of her painting, considering it closely in the neutral morning light, and thought: ah.

She had worked so hard – harder than she had ever

worked, she thought – on it. She had tried to distil some of the essence of that bright winter afternoon, when she and Florence had ridden their bicycles all the way to the Haven: she had wanted it to be luminous and exact, the sort of scene that you could almost step into. And she had failed. She had sworn at it, coaxed it, rubbed lines away before they were dry and repainted them, scraped lines away after they were dry and repainted them, and finally begun again from scratch and repainted the whole thing, all to no avail. The colours were still buttery and blurred, too thick, too rich. Portia would have licked her lips and said, 'Yum.' Kit had gone from fury to despair, then to weary resignation: it would be a useful exercise, a study, perhaps, for another painting in five years' time.

Until now. This morning, when she woke, she had come straight into this room to look at it, before she even made her first pot of tea – before she even went to the outhouse for a piss. It had been in her mind the moment before she opened her eyes, as though she had dreamt of it. Now she understood why. She had wanted to make the viewer feel small: look, she had meant to say, how beautiful it all is, how little we are, how absurd it is to think we matter. The way to serenity is merely an awareness of proportions. Looking is all very well, but the cliffs will always stand, the sea will always reflect the sky, the sky will always shine.

Now she laughed, softly, at her capacity for self-deception. Everything in the landscape loomed towards the eye, subtly drawn out of shape – and yes, the colours were edible, every shade and sheen as simple and carnal as fondant. The world was huge, but it was there to be consumed; it was all a matter of appetite, and of pleasure. It was not what she had meant, but it had a sly truth, subverting what she thought had been the message: it said, in its own voice, *look how hungry you are.*

Had she been thinking that, already, that day? Or was it only as she painted and repainted, her unacknowledged desire thickening her work like custard? She had not admitted it. Not until she saw Florence naked, water still gleaming in the hollows of her neck, and heard her say, *let me kiss you*. And then she had known . . .

Was it true, that the world in all its glory was only a backdrop for lust? No wonder there was something stomach-turning about the picture, if that was its message – but it was defiant, too, decadent and unapologetic. Would anyone else be able to see how brazen it was? If so, she would never be able to exhibit it . . . She remembered Muckle saying, in that careful, non-committal voice, *I didn't know you painted landscapes.* Yes, he had seen. Ha. She should have painted a nude and had done with it. No one would dare complain that a nude was too erotic – not anyone she knew, anyway. That would be the kind of gaffe that her friends would laugh at.

A nude, she thought, Florence nude . . .

Her breath stalled; she remembered Florence on the floor, one arm flung above her head, showing the feathery hair in her armpit, the curves of her breasts, her stomach flat, the curly mound of her pubis. Could she paint that, without her vision blurring and her hand beginning to falter? She had never painted Portia in the nude. She had never wanted to. It had seemed too predictable, too like the male students at art school who slept with the female students and then used them as models, transparently trying to recast them as muses instead of rivals; all those pictures had gleamed (she thought) with a queasy varnish that was one part lasciviousness and three parts jealousy. But Florence . . .

Florence's face. Florence's cheek, damp, with a lock of blonde hair clinging to it; Florence's eyes half closed, her lips a little parted. Yes. Kit's stomach tightened with a mixture of ambition and desire: if she could paint that, as she saw it now in her mind's eye . . .

She reached for a pencil, and then hesitated. Surely now, *now* she would be able to start again. She had slept without nightmares last night, and woken easily, gently, as she had before the War . . . There would be no more unease, no more nightmares, no more – silliness. Whatever she had thought she saw in the bonfire, or on the hill, up at the Face – it had been hysteria, surely. The effect of having been alone for too long. Of being *chaste* for too long . . . She gave a quick snort of laughter. Was that it? Simply a peculiar manifestation of sapphic frustration? All the ghosts and ghouls had been blown away, like cobwebs, after a good fuck . . . They certainly seemed distant and quaint, like the night terrors of childhood, after last night. Sex, she thought briskly, sex is always a good soporific.

Not that it had been the best sex in the world, in fact; she had not gone off, herself, only watched, breathless and tingling, as Florence moaned and jerked under her hand. What had tightened and released inside her was something else, something less physical. It was not the basic, skin-against-skin, chemical thrill of fucking; it was Florence, it was because she was fucking Florence . . .

She let out a groan. It rang out in the little room as if it came from somewhere deeper than her lungs. She had come to this cottage to be away from all that – to recover, like an invalid, between the quiet wide spaces of down and sea and sky. Not to have her heart prised open and left to glisten on the half-shell, ripe for swallowing . . .

Stop it. Today she was going to work. She would not wonder whether Florence would come today, or tomorrow, or the day after. Florence would not come. There was no point wondering. Work, that was it.

She reached again for her pencil and the pad of paper. She drew a hand, an arm, the curve of a shoulder and neck. But when she reached the line of the jaw she stopped, in spite of herself. She stared at the blank space on the paper, willing her hand to move across it with the old ease, the old unthinking lack of fear; but her body would not obey her.

Dr Manning was standing in the hallway, humming to himself. As Florence started down the stairs he looked up and raised his hand, which held something white. It was impossible for her to retreat. 'Perhaps, my dear,' he said, while Florence tried to make her face look ordinary, 'you might mention to the postman that he will persist in delivering Miss Clayton's letters to the wrong address.'

'I have mentioned it,' Florence said. 'More than once.'

'Oh. Shell shock, I suppose. Well, in that case . . .' He held the envelope out to her. 'You'll be seeing her soon, I expect? I thought about her over Christmas – no doubt she does not celebrate it, being a Quaker, but nonetheless it must be rather lonely in that little cottage. Of course you've had other duties, but I hope you have not neglected her.'

'I don't think she has missed me.'

'You must not take your friends for granted, my dear.'

Was he tormenting her deliberately? But that was absurd; if he knew, he would hardly look at her with that jovial condescension. 'Yes,' she said, with a smile, 'you're right, Horace.' Mother had always known from that smile when Florence was hiding something: but Dr Manning looked pleased.

'Take her some of the fruit my nephew sent. We shan't get through it all ourselves. And a bottle of sherry. The small one,' he added.

'That's very kind.'

'Give her my regards. I very much enjoyed the evening

we spent together. An interesting young woman. We must forgive her intemperance, under the circumstances.'

Florence did not know whether by *circumstances* he meant Christmas, or Kit's work with disfigured soldiers; but it hardly mattered. 'Yes,' she said, 'of course. I'm glad – glad you liked her.'

'Hurry along, then,' he said, with the pleased self-importance of a man doing a good deed. 'Mrs Reed will show you where she has stored the fruit.'

She blinked; but it was characteristic of Horace not to notice that she had not yet had breakfast. She glanced at the clock – yesterday she had forgotten to wind her watch – and saw that it was later than she had realised. Well then, it was good that he was oblivious, rather than asking himself why she might slope downstairs at nine o'clock, disorientated and befuddled. 'I'll go straight away,' she said.

'Good girl,' he said, and went off towards his study. The strains of 'The Holly and the Ivy' drifted down the passageway, out of key.

She was relieved to see him go; but now she was obliged to do as he had ordered. With a sinking heart she trudged to the kitchen – Mrs Reed, thank heavens, was in the scullery, grunting and clattering – packed a pomegranate, two peaches and a bunch of grapes into a basket and added the small bottle of sherry from the cupboard. It made her think glancingly of the day she and Kit had spent at the Haven, and how she had gathered her little picnic so lovingly, so excitedly; but she would not let herself dwell on that. All that was over.

She pulled on her old, shabby, thicker coat – at least it was not covered in mud – and a foolish woollen tam-o'-shanter. Her best gloves had been lost on the train, but her knitted woollen ones were in a dank lumpy ball in the pocket. She put them on too. What a fright she must be!

But there would be nothing worse than looking as if she had dressed to entice Kit into another indiscretion. She pulled the hat down over her ears and could not bear to look into the hallway mirror as she passed.

It was cold outside, with a bitter wind and low clouds. Dry leaves skittered across the road ahead of her. Her cheeks stung, and unemotional tears rose in the corners of her eyes, blurring the grey landscape. She would not knock on the door; she would leave the basket on the back doorstep and hurry away. She would have walked more slowly if the weather had not been so hostile. But she was shivering, and anxious to get home again and into the warm; so she lowered her head against the wind and did not pause until she came to the Bone cottage.

There was a light in the sitting room, a faint golden flicker that was just visible in the dingy daylight. Florence paused on the garden path, her heart suddenly hammering; then she half slid, half ducked past the window and down the narrow path at the side of the house that led to the kitchen door. She set the basket on the doorstep. There was no sound but the rushing of wind in the trees at the end of the garden. Maybe Kit was reading, or working, or asleep . . .

She hesitated. Then she turned to leave. Suddenly her throat was tight, and her feet leaden. Home again, to the vicarage; home to a long day of – what? Nothing. Embroidery and word puzzles, the endless tick of the clock and the blustery rattle of the window-panes in their frames.

'Florence?'

She spun round. Kit was standing in the open doorway, her face quizzical.

'I brought you these,' she stuttered out, pointing at the basket.

'I see. That's kind. Thank you.'

She could not think of anything else to say. She had not felt like this since she was a sixth-former in a French examination: not a single useful word came into her head, while the pressure to speak rose and rose. *Je voudrais un aller-retour pour Paris, s'il vous plait,* a childish voice suggested, a decade too late.

'Are you all right today?' Kit said.

'Yes, thank you.'

'Good.' Was that a hint of mockery?

'Goodbye,' Florence said.

At the same time, Kit started to say, 'Last night—'

They fell silent, staring at each other. Florence felt slow heat creep up from her collar and over her scalp, in spite of the icy wind. She had been sure, when she woke this morning and remembered what had happened, that she would never want to do it again. It was an abomination – unthinkable, except by the most depraved, the most perverse . . . She was not a sapphist, or a lesbian, or whatever the word was; she was normal, or more or less, she was no more one of *them* than Mother had been. And the afterglow, the fire that still ran through her at the memory of Kit's touch, was only the last lingering symptom of whatever brainstorm had taken hold of her, and made her beg to be kissed, to be looked at . . . Oh, God. *Je veux,* the same insipid schoolgirl voice prompted her, *tu veux, nous voulons.*

The silence went on and on. Kit looked at her as though she could read every thought that crossed her mind, and didn't hate her even so. At last, with a little shrug of rueful defeat, she said, 'Goodbye, then, Florence.'

Florence nodded. There it was: Kit did not want her, anyway. But she had not anticipated the misery that swept over her now. 'Goodbye,' she said again, like a stuck record.

'Goodbye,' Kit said.

'I – never mind. Goodb—' She caught herself, mortified,

before she said it a third time; but the corner of Kit's mouth had already lifted into that wry, crooked smile. 'I think it's better if we don't meet again for a while. Perhaps in a few months . . .'

Suddenly Kit laughed and stepped to one side. 'Oh, give over,' she said. 'Come inside, for God's sake, come and have a cup of tea. I promise not to molest you.'

Florence did not hesitate, even long enough to take a breath; she launched herself forward over the threshold. As she did, Kit drew further back to let her pass; but Florence's foot caught an uneven tile and she reeled sideways like a drunkard, into Kit's arms. She had not meant to; honestly, she had not meant to. But she did not recoil, even when she had got her balance again. She looked into Kit's eyes, noticing how the soft light brought out the grey-green of her irises, and the scatter of freckles over the line of her cheekbones.

Kit said, 'Florence . . .'

Then neither of them said anything more, for a long time.

'Am I getting better at – this?' Florence asked, some hours later, idly lacing her fingers between Kit's and holding their linked hands up to cast a shadow on the wall. It made a strange silhouette, monstrous and crested, with a knobbly profile. She bent her thumb, transforming the nose into a blunt beak and back again, as the firelight flickered. It was only just afternoon, but already it was too dim to make out the finer cracks in the whitewashed wall.

'"This"?'

'You know what I mean.'

'Oh,' Kit said, '*this*,' and drew her free hand lightly down the centre of Florence's body, until the fingers just brushed the line of her pubic hair.

'Don't start again.'

'Why not? Don't you want the practice?'

'Let's get up in a minute. I'm hungry. We can eat the fruit I brought.'

'All right.'

But she was too comfortable to move. There was a silence. It was astonishing, Florence thought, how different silences could be: this one was soft, like velvet, the colour of the fire-shadows that fell on the wall. It demanded nothing, it was already as complete as it could be. 'So,' she said, at last, for the pleasure of breaking it, '*am* I?'

'Better? I don't know. It isn't like playing the piano.'

'In a way it is.'

Kit laughed, a low chuckle that resonated in Florence's lungs as if their bodies had merged into one. 'OK then,' she said, 'you're showing signs of improvement. Keep working on your scales.'

'I only meant—'

'I know. I'm being unkind. Couldn't you tell that I went off – or whatever you like to call it? Don't worry.' Kit kissed her ear.

Florence shivered, with a mixture of pleasure and triumph. Lying here, naked, with Kit, she could not imagine thinking that there was anything wrong with what they had done; it was like trying to remember your monthly cramps, once they had passed. You knew they felt bad, but you could not summon the sick agony of it, you thought that after all you must have been exaggerating. 'I'm so glad,' she said. 'I thought – well, I hoped, but I wasn't sure . . . You don't mind, that I'm – that I haven't done it very much? I'm not too awfully – green?'

'I like green. Try painting the world without it.'

'But –' Florence began, raising herself on her elbow to look into Kit's face.

'Stop it, Florence. What do you want me to say?'

That you love me, Florence almost said: but caught herself, shocked. Was that really what she wanted? Or merely because it was conventional, the words a husband would say automatically to his new bride, before the shine came off their marriage? And how unfair it would be, to expect Kit to say it and mean it, when she herself was only – only . . .

She did not want to follow that thought. Partly to distract herself, she brought Kit's hand up to her lips. It was not exactly a kiss: she held it there, feeling the smooth warmth of Kit's skin, the pleasure – how strange it was – of having a mouth, and having someone else's hand to lay against it. Her breath reflected back to her tasted salty, marine.

'Shall we get up, then?'

'Yes,' she said, but she did not move, and neither did Kit. How extraordinarily comfortable it was, lying like this in front of the fire; soon the last log would have burnt down, and they would get cold, but not yet, not yet. She raised their hands again – how funny to be able to treat another person's body so casually, as if it were a puppet – and watched the shadow dance in the firelight. 'It's like a little monster,' she said.

'What?'

'Our hands. Look. On the wall.' She raised two fingers. 'Now it's got horns.' She leaned her head against Kit's. 'Now it's got a nose – there, it's like a Roman emperor, with big lips, see?' She twisted her hand, trying other angles; then, suddenly, the last log collapsed and the light died, blurring the edges of the shadow on the wall. 'And now . . . now,' she said, with mock disappointment, 'it's not a face at all, it's just – a lump—'

Kit jerked back her hand and got to her feet, so briskly that Florence's skin felt raw where Kit's body had been peeled away. She grabbed her shirt from the settee and drew it over her head. 'I need some tea,' she said, her voice muffled.

Florence sat up. 'Kit?'

Kit did not look over her shoulder. She strode to the door and disappeared. There was the sound of the range door opening, as she stoked it; then the dull clang of the kettle on the hob.

Florence got up, shivering, and dragged on her own clothes. She hesitated in the kitchen doorway; there was something about Kit's turned back that made her afraid she was not welcome any more. 'Kit?' she said again.

'I think I've run out of milk. Do you mind it black?'

'Did I say something wrong?'

'No.'

She had, of course; but she could not tell what. Desperately she went over it in her mind. She had been playing, that was all. Surely Kit would not despise her for a brief moment of childishness? No, Kit was not unreasonable or unkind. But if it was not that, then what? *It's not a face at all*, she heard herself say, *it's just a lump . . .*

'Oh, God,' she said, 'I – how awful of me – I wasn't thinking—'

'What are you talking about?'

'What a thing to say – when you must have seen men who really looked like that—'

'Shut up, Florence.'

'But I didn't mean—'

'Shut *up*.' The kettle whistled, and Kit poured boiling water into the teapot with more concentration than necessary.

Florence felt a bigger and bigger ache growing in her throat. She had been so happy; it had seemed so simple. She drew out a chair and sat at the table, telling herself sternly to be sensible. Less than an hour ago Kit had held her, kissed and touched her, Kit's face had hung above Florence's, watching, as Florence's eyes lost focus and she heard herself gasp. She wouldn't have done that if she hadn't wanted to. Even if it was not, exactly, *love* . . .

Kit put two mugs on the table, and pushed one towards Florence. They drank in silence, until at last Kit reached out to take Florence's hand. She said, 'Won't they be missing you?'

'Horace told me to come.'

'What?'

'He said that I mustn't neglect my friends.'

'Presumably this wasn't exactly what he had in mind.'

Florence laughed; and when Kit laughed too, she felt warm again. 'I wonder what he'd say,' she said, 'if he knew.'

'I hope you never find out,' Kit said, smiling; but there was an edge in her voice.

Florence blew on her tea, feeling the warm steam on her face. Kit had done this before. She knew what it was like. She had a whole lifetime – was it a whole lifetime? or near enough – of experience, of calling herself a lesbian, of navigating secret desires. What was that like? But that dangerous tone warned Florence not to ask. And did she want to know, truly? If she heard stories of Kit's other lovers, glamorous women who used depilatory powder on their armpits and did not fumble or sweat or get cramp . . . She bit her lip, and then caught Kit's eye and hoped she had not been too transparent. 'He won't notice anything,' she said, 'he probably won't even notice I wasn't at home for lunch. Phoebe—'

She stopped. She had been going to say, *Phoebe, on the other hand* . . . but she did not like the intrusion of Phoebe's name into the quiet kitchen, or the thought of her curiosity, like sticky hands rummaging through Florence's underthings.

'What about Phoebe?' Kit said, with too much interest.

'Nothing.' She took a mouthful of tea, pushing away the image of Phoebe's pale, finely-marked triangle of a face.

Kit leant back in her chair, putting her hands behind her head, and yawned.

'Do you want me to go?' Florence said.

'Soon. Not yet,' she added, reaching out to squeeze Florence's wrist as she began to get to her feet. 'If you stay here too long they *will* notice.'

'So what if they do?'

Kit let go of Florence's wrist, gently; it was worse than if she had thrown it aside, as a man would have done. 'Don't be silly.'

'You needn't worry on my account—'

'But I do. Trust me, Florence. If anyone knew, it would – would change things. You don't want that.'

There was a silence. At last Florence said, defeated, 'Yes.'

'And you can come back another time. Soon.'

'Yes. Thank you.'

'Oh, for God's sake, don't look at me like that.'

'Sorry.' Florence stood up; she would have walked out, except that she was not wearing her shoes or stockings. She blundered through the doorway to the sitting room to get them. Kit followed her.

'Florence . . .'

She fastened her suspenders without looking up. She was absurdly conscious of the margin of pale flesh above the tops of her stockings. Creamy, dimpled, soft with fine blonde hair. Obscene, much more obscene than her whole nakedness had been. She pulled her skirt down with fumbling hands, and shoved her feet into her shoes. She didn't bother to buckle them.

But when she moved towards the door, sweeping up her coat as she went, Kit didn't move out of her way. They stared at each other.

'I haven't done this before,' Florence said.

'I know that.'

'I mean – any of it. I don't know how.'

Kit held her gaze, but her eyes creased at the corners. 'Yes, I see,' she said. 'I should invite you to dance, first, and then you should introduce me to your mother, and then we should have tea, and then I should ask your father for the honour of your hand in marriage, and then there should be a wedding with orange blossom, in a lovely little flint church with a tower and a view of the sea. And then—'

'You're unkind.'

'No. I'm not making fun. You're right, it's easier when it's all mapped out. Instead we have to work it out for ourselves. Is it too hard? It's all right if it is. I understand.'

'Not too hard. But hard.' With a shameful lurch, she remembered begging, *harder, harder*, and felt herself blush. She pulled on her coat, concentrating on the buttons.

'I could say I'm painting you,' Kit said.

'Pardon?'

'If I were painting you . . .' She took hold of Florence's hands, stilling them. 'Do you see? You can tell them that's what you're doing. You can be here for as long as you like. All the time, if you want.'

She said, 'N-nude?' and wished she had not stammered.

'What?'

'Would you paint me – without clothes?'

Kit blinked. 'I didn't mean,' she said, slowly, 'that I would actually paint you. Only that you could use that as an excuse.'

'Oh.'

She had not meant to let her disappointment show; but Kit bit her lip, as if she knew exactly what Florence was thinking, and gave her hands a little cajoling shake. 'Don't be a silly billy, Florence. It isn't you. I just – I don't paint portraits any more.'

'Yes, of course. I don't mind – anyway, I expect it's very dull, having to sit still for so long—'

'We'll do other things,' Kit said, 'better things.' She smiled into Florence's eyes; then, with a sly, unexpected jab of her tongue, she licked the valley between Florence's knuckles. It was so swift Florence would not have been sure it had really happened, if it had not been for the dampness on her skin and the hot answering pulse deep in her belly.

'All right,' she said, trying to keep her voice matter of fact. 'We'll pretend you're painting me in my coat and gloves and hat, looking decidedly dowdy. "Portrait of a Surplus Woman".'

Kit laughed. 'Probably best,' she said. 'Tell them I shall need you for several weeks. Possibly months. And I am very lonely, and very sad, and it will be an act of Christian charity.'

Oh, that laugh . . . Florence had just enough breath for, 'Yes.'

'Come back tomorrow.'

'Yes.'

'Tell them that for as long as I'm painting you, you can't do anything else. You're mine. You're a muse. It's a very demanding job.'

'Yes.' *Yes and yes and yes*, she thought, and managed not to say.

Kit grinned. She leant forwards and kissed Florence's mouth, unlingeringly. It made Florence thrill more than a long passionate embrace would have done: it spoke of perfect confidence in the abundant future in front of them. 'Good,' she said. 'I'll see you in the morning.'

XII

Studies for a Portrait of a Surplus Woman (abstractions),
pencil and charcoal on paper, 1920–21

Aunt Florence's room was tidy. Too tidy, as though it had been swept deliberately clean of any clue that might hint at her secrets. Phoebe stood in the doorway, hating the room for its tidiness.

The church clock struck three. She crossed the room to the window, stepping heavily, daring Aunt Florence to appear from nowhere to berate her. But Aunt Florence was at Kit Clayton's house, being painted; or at least she said she was. Sitting still for hours, under Kit's assessing eyes . . . Could that explain her preoccupation – her infuriating *kindness,* impersonal and serene, as if Phoebe was a spoilt child who would be taken away by her nursemaid at any moment? Surely not – surely after a few afternoons of sitting still she would have grown bored . . . In any case, her mood had lasted weeks. Phoebe had waited for it to break, like a spell of fine weather; but it did not. The floorboards creaked, and she stamped harder. No one heard, no one came.

Surely something here would reveal what Aunt Florence was hiding. But the wardrobe was only full of clothes;

the books on the bookshelf were boring old classics; even her knickers and chemises were impersonal, just a scum of spinsterish cotton that Phoebe stirred with one finger. She lay down on the bed, squirming to imprint the shape of her body into the counterpane, and stared up at the sloping ceiling. She could not bear the sensation that Aunt Florence was somewhere else, doing whatever made her smile so aggravatingly to herself when she thought no one was watching. It wasn't *fair*.

She clenched her fists. There was a funny feeling in the air again: the slow unseasonal thunderstorm prickle that had built before Christmas and then dissipated, suddenly, almost overnight. It had occurred to her that it might have been the church bells ringing that had driven it – whatever *it* was – away; but it had been the day after, Boxing Day, when she had felt it suddenly clear. As if something had simply – left . . .

But now it was back. Formless, threatening, a faint taste in the back of her throat, an itch under her skin that could not be touched. She swept her hands up and down her forearms. It was all mixed up. Was it Aunt Florence, with her silly smiles and her wafting walk? Or something else, the – the gathering darkness, the thurlath . . . She clenched her teeth together. *Thurlath* was Papa's word, a scholar's word. Mrs Bone had never used it. But it didn't matter what the word was: it named something real.

She swung her feet to the floor. She paused for an instant before she left the room, suddenly drawn to throw the window wide, to peer out and stare at the slope of the down; but the Face had gone, and there was nothing left to see.

Papa's study door was closed. Mrs Reed was in the kitchen, humming in time with the familiar dull thump of a rolling pin on pastry. Phoebe walked loudly past, daring someone to ask her where she was going. Nothing. She might as well not exist. She took her coat and hat and gloves, opened the front door and stepped out into the freezing afternoon.

She walked briskly, as if she were at school, being shepherded along the road to the playing field by the gym mistress. When she came to the Bone cottage she paused at the gate, her hand on the latch. Was it possible that Aunt Florence was not here at all? That the story of Miss Clayton and her picture – the masterpiece in oils that Papa jovially claimed he could not wait to see – was only a cover for . . . for what? Something else, something secret . . . A man, she thought. Could it be a man? Staid, gawky Aunt Florence, with a man! Tonight, at dinner, she would wait until a pause in the conversation and tilt her head guilelessly. 'Oh, Aunt Florence,' she would say, as if it had only just occurred to her, 'I walked past Miss Clayton's house today, but you weren't there. Miss Clayton said she hadn't seen you at all this week.'

She lifted the gate, went up the garden path and around the side of the house to the back door. Last time she had been here, when she delivered the parcel, she had had to use the spare key. But now the door was unlocked. She reached out to the teapot as she passed the kitchen table. It still held a lingering trace of warmth.

She mounted the stairs, listening. The studio door was open. The studio was empty, and a little ghostly in the grey light. Through the doorway she could see a corner of the room set up as Aunt Florence had described: a straight chair, the bare rectangular lines of the window. There was a book on the floor, splayed face down. And –

She peered at the dim puddle of fabric on the floor, and recognised Aunt Florence's blue dress, the one from Dale and Kerley's. What was it doing there? It was not as if Miss

Clayton had a lady's maid, who would sweep it up and take it away to be laundered.

There was a murmur behind her. She whirled round, afraid someone had crept up on her. Another murmur, and a creak, like a footstep. But no one was on the tiny landing.

There was someone in the bedroom. She heard it again, a low note like a pigeon cooing, but human. There must be words, but she could not hear them. Unless – could it be weeping? She narrowed her eyes, staring at the bedroom door as if she might be able to see right through it, if she concentrated. There was a weight in her chest that she could not name. If she tiptoed downstairs now, she could get away without anyone knowing she had been here. But she did not move – or, rather, she moved in the other direction, stepping closer to the bedroom door, laying her hand gently on the doorknob. She put her face into an expression of polite, apologetic enquiry. *Oh, excuse me. I was hoping to find Aunt Florence. I'm sorry if I took you by surprise . . .*

Her hand tingled, in time with her pulse. Then, slowly, as quietly as she could, she opened the door.

She saw a bed. Two people. A face with an open mouth, the face making the noise.

Aunt Florence. The face was Aunt Florence. There was bare skin – a bare breast, a purple upward-poking nipple – her arm thrown above her head, a furry glint in the armpit. And lying beside, over, above her, another body – Miss Clayton, still dressed, her short hair falling over her face, her hand busy under the tangle of bedclothes.

Aunt Florence made the pigeon sound again. Her eyes were open but she had not seen Phoebe. Miss Clayton did not look round.

Phoebe drew the door shut, quite calmly, without making a noise. She wiped her hand on her coat as if the doorknob were greasy, and walked down the stairs.

As she opened the door to the kitchen there was a thump behind her, at the top of the staircase, and Miss Clayton called out, 'Hey!'

She turned. Perhaps she should have been quieter. She did not much care. She stared up into the shadows, and said, 'Hullo.'

'What the hell are you doing?'

'Papa asked me to tell Aunt Florence that dinner will be earlier today. Mrs Reed wants to go to the Picturedrome later.' The lie came fluently; in fact, only part of it was a lie. 'Is she here?'

'She – yes. Yes, I was just sketching her. Upstairs.'

'Oh. Can you tell her for me?'

'Yes. Why didn't you knock?'

'I called out. I suppose you didn't hear.'

Miss Clayton pushed her hands into her pockets. 'Did you— ? I thought I heard you come upstairs. Were you listening at the door?'

'I was just leaving. I didn't think anyone was here.'

A silence. Neither of them moved. At last Miss Clayton gave a curt nod. 'I'll tell her. Once I've finished my drawing.'

'Thanks.'

'And next time – don't disturb me while I'm working. I don't like distractions. If no one comes when you call, go away. Got it?'

'All right.'

'Good. Run along, then.'

She did as she was told. She felt Miss Clayton glare at her back, long after she had emerged into the garden and shut the door; it sent a tingle down her spine and into her thighs. She walked until the house was out of sight – or would have been out of sight, if she had looked over her shoulder, which she didn't.

Then she stopped, and shut her eyes, and tried to remember exactly what she had seen.

'She's gone,' Kit said, shutting the door.

'Oh God,' Florence said, 'did she see – what did she see? Oh God – Kit—'

'Nothing. I was wrong, she hadn't come up the stairs. Nothing, Florence, nothing, it's all right, I promise.'

Florence stared at her, biting her lip, her eyes wide. 'You're sure?'

'She didn't see anything.'

'But the door, you said you heard—'

'It was a mistake. She can't have seen anything.'

Florence held her gaze; then, with a great outrush of breath, she bowed her head over her bent knees. 'If she saw . . .'

'Oh, buck up, Florence,' Kit said, more sharply than she meant to. It was not Florence's fault that she was afraid; she had not had a lifetime to grow weary and impatient instead. 'She didn't. And even if she did – no, stop it – I told her I was drawing you – even schoolgirls know that life models are nude.'

Florence nodded. 'Yes,' she said, shakily. 'Yes, I suppose so.'

Kit meant to sit down on the edge of the bed and take her hand; but as soon as she moved, Florence got to her feet, clutching the sheet to her body as if Kit had not seen it a hundred times.

'I must go,' she said.

'Yes,' Kit said. 'Actually she – Phoebe – said to tell you that dinner was earlier tonight. Someone's going to the pictures. I don't remember the details.'

But Florence had already disappeared through the

doorway to the landing. There was the rustle of clothing as she dressed, then the clunk of her shoes. 'Goodbye, then.'

'Goodbye.' If Florence stayed longer, it would only be to go over and over what Phoebe might have seen – to repeat, neurotically, the conversation they had just had; and yet part of Kit longed to beg her not to go, or at least not to go like this. She resisted it. 'Tomorrow?'

'Tomorrow's Sunday.'

'Monday, then.'

'Yes.'

They had, recently, got into the habit of kissing each other goodbye; but now Florence only gave her a polite, unseeing smile, and fled.

Kit followed, too late to call after her. It was almost twilight. Something – some trick of the light, as if the air shimmered above the place in the garden where the bonfire had been – made her lock the kitchen door. The teapot was cold, and she boiled more water and brewed more tea. Eggs tonight, she thought, scrambled eggs and mashed carrot, and fruit cake . . .

Florence would be all right. Florence would be fine.

She began to rake her hands through her hair, smelt the fresh salty scent of sex on her fingers, and hesitated. Who would notice, who would care? But she washed her hands, and then superstitiously wished she hadn't. If that was the last time . . . She dried her hands. A breeze rattled the door and she checked it was locked. Yes, locked. No need to check again. She checked again.

She said aloud, 'Damn. Damn, damn.' Silence. She was a bundle of nerves; and not only because of that damned – that *bloody* child barging in where she was not wanted . . .

Portia's letter crackled in her pocket. She tapped it through the material of her trousers, trying to resist rereading it. Not now, not as the night closed in.

She pulled it out and unfolded it. It would have been too dim now, in the lightless kitchen, to read it, if she had not already known what it said. She skimmed past the *darling, surely you would like some company? you must be going positively bats!* and the *don't try to pretend you don't ever think of how things were* to the last few paragraphs.

Has Muckle written to you since you last saw him? I hope he has. Oh Kit, I am so anxious about him! I expect he has told you everything, he is so in love with you (just like everyone else I suppose), he talks about you all the time and I know he tells you things that he doesn't tell anyone else. Oh dear I am rambling. But no one knows where he is. Or rather it is all mixed up, his landlady says he came back to his flat with another man, at first I thought she meant Septimus but he is in Oxfordshire, holed up like a hermit, and he swears he hasn't been near London at all. Anyway none of us have seen Muckle since he left yours and if he is there he won't answer the door to us. Did something awful happen my dear? Or is it the War, the damned War again? Is it possible that he is shell-shocked now, even though he was all right before? Or could something awful have happened to him?

It can't be true, but I am going to tell you anyway.

Oh darling, there was a cat – the landlady's cat – and they found it hanging from a hook in the little yard at the back of the house, and the landlady said it was Muckle and she was afraid of him, and even more of his friend who was still there with him, and she said the cat was not just dead, it had been skinned – alive, she thought – oh I cannot believe I am writing this! We know Muckle, don't we, he is a kind gentle man and even if the War hurt him inside it could not have been so hidden for so long. And she says that she only sees him and his friend at night and she is too frightened to speak to them. And she dropped horrible hints, you would think he had been murdering people – but it was not that exactly, she seemed to think he was almost not human any more. She said something that made me think of the old story of the golem, you know, horrid shambling creatures made out of earth – or rather rotting trench mud, do you remember the stink on the men's uniforms—

No no no oh I will stop it now, I think I am simply missing you my darling and worrying because life does not feel right without you here, promise me you will come back soon, and write, WRITE! You must be working and I want to know what you are working on. And then I will forget about Muckle and let him be, I am sure he is perfectly all right really except maybe missing you and I know what that is like, sometimes I feel like I could torture a cat myself. Ha ha of course I am joking. Oh God I will stop writing now, I miss you darling, lots of love.

She should not have reread it. She should not even have kept it. With a sudden impulse she leapt to her feet, screwing the paper into a ball, and dropped it into the range. But as soon as it had burst into flames she grabbed for it, too late. She caught her wrist on the hot edge of the range door and jumped back, cursing. It was worse, now, without the actual words in front of her. What had Portia said, exactly? *It was not just dead. She is too frightened to speak to him. Creatures made out of trench mud . . .*

She held her burnt hand under cold water. Don't think. Portia had said she was mistaken. She must be mistaken. Muckle would never hurt anyone.

Yes, he would. He had hurt Florence, hadn't he?

She rolled her shoulders, trying to slough off the sensation of something settling on her. Maybe it was better that she had burnt the letter after all. That was it. It had gone up in smoke. Gone. Like Muckle himself, who was miles away – like poor dead Julien, and the others . . . She did not have to think about them. She did not want to.

She was still standing at the sink. She bent over it and splashed her face with water. She focused on the feeling of it trickling down her cheeks and dripping off her chin. She was afraid. Why shouldn't she admit it to herself? Afraid, not of faces, but of what went on behind them.

But that was weak, and cowardly. One day soon, she told herself, she really would ask Florence to sit for her. What had Florence called it – *Portrait of a Surplus Woman*? Yes, that was it. *Portrait of a Surplus Woman.* She could imagine it perfectly: Florence demure, level-eyed, lovely. Before the War it would have been easy.

Not today, or tomorrow, she thought. But one day. Perhaps.

XIII

Single Flame, charcoal on paper, 1921

By the last period of afternoon school the windows in 5a's form room had steamed over entirely. One of the girls had draped her wet blazer over the radiator at the back of the room, and the smell of damp wool permeated the whole corridor. Beatrice Timothy, catching sight of it, wondered wearily whether to ask who the culprit was and berate her – such things were, naturally, forbidden – and then decided, just as wearily, to pretend that she had not seen it.

She hated February. Christmas had been quiet – oh, say it, it had been lonely! – but it had marked a friendly pause in the turning of the year. Now the world had reached its lowest point, the long miserable tail of winter, and it was hard to believe in the prospect of spring. The classrooms were draughty and cold, with pockets of furious heat next to the radiators and pipes, and the girls grew restless and prickly, like cooped-up animals. Today they were pink-faced, with the repressed feverish hilarity that meant they'd played up in their previous lesson. She drew her hand over her forehead, trying to ease the familiar tightness around her temples, and said, 'Settle down, please.' It had some effect, although not very much.

She often tried not to dislike 5a. They were not bad girls, individually. But there was something in the collective alchemy – the three or four ringleaders, their followers, and then the odd, aloof outsiders like Lettice Brown or Phoebe Manning – that made them more volatile and more spiteful than the other fifth-formers. Especially on a rainy February afternoon . . . She said, more sternly, 'Settle down,' and glared until a temporary atmosphere of calm descended on the classroom.

'Open your books, please,' she said, and there was a reluctant rustling of pages. Elizabeth Steadley put her chin in her hand and blinked up at her, her dark eyes insolent. Beatrice let her gaze sweep past, with the impassive lack of acknowledgement that she had cultivated so determinedly. 'Can anyone,' she said, resisting any hint of sarcasm, 'can anyone remind me where we finished reading last time?'

Rosamund Jenks – thank heavens for children like Rosamund! – put up her hand and said, 'The end of Act Three, Miss Timothy.'

'Yes, indeed. Now – yes, Elizabeth?'

'Can I ask a question, Miss Timothy?'

'Is it pertinent to Shakespeare?' She should not have said it like that; she felt, rather than saw, the class swap glances. 'Very well, then.'

'I adored what we read last week, Miss Timothy,' Elizabeth said. 'I simply *adored* it. So I borrowed my papa's copy to read it again. But there were some things I didn't quite understand. Could you explain them?'

'I'm not sure—'

'There were some phrases that weren't in my school copy.' She had the book ready: she did not have to search for the right page before she said, 'For example, Miss Timothy, what is a *maidenhead*, please?'

Beatrice said, quite coolly, 'I imagine you are familiar

with the concept of virginity by now, Elizabeth. Hasn't it been mentioned in your Bible Studies class?'

'Yes, but . . .' She bit her lip, wishing no doubt that she had started more gradually. 'This bit, here, about "true love acted simple modesty". Can you explain that?'

'Do I need to?'

'Well . . .' She exhaled, tilting her head. 'But why isn't that bit in our books, Miss Timothy?'

'Because it is considered unsuitable for school children.'

'Is that because it's about— ?'

'Because it is about a wedding night, and surely even *you*, Elizabeth, must by now be aware that what happens between a man and his wife on their wedding night is not suitable for innocent ears.' She said it all on one breath, without giving herself time to think. For a brief moment it had the desired effect: Elizabeth slumped a little, her cheeks flaring, and one or two of her friends giggled. But it was as though the words were on a thread, and an unexpected hook caught in her throat long after they had come out of her mouth. A wedding night. She, Beatrice, should have had a wedding night.

She got to her feet and walked to the window. The oaks on the other side of the playing field tossed in the wet salt wind that blew in from the sea. The class murmured, behind her. It was foolish to turn her back on them for so long, but she was so tired of being on guard all the time, so tired . . .

'Miss Timothy?'

'One moment,' she said, without glancing over her shoulder. She knew she did not have time now to think about Frank, or the wedding she should have had. The trick was to focus on the lesson – this hour, these particular sixty minutes – and the girls. Neither the past nor the future, not the fact that she would have to work for another twenty-seven years straight to gain her pension nor the rage that rose through her as the children whispered and began to flick inky pellets. Anyway, that was hardly the worst thing in the world. No, the worst thing in the world was dying alone, ripped apart in a wilderness of moonlit mud . . .

She clenched her fists. She would not disgrace herself in front of the class. In a second she would turn to them and speak perfectly normally. Frank would be proud of her; in his last letter he had talked about courage in the face of the enemy. She counted down, *three, two, one*, and then spun briskly on her heel, as if she had only paused to watch some fleeting phenomenon outside. 'Now, girls—'

'Miss Timothy?'

It was Phoebe Manning, her arm raised. 'Yes?' Beatrice said.

'You said it wasn't suitable for children. But we're older than Juliet.'

'Well –' She stopped. There was something about Phoebe Manning, and the way her face flickered arrestingly between ugly and handsome. You never knew what she was thinking; you never knew whether she asked her questions out of malice or simple curiosity. 'The historical Juliet lived a long time ago,' Beatrice said, 'when girls were married very young.'

Phoebe nodded, her eyes level and unwavering: recognising the answer, without accepting it. She said slowly, 'But—'

'Let us turn to the beginning of Act Four. Rosamund, please read Friar Lawrence – Elizabeth, Paris – Phoebe, Juliet.' At least Phoebe could be relied on to read the text as if it meant something. 'No more questions, please.'

Rosamund bent her head obediently and said, tonelessly, 'On Thursday sir the time is very short.'

Elizabeth said, with the same intonation – mocking or simply inept, it was difficult to tell – 'My father Capulet will have it so and I am nothing slow to slack his haste.'

Beatrice sat back in her chair, pinching a pen between her finger and thumb. Her head was aching badly now. How would she bear another twenty-seven years of listening to schoolgirls rattle through Shakespeare as if it were the times tables? She heard whispers begin in the back row, next to the window, and stared in that direction – Winifred Whelan and Jennifer Stark, of course – quelling them; but as soon as she looked away they began again. As Rosamund and Elizabeth ground slowly through their scene the noise grew, until she could not ignore it any longer. She brought her hand down sharply on the desk. 'Enough!'

Rosamund droned, 'I would I knew not why it should . . .' and looked up, belatedly realising that she was the only one speaking. She flushed and fell silent.

'Is there something amusing you, girls? Something you would like to share with us? Winifred? Jennifer?'

They both looked down, with identically demure expressions. Beatrice wanted to stride down the aisle and slap them both. Instead, she said, 'No? What a surprise. Very well, then. If you disturb the class again I shall ask you to leave.'

Winifred looked up. 'Miss Timothy . . .'

'Yes?'

'Will we understand it, when we're older?' She sneaked a glance at Jennifer; then, with a noise like a punctured bicycle tyre, they both hissed with repressed mirth, their cheeks growing redder and redder, until finally they exploded into a spluttering, braying laugh. The girls beside them began to giggle too, in sympathy; then, with horrible inevitability, the whole form was laughing, emboldened by one another. Beatrice felt sweat break out in her armpits. If she raised her voice, and they did not quieten – if it only goaded them on . . . that would be fatal, they would never listen to her again. Another twenty-seven years, she thought, and a kind of panic went through her, mixing with fury, making her light-headed.

She shut her book. It did not make much noise, but the girls in the front few rows noticed, and watched her more closely. They were still clutching their ribs and ostentatiously wiping away tears; but with less conviction.

She said, quietly, 'I am rather glad you all find it so funny.'

Slowly, gradually, the laughter died.

'I suppose,' she said, 'it is natural for a teacher to imagine that pupils like you might begin to understand *Romeo and Juliet*. I will confess that I imagined that as well as achieving the necessary level for your Junior Certificate, you might find that Shakespeare's poetry was worth reading for its own sake. I even imagined that you – some of you, at least – would find that it spoke to you of your own hopes and dreams, your youthful joys and tragedies, your wonderful world-changing loves.' She had laid it on thick: but they were too bemused to laugh now, their interest caught by the edge in her voice. 'What better play, I thought, to read with a class of young ladies, as they tremble on the threshold of real life? Let it sing to them of their birthright – that is, the divine, erotic, sublime passion between men and women, husbands and wives . . .' She let the words hang. Then she shrugged. 'But yes,' she said, 'I am very glad I was wrong.'

She glanced round, without seeming to. Elizabeth pouted and played with a pencil. Phoebe was sitting very still, with steady cat-like eyes.

'How many of you will get married?'

The girls exchanged glances; almost all of them smiled, with varying degrees of condescension. A few stirred, as if about to raise their hands.

She did not wait. 'How many are in this class?

Twenty-five? Let's call it thirty. So, three of you. Three. No, put your hand down, Rosamund. I am not asking you. It is a fact. No more than three of you in this room will find a husband.'

The girls in the front row shifted uneasily on their chairs. Their faces were sombre now, resenting her for their own confusion.

'I am not guessing. It is a statistical fact. Only one in ten of the girls at this school will be able to get married. *One*,' she repeated, 'in ten. Nine out of every ten of you will be alone. Will live alone. Die alone.'

Elizabeth's mouth had slackened. Beatrice had never seen her looking so young, so devoid of what Frank would have called 'side'. It was a small victory.

'How cruel it would be,' Beatrice said, 'to instil in you any hope of experiencing a great love – a *grande passion*! How thoughtless we are to prescribe great literature, when it will only show you what you will never have. How much we must pray that you all remain exactly as you are, like children. Your lives will be so much smoother if you keep your hearts very small and closed and incurious. Pour all your energies into other things, girls. Be content with your silly jokes and your petty rivalries and your trivial meannesses. That will make it easier. Perhaps if you began to understand the depth of the wrong done to you . . .' She stopped. It was the same wrong that had been done to her. It was not as bad as the wrong done to Frank, to his brothers, to hers; but it was a wound, an amputation, a disfigurement that would never be healed.

She drew in her breath, slowly, while the girls stared up at her. She had had years to get used to the idea. But no one had told them; not until now.

'There will be no bounty as boundless as the sea,' she said. 'There will be no true love enacted. There will be no Romeo, lying on the wings of night like new snow upon a raven's back. No Paris, even, no dull, decent man who might be at least good enough . . . You will be single women – spinsters – a cohort of surpluses. You are a superfluity. You were born to be wives and mothers. Now that the men are dead, you serve no purpose.' *You*, she had said. It should have been *us*. But she was not feeling generous; and it would be no comfort to the girls, anyway, that she formed one of their number. It would probably be worse. 'So please feel free to giggle at the idea of erotic love. Snigger away, girls. Guffaw at the poetry, roll your eyes at the tragedy – and whatever you do, make sure you do not *feel*. Because the story of Juliet is your own story, the story of most of you here, except that you won't die in triumph like the meeting of fire and powder, you will slog on and on, unloved and exhausted. And all you can do to numb the pain will be to pretend to yourselves that really you are not missing very much at all.'

There was silence. It was not as silent as a tomb, but as silent as a classroom, a February-afternoon classroom that stank of wet wool and grimy girl-child.

'With that in mind,' she said, and for the first time she disliked what she heard in her own voice, 'shall we continue? No matter what else your futures may hold, there is the Junior Certificate to be thought of.'

No one moved. It was not disobedience. They were still staring at her.

'Rosamund,' she said, making the girl jump. '"I would I knew not", I believe.'

Rosamund bent her head and turned the pages of her book as if it were not already open on the scene they had been reading. Beatrice waited until she had fumbled and found her way back to the right page. Normally, the girls would shuffle and whisper; now they did neither.

'I would I knew not why it should be slow'd,' Rosamund said at last. 'Look sir here comes the lady toward my cell.'

'Happily met my lady and my wife,' Elizabeth said.

'That may be, sir, when I may be a wife,' Phoebe said, her voice clearer than the others. She raised her head and looked straight at Beatrice.

Elizabeth ploughed on, 'That may be must be love on—'

But suddenly Beatrice was so weary she could have put her head down on the desk and slept. 'Never mind,' she said, cutting through Elizabeth's drone. 'Read the rest to yourselves in silence. When you have finished the scene, an essay: "What is the place of love in the aftermath of *Romeo and Juliet*?" You may complete it for your prep.' Belatedly the girls scribbled down the title. Then another silence fell, duller, more ordinary.

She drew a stack of exercise books from her drawer and began to mark them mechanically: 3b's grammar exercise from Tuesday. They had struggled. She ran her pen down the margin, leaving neat crosses in red ink, the occasional *Foolish error!* or *Revise the difference between subject and object, please.* She did not look up at all. Let 5a do what they wanted, she was too tired to care. But for once, it seemed, she had won. The subdued silence continued, thick as felt, until finally the bell rang for Prayers.

'Quietly,' she said, getting to her feet, and then, '*quietly*, I said,' as they pushed past her to the door, beginning to chatter in an undertone as soon as they had got into the corridor. She gathered 3b's exercise books together. Her head was aching worse than ever.

'Miss Timothy?'

She looked up. Phoebe Manning was standing beside the dais, her hands clasped demurely in front of her gym slip. 'Yes?'

'I wondered if I might ask you something.'

A twinge of pain shot across her temple. She knew better than to suppose it was about *Romeo and Juliet*. But it was only what she deserved, after losing her temper; she should have held her tongue. She said, with a sigh, 'Yes?'

But Phoebe, usually cool and ready with her questions, hesitated. She glanced at the door, where the last few girls clustered, waiting for the rest to move along. Beatrice called to them, 'Tell Rosamund to take you to Prayers. I'll be there in a moment.' It was not allowed for the Head of the Form to lead the girls away without a mistress to bring up the rear, but they would not play up, not in this mood. She said, 'What is it, Phoebe?'

'It isn't true,' Phoebe said slowly, 'that none of us appreciate literature.'

'No, well, I was uncharitable, perhaps.'

'But is it true that only one in ten of us will know what it's like, to love someone? Like – *that*?'

Here it was, then. In the heat of the moment it had been easy to say it, and relish the effect it had: now her blood had cooled, and with it her desire to hurt. She looked into the child's face, and away. Really, Phoebe was not a child; in only a few years she would be a woman. She said, conceding defeat, 'I was wrong to say so. Let's say no more about it—'

'But is it true?'

That stopped her. The corridor outside had emptied, and the door swung shut. It was too late to hedge: she could simply tell the truth or lie. She said, 'I'm afraid it is.'

'Because—'

'Because so many young men have been killed. You know, at the end of the War, there was hardly a single one of you who was not wearing mourning. And every brother, every cousin would have been someone else's husband, in time. It is simple arithmetic. They say at the next census there will be two million women with no hope of a husband. I am one of them, too.' If she had anticipated a flicker of sympathy, she had been mistaken: Phoebe hardly blinked.

'Yes, Miss Timothy,' Phoebe said. 'I understand that. The men are dead, so we can't all get married. But isn't there a – a gap in your logic?'

'In what way?'

Phoebe frowned. If she had been born twenty years ago, Beatrice thought, suddenly, that frown would have served her well: how unexpectedly winsome it was, that single elegant crease between her brows, how the young men's hearts would have melted! And now her beauty was all for nothing. Unless she was lucky – yes, perhaps she would be lucky. The one in ten . . . Beatrice felt a wave of dislike.

'You don't have to be married,' Phoebe said, 'to experience erotic love. Do you?'

Beatrice felt her cheeks flush. Did she mean – surely she meant the emotion, not the – the act? Even so, it was unbelievable. What a question, and from a vicar's daughter! But she could hardly report Phoebe without having to answer awkward enquiries from the headmistress, and betraying herself in the process. She said, very stiffly, 'I do not think that is a suitable question from a young lady.'

Phoebe did not seem to be affected in the slightest by Beatrice's disapproval. She said, 'No, I don't suppose you do, Miss Timothy. But it is a pertinent question, isn't it?'

'If you mean to suggest that – that what Juliet feels for Romeo might have any place outside the sacred contract of marriage—'

'"Spread thy close curtain, love-performing Night,"' Phoebe said, almost dreamily, '"That runaways' eyes may wink and Romeo / leap to these arms, untalk'd of and unseen . . ."'

'I am perfectly familiar with the play, thank you,' Beatrice snapped. Phoebe had been quoting a part that had been censored from the school edition. Had they all been giggling over Elizabeth's copy, for heaven's sake? 'That passage refers to the proper desire of a bride for the bridegroom – there are no other circumstances in which . . .' She stopped, waiting to be interrupted; but Phoebe only gazed at her, attentive and patient. 'In which,' she started again, helpless, angry with herself, 'in which those things would – would apply. No healthy woman would – would feel such things for a man who was not – not already her—' She stopped again. It was as if Frank was standing behind Phoebe, a mocking glint in his eye. *When I shall die, take him and cut him out in little stars . . .*

Phoebe lowered her eyes. 'No,' she said.

'Was there something else? The bell for Prayers—'

'A man,' Phoebe said, without looking up.

'Yes?'

'You said, feel those things for a man. But what if it were not a man? Might it still be the same thing then?'

'If boys were old enough to be killed in the trenches,' Beatrice said, 'we may as well call them men. Why, is there . . . ?' She bit her tongue. She did not want to know. She put the key of her desk into her pocket and swept towards the classroom door, deliberately ending the conversation. 'Come, Phoebe, we'll be late—'

'I mean a girl. A woman.'

Beatrice did not answer. She could not have heard correctly. A faint voice cried out, echoing in a far corridor, and rubber soles squeaked on a polished floor. There was a crack in the lowest pane of the door, a neat line through the corner of the pebbly glass. She had never noticed it before; she found her eyes were drawn to it now, as if it were a flaw in her own vision.

'Is it still the same thing, with a woman?'

She turned round. That face, impassive, utterly self-possessed! 'Why would you ask – *that*?'

'Is it? Can you love a woman that way?'

She drew a breath. If it were Elizabeth Steadley asking, she would know how to respond: brisk, dismissive, refusing to rise. Why couldn't she summon the same self-possession now? 'Such a thing would be – obscene,' she said, trying to keep the words flat.

'But you might feel it all the same.'

'I would not – I would never—'

'Not *you*, Miss Timothy,' Phoebe said, with the flicker of a smile. 'Someone else.'

'I cannot possibly say what other women might feel. There are perverse – horrible – vicious elements in society. I cannot deny that. But you must not sully your mind – you must not – to suggest such a thing, at your age . . .'

Phoebe let her stammer to a halt. Then she nodded, as if to fix the answer in her mind, and walked past her to the door. As she went into the corridor she turned back, with a polite, impersonal smile. 'Thank you, Miss Timothy,' she said. 'That was all I wanted to know.'

XIV

Further Studies for a Portrait of a Surplus Woman (abstractions), pencil and charcoal on paper, 1921

At nine o'clock Florence yawned, and laid down the embroidery she had been holding. There was the heavy Sunday-evening tick of the grandfather clock, and the rustle of the fire; it was restful, she could have fallen asleep on the settee, but then she would wake up here tomorrow morning, stiff and freezing. She closed her work basket and got up, stretching her arms above her head. Her hands tingled as the blood flowed into the fingers. Oh, her hands! She noticed them now, their cleverness, their usefulness. The things they could do – what a pleasure it was, to have hands, to have a body . . . She laughed softly. Had Imogen felt like this, when she was a newly-wed? No, surely not. Not with Horace . . . Florence wrinkled her nose as if Imogen were alive and standing in front her, one hand fluttering to her mouth to cover her smile.

She went down the passage to the kitchen for a drink of water. She did not bother to light a lamp. She stood in the flooding moonlight beside the window to sip from her glass. Then she prised open the biscuit tin and ate one, then two of Mrs Reed's shortbread. She had never had such an appetite as she did now. It made life worth living – all this, this silvery darkness, the sugar on her tongue, the joy of knowing that tomorrow was Monday again and she would go to the Bone cottage to see Kit . . .

The church clock struck the quarter, and she rinsed the glass and put it back in the cupboard. Then she made her way back along the passage. Horace's study door was open. Had it been open when she came past the first time? She paused in the sliver of lamplight, and looked through the gap. He was at his desk, frowning down at a book of sermons, half-moon spectacles halfway down his nose. He looked like a character from Dickens. She leant on the side of the door, and smiled. 'Goodnight, Horace.'

He jumped. 'Florence,' he said, as if he had not seen her for years. 'My goodness.'

'I'm going to bed now.'

'Yes. Yes, of course. Wait – just a moment, since you're here – come in, my dear.' He took off his spectacles and gestured with them.

'Now?' she said, stupidly.

'Please. Sit down. I want – there is something I would like to – please.'

'I'm just going to bed. Perhaps tomorrow— ?'

'No, no, please. It won't take long.' He pointed again, jerkily, at the chair on the opposite side of the desk.

She stared at him. Then, slowly, she sat down in the chair. She should not have eaten the second shortbread; she felt her stomach churn.

He picked up his fountain pen and screwed the cap off and on again. He cleared his throat, but didn't speak.

She laced her fingers together in her lap. 'Is anything wrong?'

She had been hoping – assuming, even – that he would chuckle, and shake his head. Perhaps he only wanted to ask something about the sermon; he had been known to want her advice on which Bible verse to include. But instead he coughed, and thumped his chest with his fist. 'Forgive me, my dear,' he said. 'Sundays are bad for my lungs. The church gets very cold during evensong.'

'I do hope the weather improves soon.'

'Yes, indeed.'

A silence. There was a thread of embroidery silk on her skirt. She picked it off, and noticed that her hand was not quite steady. 'What is it, Horace?'

'I – er – I must apologise,' he said, and began to straighten the objects on his desk, one by one. 'You would expect a vicar to be able to speak frankly, would you not? After so many years of counselling his parishioners . . .' He picked up his blotter as if he did not know what it was for, and laid it down again, lining up its corners with the leather panel on his desk.

She waited.

'Yes. Ahem. Well. Florence, my dear . . . I take my obligations very seriously. As your spiritual director and – well, as your brother-in-law, your closest male relative. I regard it as my duty to understand you, and protect you, and – indeed – l-love you.' He stammered on the word, and then recovered with a strained smile. 'I learnt long ago that it is not an intrusion but an act of devotion to observe those around me, and speak when it is necessary.'

'Horace—'

'No, no, don't interrupt.' He coughed again, holding up his hand when she leant forward to offer help. 'Excuse me. Now, where was I . . . ? Yes. Yes, it has come to my notice that there has been . . . a change. In you, I mean. A difference. That is true, is it not?'

'I don't know what you are talking about.'

He blinked, and began to fuss again with his pen, wincing

as it left ink on his fingers. 'I mean that – you seem . . . happier.'

'No,' she said, as levelly as she could, 'I don't think so, particularly.'

'Come now, Florence—'

'Honestly, I—'

He gave a sharp barking laugh, and then wilted a little, as if embarrassed by the sound of it. 'Well naturally,' he said, 'naturally, you could hardly admit . . . Let us not argue about it.'

She looked down at her clasped hands, her fusty skirt, her crossed ankles. If only she were not here – if she were anywhere else, anywhere at all . . . She said, 'I'm very tired, Horace. May I go to bed?'

'When I have said what I want to say. Hear me out, my dear. You need not reply, merely listen.' He grimaced slightly. 'Where was I? Ah yes . . .'

She did not remind him.

'We did not know each other very well before your mother died, did we? Since Imogen was taken from us, and you had no reason to visit . . . we hardly saw each other. I am not blaming you, of course. Your mother needed you, and Phoebe – well, Phoebe was not your responsibility. When you came to live here, you were almost a stranger. It was peculiar for me,' he added, with a dry little smile, 'seeing a woman about the place again. Not a young woman, not in the first flush of youth, but still – well – attractive, if you'll pardon the term . . .'

Why wouldn't she pardon the term? She clenched her jaw and went on staring at her hands.

'Yes. Well. When you arrived, you were grieving, were you not? You had lost everything you cared about. I wish I had been kinder to you – you must have thought that I did not understand—'

'Horace, you were perfectly—'

'No, I should have made more effort. I regret that now. I should have extended a warmer welcome – the embrace of Christ – but never mind. What I am trying to say is that you were miserable. It is only now that I see that. And I owe you an apology.'

'Really, there's no need – if that is what you wanted to say to me—'

'No. I mean, yes, but that is only incidental. Let me finish.'

She sat back, the brief flush of hope fading.

'In the last few months I have seen you change. You may deny it – of course you will deny it, it is not an easy thing to admit – but I can see it. I remember my old rural dean, when I was ordained, telling me that I should look out for certain signs, especially in young women. A lightness of step, he used to say, a trick of smiling at nothing, a new attention to their garb and appearance – and most of all, a certain indescribable . . . blossoming.'

He waited until she was forced to raise her eyes to his. She could not remember how to make her face look quizzical, although she tried; and what he saw seemed to confirm his suspicions. 'Oh, my dear,' he said, 'it is very common. Devotion is a woman's purpose, is it not?'

'I . . .' But her tongue stuck to the roof of her mouth.

'No. Say no more. I am not seeking to embarrass you, only to . . . Let me go on.'

Let him. She told herself that she could get up and leave the room, or grab the glass paperweight from his desk and hurl it through the window into the dark. She was as likely to do the one as the other. 'Please do.'

'It is a delicate matter, of course. But I would be remiss if I had not noticed. You are . . .' He glanced at the paperweight, huffed on its smooth curve and polished it with his sleeve. When it was clean he cleared his throat. 'You are – forgive the direct question, my dear . . . Are you – in love?'

She could not move. For a second all she felt was pure regret: she should have broken the window while she could. Then, as he leant forward, scrutinising her, she felt the blood rush into her face and neck – and everywhere, heat rising to every inch of her skin, humiliating, betraying her more completely than any word could have done.

'You can tell me, Florence.'

'Did Phoebe—? Never mind,' she said, hoarsely: that would be the final straw, if she found that after all Phoebe had seen— had told him . . . 'Horace, please – don't –'

'A simple yes or no will suffice. I am not mistaken, am I?'

She breathed in. 'No.'

'No, I am not mistaken?'

'No, Horace, you are not mistaken.' The humiliation was so strong that she shut her eyes.

She heard him cough. When at last she forced herself to look at him again, there were blotches of colour in his cheeks. He could not hold her gaze.

'I suppose,' she said, 'you think it is a terrible sin?'

He grimaced, as if she had made a joke. 'Misguided, perhaps,' he said, 'but – well, the dictates of the human heart – a young woman, in her prime – who can blame you for wanting . . . ? I venture to say I can understand—'

'How can you possibly— ?'

'You are too hard on yourself, my dear. If your own conscience – but never mind that. I am not going to chastise you.'

She clenched her jaw, and went on looking at him. Her eyes were hot, stinging. Now she saw that there was a tiny smile playing around the corners of his mouth. Was he – yes, he was *pleased* with himself. She curled her fingers into fists. The paperweight was within arm's reach; but what good would it do now?

'I am glad you were honest with me, Florence. Then perhaps I may be honest with you in return.'

He seemed to be expecting an answer. She raised her shoulders an inch and lowered them again.

'It is a very strange thing,' he said, at last, 'to discover the existence of such feelings, when you are an old man, as I am. No, do not contradict me, my dear, we must tell the truth to each other. I feel as though I have spent the last few years half asleep . . . But that is not important. These last few days – since I allowed myself to realise what was happening – I have asked myself, over and over, where my duty lay. I have prayed, of course. I have wondered what Christ would have told me. And tonight, during evensong, I believe I heard the answer. Would you like to hear it? It is – love.'

A pause. He smiled at her, as if expecting congratulation. She said, 'Love?'

'Love. How pure it is, really! The sacrament of marriage is blessed – it is the mirror of the union of Christ and his Church. He would never forbid that which brings us closer to each other, or to God.'

The world wavered a little. She exhaled until it was steady again. Did he mean . . . ? The floor beneath her feet was like the first solid ground after a shipwreck: marvellous, hardly believable.

'Have I – no, perhaps I have not made myself very clear. Forgive me. This is a very . . . unusual situation.' That smile again, as if he had practised it beforehand. 'Well. No doubt this is not how you might have – that is to say – ahem.' He clasped his hands as if he was going to recite a prayer. 'Will you marry me, Florence?'

There was a silence. A tawny owl cried, 'Kewick, kewick,'

in the tree outside. A female, she thought, irrelevantly; a moment later the male answered, its call softer, ghostly.

She drew her hand across her forehead. 'Horace,' she said, with an effort, 'I'm sorry – I—'

'You're overwhelmed, of course. Quite understandable. This has all been very sudden.'

'I don't understand – why would you— ?'

'It would be selfish of me – cowardly . . .' He stopped. Suddenly he winced, drew off his spectacles and began to polish them on his handkerchief. 'Oh dear,' he said. 'I have messed this up most awfully, haven't I? As if I were merely trying to do you a kindness.' He put his spectacles back on his nose, and looked at her through them. 'I am honoured by your regard for me, Florence. I do not deserve it. But if Providence has disposed you to give your heart to me, then it is a gift I will not throw away. I will receive it gratefully, with open hands. I thought, when I buried Imogen, that I would never marry again. And of course I never imagined – it has hardly been ten years, since a man was allowed to wed his wife's sister . . . But now I cannot turn away from your need, and I do not wish to.'

'You want me,' Florence said, as though the words were pieces of a puzzle, to be fitted together one by one, 'to marry you? Because I— I have fallen in— because I love – *you* . . . ?'

'Yes. Yes, indeed. Forgive my clumsiness, my dear. I wish I were a younger man – a more romantic man – but what I lack in energy I hope I have gained in experience, and wisdom. I will be a faithful husband – a guide, a counsellor – and perhaps . . .' He coughed drily into his fist. 'Perhaps – should you desire children – well, I see no reason why that should not, God willing, be possible . . .'

Florence put the back of her hand over her mouth. She had a horrible urge to break into laughter. She must not, she must not . . . She squeezed her eyes shut. When that did not help, she took a fold of her skin between her teeth, and bit until she felt water seep out between her eyelashes.

'It is a great deal to take in, when no doubt you had no inkling . . . There is no need to answer me now. You are tired. Go to bed, my dear.'

'Yes,' she managed, 'thank you, Horace. I am very – it was – yes. Good night.' She stood up and stumbled to the door. She did not dare look at him over her shoulder as she pushed it open and staggered into the cold darkness of the passage. She shut the door and leant against the wall. The dado rail dug into the small of her back. She imagined him sitting back in his chair, polishing his spectacles, replacing them with a satisfied nod: it had gone as well as might be expected, between a spinster and a senescent widower. The image brought the threat of laughter back into her throat and she put her hand over her mouth again. What would Kit say, when she related the scene?

She must not think about that now. No, not until she had regained the safety of her room, where she could bury her face in her quilt and shriek like a first-former . . . She hurried up the stairs with as much urgency as if she wanted to be sick. She almost ran past Phoebe's door – which was open a crack, as it always was – and up the final flight of stairs. Then, at last, she threw open her bedroom door and collapsed on the bed. Oh, God, poor Horace, poor pompous Horace!

But in fact, once they were released, her giggles did not last very long. After a while she rolled over to stare up at her sloping ceiling, and felt the last tears of mirth slide down her temples and slowly dry. She had been so afraid. It had been an awful feeling, like having cheated at an exam. Knowing that you had no possible defence, no recourse except to hang your head in shame. Having to say, *no, you are not mistaken*, and mean: *I have sinned*. She shivered. She had come so close to admitting—

Thank God she had not. Thank God she had not stammered out some incriminating phrase, some justification – even a pronoun, the wrong pronoun, *she* instead of *he*, or *you*! She had come within a hair's breadth of calamity. And escaped it. Just.

She blew out her breath, bringing her hands up to her face.

After Phoebe came to the cottage . . . She had been so afraid that Phoebe had seen – something. Had seen – oh, for heaven's sake! – had seen her naked, wanton, moaning, while Kit hung above her, one hand between her legs, with that half smile, that attentive look in her eyes. If she had seen *that* . . . Those first few days had been excruciating: watching, trying not to watch, trying not to show she was watching. But Phoebe had not acted any differently. She had not even seemed to notice Florence's covert scrutiny. And at last Florence had relaxed: Kit had been right, after all. Phoebe could not possibly have seen anything.

But she might have done. If she had come up the stairs and opened the door, she would have done. It had only been chance that saved them. Another time – next time . . .

They would never be safe. Locked doors, locked tongues. And always, even so, the consciousness of danger, waiting for the smallest slip.

She sat up, folding her knees to her chest. Liquid trickled suddenly between her legs, warm, flooding the fabric of her knickers. Damn. Her *friend*, as they had called it at school, although it did not feel very friendly. She swung her legs off the bed and stripped off her underthings, leaving them in a heap on the floor. There was not much blood, really; it always felt like more than it was. She poured water into the basin on the washstand and wiped herself clean. Then she rinsed out the flannel, dripping pink water into clear, the colour fading almost to nothing. She stared down at it, swirling her hand in the water until the trace disappeared. She felt new wetness run down her leg, and stop at her ankle. She did not move.

Last month . . . Last month when it came, she had told Kit, painfully, struggling for words. She could not have borne it if Kit had recoiled, furious at not being warned; so she had stammered out, 'I'm sorry – I'm afraid I – I'm not – clean . . .' Then she had blushed, terribly, as Kit looked baffled. 'I mean I'm – bloody,' she said. 'There's blood.'

But Kit had not minded. Later, in bed, she had raised herself up on her elbows to smile from between Florence's thighs, and her mouth had been edged with smears of red, like an animal. Florence had felt a jolt of shock and disgust, mixed with desire. It was as though there were no decent limits, no rules, no taboos . . . as though she and Kit were nothing more than bodies, appetites, living meat. It was one thing not to be ashamed of your menses: quite another to taste them on your lover's lips. But she had, she had not protested or turned away from Kit's kiss – and she had liked it—

Another gush. It was heavier, this time, and she bent swiftly to scrub it away before it stained the floorboards. It had been Imogen, not Mother, who had told her about the menarche, and what it meant. They had been sitting in the garden, watching the clouds build up on the horizon, and she had taken Florence's hand and squeezed it. 'Don't worry, darling,' she had said. 'When you become a woman, your body makes a soft little bed for a seed to grow in. When you get married, the seed can grow into a baby. But until then, every month it does a little spring clean. The blood that comes out isn't like the blood when you cut yourself. It's just the red cushiony baby bed coming out.'

Then she had dipped her head to Phoebe, who was asleep on her lap, and kissed the top of her head. 'One day you'll have a baby too, and it will all be worth it.'

What would Imogen say now? If she knew Horace had . . . ?

She scrubbed harder, until her leg was rosy, almost raw. *One day you'll have a baby too.* She balled up the flannel, threw it into the basin with a splash, and sat back on her haunches. She was not sure it would be funny, after all, if she told Kit about Horace, and the misunderstanding. Maybe it would be better not to mention it.

Slowly she got up and went to her drawer to look for a rag. As she passed the window, she glanced sideways as though someone outside had tried to attract her attention: but it was only her reflection, of course, clear against the black backdrop of the February night.

She did not look again. She went to the drawer and bent over it, wondering why she was suddenly fighting tears.

'You know,' Florence murmured, 'such a funny thing happened.' Kit had thought that she was asleep, until she spoke. It was afternoon, and they were lying in Kit's narrow bed, naked, while the last of the daylight slid over the ceiling, the oblong shape cast by the window growing thinner and longer. Now that she knew Florence was awake, Kit eased her arm out from under Florence's head and massaged the feeling back into her numb hand.

'Oh yes?'

'Yes,' Florence said, 'I wasn't going to tell you, but – oh, this bed! Shall I— ?' She tried to give Kit more room, but as she squirmed sideways her foot struck Kit's shin. 'Oh, bother – sorry—'

'Ah – wait,' Kit said, clutching the blankets, 'I'm a bit . . .' She tried to lever herself back into position; but it was too late, and she slid sideways, onto the floor. She landed on her back with a thump, and Florence came with her, landing in a squealing tumble of flesh and bed linen. They both began to laugh. 'Damn it,' Kit said, trying to find a more comfortable place to settle her buttocks, 'I haven't been so bruised since I rode with the Quorn before the war.'

'Oh! Did you . . . ?'

'God, yes. There was this amazing filly. Palomino, I think it's called. Golden-haired. Muscular and elegant. Took her hedges early. She— oh, Florence,' she said, 'I'm only joking. I've never been on a horse in my life. You're so wide-eyed, it's delightful—'

'You beast,' Florence said. 'You're a horrid, horrid beast.' She began to giggle. She had a lovely giggle, helpless and untrammelled. And it was contagious, so now they lay side by side, on their backs, hand in hand, laughing. Kit could not remember the last time she had done this, laughed like this: not since before the War, surely, when she first met Portia, or when she was a child, with Mama, drawing silly monsters together . . . At last, when they grew quiet, Florence laid her head on Kit's shoulder, and Kit stroked her hair.

Florence said, 'I love you.'

Kit did not let her hand pause. She kept stroking, maintaining the same steady rhythm. Perhaps Florence would think she had not heard . . . But she could feel the answer she wanted to give pushing up into her throat: like some physical imperative, like wanting to vomit or burst into tears. When was the last time she had said *I love you too*? Or even the word *love*? And would it be true, if she did say it? Or would it be only a comforting fiction, a piece of cowardice, to avoid hurting Florence's feelings?

But she had let the silence go on too long. Florence sat up, shaking off Kit's hand easily, as if nothing out of the ordinary had happened. 'But I was going to tell you about the funny thing, wasn't I?' she said, bringing her knees up and smiling. 'It happened the other night. I was just on my way to bed and Horace called me into his study. I felt like a schoolgirl about to get a demerit mark.'

'I can imagine,' Kit said. Florence had said, *I love you*. Oh, why hadn't she answered? If she had answered . . . She blinked and tried to concentrate on what Florence was saying now.

'He gave me a little sermon,' Florence said, resting her chin on her knees. 'About love and marriage and things. I thought he had found out about us, somehow. My heart was absolutely hammering. But then it turned out—' She tilted her head and gave Kit a different kind of smile, a quick awkward spark of a smile, and stopped speaking.

In the pause a cold draught went down Kit's spine, making her shiver, and she sat up too and drew a blanket up over her shoulders. 'Yes?'

'Actually,' Florence said, 'actually he offered to marry me. Just think,' she went on, without pausing, so that Kit almost thought she had misheard, 'all the time I was sitting there afraid he was talking about you, and actually he was talking about himself. He thinks I'm dying of passion for him, and it's the least he can do to offer me his hand in marriage. Isn't it silly?'

Kit pulled the blanket tighter round her chest; but it did not warm her. 'Silly,' she repeated. 'Is it?'

'Well – he's so old. And pompous. And he was married to Imogen. But he thinks I'm head over heels in love with him. I suppose because he's the vicar, and I'm only a lowly parishioner – a spinster, living on his charity – like Jane Eyre or something—'

'He thinks that you won't get a better offer,' Kit said. She threw off the bedclothes, reached for her knickers and shirt and put them on. Halfway through she saw that she had put the buttons in the wrong holes, but she did not bother to undo them.

'Yes. That's it, exactly. He thought I would be *grateful*—'

'And he's right. Isn't he?' There was a silence. Kit found her trousers and jumper and finished getting dressed. When she glanced over her shoulder she saw that Florence was staring up at her. 'What?'

'I'm not grateful.'

'He's right that you won't get a better offer.'

Florence laughed. It was the sort of laugh that Portia would have called *the tinkling of silver bells*; but it was more like something fragile hitting a tiled floor. 'Oh, Kit, don't you think you're a better prospect than Horace? I do.'

'I'm not offering to marry you, am I?' Kit picked up Florence's underthings and held them out to her. Florence plucked them out of her hand and began to dress, her head lowered. 'All I'm saying,' Kit said, 'is that it's different.'

'I know it is,' Florence said, without looking up.

'He can be your husband. You'd be respectable. Safe.'

'Stop it!' Florence stumbled to her feet. 'I only told you because it was funny – it's a joke, can't you see that? A man more than twice my age, compared to *you*—'

'He could give you children.'

Florence flushed, so deeply and swiftly it was as though a red curtain had been drawn across the window. There was a pause. She looked around for the rest of her clothes, and began to gather them up and put them on. When she sat on the bed to fasten her stockings she did it by fumbling under her skirt, as if Kit would be shocked by a glimpse of her thighs. 'You sound as if you think I should accept,' she said, at last.

Kit gave a tense jerk of her shoulders that was not quite a shrug. 'It's up to you.'

'I know that.'

'Don't turn him down for my sake.' She went to the window: not to look out, but because she did not want to see Florence's expression. 'Don't ruin your life because you're afraid of hurting me. I shall be perfectly all right. Marry him if you want.'

'I will, if I want!' Florence drew a long breath. 'Kit,' she started again, more levelly, 'you don't really want me to— ?'

'Oh, give over,' she snapped, and swung round. 'You're a normal woman, Florence. Why on earth *would* you choose me? You'd be a fool. A lifetime of hiding and denying, of silence – getting old with nothing to show for it, no family, no pension, nothing but two dotty spinsters living alone in a cottage—'

'There'll be lots of women like that, now.'

'Not through choice!' She should not have raised her voice, but it was too late now. She flourished her arm at the mess of sheets, the naked bed. 'If you think that this will last – that *this* will make up for everything else . . .'

'What if I do?'

'Then you're a fucking idiot.' She clenched her fists. Oh, Christ. It was true, why should she regret saying it if it was true? It was a kindness, really: Florence had never been in love before, she had never known the slow slide from euphoria into familiarity, the fading intensity, the moments when you noticed, horrified, that the thrill had died, and at best there was only weary affection, like a slipper that had worn to the shape of your foot. Just because it felt eternal now, as if they were two miraculous, asymmetrical halves of one whole . . . It was a mirage. When Florence stopped loving, as she would, inevitably – when she remembered that she was a normal woman, with normal appetites, normal ambitions – then she would regret giving up the rest of the world, merely for Kit. It was only fair to warn her.

But she had gone white, as if Kit had raised her hand to strike her. 'I see,' she said. 'Well, then, there's no more to be said, is there?'

'Florence . . .'

'No, there's no need,' Florence said, as if Kit had been about to apologise. She gathered up the hair that had fallen on her neck and pinned it into place. Then she stood up, glancing round – and that glance made Kit's insides turn over, because it was the careful, thoughtful look of someone leaving a hotel room, making sure nothing was left behind.

'Florence – all I meant was –'

Florence took a step towards the door. 'You are quite right. You know much more about this kind of thing than I do. You have years of experience.'

It was hard to tell whether she meant the emphasis on *years* to sound disdainful, but it did: as if Kit were as grimy and jaded as a worn-out whore. Kit stepped aside.

Florence went out into the little passage at the top of the stairs, and paused. The door to the studio was open, the room beyond dim and still. 'Well, at least,' she said, 'there isn't a portrait of me to give up on.'

Kit steadied herself against the upright of the doorframe. She had the dizzying sense that the floor and ceiling were sliding away in different directions, faster and faster. If she could only catch at the right word like a rope and pull them both back to safety . . . 'Florence,' she said, with an effort, 'stop it. You are twisting everything.'

'There's nothing to twist, is there? You've told me quite plainly what I should do. I'll leave you alone. Then maybe you can find someone else. Someone beautiful enough to paint.'

'Oh, for God's sake, Florence!'

'Quite right,' she said, with a tremor in her voice that might have been distress or mockery, 'shout and swear at me, just like a man. I am a normal woman, after all, aren't I? I suppose that must be what I really want.'

'I didn't mean to make you angry—'

'But I'm not angry. Why should I be? Much better to cut me down to size now than let me go on thinking we were— that you cared for me at all.'

'Don't be idiotic, of course I care for you—'

Florence swung round so suddenly Kit steeled herself for a blow. 'No,' she said. 'No, you don't. How can you care for something you don't want to look at? If you loved me, you wouldn't flinch at the thought of painting me.'

Kit began to say, 'That isn't . . .'

But the last burning inch of rope had slipped through her fingers, and Florence was already gone, marching down the stairs without looking back.

Florence walked home quite steadily, her head held high, her steps as smooth as if she were back at school, in a deportment lesson. Mother would approve, she thought – if not of the circumstances, at least of Florence's straight back and strength of character. She came to the vicarage, went inside, hung her coat and hat on the hook, and brushed a crease out of her skirt. She did not need Kit. She did not need to be loved at all.

The house was very quiet. Mrs Reed was in the kitchen, no doubt, and Phoebe was at school. Horace would be in his study, or visiting parishioners.

She did not know what to do now. What was there to do – what *had* she done, before she spent every day at Kit's? Read, and embroidered, and taken long walks. Was that really all? Her only excitement had been the weekly trip to Eastbourne, to change her library books. Even if she had wanted to, it was too late to go to Eastbourne today.

She swallowed, hard. Surely she could find some way of making herself useful. She might sort through the mending basket – or do some light dusting – check the curtains for any repairs that should be done before the spring . . . Or she might make decorative spills or a *decoupage* tea tray, or cut some paper dolls for the village children. What mattered was to keep yourself busy. Not to think about— not to remember that another life was possible, and had been yours—

She went into the drawing room. What a horrid, dingy, oppressive room it was, with its heavy Victorian furniture and dusty knick-knacks. And that vile tapestry ottoman! She had sat there the night Kit had come to dinner, just before Christmas – sat there and gazed like a handmaiden, almost laughing at the unfamiliar sight of Kit wearing a dress, her heart light as a blown glass bauble. If she had known then . . . Had that been the beginnings of love? Or had it started long before? Was there really such a thing as love at first sight – before first sight, even, at the moment when she saw Kit's shirts belly in the breeze, that morning last autumn— ?

It didn't matter when it had begun. Today she had said *I love you*, and there had been no answer but silence.

I'm not offering to marry you, am I?

Very well then. She would marry Horace. She would live in this house – *her* house, forever. She would make the best of it, and Kit would be sorry. She looked round at the clumsy furniture, the faded curtains, the view of the muddy lawn. It would be *hers*. She would get the sofa patched – she would change the curtains and the rug – paint over the wallpaper. She would swap the positions of the hard chair and the armchair, so that you could sit by the window in comfort; she would find a better picture for the wall than that awful print of a hunting scene. And that vile, vile ottoman . . . ! She had opened it once and knew it contained papers and ephemera, Imogen's old theatre programmes and dance cards and photographs. Even if she could not throw it away, she could get it reupholstered in something pretty. For now she might simply push it against the wall and pile it with cushions.

She dragged it a foot or so sideways. But it was unwieldy as well as vile, and her arms began to ache almost instantly. With a sound halfway between a grunt and a cry she sat back on her haunches and gave it a final, childish shove. She meant, if not to ram it viciously into the skirting board, then at least to tip it over; but only the lid flew up and fell open, landing on its hinges with an unperturbed thud. Florence wanted to kick it, but that would mean getting to her feet, and anyway the spasm of fury had passed, leaving a sense of her own ridiculousness. She leant over to shut it again, and paused. The piles of papers inside were the same jumbled, overlapping mess she had seen before: orders of service and envelopes, *Baby's first hair*, a bundle of letters tied with a mauve ribbon . . . But on the very top, catching her gaze, was a picture of Imogen on the day of her wedding.

She was standing in front of the plain east window of Haltington church, her wide hat behind her head like a halo, her hands invisible behind the bouquet of roses and maidenhair fern. The photographer had been either clever or lucky: he had caught her just as she broke into a real smile, so that her eyes were wide and her mouth soft. She might have been about to ask, with delighted emphasis, where her *husband* had got to; or to call out to Florence not to look sulky, it would be her turn next . . . The whole church seemed to glow, as if she were so young and beautiful and happy the world itself was alight with it.

Florence's eyes stung. The face in the photograph was frozen, forever silent, forever behind the glass pane of memory. She reached out her fingertip and touched the sepia shadow on Imogen's cheek; and at last, like rotten lace ripping, she began to cry.

She did not need to worry about disturbing anyone. She wept until she felt dried out and empty, and her face was raw. Then, wearily, she tidied up and got to her feet, pushed the ottoman back into its previous place, and straightened her clothes. Of course she would not redecorate; she could already see Horace's wondering frown if she suggested it.

But before she left the room she darted back, and took Imogen's photograph from the ottoman, and set it on the mantelpiece beside the clock – not quite knowing, as she did it, whether it was an act of penitence or defiance.

XV

Sketches, pencil on paper, 1921

Florence was woken by a child, calling. She had been dreaming of Imogen, and for a little while the voice was part of the dream, until finally she floundered into wakefulness and it was real. A child. 'Mamma,' it said, 'mamma . . .'

She sat up, squinting into the dark, straining her ears. It could not be a child, there was no child in the house, except Phoebe—

Phoebe. Could it be Phoebe?

'Mamma . . . ?' Yearning, bewildered. The stress on the first syllable, the way an infant would say it. An abandoned infant, an infant who could not believe that the world was so bleak, so cruel as to take its mother away. But – she grimaced, holding her breath to listen – yes, maybe it *was* Phoebe, a Phoebe she had never heard before . . . She lay down again, pulling her pillow over her head to muffle the sound. Then, groaning, she flung it aside and got to her feet. She reached for her dressing gown, but before she could put it on she heard the creak of footsteps on the landing below, and then the soft patter of feet going down the stairs. She hurried out into the passage, shoving her arms into the sleeves of her dressing gown as she went, and looked over the banisters. There was a faint moving pool of lamplight, and a shadow. It crossed the hall and turned down the passage towards the drawing room. 'Mamma?' the voice said. It was Phoebe, Florence was sure of it now, but that childish note was still there, raw with disbelief and longing.

'Phoebe?' But the light and its trailing shadow had already disappeared into the drawing room. She crept down the first flight of stairs, and hesitated. It was cold; she wanted to get back into bed and draw the covers over her head. She repeated, 'Phoebe?'

It was silent now. She told herself that if she heard that plaintive cry again, she would go and see what was wrong; but she did not. The pause stretched longer, until it must have lasted minutes and not seconds.

Had she really heard it? Or had it been a remnant of a dream? She had gone to sleep thinking of Imogen, and weddings, and babies, and then . . . She shivered, hugging herself. She would count to five, and if it was all quiet she would go back to her room.

There was a crash. She reacted automatically, almost flying down the stairs, her mind catching up as she rounded the corner and started down the passage. A vase? A decanter? The drawing room door was open, and firelight spilt through the gap, flickering. There was a scratchiness in the air that irritated her eyes and throat. Smoke. *Fire*—

And then she was in the room, and moving too quickly to think. Fire – yes – a patch of flames, the stink of oil, black smoke in gouts pouring up to the ceiling, air thick and fierce as acid . . . She ducked to the settee, fumbled for a cushion, and crouched to beat it against the raging flames on the hearthrug, her arms stretched, her face averted. It would not work – what else was there? – and such heat, hot as an oven on her face and chest! The smell of singeing velvet – something acrid – she wrenched off her dressing gown, that was thick padded silk – threw it down, and beat and beat with the cushion as the flames started to eat it into holes. It seemed to last an eternity, while horrid seeds of black and gold sprouted and spread; then, at last, it was over, and the room was dark. She staggered, and put a hand against the wall. The afterimage of flames spun and drifted in front of her eyes. Her hands hurt. Her lungs hurt, too.

There was someone there, with her. Phoebe. She said, shakily, to the silhouette, 'Light the gas, will you? Carefully.'

There was movement, a spurt and a flare, and then the gas hissed and steadied and she could see again. The smoke had begun to clear. Her dressing gown was a heap of sad rags and ash, more black-edged holes than fabric. There were plumes of soot reaching up the chimney breast to the ceiling, and scattered shards of burnt debris on the hearth. But it had been a small fire, really; it might have been much worse . . . Thank heavens for Mother, and how anxious she had been about the air raids in London: 'Yes, but Florence,' she had said, 'if there were a fire here, and when we called for help no one came . . .' She had insisted that Florence be ready, as if a blanket or a sand bucket would protect them against the worst the Kaiser could throw at them. 'Practice,' she had insisted, 'we must make it second nature!' Florence felt a sudden rush of guilt and grief. Poor Mother; had her hysteria saved them all, tonight? She drew her forearm across her stinging eyes.

'Aunt Florence?'

She turned to Phoebe, ready to berate her. It was her fault, it must be, if she had not been out of bed, wandering . . . But as she opened her mouth she saw something unfamiliar in her niece's face: something softer, less sure of herself. She sat down in the chair furthest from the fireplace, and took a deep painful breath, leaning forward to try to ease her chest.

'Are you all right?'

'I think so. Are you?'

Phoebe's eyes widened, as if the question surprised her, but she did not answer. Instead she took a few steps towards the remains of the fire, looking around, surveying the damage.

After a moment Florence said, 'What happened?'

Phoebe shot a look at her. She shrugged.

'Did you have a bad dream? I thought I heard you. That's why I came so quickly. I was already on the stairs.' She should not have said so much without pausing. She tried to catch her breath and coughed, tasting charred grease and metal.

'In a way,' Phoebe said; but for once she seemed uncertain. 'I think it started with a dream.'

So it had been her, saying *Mamma* . . . 'About Imo—your mother?'

'Yes.'

'Were you sleepwalking?'

'I don't know. I don't think so.' Phoebe twisted her fingers together and looked down at them. 'I thought I heard Mama. I thought she was here, waiting for me.'

'And then what?' Florence cleared her throat again, forcing herself to swallow the foul-tasting phlegm. 'You came into the parlour, because you'd dreamt that she was here, and then . . . Did you see how the fire started? Did the chimney catch . . .?' She blinked, trying to ease the soreness in her eyes. Somehow the fire in the grate had spilt out into the room. Where was the fireguard? And why, so late at night . . . ? 'Phoebe? Did – did *you* . . . ?'

Phoebe looked down.

Florence said, 'You – tried to start a fire?'

'I dropped the lamp,' Phoebe said.

There was a silence. Florence got to her feet. Her head spun, and she waited for it to stop before she stepped over the rug, bent carefully and gathered up her ruined dressing gown. There were curved shards of broken glass on the hearth, glinting in the corner beside the fire irons. She had been lucky not to stand on any of them. She crouched down, filled with a sudden, cold suspicion. In the grate, lying in the jumble of old embers, was a thin margin of blackened paper: the very edge of a plain church window, a sooty patch of sepia lace.

'Why did you leave the photograph there? You took it out and – and *looked* at it . . . It was your fault,' Phoebe cried out, her voice cracking. 'How could you? It wasn't yours – I was keeping it safe, and now it's gone—'

Florence spun round, resisting the impulse to hit out. Her hand was smarting, the scorched skin raw. Oh, but how she wanted to—

Phoebe met her gaze. Tears brimmed in her eyes. She blinked, and they spilt down her cheeks. Her mouth trembled.

Florence clenched her jaw. But she could not hold on to her anger: it slipped through her fingers like water. She could not remember having seen Phoebe cry, ever. Not even at Mother's funeral, when she had taken the child's hand, and it had lain so lifelessly in her own that she had let go almost immediately. 'I'm sorry,' she said. 'But why? Oh, Phoebe . . .'

'It wasn't Mama,' Phoebe said, 'it wasn't . . .'

'No, it's only a picture,' Florence said. She wanted to reach out; but not to hit her, this time. 'It's all right. Only a picture.'

'No – I mean . . .' She bit her lip. Her eyes slid past Florence to the fragment in the grate, then came back to Florence's face. They watched each other, drawing breath in unison, and Florence saw her decide to tell the truth. 'I had to get rid of it. I saw—'

'Good Lord,' Dr Manning said, from the doorway. 'What in heaven's name happened here?'

Florence swung round. Damn him, *damn* him! She wished she could slam the door on him, his blinking eyes, his belted, paunchy dressing gown, and his stupid, stupid air of taking charge. 'I put the fire out,' she said, with all the patience she could muster. 'There's no danger now. You can go back to bed.'

'But what on earth *happened*?' He took a few steps into the room, fumbling for his spectacles. He put them on and stared at the blackened mantelpiece and scorched hearthrug. 'My God, what a mess . . .' He looked round, bewildered. 'I don't understand.'

But there was no chance, now, that Phoebe would make a clean breast of anything. The glimmer of frankness in her eyes had disappeared as if it had never been. 'It was an accident,' Florence said, wearily. 'Phoebe was sleepwalking.'

'But how— ?'

'Please, Horace. Let's talk about it in the morning.' She pushed her hair off her face – or rather, tried to; but new, ferocious pain surged through her hand, and she winced and cradled it to her chest. The other wasn't as bad, but it prickled, like sandpaper; her cheek felt the same, tight and tingling.

'Are you hurt?' Dr Manning said. 'Florence?'

'Not badly.'

'But you . . .' He fussed in his pocket, and drew out a crumpled handkerchief, not quite clean. 'Here . . .'

'No, thank you, I'll bathe it properly before I go back to sleep.'

He looked crestfallen for a moment; then he swung round to address his daughter with sudden fury. 'Phoebe, you foolish girl! How *could* you? What sort of accident— ? Look at your aunt, look at this room! What an appalling mess – what danger – you might have burnt us all in our beds. Well? You had better explain yourself.'

'I don't remember,' Phoebe said. 'I was dreaming.'

'What nonsense – you cannot possibly have done *that* while you were asleep—'

'I did.'

'Thou shalt not bear false witness,' Dr Manning boomed, as if he were in his pulpit; and as if she were in the family pew, Phoebe lowered her gaze, expressionless. It seemed to enrage him more. 'Whatever you did, adding more lies—'

'Horace, please,' Florence said, 'it's late and we've all had rather a shock. We can get to the bottom of it tomorrow, when we've had more sleep.' She held out her hand, gesturing to Phoebe. 'Come on, sweetheart—'

Phoebe recoiled, her eyes narrowed. 'You needn't defend me,' she said.

'I wasn't – I only thought—' She took a breath, desperate to recapture that swift, unexpected intimacy: but the mask had dropped over Phoebe's face again. 'Never mind, let's just—'

'You must not speak to your aunt like that,' Dr Manning said. 'I will not permit—'

'Horace, don't be hard on her,' Florence said, with a painful wave of her hand, 'I'm sure Phoebe didn't mean to be—'

'Yes, I *did*,' Phoebe said, with a tilt of her chin, 'and you can stop ordering Papa about, too. This isn't even your house—'

'Be quiet!' Dr Manning had raised his voice; there was a silence. 'I'm horrified by your manners. Your mother would be ashamed of you. Not to mention – well, you might as well know now. Florence is going to be your stepmother.' He added, with an air of victory, 'I hope *that* at least will instil some respect.'

Phoebe stood very still. At last she turned her head and looked, not at her father, but at Florence. If there had been a moment to deny it, it was then; but Florence could not bring herself to speak.

'You had better apologise,' Dr Manning said. It was the first time he had ever chastised Phoebe in front of Florence; and what a time, Florence thought, what a time to choose . . . Anything she could say would make things worse. Her eyes were stinging worse than ever. That was the smoke, of course.

'I'm sorry, Aunt Florence,' Phoebe said. She could not have made it sound less sincere.

'Very well,' Dr Manning said, 'now go to bed. We'll talk about the rest in the morning.'

Phoebe slipped between them, out of the door into the passage. Her footsteps went up the stairs, light and steady, giving nothing away.

'Well, my dear—'

She should have stayed and made inconsequential, reassuring conversation about fire precautions and growing pains, or thanked Dr Manning for his thoughtfulness, and said earnestly that she hoped, one day, to do justice to Imogen's memory. Or, even, told him gently that she was not sure, she was conscious of the enormous honour he had done her, but she could not bring herself to demand so much of him, at his stage in life . . . But no words she could think of could have got past the thick barrier in her throat, a sore plug of soot and mucus and misery; so she simply turned and followed Phoebe, feeling like a child herself, unable even to wait to hear what he was going to say.

Being in disgrace did not especially bother Phoebe. It was not very different, really, from how things were when she was not in disgrace. Papa made an effort to be distant with her, but as he was not particularly interested in her at the best of times she did not feel much loss. It was nice, in a way, when he was kindly; but it was always a vague sort of kindliness, the sort he would turn on his parishioners out of duty or pity. At least now he looked at her. She was almost glad when she caught his eye over the silent breakfast table, and he looked surprised and displeased: for once he was genuinely seeing her, as she was. She stared down at her plate and cut her toast into smaller and smaller pieces.

Aunt Florence did not come down from her bedroom. Phoebe did not think her burns had been very bad, but Papa spoke with a hushed voice and closed doors with elaborate delicacy, and Mrs Reed fussed with bandages and iodine and bowls of broth on trays. Once Phoebe tiptoed up to the top landing and stood quite still, listening: was there a sound from inside the room, or was it only the blood pounding in her ears? What was Aunt Florence doing in there? Was she asleep, or reading, or thinking? And if she was thinking, was she thinking about marriage, about being Phoebe's stepmother – or about that fumbling unnatural embrace in Kit Clayton's bed?

If she knocked on the door, and went inside . . . But what would she say? She was not sorry; she did not want Aunt Florence to get well soon. When Mama was ill, she had sat on the bed, holding Mama's hand. Mama had promised a picnic, and sweets, and then given her a fluttery nuzzling kiss under her chin that made her giggle and squirm. Was that a real memory, or was she making it up, because she wanted to believe it? And then Mama had died.

Aunt Florence was not going to die. She was not even badly burnt.

Phoebe put her hand against the flat wood of the door and shut her eyes. It was not her fault. She could not have done anything differently.

Mama's photograph—

She did not want to remember that. Not the picture, or the dream – had it been a dream? – that had made her leave her bed, and creep downstairs. Not the strange, heartbreaking hope, or the way it turned to nightmare, when she looked at Mama's picture and saw . . . There was no use dwelling on it; it was over, the picture would never look at her like that again. And Aunt Florence – well, she would not have understood, it was just as well Phoebe had not managed to explain. Aunt Florence, who was going to be her stepmother, although she had been in Kit Clayton's bed . . . Could it be true? Surely she would not do it, she would not marry Papa, when . . . ? But she had not denied it. She had met Phoebe's eyes, tremulous and guilty. Yes, it was true.

Phoebe turned away and went downstairs, not bothering to tread quietly; and when Mrs Reed left a tray unattended at the bottom of the stairs she licked her finger lingeringly and stirred the soup with it.

The days dragged on. At last Aunt Florence got up, but she did not speak very much, or go out; she sat in the parlour with her book, her back turned to the chimney breast, where a wash of ashy grime still marred the wallpaper. Phoebe watched her from the doorway for minutes at a time, but never saw her move. On Sunday she said that she was not well enough to go to church, and Papa said, 'Of course, my dear, you must not exhaust yourself . . .' and patted her shoulder. There was a new gleam in his eyes when he looked at her; it made Phoebe's stomach twist to see it.

Phoebe, naturally, was not excused from going to church. Papa did not actually ignore her on the way there; he merely walked ahead with overstated dignity, without looking round. It was a mild day, clear-skied and golden, with a breeze rustling the wintry grass and making tree branches click overhead; and on a sudden impulse, as they approached the lychgate Phoebe ducked into the ditch and up the slope, hurrying to get to the nearest clump of trees before Papa noticed her absence. She waited until he had gone into the church – he had not even glanced behind him, had he forgotten about her entirely? – and then climbed the hill, turning back to look down towards the vicarage. The wind blew softly into her face. She unbuttoned her coat and let the air slide its fingers into her dress.

Would he realise that she had slipped away? Well, if she was already in disgrace . . . With a sudden sense of defiant freedom she ran forwards, letting her coat flare out behind her like wings. She came over a ridge in the chalk, and stopped, looking down at the Bone cottage.

She did not exactly mean to walk towards it; and she did not know until she had come to the back garden, and lifted the latch of the gate, that she meant to walk up the overgrown path to the house itself. The kitchen door was open and she could hear the clatter of pots inside; as she approached she saw a shadow cross back and forth, dim in the dim room.

Last time she had been here, Kit had sworn at her and told her to run along; but now she did not care. She felt older, wiser, more worldly. She knocked on the open door, and stood in the sunlight waiting to be acknowledged.

Kit had just dumped an armful of crockery in the sink. She spun round, squinting; then she started forwards, wiping her hands on a cloth, saying, 'Where have you been? I thought . . .' Then her smile slid off her face. 'You,' she said. 'What are you doing here?'

'Good morning, Miss Clayton.' Too late, she thought she should have said *Kit*.

'Where's Florence? Is she— ?' She stopped, biting off the question as if it might betray her.

'She's at home. There was an accident.' Phoebe saw fear leap in Kit's eyes. She paused for a moment, a tiny moment, before she added, 'It isn't serious. Aunt Florence hurt her hand. I expect that's why she hasn't written to explain.'

Kit exhaled, slowly. She folded the cloth she was holding, very carefully, and hung it on a hook beside the sink. 'I see,' she said. 'Well, I'm glad she's all right.'

'I expect she'll be recovered soon.'

'Good. Well, will you say to her that I – I hope she isn't in pain? And thank her for sending you to tell me.'

'She didn't send me.'

Kit blinked. 'Well then – why—'

'I thought you might want to know.'

They stared at each other. Kit nodded. 'I see,' she said. 'Thanks.'

A gust of sweet-smelling wind touched Phoebe's face, blowing a curl of hair across her eyes. She pushed it away. Kit had turned to collect a handful of paintbrushes and a jar of drab green-brown water, moving with unhurried deliberateness as if she were alone. As she took them to the sink and began to rinse the brushes, Phoebe said, 'Did you know that she is going to marry my papa?'

Kit paused, her fingers frozen underwater as they splayed the bristles of a brush; then she went on, steadily, and held the brush to the light to examine it for traces of colour. But when she set the brush aside, it was still stained grey-green, not clean at all. 'Is she,' she said, but it was not exactly a question.

'If you don't believe me, you can ask her.'

Kit sat down, folding her hands on the table in front of her. She had a watery smear of paint across her forearm, below the roll of her sleeve, the indeterminate colour of an old bruise. Phoebe wanted to lean forward and touch it. 'No need,' she said, at last, 'I knew already.'

Phoebe did not believe her; but she was glad Kit had lied, because it meant she was worth lying to. 'I'm sorry,' she said, not meaning it.

'Why?'

'Because you – I suppose it isn't very nice to hear,' she said, 'that she's going to marry someone else.'

Kit held her gaze. 'Someone *else* . . .' she said, and suddenly she gave a crooked, unamused sort of smile. 'It's all right, Phoebe. I told her to marry your father, since he'd asked her. I could hardly marry her myself, could I?'

And there, just like that, it had been said aloud. Acknowledged, between the two of them, and the world did not change, nothing ghastly happened, the wet cloth dripped, the brushes on the sideboard went on oozing coloured water.

'Were you really painting her?' Phoebe said.

Kit winced; then, as though she had nothing left to lose, she laughed. 'No.'

'Why did you lie?'

'Why do you think?' Belatedly Kit seemed to notice the paint-shadow on her arm, and rubbed it away.

Phoebe watched until Kit's fingers grew still. Long fingers, with short, blunt nails: too capable to belong to a lady, too beautiful to belong to a man. What would it be like, to feel those fingers inside you? She said, 'You'll be lonely.'

'I'll take my chances, thanks.'

'I'll come to visit you. To make sure you're all right.'

There was a pause; then Kit smiled, in wry, unhappy defeat. She said, 'I suppose you can come now and then, if you must. As long as you're quiet.'

'I won't tell Aunt Florence—'

Kit said, too swiftly, 'Tell her if you want, I don't mind.'

Ah. So that was why she had conceded so easily . . . But it didn't matter. In any case Phoebe resolved that she would *not* tell Aunt Florence. It would be her secret, her silent revenge for Mama's photograph; and she did not want to risk being forbidden to come. 'I'll see you tomorrow, after school, then,' Phoebe said.

'If you insist.'

Kit put her elbows on the table and rested her forehead against her clasped hands. She shut her eyes. Phoebe stood still, watching her, prolonging the moment before she said goodbye. Far away the church clock struck the hour, sweet and triumphant in the mild air.

Kit should not have agreed to let Phoebe visit her. She asked herself, lying awake that night, why she had. Or, at least, she pretended to – but she knew that the true answer was simple, and shameful: she hoped that Florence would hear of it, and be jealous. If Florence had only written! But why should she have done? There was nothing to say. She had done what Kit had told her to do, hadn't she? And Kit . . . well, what could she have said, in return? *I didn't mean it. I didn't think you really would agree to marry him. Please come back . . .* And thereby, she thought, ruin Florence's chances of a happy life. No, she must not try to bring Florence back to her; it was not fair to try to rekindle their affair, when Florence had made the right choice.

And Phoebe . . . Before the War Kit would have yearned to paint her portrait. She was a mystery, an enticing, treacherous mystery, conscious of her own power; when Kit gazed at her, she gazed back, reversing subject and object. What a painting Kit could have made, if she had had the stomach for it! But that was all over. She did not draw people any more – not even gorgeous, enchanting children, children with that elusive perilous gleam. Once Phoebe would have been a perfect model; now she was a perfect nuisance. Kit groaned, and pushed her face into her pillow, resolving to send her straight home the next time she came. A brisk *sorry, I'm working* – or better still, a day out, so that Phoebe arrived and found the door locked, and the house dark and cold, and left again, without a fuss . . .

But somehow, in the morning, the prospect of going out in the rain did not attract her, and her solitude weighed more heavily than it should have done. By the afternoon she was bored and restless. After an hour of trying to sketch she flung down her pencil and turned away from the arrangement of jars she had set up as a still life on the studio table; she stood at the window, staring out, and when the church clock chimed she realised she was watching for Phoebe to come up the path. She was still, she thought, determined to send her away – she only wanted to get it over with, and then she would be able to concentrate . . . But when at last Phoebe arrived – by the time Kit had descended the stairs, she had dropped her satchel in the corner of the kitchen and settled herself in the chair beside the range – Kit did not jerk her head at the door and dismiss her, as she had planned.

'Hullo,' she said. 'You can't stay long. I'm working.'

Phoebe met her gaze, undeceived, and smiled. She folded her legs up onto the chair and linked her hands around her knees. Her hair had come out of its plait, and wisps hung around her head, shining. She looked very young.

Kit bit her lip. After all she did not want to – could not, somehow – tell Phoebe to leave. With a sudden inspiration she said, 'Do you want a cup of tea?'

'Real tea? Yes, please.' It was only when Kit had made the tea in two steaming cups and put one into Phoebe's hands that she added, 'Papa won't let me drink real tea. He says it's a stimulant unsuitable for young ladies.' She smiled at Kit's discomfiture, and raised the cup in a mock toast.

Kit leant against the window sill, drinking from her own cup. With every moment that passed she knew she was making it easier for Phoebe to come again – it was like feeding a stray cat – but she felt reckless and lonely. Phoebe sipped her tea, quiet, unexpectedly undemanding; and in spite of herself Kit imagined again what a picture she would make. If only . . . But no, that was impossible.

After a long time she said, 'What was the accident?'

'Which accident?'

'Florence hurt herself, you said. When you came to see me yesterday.'

Phoebe took a mouthful of tea, with a considering look. Perhaps it was only that she had never had tea before, and was savouring the taste. She leant back, letting her head loll against the wall behind. 'There was a fire. Aunt Florence put it out.'

'A fire?'

Phoebe nodded.

'What sort of fire? Christ, was Florence . . . ?' Kit set her cup down and hot tea slopped over her hands, but she hardly felt it.

'Only a little one,' Phoebe said, with a quirk of her head. 'She's all right. Honestly.' She added, without malice, 'Don't you think you would know if she wasn't?'

It was probably true. Mousy little Hannah Smith had been that morning to drop off the clean sheets, and she would have said if something had happened to Florence. But Kit should have asked sooner than this, how could she not have *asked*?

She knew how, of course, or rather why. She subsided against the window sill and picked up her cup again, trying not to hear reproach in the silence. Mainly to break it, she said, 'What happened?'

But Phoebe stared out at the sky and the bare branches of trees, the corners of her mouth pulled in. 'Nothing very much,' she said.

'But what?'

'Do you care?' She turned her gaze on Kit.

'Of course—'

'About Aunt Florence, yes, I know,' she said, with swift patience. 'But do you really care what happened? Or only that Aunt Florence is perfectly recovered?'

'Well, I . . .' Kit stopped. Phoebe did not move, or speak; only waited, with that ageless, impassive curiosity. 'OK, then. Tell me.'

Phoebe drank from her cup. Then she held it between her hands and looked down into it; Kit had not left the tea leaves in it, or she might have thought Phoebe was telling her fortune with them. She said, 'It was late at night, I don't know what time exactly. About midnight, I think. I'd been asleep. I dreamt of Mama. Then when I woke up I heard her, calling me. At least . . . I don't know if I heard it, exactly, but there was someone saying, *sweet one, darling, come here, darling*. That's what Mama used to say,' she added, with a sudden glare, as if Kit had smirked. 'I don't remember her voice, but I remember that.'

'You were still dreaming, you mean?'

Phoebe raised one shoulder with childish grace, dismissing the question. After a moment she went on, 'I went downstairs. I took a lamp. I followed the – the calling. It was coming from the parlour. When I went into the room . . .' She stopped and drew breath, carefully, as if it were a tactic they taught at school, in elocution lessons. 'Aunt Florence had put a photograph of my Mama on the mantelpiece. When I saw it . . .' She tapped the cup with her fingernail, as if she were testing how easily it would break.

Kit waited.

'Do you remember Papa talking about the Face? And the – the . . .'

'The thurlath,' Kit said, 'yes.'

Phoebe met her eyes. 'The thurlath,' she repeated. 'The hollow ones, the ones who come looking for faces without souls. Papa thinks it's only a story.'

Kit looked out at the road below, determined not to betray the leap of unease in her gut, the thudding of her heart.

'The picture was coming alive,' Phoebe said. 'I saw it. It hadn't yet, but . . . It's hard to describe. I don't mean that it was moving. But it was going to . . . it wanted something. It wasn't Mama,' she added, suddenly fierce, 'it looked like her picture, but it wasn't. And whatever had been calling me wasn't her, either. It was someone— something else.'

Kit said, a thurlath? and then realised she had not said it aloud.

'I knew if I went any closer . . .' Tap, tap, her fingernail went against the china cup, tap tap. 'It wanted to get hold of me, I think. Take me.'

Kit cleared her throat. 'What happened then?'

'I put it in the hearth and dropped the lamp on it.'

'You did *what*?'

Phoebe smiled, a little: it was almost the look Muckle had had, once, when Portia asked why he wouldn't talk about the trenches. 'I had to destroy it,' she said, 'before it happened.'

Kit stared at her. Then she laughed: she felt like the cup, suddenly cracking. 'You set fire to your mother's photograph?'

'Aunt Florence put the fire out. But it had gone by then. Whatever it was.' Phoebe met her gaze without blinking. 'You don't believe me.'

'Don't I?'

'Do you?'

There was a long silence.

'No. No, of course I don't. A thurlath . . .' Kit shook her

head, swept her hair off her face with both hands, laughed again.

But Phoebe did not seem to hear. 'Papa thinks that writing a book about something makes it safe. Giving it a name. Once it's written down and labelled . . . Sussex folklore. Quaint, but with its own logic. Predictable. A metaphor,' she said, with an ironic twist on the word.

'And you think . . . ?'

'I don't think Papa would know what to do, if he saw what I saw.'

Kit might have said, 'What you *thought* you saw.' Instead she said, 'Were you afraid?'

'Yes, of course.'

And yet she had thrown an oil lamp without hesitation, minutes after waking from a nightmare; and recounted the story, now, with that level sang-froid . . . Kit said, 'Phoebe, you don't – really – think—'

'I had better go now. Thank you for the tea,' Phoebe said. She got up to leave, putting down her cup, still unchipped, unmarked, unbroken.

XVI

The Widow, candle wax and spent matchsticks, 1921

That Saturday evening Hannah laid the table for two, as she always did, in the little room at the front of the cottage. She set out the best china, the knives and forks of good Sheffield steel, and the two precious mismatched sherry glasses. In the middle she put a candle, and lit it. And, as she always did, she ate her meal alone, making bright conversation, telling the empty place opposite that the eldest Wood girl had had her baby and the paint on Sally Jenson's windows was peeling again and there had been a terrible quarrel because Billy Robb had said the Half Moon was watering down its beer. But the weather was looking better for next week, and that was good news, wasn't it?

There was a pause, while she got up to clear away the remains of her rabbit pie; then she came back again with the jam roly-poly. The jam was good and sweet, from before the War – the last pot, from the last batch Hannah's mother had made – and it was raspberry, Jack's favourite . . . 'Dig in,' she said, and cut herself a slice. She wished she could have afforded cream, but she chewed and smiled dutifully, swallowing the heavy pastry and making a little *mmm* of satisfaction after it had gone down. 'Oh, and I saw Florence

Stock outside the vicarage,' she said, putting down her spoon. 'That woman looks through me like I'm nothing.'

She bit her lip. That had been an unladylike, unkind thing to say, even though Florence Stock was stuck up and thoughtless and no better than she should be. Jack's mother would purse her lips if she were here, pretending she had not heard; it would be one more item on the list that showed Hannah was not good enough. Jack would not have understood, either. Before he was wounded he would have given her a benign, wondering frown, as if he could not imagine disliking anyone; after – well, after he was wounded he often looked right through her himself.

There was a silence. She could not have explained what she resented about Miss Stock, nor her suspicions about what she got up to with that funny artist from London, with the men's clothes and short hair. She had never dared to discuss Miss Clayton's sheets. Once, when she was bundling the dirty linen into the hot water, panting and sweaty, she had let herself wonder what it was like, what they did together: what *was* there to do, when there was no – well, no long thing to go into the – the hole? She had racked her brain, mulling it over until her insides went funny. She might have stood there forever, lost in imagination, if she had not burnt herself and come back to where she was with a painful jolt. She could never have told anyone about that. Even if all she had said was to say, innocently, that Miss Clayton's monthlies seemed to come twice as often as they should . . . It wasn't only the indelicacy. Any mention of blood would make Jack – well, she must not, that was all. She said, 'She's going to marry the vicar, did I tell you? I can't think why he asked her.' Oh dear, unkind, she was being unkind again!

She looked down at her plate and the half-eaten slice of pudding that lay on it like a waning moon. The candle flame was reflected in the smeared bowl of her spoon, along with the linen-covered table, the glasses, the flowered curtains at the window and the night outside. She got up, clearing the dirty plate and the clean one, the dirty glass and the clean one, the dirty spoon and its clean, untouched twin. She took them into the kitchen; but tonight she did not wash them immediately, she only piled them on the side beside the sink. The range needed stoking, but she did not do that either. Above it, the laundry hung just below the ceiling on its rack, sagging and dripping. Her arms still ached from hauling it up there. She turned, leaning against the cold copper that stood in the corner, and looked through the doorway at the empty chair.

'Jack?'

Tonight the answering silence was heavier than usual. She clenched her hand on the locket that hung around her neck, squeezing and squeezing as if it could stop her being swept away. The chain bit into the back of her neck, but for once the pain did not help. 'Jack,' she said, *'Jack . . .'*

What would Jack's mother say, if she could see her here, raising her voice to no one? Nothing, probably. Only a wrinkled nose, a dab of the lace handkerchief to her lips, a little cough of disdain. How she had despised Hannah – even more, after Jack came home, after—

Hannah took a step forward, staring at the chair as if there were really someone sitting in it. If she squinted through her eyelashes, she could almost see his silhouette. Not as it had been after he came home the last time, but how it had been on their wedding day. He would have leant forward with one elbow on the table, smiling at her. He would have told her to come over there, and patted his thigh to show that he meant her to sit on his lap. She would have danced towards him, eager to obey, to throw her arms round his neck and let him—

She reached out, without looking. Her fingers closed on something smooth and curved.

She flung it. It smashed against the wall. Blue and white shards exploded towards her, streaks of candlelight sliding over each one as they flew.

'How could you – how *could* you, Jack—?'

He should have been there. He had *chosen* not to be there. He could quite easily have been sitting in that chair, eating jam roly-poly, nodding as she passed on the village gossip. He would not have been the same as when she married him, of course: for one thing he would have been eating with his left hand, spilling jam and crumbs down his front as his fork trembled in his grasp, cursing at her through gritted teeth if she so much as offered to help. He would not have wanted her to touch him, much less kiss him; and even if he had, he had not exactly had a lap for her to sit in . . . But that was not the point. She had wanted him there – she *did* want him there – even as he was, even legless and one-armed, even glaring at her and shaking so hard he could hardly get his words out. She had loved him. She had still loved him. If he had only let her love him, instead of . . .

And now she didn't even have a widow's pension! Not even that. So she was reduced to washing filthy sheets for filthy women, all because Jack was too cowardly to go on—

She put her hand over her mouth. The shards of the china plate lay on the floor, the two bluebirds broken apart, the willow tree split down the middle as if by lightning. Oh, Jack . . . She had been so utterly in love, so swept away by joy. Her wedding day had been the happiest day of her life, in spite of the fact that she had only had her old blue Sunday dress to wear and a bunch of roses picked from the garden, and Jack was only home for a few days . . . She had almost been glad of the War, because without it he might have waited and had time to find another girl, a prettier, cleverer girl, the kind of girl he deserved. She had stood at the altar with her heart in her mouth, unbelieving, waiting for him to turn tail and run. But instead he had smiled down at her, and said *I will*, and afterwards at the Half Moon he had made a speech and said if he died at the Front his last thought would be of her.

Had his last thought been of her? No. He had not even cared enough to wonder who would have to clean the wall behind him.

She pushed her fingers into her mouth and bit down. She had never raised her voice to him while he was alive. She had tried to be an angel – because men wanted angels, didn't they? When he threw a vase of flowers at her or pinched her thigh as she shaved him or whistled 'Whiter Than the Whitewash On the Wall' for a whole day with endless vicious energy – whatever he did, she had smiled and spoken softly and never reproached him. Her forbearance was nothing, faced with his sacrifice. He had earnt that at least. Until—

She bit harder and harder, tasting salt. It wasn't fair. It wasn't *fair* . . .

Something snapped. At first, at the stinging jolt of it, she thought it was her heart breaking. But her other hand slid down her bosom, still clutching her locket, and a moment later she felt the broken ends of the chain slithering past her collar. She heard herself make a sound as though she had been struck: the sound she had never made when Jack *did* strike her. Her locket . . . Jack had given it to her before he went away the last time, and she had never taken it off, not even in the bath – and now it was broken, she had broken it, it was her fault, if she had not let herself get angry—

She stumbled towards the door. She did not know where she was going, only that she wanted to get out. She could not breathe inside this house, she could smell Jack's death, the scent of blood and brains and shit. The cold air hit the back of her throat as she stepped outside, but she did not stop. There were lights in the Holders's cottage and the old smithy; further along the houses gave way to hedges, but there was enough moonlight to see by.

Momentum carried her to the place where the road curved between the ditch and the down. There, at last, she staggered slowly to a halt. She was breathing in great gasps, as if invisible hands had been pressing on her throat: but here she could finally get a full lungful of air, and exhale it again without bursting into fresh sobs. Her hand was aching. She had kept it pressed against her heart as she ran. Now she lowered it, and uncurled her fingers. The silver oval lay in her palm, smeared with sweat in the moonlight. Somehow she had lost the chain entirely. She blinked, and tears rolled down her cheeks and dripped off her chin.

With sticky, trembling fingers, she undid the clasp. Jack's face looked up at the sky. It was the first – the only – photograph of him in uniform. It had been taken just after he signed up, and his moustache was still rather thin at the edges, his eyes unclouded, his smile as wide as a schoolboy's. Another sob rose in her throat, and she clenched her jaw, repressing it. That was the real Jack. He could not be blamed for what happened to him.

And he would not blame her, either. He would draw her into his arms and kiss her hair, the way he had when she saw him off at the railway station. *Don't cry, dear.*

She ran her thumb over his face, more tears welling up; but they came and spilt easily, without threatening to tear her apart. She could not remember the last time she had actually looked at his picture. Old Mrs Bone had warned her not to dwell on it, before she died – the interfering old witch . . . Hannah felt a fresh surge of resentment, remembering how the old woman had leant over her and tapped the photograph with a horny fingernail. 'You be careful,' she'd said. 'The brightest light casts the strongest shadows.'

Hannah had jerked the locket away, although it still lay open in her hand. She said, 'I don't know what you mean.'

'I mean, *put it away*,' Mrs Bone said. 'You don't want to attract attention.'

Hannah had turned down the corners of her mouth and shaken her head, to show that she still didn't understand. Then she had got up from the bench where she had been sitting, to go home. But Mrs Bone had caught her elbow.

'You ever seen how us old ones gather round to hear the gossip when girls like you get married? It's hot, young love. It's strong. But it isn't just people who come out of the shadows, wanting to get warm.' Suddenly she had reached out and flicked Hannah's cheek, just where a sculptor would have put a tear on a weeping angel. 'You think you can stare at that picture forever, wanting and wishing? You listen to me, girl. If you keep on eating your heart out, there'll be things coming to take his face and wear it.'

Hannah had snapped the locket shut and swayed backwards, out of her grip; but old Mrs Bone followed her, nose to nose. 'You don't want to meet them,' she said, 'trust me. So you be a good girl and put that picture away. Look at it once a year if you must, on his birthday or your wedding anniversary. Cry a little if you must. Then close it again and try to forget what he looked like.' There was a silence, and she had smacked her lips against her teeth. 'You're not from round here, are you? Where . . . ?'

'Alfriston,' Hannah said, indignant, because it was hardly a foreign country.

'Well, *he* was a local boy. *He* should've known better. Foolish.' She sighed. 'Ah, you young 'uns, you don't know when to be afraid. One day the chalk will lose its power, and then . . .' She had hesitated, as if there were more she could say; but then she had hissed out her breath and turned away, and left Hannah gaping after her like a scolded child.

But now the meddling old mare was dead – and much good had it done her, all that muttering and silliness! It hadn't saved her from falling down in the dark, and being found in the morning with her eyes frozen open, had it? They had all been scared of her, but now there was nothing to be scared of. And anyway the worst had already happened – to Hannah, to Jack, to all of them. What was there left to dread? Hannah could look at Jack's picture for as long as she wanted. Why not?

And she did, now. That smile . . . Oh, what wouldn't she give, to see him like that one more time! The moonlight made everything seem flat, as if the whole world were printed on paper; it played tricks with Hannah's eyes, as though the photograph were not a thin surface but a window, and a tiny version of Jack were imprisoned in the silver chamber. If she could let him out . . . She drew in her breath, and held it. The atmosphere was so still she felt as if she were on the brink of a great discovery.

She bent closer, squinting. There was something under the photograph. Or rather . . . she could not have put it into words, exactly: but it was as if there was impossible depth, not inside but somehow *behind* the picture. She turned her hand over, half expecting to see some glimpse of infinity. There was nothing, of course, but the sensation did not go away. Now it was in the air around her, in her ears and nose and mouth, almost audible, almost tangible . . . She lowered her gaze again, to Jack. Jack's smile. Jack's eyes.

Oh, she thought.

It was like a moment in a dream. *Was* it a dream? It had to be, because it could not be real. But if it was a dream, it was not like other dreams. She touched her thumb to her wedding ring, feeling the solid edge of it against her skin.

He was there. He was looking back at her.

He was not the same size as his picture. Or – was he? Yes – he was inside the locket, in her hand – but somehow he was only small as people in the distance are small. She could see him clearly, inside the frame – but at the same time he was approaching, gathering life, solidity, *reality* as he came . . . She could not have described it, any more than she could describe any other dream (*was* it a dream? it had to be) but it was there in front of her, happening, and even though she did not understand it she felt her heart expand, like a dry scrap of sponge dropped in water. *Jack*, she thought, and abruptly she was full of terror that if it was a dream she would wake up. But she did not.

There was a sort of shimmer. It might have been a wakening, only she was still where she had been, and – oh, *oh* . . . She was dizzy, swaying on her feet, but it was real, it was not a dream, how could it be? He was there. His uniform, his fluffy-edged moustache, his smile. His arms and his legs – well, his whole body was rather shadowy, but that hardly mattered, she did not care. She said, 'Jack . . . ?' and heard her voice catch with incredulous joy. Had she died, at dinner? Was this heaven? She wouldn't have thought she'd been good enough to go to heaven. She reached out, giddy, her head spinning.

Jack was standing in front of her. There.

He did not embrace her, or speak. She had the sense that he did not know how. His smile did not flicker, and for the first time she saw that his face was not entirely right. It was him, his face – who else could it be? But at the same time it was not. It was like a mask printed on paper, wrapped round a sphere: the contours did not sit quite where they should, and the shadows were wrong. She pushed her thumb harder against her wedding ring, because perhaps after all she *could* bear to wake up. She did not wake up.

She said again, 'Jack . . . ?' Her hand took hold of his sleeve and tugged, to get his attention, and what should have been khaki wool was slick and soft, like the skin of an overripe greengage.

He turned his eyes to her. He had looked at her before, as he came into being; but now, for the first time, he saw her. There was an instant, hardly as long as a heartbeat, when she could not move, when hope was balanced against horror, poised on an exquisite knife-edge.

Then it was over: and she knew, with swift appalled certainty, that it was not Jack; that whatever was wearing his face was not, had never been human; and that whatever it was it did not have any sense of honour, or mercy – or any awareness at all save a deep, insatiable appetite for suffering.

She did not know much, after that. A kind of numbness crept over her, like the clumsy deadness of a cramped limb. She did not exactly obey the thing, but she found herself drifting with it, as if it had sucked all volition out of her, along with her fear. Time passed, dragging uncomfortably at the roots of her hair and the beds of her fingernails. The road reversed itself, sliding under her feet, and the old smithy and the Holders's cottage went past, their lights a feeble parody of comfort in the bleak evening. She came to her front door and opened it, or perhaps Jack—*it* did, with its blurred fingers, and they went into the house. She remembered that in another life she had cared about the best china and the plate she had broken; but it was like something in a newspaper, a story that had happened to someone else. So was the room, the candle, the seat where Jack had sat, all distant and veiled, a memory of a memory . . . She could not do anything but submit to the *thing*. It was still smiling.

She went into the kitchen and unlooped the cord of the laundry rack from the hook on the wall. She did not know any more whether the thing was behind her, watching with its eyes, or whether it could simply watch with its mind as it moved on somewhere else, already searching for the next person. It did not matter. With one arm she put her whole weight on the cord, holding the rack where it was; with the other hand she wrapped the cord around her neck. Then, when it was tight, she let go.

XVII

Still Life: locket, mud (unfinished), charcoal on paper, 1921

Abruptly Kit was awake, staring into the dark of the Bone cottage, rigid and freezing. A breath, another breath. She uncurled her fingers, focusing on the tiny blind no man's land of sheet and blanket. With an effort she reached for the matches, found them by touch, and lit her candle. It was not much light, but it was enough: the room was gold and shadowy, empty, familiar. She sat up and linked her arms round her knees. Her face and chest were clammy. She could smell the sourness of her sweat. A nightmare, only a nightmare.

She took a deep breath. She had almost forgotten what they were like. Things had been better, while Florence – while they – while the two of them were lovers. Florence – even the thought of Florence – had been a bulwark against the terror. Every night, after she went home, blowing a kiss up to the studio window as she rounded the bend in the road, Kit had slept deeply, dreamlessly, like a drunkard after a long binge. Occasionally, when she did wake, she found herself smiling, remembering Florence before she remembered anything else. That didn't make her smile any more. But it was not Florence's fault that the nightmares had come back. That unlooked-for peace had been too good to last. All of it, she thought, had been too good to last.

She was cold. The shirt she had slept in was stuck to her, wet all the way through. She forced herself to get out of bed, and rummaged in the drawer for another one. The air was raw on her skin, and when she blinked her mind's eye caught a glimpse of a white, blind face, its mouth gaping, alive . . . She would not be able to sleep any more tonight. She dragged the fresh shirt over her head, and found her trousers. She pulled a blanket from the bed and wrapped it round her shoulders like a cloak. Then she picked up the candle and went downstairs to the kitchen. It was beginning to get light behind the bare trees. Light at this hour! Spring had seemed to come late this year: it still felt like the arse-end of winter. Still cold, although the days were longer. Still too early for any kind of hope . . .

She stared at the lacework of branches and the flat sky behind. It had gone past blue; now it was grey. On a sudden impulse she pushed her bare feet into her boots, grabbed her coat and went into the garden. The air was milder than she was expecting, damp and fresh, and she was glad she had come outside. She stooped to tie her laces, pushed her hands into her pockets, and walked round the side of the house, through the front gate and out onto the road.

As she walked, the exercise made her warmer; she felt her lungs expanding and the tingle of blood in her cheeks. She was not quite cheerful enough to whistle, but she felt stronger, more determined. The image of the plaster mask was fading now. Only a nightmare. She would be fine. She had lived without Florence before, she could do it again; life without Florence could hardly be worse than the War . . .

She came to the corner where the main street met the

Alfriston Road, and stopped. There was a group of people clustered outside the furthest cottage. One was Dr Manning, and one was the doctor, with his bag. A young woman with a baby on her hip was shaking her head as she comforted another, older woman. Their voices drifted in the damp breeze, coming and going on the gusts. Kit heard Dr Manning say, '. . . inquest, I suppose,' and the doctor nodded. The older woman gave a whinnying sob, and the younger one rolled her eyes a little as she went on patting her shoulder. '. . . don't deserve this,' she wailed. 'Won't it ever stop? What on earth did we fight the war *for*?'

Kit wanted to turn away. Someone was dead, it did not matter who or how. But she stayed still, staring, until the little group broke up and the two women – with the baby still sitting wide-eyed on the younger woman's hip – came towards her. Usually the villagers did not say good morning, let alone stop to speak; but when Kit put out her hand and blurted out, 'What happened?' they drew to a halt, glancing at each other.

'It's Mrs Smith,' the younger one said. 'There was an accid—'

'Killed herself,' the older woman croaked, at exactly the same moment. 'Oh, I can't bear to think of it! Just like her husband, when he came home – only he had a reason, he didn't want to live with no legs and one arm and you can't blame him—'

'Hush now, Ma,' the young woman said, sharply.

But the other woman went on, leaning towards Kit in a waft of rancid breath. 'I found her this morning – she strangled herself in the kitchen – oh, it was horrible, heaven knows I'll never see a wet sheet the same way again—'

'Stop it!' The young woman pulled her away. 'An accident,' she repeated, glaring over her shoulder as she marched her mother down the road.

Hannah Smith. Pale, softly-spoken Hannah Smith, with her washed-out prettiness and watery eyes. She had never said very much, hardly more than *please* and *thank you*, but she had always returned Kit's sheets as clean as a new sketchpad, and accepted the money for them with a duck of her head as if it were alms. Then she would scurry away, clutching at the locket round her neck, her long black skirt trailing in the mud. Kit took a foolish step towards the cottage – the front door was still open – before she mastered herself. Whatever kind, clumsy thing she might have said, it was too late now. But Christ, what a way to go! Surely there were quicker ways, if you wanted to end it all . . .

She swung round and strode onwards, without knowing or caring where she was going. If only she could see Florence! For a moment she actually considered knocking on the door of the vicarage. She would apologise – say whatever it would take for Florence to forgive her – anything, if it would make Florence take her into her arms . . . But she did not turn back. It was not that simple. Florence was engaged to be married, and Kit did not need her pity. She would not cringe and beg.

She came to the end of the village, to the place where the road curved on its way to the sea. From here you could look back past the church, to the distant slope of the down where the Face had been. In the dull grey light it had disappeared entirely.

Something gleamed in the middle of the road. She stooped to pick it up.

It was Hannah Smith's locket. She recognised the engraving on the front. Had it been thrown away, or only lost? She hesitated. Then, because Hannah was dead and could not mind any more, she undid the clasp.

She was expecting to see a photograph of a young man in uniform. She braced herself to see the brave, universal smile of a soldier going to war, pretending to be a hero. Or it might be a drawing, or a painted miniature, or a brief, scrappy lock of hair. She held the locket very carefully as she parted the two halves, in case anything fell out.

It was a photograph; but there was a stain across it, where the face should have been.

She squinted at it. In the background, a little out of focus, were trees, with the sun shining through the leaves, and the soft shape of a church tower, and the horizon. But the whole foreground was obscured by a dark irregular blotch, a burn or an ink blot. Poor Hannah Smith! Had this been the only picture she had of her husband? And she had kept it anyway, close to her heart, even though it was spoilt . . .

Kit was about to snap it shut again, and lay it carefully down in the road where she had found it; but as she did so, she saw that the edge of the frame had left a sooty line across the pad of her thumb. Perhaps she had jumped to the wrong conclusion, perhaps the damage was new. She touched the photograph gently with her index finger, testing to see if it would wipe away. It did; at least, her finger came away dark. The stuff was slightly sticky, like eye-black or the grease from charred meat. She wiped it hastily on her coat and then wished she had not, because it stank, with a putrid undernote like gangrene. The paper had felt thinner than it should, almost damp, clinging like a cobweb to her finger. Perhaps something had dissolved the ink on the surface, and it was bleeding . . .

Carefully, without knowing why it mattered, she fished for her handkerchief and dabbed it over the black stain, trying not to tear through the photograph. The smell rose, so strong she could almost taste it. For some reason it reminded her of Paris, and her nightmares, but she did not give herself time to wonder why. After a few seconds her handkerchief was ruined. She threw it away without a second thought, staring down at the picture. She had not managed to erase the shadow entirely, but now all of the photograph was more or less visible. It was distorted, as if seen through old wavering glass, bulging towards the place where the stain had been thickest, but the foreground was clear, and sharp-edged. It showed the yard in front of the church, in the sunlight, on a spring day long ago; and it was empty.

Her mind stuttered. What— why . . . ? But before the question took shape, a deeper, colder part of her knew the answer. Of course it was not a picture of no one, standing in front of the church. Why would Hannah wear a photograph of no one?

It was simple. There had been a man in the photograph, and now there was not.

She flinched, and the locket fell to the ground. It was not possible. It was hysterical, even to think . . . But as her hands rose to her face, she caught that stench again, the gas-gangrene stink of decay; and in spite of herself she imagined something – something with a stolen face, heroic, grinning – a *thing* – rising through the layers of silver and gelatin, dragging the whole photograph out of shape, until finally it tore itself free. An unclean, appalling thing, leaving foul traces of its touch as it came . . . And then, *then* where had it gone?

She took a few wavering steps towards the verge, on spongy legs. It was impossible. She was worse than Septimus hallucinating corpses at King's Cross. The picture had corroded somehow, that was all – and Hannah – Hannah had ended up dead in her own kitchen, by her own hand . . .

When her vision cleared she was sitting on the grass, her head between her knees. For a long time she watched the tangle of roots and long leaves, where nothing moved but the slow slide of a dew drop, where the shades of green and brown seemed to separate into finer and finer distinctions of colour and light.

Her old drawing teacher had died long ago; but in her head, apropos of nothing, he looked at her sternly over his spectacles. *To be a good artist,* he had said to her once, *you have to look past what you're expecting, and see what's there.*

XVIII

Landscape with Face, watercolour on paper, 1921

Florence sat in the drawing room, trying to darn a sock. Now that her hands were better, she had no excuse not to be useful; she tried to smile as she did it, even though no one was watching, sustaining her expression with the same dutiful constancy as she would have sustained a note in a hymn. How she hated socks! She had tried to knit so many in the early days of the War, and made nothing but a limp mess of grey knots; she had thought darning might be easier, but there was something about the shape, and the thought of Horace's feet, that set her teeth on edge. Although they were clean, the memory of damp, gamy heels and horny toenails seemed to cling to them, like a smell. But she was grateful – happy. Most women did not have a man to look after; certainly not a fiancé . . .

Her fiancé. Once the word would have been intoxicating, redolent of yearning and excitement. It made her think of those schoolgirl games they played in the first form, bending their heads over an exercise book and calculating the number of letters in names: *who will I marry, when will I marry him? How many children will we have?* It should at least have reminded her that she was important after all, she was not destined to be boring lonely Florence Stock but someone's wife. The vicar's wife – Horace's wife . . . Like Imogen. When Florence was a little girl, she had always hankered after everything Imogen owned: her pinned-up hair, her frocks, her beauty. Now she squinted her mind's eye, recalling that childish envy, and tried to summon a faint veil of glamour to draw across Horace's real face. Imo had loved him: and that was almost, almost enough to make him seem handsome – almost enough to make her think she might, one day, be able to love him too. *Fiancé*, she repeated to herself, trying to imagine how Imogen would have said it, *my fiancé* . . .

She could hear his voice now, muffled by the wall between the drawing room and the study: a long drone, with the same inflection that he used for his sermons. After what seemed a long time, it was overlaid by another voice, a woman's, rising higher and higher. A crescendo was followed by a pause; then the woman spoke again, while another female voice burst into sobs. Florence bit her lip, listening. There had been a lot of weeping over the last few days. Poor Hannah Smith had not struck Florence as the sort of person who had many friends, or was generally loved; but her death had been horrible, and it was hardly surprising that so many people were upset. Since it had happened a steady stream of parishioners had come to see Horace, all with gaunt faces and – apparently – short tempers. On the first few occasions Florence had knocked on the door to offer tea; but every time she had been sent away, and the looks that she had received told her plainly that she was still a newcomer to Haltington, and this was not her business. But *why*? she thought now, setting down her darning, after all she had been here for years, and she was going to be the vicar's wife . . . Surely she could offer a different sort of comfort – feminine, maternal?

She got to her feet, and walked softly into the passage. But both women's voices were raised now, while Horace's thin baritone grumbled underneath like a bad harmony; if she knocked and went in, they would all turn and stare, suddenly united in common outrage at the interruption. She stood undecided, chewing her lip, and after a moment the voices quietened again until she could make out distinct words. 'Mrs Flitworth,' Horace said, with a sigh, 'you have my heartfelt sympathy. It must have been a terrible shock when you found her. But we must put our faith in God—'

'But, Vicar, can't you *do*—'

The other woman burst out at the same time, 'I told you it would be no use, Jenny—' and then for a few moments there was a jumble of argument, an overlapping back and forth that made it impossible to make out what they were saying.

'. . . our *faith*,' Horace repeated, 'in *God*!'

He had almost shouted it. Now there was a silence. 'Very well,' Mrs Flitworth said, with great dignity – Florence imagined her clasping her hands below her bosom, and tilting her chin – 'in that case, Vicar, we won't intrude on you any longer.'

The door banged open. Florence stumbled backwards, caught off guard; she had expected a longer leave-taking, and it was too late to pretend she had not been standing directly outside. She smiled weakly as the two women passed her, looking her up and down as they went. Both were red-eyed, but the impression they gave was not of grief but fury, as if Horace had not only disappointed but insulted them.

They did not wait to be seen out. The front door slammed, setting off a faint echo from the grandfather clock in the hall. Horace said, 'Oh, these— these *bloody* . . .' and stopped. There were footsteps, and he came into sight through the doorway. He looked older than ever. 'Florence? I did not know you were there.'

'I came to see if I could— if there was anything you needed.'

'That was kind.' He paced to the window and stared out at the muddy lawn.

It was not exactly an invitation, but it was better than nothing. She took a few diffident steps into the room. 'I suppose,' she said, 'it is very difficult. About poor Hannah Smith's funeral, I mean, when she— when some people say it wasn't an accident . . .'

'Ha!' Perhaps his own venom had shocked him, for he cleared his throat as if it had been involuntary, like a cough or a sneeze. 'If only it were that,' he said. 'No, suicides have been buried like everyone else for nearly forty years, my dear.'

'Mrs Flitworth seemed very . . . cross.'

'Oh, this *place*!' he said, spinning on his heel and flinging his arm in the air, as if to appeal to heaven. 'I remember when I was offered the parish – I was pleased, you know, I might have gone to Birmingham! I wish I had. I never thought it would be more benighted here – more superstitious – than the city slums.'

'I thought you liked the superstitions?'

'As a scholar,' he said, 'I find them quaint. Charming, even, in their place. The Face is picturesque, and the thurlath are like something out of *Ghost Stories of an Antiquary*. But for people – apparently sensible people, in the twentieth century – to *believe* them . . . ! It's absurd. They think this terrible thing with Hannah Smith is somehow— well, goodness knows what they think. And they are importuning me to behave as if I think so too. Do you know, as a concession, I offered to write to the bishop? I said I could ask if it would be unbecoming for me, a minister of Christ, to go up to the Face and – well, take a spade and clean it up a bit, just to keep them happy. And do you know what they said? That it would be no use! *That's* the sort of gratitude I get, for indulging them against my better judgement.'

'I see,' Florence said.

'It is infuriating to see them in the grip of this hysteria. I don't know what to do.' She drew breath to answer, but he ploughed on; it had not, after all, been a request for her advice. 'As if there were anything different about what they suffer here, compared to the rest of this country! There is nothing especially terrible or haunted about this valley, it is exactly like everywhere else—'

'I thought you said the Downs were special,' Florence said, 'because of the landscape. Like sacred ground—'

'Oh, for heaven's sake, Florence!' He threw himself into his chair. 'Everywhere has its stories. Everywhere is ancient, come to that! They are like stupid children, imagining that their particular nightmares are real. You surely do not think,' he added, with sudden sarcasm, 'that I should perform some kind of *exorcism* at their behest?'

She realised just in time that it was not a rhetorical question. 'No,' she said, 'no, of course not. I am sorry, Horace.'

He inhaled, laying his hands flat on his desk as if to steady it. 'Poor little Hannah Smith,' he said at last. 'I married them, you know, in 1916. Ours will be the first wedding in Haltington since then.'

'Oh.'

He sighed and bowed his head. 'Forgive me, my dear. I felt so useless during the War. When it was over, I thought that I could go back to serving my little flock, as I had done before . . . but now this! If they do not trust me . . . I sometimes wonder if I have outlived any purpose I might have had.'

'Oh, Horace . . .' She did not think; she found herself beside him, taking his cold, bony hand in her own. 'Of course you're not useless. You mustn't think like that.'

'Certainly,' he said, rallying, 'I can be good to you, my dear. That is something. To know that I can support you, uphold you – give you children, perhaps—'

'Yes,' she said, too quickly, 'yes – there will be children, won't there? That's what marriage is for, isn't it—'

'We will accept the workings of Providence,' he said, his hand stiffening a little in hers. 'Naturally you hope to be a mother. That is to your credit. But we must submit to the will of God.'

'Yes. Yes, of course. That's what I meant.' She clenched her jaw; it would not be tactful, to talk too much about children, too soon. 'We will have faith,' she said, 'together.'

'Quite,' he said, and – a beat too late, like a bad musician – he patted her hand. 'Quite.'

She looked into his eyes. Poor Horace, doing his futile best for his parishioners, and for her. It was not his fault he was not Kit. It was not his fault that everything she wanted from him was because he was male, and not because of any quality of character or affinity between them. It was not his fault, that no one loved him. He was kind. He would look after her. He would marry her. God willing, he would give her children . . .

Without thinking, she leant forward and pressed her mouth against his.

She did not know what she was expecting. Indeed, she had not had time between the intention and the action consciously to expect anything: it was only when he cleared his throat, his closed lips moving under her kiss, that she knew she had anticipated something else. She still, in spite of herself, shifted towards him, fumbling for his hand and drawing it towards her breast, so that he could cup it gently with one hand while he slid the other arm around her, and took her weight. But he did not – of course he did not, he was not Kit! Instead he grunted and stiffened, his fingers splaying into a jabbing fan, and swayed backwards in his chair as if the meeting of their mouths was likely to smother him; and then they were staring at each other, frozen, and Florence wished she could die.

Mother had told her once that she must never let a man get too close to her, unless he was her husband. They could not control themselves; it was not that they were evil, only that the force of their passions could overwhelm them, and it was Florence's job to ensure that they were never tempted. Like Kit's friend, the one who had kissed her in the road, and then tugged at her blouse. That horrible struggle had been her fault, because she should never have been so familiar with him in the first place. She should have known better. But now—

Now, when she wanted Horace to behave like a man, he did not. How easy, how shockingly easy it would be if he kissed her back. If he kissed her and caressed her and – and *took* her, not like Kit but like a man! Even there in his study, on the threadbare rug, under the foxed Victorian prints . . . She could have lain back and pretended not to be there at all, letting him do his business – and then tomorrow, tomorrow there might already be a seed taking root . . . It would be worth it all, then. She could stand at the altar glowing with her secret, knowing she had made a good bargain. But he did not behave like a man in the slightest, he only looked at her in utter amazement, shocked at her lack of decency – although it struck her, then, how very like a man *that* was.

With a sigh that seemed to come all the way from his ankles, he disengaged himself from her entirely. He said, 'Florence, this was— most unlooked for . . .'

She could not answer. What on earth had possessed her? She could not even mutter an apology.

'And,' Horace said, as if it had only just dawned on him, 'in broad daylight . . . !'

For an instant she considered taking the dried flowers out of the arrangement on the window sill and cramming them into her mouth, to give herself the excuse of lunacy; an asylum in Eastbourne seemed, in that moment, preferable to life with Horace. But she was not mad. She got to her feet, noticing a ladder in her stockings as she stood up. Somehow she managed to say, 'I had better leave you to your work.' Then she left, shutting the door behind her very gently, hating him and herself with a force that made her ears ring.

Mother would have said that she did not deserve such a good man. But Mother would have been wrong. They deserved each other. She deserved a man who looked at her as if he were just about to impose a penance; and he deserved a wife who would lie rigid underneath him, yearning for a lover of her own sex.

She could not bear to stay under this roof. She went into the kitchen and out of the back door before Mrs Reed had time to look up from her pie; she strode across the lawn to the gate, wrenched it open, and half stumbled and half ran through the band of trees, and out into the wide grey light of the bare hill. She had no hat nor coat, but she was sweating, and her collar and cuffs felt as tight as bandages. She paused, at last, fumbling for her buttons.

From here she could look down and see the vicarage in its hollow, its flint walls dark, the garden touched with the first transparent green of spring. A wave of claustrophobia swept over her. Would she spend the rest of her life in that house? *Could* she . . . ? Her gaze slid sideways, past the scattered roofs of the village and the Half Moon with its column of smoke, to the closed, unlit windows of the Bone house. What was Kit doing, at this moment?

She had wanted to believe that love was enough; and Kit had said to her, *Then you're a fucking idiot.*

She threw her head back, and shouted. Her voice was flat and harsh and loud enough to shock her, as though she had discharged a gun; but that only made her put her head back and yell again. Let them all hear, and think she was crazy. Let Kit hear! Damn them all – Kit, and Horace and Mrs Flitworth, and Phoebe, and Imogen who had died, and Mother who would turn in her grave – all of them, damn them, even poor Hannah Smith who had never liked Florence anyway . . . She spun in a circle, bellowing her fury into the unresponsive air. The ground was irregular underfoot, and as she caught the heel of her boot she went over on her ankle, and her wordless cry changed to a yelp of pain. Damn it, damn . . . She dropped to one knee. The Face, the bloody Face! It was only just visible – a few bald patches of chalk under stringy grass – but clear enough to see that she had been standing on it, and that was why she had missed her footing. And damn you too, she said to it, and then aloud, since she could: 'Damn you, *damn* you, you stupid – bloody— ! Why don't you – just *fuck off*— ?' She was not sure she had ever said *fuck* before; or not as an oath, anyway. She pounded on the ground with her fists, still swearing, until her hands hurt and she was out of breath, sore and sweating and foolish.

She sat back on her haunches, panting. Surely something must happen now. Surely her anger must have changed the world, somehow. There should be a cataclysm, or a climax, or at least an answer. But there was only silence, and the pain in her own hands, the scent of salt from the sea and the dead chalk underneath her, made of ancient, countless bones.

Kit sat in front of the fire, holding Hannah's locket, watching the flames. She had hardly moved for three days, except to the outhouse and to make tea – and, occasionally, to fetch wood from the log pile. She could not eat or work, and if she slept it was only the slow drifting of her mind, a long dazed blink between leaping flames and glowing embers. The only reality was the endless need to keep the fire burning; but no matter how high she stoked it, she could not get properly warm. Even Hannah's locket did not seem to take on her body heat; it sat in her palm as slick and cold as if she had only just picked it up.

She could not stop thinking. She could not chase away the image of Hannah, hanged in her own kitchen. She remembered Phoebe, saying her mother's picture had come alive; and the smoke that had coalesced around Julien's mask as it hung in the bonfire; and Horace's description, *a wandering, hungry thing that resembles a man* . . . Whenever there was a noise outside she jerked upright: imagining first Hannah knocking, ready to ask with that ducked-head timidity for Kit's dirty laundry, and then— then someone, something else . . . If only Florence would come! Kit would have welcomed her shamelessly, apologised shamelessly, pulled her into her arms and kissed her shamelessly. That, at least, would have driven away this stubborn chill. But she did not expect Florence to come, really. It was too late for that. No, what leapt inside her when she heard the rattle of the garden gate was not anticipation but dread, so that she clutched the arms of her chair, bracing herself. Not Hannah, but . . . Then, as the silence rose again, and she knew the sound had only been a gust of wind or a bird calling, she sank back down. She did not open the locket; she wanted to believe that the empty picture was only out of focus, that the stain had only been an ink blot, after all, and that her fear was not rational but neurotic. It would pass. There was no such thing as a thurlath; there were no hungry spirits, there was nothing that could take on an inanimate likeness, and come alive, come seeking . . .

She could run away, she supposed, the way she had finally run back to London when she could not bear Paris any more. The prospect of a London hotel – with central heating and snowy bed linen, Martinis and mock turtle soup – made her shiver with longing, wishing she could snap her fingers and be transported there. But she could not bring herself to stand up, let alone pack and walk all the way to the station. And, she thought grimly, she could not always run away.

After a while – it was morning, or maybe early afternoon, although she was not sure which day – the fire died down and she saw that the log basket beside the hearth was empty again. For a long time she looked at it, huddling in her blanket, hoping it would magically refill itself like a porridge bowl from a fairy tale. Then, with a groan, still wearing the blanket around her shoulders like a cloak, she got to her feet and carried it outside. It bumped against her heels as she trudged to the woodpile. She slung in as many logs as she could manage, and then staggered back into the kitchen with it, her teeth already chattering. She paused beside the range, setting the basket on the nearest chair, and reached for the kettle. More tea would warm her up. Then she ducked to the cupboard and took out the bottle of brandy instead. She poured a slosh into an enamel mug, and, on second thoughts, filled it to the brim.

The back door opened. She whirled round, so quickly the brandy slopped over her hand; and then huffed with relief and sucked the liquid from her fingers, because it was only Phoebe. 'Shit!' she said. 'You made me jump.'

Phoebe stepped neatly into the kitchen and shut the door behind her. 'Hullo,' she said.

'What are you doing here?' She tugged at her collar with her free hand, hoping that Phoebe was too far away to smell the faint unwashed scent that clung to her skin.

'I came to see if you were all right.'

Kit gave a bark of laughter. 'Bless you,' she said, with a heartiness that she did not feel, 'I'm perfectly all right, thank you. Why shouldn't I be?'

Phoebe did not smile. 'Did you hear about Hannah Smith? She's dead.'

'Yes, I heard.'

There was a silence. 'You know—' Phoebe began to say.

But Kit could not let her finish; she could not bear to hear it said aloud, it would make it real, they would look at each other and she would not be able to deny it any more. She said, wildly, 'Shouldn't you be at school?'

Phoebe hesitated, as if she was not deceived by Kit's attempt to change the subject, but after a moment she shrugged. 'There weren't any lessons this afternoon, there was a country dancing competition. Our form was doing "Mr Beveridge's Maggot". They won't care that I wasn't there.' She leant on the back of the chair, twisting one ankle round the other.

Kit licked the last trace of brandy off her hand, and then drained her cup. It slipped down easily, like water but warmer, sweeter. That was the ticket. She should have thought of alcohol earlier, instead of brewing interminable pots of tea. She savoured the fire in her mouth and throat. Already it had drawn a soft curtain between her mind's eye and the memory of Hannah's locket. She could feel the small weight of it in her pocket, but it was not cold any more, she had probably imagined that. 'Well,' she said, 'I'm all right. Don't worry about me.' She refilled the cup, refusing to meet Phoebe's interested gaze. Why shouldn't she get drunk, in her own house, if she wanted to?

'Do you want me to leave?'

'No! Please stay—' She cut herself off with a laugh, but it was too late. Phoebe was looking at her with a new expression, something between curiosity and triumph. 'If you want,' she added, without conviction. Christ, how she wanted company! Florence would have been best, but anyone would do.

'Can I have one?'

'What?'

'One of – whatever you're drinking.'

'You want *brandy*?'

'Only a little. A taste.'

'Phoebe, your father wouldn't let you have tea. I hardly think—'

'But you did.' Phoebe added, with a glint, 'And you don't care what my father thinks of you.'

'I don't want to get a name for corrupting innocence.' But she knew as she said it that she would give in. One taste would hardly hurt, would it? Her own mother had given her wine and water at Christmas and New Year from when she was six; not enough to intoxicate a gnat, but as a rite of passage. She thought of her mother's hands, pouring, and the dark cloud of wine spreading into the water. Mother's hands had been beautiful, slender and smooth and covered with rings that blazed in the candlelight. You would have thought they would be as heavy as gauntlets, but her touch was so gentle you hardly felt it. *Merry Christmas, darling . . .*

Kit reached for another cup, took the bottle out and poured a bare half-inch into the bottom. 'Shall I top it up with water?'

'No, thank you.'

'Here. *Santé*.'

'Thank you.' Phoebe took the barest sip, and narrowed her eyes, considering.

'Good?'

'I'm not sure yet.'

Kit balanced her cup on the logs in the basket and carried

the whole thing carefully into the sitting room. She knelt down in front of the hearth, among the mess of torn newspaper and advertising leaflets, to stoke the fire.

Phoebe appeared after a moment, her eyes already shining, her mouth rosy and wet. She sank on to the hearthrug opposite Kit, her legs folded neatly underneath her, her gymslip riding up over her black stockings. Kit brushed the flecks of wood and bark from her trousers and sat back on her haunches. When she looked at Phoebe she did not want to look away. Perhaps it was the brandy, adding a softening glimmer to everything she looked at; or perhaps it was simply that Phoebe was so beguiling. If that were a picture – if you had got the colours right – you could stretch out your hands and warm yourself by it . . .

Phoebe met her gaze. 'Am I beautiful?' she said.

Another time Kit would have told her not to fish for compliments. 'Yes.'

'More beautiful than Aunt Florence?'

'Much more beautiful than Florence.' There was satisfaction in saying it; and why shouldn't she say it? It was true.

'Do you love her?'

'No.'

'Did you love her?'

'No,' Kit said. 'Let's not talk about Florence.'

'Why not? If you don't love her—'

'It's boring, that's all.'

Phoebe lowered her gaze. She lifted her cup to her mouth with a sort of steady concentration, as if it might be dangerous.

'When you're older,' Kit said, 'you'll understand.'

'That's what Miss Timothy said.'

'Who?'

'A mistress at school. She said we couldn't understand erotic love. I asked why not, when we're older than Juliet.'

'Did you?'

'It's true. Juliet was fourteen.' She turned her cup thoughtfully in her hands. 'Miss Timothy said we would never feel it, now that all the men are dead.'

'She's probably right. There've been articles about it in the papers.' Portia had mocked them in her letters: *the Mail is awfully, thrillingly terrified of the natural consequences, I think they must imagine hordes of marauding women so desperate for cock that they will pounce and paw at any man who comes within ten yards. Ugh! I on the other hand rather approve of the situation. Most women would be better off with some sensible, well-brought-up Lesbian after all . . .*

'Come, loving Night,' Phoebe murmured, 'come, loving, black-browed Night . . .'

'I beg your pardon?'

Phoebe smiled, and Kit found herself looking away in a sudden, strange confusion. 'I like this,' Phoebe said, 'the brandy,' and Kit heard her swallow.

'Don't drink it too fast.'

'I'm not. It tastes like Christmas pudding. Papa says that the Quakers called Christmas pudding the invention of the Whore of Babylon.'

Kit snorted. Dr Manning wouldn't have known the Whore of Babylon if she had offered to suck his cock; but at least she caught herself before she said so.

'I don't think,' Phoebe said, 'I want to get married. I don't like men at all.'

'Well, you don't know any, do you? Only your father. And Christ knows— I mean, not every man is like that. You'll be one of the lucky ones, you'll see, with your face—'

'Do you know lots of nice men?'

'Some,' she said, although after Muckle she was not sure she could trust any of them.

'And do you want to marry them?'

Kit opened her mouth, and shut it again. 'That's different.'

'Why?'

'Because – I'm different.'

'Why are you different?'

'Oh, come on, Phoebe.' Kit shook her head, half laughing, and gestured at herself: her short hair, her trousers, her dishevelled, open-collared shirt. But Phoebe only tilted her head and waited. There were tiny leaping flames reflected in her pupils, almost too small to see; Kit wondered suddenly if all the light in the room came from those eyes . . . 'I mean,' she said, finally, 'I'm not like your Aunt Florence. She wanted me because there was no one else. I saw it in her eyes the first time we met. She wanted to want me. I could have been anyone. I'd do, that was all. Then your father offered her what she really needs. She can be someone's wife.'

'And you?'

'I want . . .' Too late, she wondered if it was wrong to be talking like this to a child, even a child as clever as Phoebe. But then, if they had been studying *Romeo and Juliet* . . . 'Just love,' she said at last. 'Love between equals.'

'Between women, you mean.'

'I – yes,' she said, conceding defeat. 'I'm what the medical books would call an invert. That means that – that there's something inside me that bends the wrong way. I can't help it.'

'Do you want to?'

She had turned to stare into the fire, searching for words; now she shot a look at Phoebe's face. Could she – should she . . . ? But she could not summon the energy to make up a lie. 'Not exactly. But it would be easier. Simpler.'

'Not if there aren't any men.'

'Well, no. No, I suppose now – maybe now it's – useful.'

She found herself laughing. Was she really talking like this to a fifteen-year-old, a vicar's daughter?

'You can have *love between equals*,' Phoebe said, with precise emphasis. 'And it doesn't matter that there aren't enough men. You can have –' she drew a breath '– true love acted.'

'What?'

But Phoebe did not repeat the phrase. She drained her cup and held it out, a little breathless. 'Can I have some more?'

'Phoebe! No.'

'I think I must have a naturally strong head.'

'Don't be absurd. And even if you did, you can't go home stinking like a sailor.'

'I don't have to go home for ages. Papa didn't know about the country dancing, and he thinks I play lacrosse after school.' Kit smiled at the thought of Phoebe pelting up and down a lacrosse pitch, yelling, and Phoebe caught her eye, acknowledging the incongruity. 'We've got hours yet.' She got to her feet, unfolding herself with a grace that was the very opposite of a lacrosse fiend's blunt muscularity. She picked her way fluently through the scattered scraps of paper to the door, plucking Kit's cup from her hands as she went, swinging both by the handles as she disappeared into the kitchen. There was the sound of the cupboard door, and the bottle thumping on the table. Glass chinked on a brim; liquid glugged.

'I mean it,' Kit called, struggling to her feet, 'you mustn't have any more.'

Phoebe came back in. 'Look,' she said, 'only one cup,' and put it into Kit's hands with exaggerated care.

'Thank you.' She had not wanted any more, but now there was nothing to do but to drink it. This would be the last one. Whatever happened, she was not going to end up like one of the shell-shocked dipsomaniacs that Portia insisted on buying drinks for in the Café Royal. She sank down on to the settee, pulling the blanket closer around her shoulders.

Phoebe smiled. She put another log on the fire, and jabbed at it with a poker until it gave out a fountain of sparks. Then she sat easily at the far end of the settee, stretching her legs out until her stockinged feet lay in Kit's lap, as if it were the most natural thing in the world.

The grey of the sky outside was starting to turn blue. The window pane rattled as the trees swung in the wind. After a moment Phoebe leant her head back against the cushions and shut her eyes.

Kit did not move. She had lifted her left arm awkwardly as Phoebe settled herself, and now she did not quite know what to do with it, with Phoebe's feet in her lap; but it was too late to protest, or make an excuse to get up . . . She looked at Phoebe's feet, feeling their heat where they weighed on her thighs. One stocking had a hole in it, and a single pink toe peeped out, neat and childish. A grown-up would be embarrassed, but Phoebe had not even seemed to notice.

Was she asleep? Kit held her breath, listening. No sound but the fire and the wind, and – yes, there – the very softest note of all, Phoebe's exhalation, quieter than Kit's own heartbeat. The outside world receded. It was as if beyond these walls everything had ceased to exist: there was no Haltington, no Sussex – no place where Hannah Smith lay, her body waiting to be buried, no Muckle, no Face carved into the down. There was only this moment, vital and precious. Suddenly Kit remembered sitting with her mother, like this, beside the fire – although she had been younger than Phoebe, she had only been twelve when her mother died. What was it like, to have a daughter? To sit in silent companionship, with a child you loved more than anything on earth? A different sort of love, the sort of love Kit would probably never feel. No wonder Florence wanted . . . No. No more of that. She took a deep breath, as if she were bracing herself for a pain: then she let herself relax, taking pleasure in the simple weight and warmth of Phoebe's feet on her lap, her stillness, her mere presence. The contact of two bodies, without demands or expectations, as simple as a cat and its kitten, as brandy and firelight. With a strange, hesitant joy she lowered her arm and let her hand rest – gently, so gently she could hardly feel the moment when she made contact – on Phoebe's ankle. Phoebe smiled, without opening her eyes.

How lovely she was, Kit thought. What a portrait she would make, just like that: her face lit by the fire, her hair falling out of its plait and shining as if sparks were caught in it, while the cold daylight outlined the window on the other side of the room . . . *Study in Gold and Silver*. Oh yes, Kit would like to paint that, to paint her . . . Not another bloody still life. *That*. She felt a deep, unmistakable ache of ambition rise in her chest, raw as the onset of flu. A real painting could never be as good as the one she could see now: but it would be real.

She shifted in her seat. Phoebe murmured, and lifted her feet a little to allow Kit to move and resettle. Those planes of skin and shadow, her cheek, her forehead . . . ! Ever since Paris, Kit had despised the thought of portraiture: what was it but a covering, a painted surface over the terrible fragility of it all, the ease with which bone could be crushed in on itself, eyes could be blinded, tongues ripped out? But now . . . was there, after all, something to be said for simple beauty?

Her heart had started to pound. She felt her breath become shallower and faster, and tried to master it. Florence had been beautiful, and she had flinched from painting

Florence. Why was this time – why was Phoebe different? But it was, she was. Was it the brandy on an empty stomach, softening everything, reducing the universe to this enchanted circle of firelight? Or Phoebe herself, not only her perfect face but her youth, her self-possession, her lack of fear? Or something else?

She thought: *hope*. It caught her off-guard, as if she had never heard or said the word before. She knew she had tensed, because Phoebe's eyes flickered open in a brief look of enquiry. 'Sorry,' she said. And before she could think better of it, she leant sideways, stretching for the nearest scrap of waste paper. She caught it by her fingertips, and then dug in her pocket for the nub of pencil that was always there. She was afraid – as afraid as the first time she went into the Antiques Room – but she was not sure whether she was more afraid of drawing or failing. Best not to dwell on it; best to ignore the fizz of nerves in her fingers, and her breath coming short. She laid the paper against her knee – it was an advertising leaflet for biscuits with a blank space on the last page, just large enough – and with a trembling hand drew a rough pencil line.

How easy it was, the first line, the first shadow! She did not dare stare too long at what she was doing, in case she jinxed herself; instead she kept her eyes and fingers moving, and let the shapes emerge on the paper as if they were invisible ink, drawn out by the heat of the fire. *Was* it only drunkenness, and Phoebe's elfin loveliness? Or was it something else too, something about Hannah's locket, and the chill outside, and not wanting to be ruled by fear? She was so tired of being frightened . . . Or even something less valiant, because Florence had wanted to sit for her, and Florence had not bothered to come? It didn't matter. She let the pencil go where it wanted to go, and saw that it knew better than she did.

After a long time – or what seemed like a long time, although she had always sketched quickly, and perhaps it was only a few minutes – she let her hand come to a halt.

It was a good drawing, in spite of the jaggedness of the lines and the wavering dent in the paper where she had been resting it on her knee. Not a masterpiece, but a good drawing – a start, she thought, with sudden incredulous triumph, a start, only a start . . . ! She felt her throat tighten, like the prelude to a shout of victory.

Phoebe opened her eyes. Swiftly Kit shaded one iris, a darker ring around the rays that encircled the pupil, before Phoebe frowned and sat up, reaching out. 'What are you doing?'

'A drawing.'

'Of me?'

'Do you mind? I said you were beautiful.'

There was a silence. Phoebe stared, not at the paper, but at Kit, her expression unreadable. For the first time Kit wondered if it had been a terrible liberty, to sketch her without asking first. But it was not mere pique in her eyes; it was more considering than that, as if she were contemplating a mental arithmetic problem.

Kit said, conscious of her cowardice, 'I have to go outside.'

'Outside? Oh. Yes.'

'Too much brandy,' she said, thinking she was joking; but as she moved to the door, letting the drawing flutter on to the hearth rug, she felt her head spin. Damn it. Perhaps she should eat something, after all. 'I won't be long.'

Phoebe nodded. Cravenly Kit smiled at her, reaching out with her fingers as if to pluck a thread that stretched between them; and after a second's hesitation Phoebe smiled back, as if she could see the same thread gleaming in the firelight, fine as her hair.

Kit pissed as quickly as she could, and hurried back towards the house. There was an unpleasant elasticity in her knees, and she slowed down, in case she tripped and went head over heels. Under the heavy afternoon sky was the high sweep of the down where the Face had been. It was gone now. She paused, briefly forgetting her drawing of Phoebe, to look. She told herself it had been gone for a long time; but there was a curious absence, a new flatness to the grass, like a velvet dress packed away after a death . . .

She pushed open the back door and slammed it behind her. She rubbed the goosepimples from her arms, blowing air through her lips. Only the cold. And too much brandy. Her cup was on the table, with an inch of liquid left in it. She picked it up, then put it down again without drinking. Enough was enough. She was drunk already; it was time to send Phoebe home, and go to bed herself. Or, at least, sit alone in the parlour, poring over her drawing, marvelling at it . . .

She put her hands in her pockets – why did it take an effort of will not to drink, when she was not a drunkard? – and shouldered the door open to the sitting room. 'Phoebe,' she said, 'it's getting late—'

She stopped.

Phoebe had drawn the curtains, and built up the fire so that it blazed, throwing golden light and shadows into every corner. She had moved the settee, so that it faced the door. And she was lying upon it, naked.

She was exquisite. Kit saw that, even through the haze of disbelief: slender and leggy, almost flat-chested, her skin so pale and fine-grained that the pressure marks left by suspenders and bodice stood out like dark blossom. She had one hand over her sex, like a classical nude; but as Kit stared she took it away, and put both arms behind her head, lifting her breasts – the beginnings of breasts – into sharper relief. Kit did not look at the place she had uncovered, the place between her legs.

Kit took a very, very slow breath. 'What are you doing?' she said.

'Acting true love.'

A silence. In the road outside there was the roar of an automobile. Its headlamps swept past the curtains, changing the timbre of the light for an instant before it went past. Kit swallowed, conscious of the thick mechanism of throat and tongue as if they did not belong to her. She said, 'Do you want me to draw you again, like that?'

'Draw me, or – whatever you want.'

'What the hell does that mean?'

Phoebe flinched; but she held her pose, defiantly statuesque. 'I'm more beautiful than Aunt Florence,' she said. 'Don't you want me?'

'Phoebe – you're a *child* . . .'

'I'm older than—'

'Older than Juliet, yes, you said, but you're not— oh, Christ, never mind – Phoebe, please put your clothes on. I'm drunk – *you're* drunk – and I think you should go home.'

There was a silence. Phoebe did not move. Kit gazed at her helplessly, suddenly wondering what on earth she could do if Phoebe simply refused to get dressed. She could hardly call the police . . . Then – oh God – a terrible, excruciating desire to laugh swelled in her lungs. Honestly, what was it about her that made these women strip to the skin and proposition her? Was it sheer animal magnetism? Or what Portia would call her chemical thingummies? She put her hand to her mouth and clenched her jaw. She must not laugh; Phoebe was a child, it would be cruel to laugh . . .

There was a knock at the front door. Kit jumped and swung round, her heart thudding foolishly. Thank God the curtains were drawn. But who was it, this late in the day? Not the postman, or the baker's boy . . .

'Don't open it, please, Kit, please don't—'

She hissed, 'Of course I won't. Keep quiet, they'll go away.' They stood, listening and rigid, until a knock came again, and the tap of fingernails on the windowpane; and then, after an eternity, there was the click of heels on the path, retreating. Simultaneously they both exhaled, and Kit realised that they had been staring at each other, unblinking, all that time. Phoebe was no longer draped seductively over the settee; instead she was bolt upright, clutching the edge, her eyes wide.

Kit no longer had any desire to laugh. She looked around for Phoebe's school uniform, and saw it in a neatly folded pile beside the hearth. She picked it up and threw it into Phoebe's pale naked lap. 'Get dressed, for God's sake.' Then she turned her back to go into the kitchen, biting her lip so that she did not say anything that she would regret.

But there was the sound of bare feet behind her, and a hand caught her sleeve. 'I'm sorry, Kit. Please don't be angry—'

She shook her away. 'Aren't you cold?'

Phoebe hugged herself, shivering, but she didn't stoop for her fallen clothes. 'Please. I thought you would like it—'

Kit dragged her hands through her hair. 'Why on earth would you think that?'

'Because you . . .' Phoebe trailed off, gesturing to the room, the fire, the settee. 'You gave me brandy,' she went on, at last, her voice wobbling, 'and drew me, and stroked my ankles . . .'

Kit opened her mouth, and shut it again. She had done those things, yes, but not because – how could Phoebe think—? With a sudden sick lurch, she saw herself as Phoebe must have done: louche, drunken, foul-mouthed. Predatory. 'No,' she said, 'it wasn't like that. You misunderstood.'

'But—'

'You *misunderstood*.' She curled her hands into fists, resisting the anger. It was not Phoebe's fault. It was her own. Sitting there, smug, full of self-congratulatory dreams of mothers and daughters, when she had no right . . . What a bloody fool she had been. Of course Phoebe had been confused. She was only a child, a child to whom she had given strong drink, talked of love—

'I'm sorry,' Phoebe said. Tears rose in her eyes and slid down her cheeks.

'All right. Just get dressed.'

She sniffed and nodded. Another gust of wind rattled the windows and the latch of the back door.

Kit collected up the scattered stockings, school uniform and underwear, and pushed the bundle into Phoebe's arms. Her hands touched the skin over Phoebe's collarbone, and Phoebe flinched. 'Here,' she said, as steadily as she could, 'put them on, and then you should go home.'

Phoebe held her gaze. She said, with an odd tearful insolence, 'Are you going to watch me?'

Oh, for God's sake! 'No,' she said, spinning round, 'no, of course not – just put your fucking *clothes* on—'

She stopped. A shadow slid across the kitchen floor, a shape crossing in front of the lamp. Her heart missed a beat. She started to step forwards to slam the door shut, but her limbs would not obey her; and then it was too late.

XIX

Journey at Night, charcoal on paper, 1921

'Kit, darling,' Portia said, 'you really are full of surprises.'

'Portia – what are you – you didn't – I wasn't—'

'Expecting me? So I gather.' If there was one thing she prided herself on, it was her presence of mind; so it was some comfort to know that she was the only one in the room not gaping like a mooncalf. She put down the lamp she had taken from the kitchen table and slid her cigarette case from her pocket. 'What a beast of a drive,' she said. 'Horrid weather, too. I'd much rather have good honest rain than this wishy-washy mizzle. Oh! How rude of me, I do apologise. Portia Forbes-Lascelles.' She held out her hand to the girl.

'This is Phoebe Manning,' Kit said.

'*Enchantée*, I'm sure.' The girl stared at her, silent, her clothes clasped to her breast like a sculpture of Diana bathing. Under different circumstances Portia would have given her a sympathetic wink – she remembered being caught *in flagrante* herself, when she was about the same age – but now, here, she had no inclination to be kind. She shrugged and plucked a cigarette from her case. 'Please,' she said, when she had lit it, 'please, don't mind me. Carry on with – whatever you were doing . . .' She drew a smoky flourish in the air.

Kit said, in a low, taut voice, 'Phoebe is my model.'

'Is she? How thrilling.' She looked around, pointedly, until she saw a scrappy little sketch on the hearthrug. 'Oh,' she said, nudging it with her foot, 'what a pity the paper was only big enough for her face . . .'

Phoebe made a noise that was halfway between a yelp and a sob; then, with frantic fumbling hands, she began to dress, dragging her clothes on higgledy-piggledy.

'Oh!' Portia said. 'School uniform! I didn't know you liked that sort of thing. I could have worn mine for you, darling, if you'd told me—'

'Shut up, Portia.'

Phoebe ducked for her shoes and crammed her feet into them. It was sickening how beautiful she was. Portia could practically feel her own chin sagging and her wrinkles deepening as she looked at her.

Kit said, 'Where's your coat, Phoebe?'

'I don't— there,' she said, looking up from her tangled shoelaces to jerk her chin at where it lay over the armchair in the corner of the room.

Kit swept it up and held it out for Phoebe to put on. Phoebe shoved her arms into the armholes, breathing hard. 'Thank you – I'm sorry –'

'When you get home, go straight to bed. If anyone sees you, tell them you're ill. Do you understand?'

'Yes.'

'Oh, Kit. Is she *pissed*?'

Kit spun round. 'I said shut *up*.'

Portia stepped backwards, fluttering a hand theatrically over her breast. 'There's no need to be so exercised, my dear. You know you can trust me with all your secrets.'

'Don't . . .' Phoebe paused, her glance flicking back and

forth between them. Finally it settled on Kit, and her sweet little mask of a face was full of pleading. 'Kit . . .'

'It's all right. Portia knows perfectly well it isn't true.'

'But, Kit darling, I don't know that at all. What would anyone think, stumbling in on you like this? A naked woman—'

'A naked *child*,' Kit snapped, 'and in case you haven't noticed, I am fully dressed.'

'That's never stopped you before—'

'Portia, *enough*!' Kit snatched the cigarette from her lips, and flung it into the fire. Portia recoiled, catching her breath, and Kit grabbed her shoulders, hard. 'Don't be an idiot. Look at her! She's a child, a *child*, damn it. She was being stupid, that's all. You really think that? That I'd fuck – *her*?'

Portia slid her gaze past Kit's face, to Phoebe. Oh, that had stung – and that meant that Kit was telling the truth, after all. She turned aside, concealing her shameful rush of relief.

'Kit,' Phoebe said, her voice high and miserable, 'I'm not – not a child—'

'For God's sake!' Kit shouted. 'Will you just fuck off home, Phoebe?'

There was a silence.

'I'm sorry,' Kit said, 'I didn't mean—'

'Not at all,' Phoebe said, brittle as a polite hostess after a breakage. 'Please don't mention it.'

'Forgive me – Portia is an old friend, but her sense of humour—'

'I'll go now. Goodbye. Goodbye, Miss Forbes-Lascelles.'

'Goodbye,' Portia said. The girl had such entrancing dignity. Anyone would think it was Portia who had been scrabbling around in the nude. She watched Kit watch Phoebe as she swept past them into the kitchen. Then there was the sound of the back door opening and closing, and a blast of freezing air. Finally Kit inhaled, and met her eyes.

'Portia—'

'Well, what a welcome, darling.' She smiled, with the particular smile that had always, in the past, made Kit soften.

But Kit rubbed her forehead and did not smile back. 'What are you doing here? Why didn't you tell me you were coming?'

'You would have told me not to come. And now I've seen why.'

'I've told you, Phoebe got things wrong,' Kit said. 'I went to the outhouse, and when I got back she was just – lying there. Naked.'

'That must have been rather a shock.'

'It was.'

Portia laughed. Kit frowned at her; then, her mouth twitched, and with a half-repressed splutter she began to laugh too. Portia had forgotten the deep ringing tone of her voice, and the lovely masculine abandon, the lines of her neck as she threw her head back. Oh, Lord, Kit could make her forgive anything, any number of unanswered letters, any number of naked nymphs . . . She held out her hand and Kit took hold of it, warm skin and bone, the gusts of laughter shaking them both.

Something crashed through the window. They spun round, forgetting their shared mirth. A stone as large as Portia's fist lay under the window, amid shards of glass. A flint, worn smooth. Kit crouched to pick it up. 'Oh dear,' she said. 'I suppose she has every right to be angry with me.'

'Hell hath no fury,' Portia said, crossing cautiously to the wall beside the window and pulling the curtain aside. The front garden was empty, but in the dusk she could just make out a slight, fair-haired figure hurrying away down the road. 'The young ones are the worst. Don't worry, she'll get over it. As long as she doesn't touch my car.' She turned back to Kit, and winked. 'Such melodrama, darling! I imagined you here all alone, like a nun in a convent. And instead . . .'

'From what you've said about your education, it isn't too dissimilar to a convent, is it?'

'Oh Kit, darling, I have missed you.' It was too early to try to kiss her; Portia glanced at her watch, wondering if another ten minutes might do it.

'Yes. Well.'

'Don't say you've missed me, I know it isn't true.'

'Of course I have. In a way.'

And there, that was it: honesty, suddenly sparking between them, a leaping electricity that was unlike anything else. Portia lit another cigarette. She held out the case, and Kit sighed and took one, letting Portia light it for her. They blew identical plumes of smoke towards the dying fire.

'Why didn't you answer my letters?'

Kit raised her shoulders and let them drop again, as if she had braced herself to take a burden and found it too heavy.

'Did you get them? The one about Muckle?' she added, before Kit had time to answer: that was the one that mattered, the one she had thought would force Kit to break her long silence.

'Yes.'

'And you still didn't answer.'

'What should I have said?'

'You might have told me how he was, with you. Or that I was worrying too much. Or – oh, I don't know, Kit! I've been so lonely. I thought you'd care about him, at least. Maybe that was stupid, when you didn't care about anyone else, even Julien. Or me. You left so suddenly – you didn't even tell me your *address* –'

'Because I didn't want you to know where I was.'

The honesty had tipped into something else, something with a sharper edge. Portia took a long drag of her cigarette, weighing up the risk. 'Fair enough,' she said, at last; she did not want to be thrown out before she even touched Kit's lips. She finished her cigarette, cast the butt into the embers in the grate, and stooped to pick up the drawing that lay on the floor. It was quite good – in fact, it was *good*. She said, 'This isn't bad, darling.'

'Thanks.'

'She really is very pretty.'

'It's the first portrait I've done since Paris,' Kit said, 'it's only a beginning.' But her tone forbade any more questions. It was just like Kit, of course, to come out with something like that, and then look at you with narrowed eyes as if curiosity killed the cat.

Portia propped the drawing – why on earth hadn't Kit used a sketchpad? Beneath the face a fatuous line of print asked WHO ATE ALL THE ROMARY'S? – on the mantelpiece, wrapped her arms round her ribs and shivered. '*Sacré bleu*, it's cold.' When she had come in, the room had been cosy, full of flickering firelight; but now she had chills creeping up her backbone, and an irrational sense that whenever she looked away the shadows began to move on their own. Perhaps it was the draught from the broken window. 'Christ!' she burst out suddenly, unable to restrain herself, 'this place! It's so utterly, utterly dreary. How can you bear it?'

'It's all right.'

'No, it isn't! Oh, you *idiot*, darling, your teeth are chattering. It's *freezing*. There's a broken window and a draught like something from Dante. Honestly. Get your coat and get in the car with me. We needn't go far. We'll stop at the first nice little place we come to. Don't you want a hot bath, and a hot dinner, and a hot—'

'Bed?'

'If you want,' Portia said, and smiled. She gave Kit a coquettish look through her eyelashes. 'I was going to say, a hot toddy. Come on, darling. Don't argue any more.'

Kit stared at her, her eyes flicking back and forth as she searched Portia's expression for – what? It was hard to know. But after a moment she said, in a low voice, 'Very well, then.'

Portia nodded. She would have preferred more enthusiasm, but any victory was better than none; the important thing was to be away from here, and alone together. She said, briskly, 'Jolly good. Get your gear, then.' She had meant pyjamas and toothbrush, or whatever Kit was likely to need for the night; but Kit nodded, got up, and merely grabbed her coat from a hook in the kitchen before she flung open the back door. So she was eager to leave, after all – just not, Portia thought, eager to admit it . . . She picked up her own hat and gloves and followed Kit into the blustery twilight.

The wind bit into her face and fingers. She bent her head and fumbled with her gloves as she walked down the path to the car. Kit was already settling into the front seat, hunched over, her teeth chattering. Was it foolish to drive away, now? Would it be more sensible to build up the fire and hunker down in front of it, wrapped in blankets? Portia hesitated, wondering; but Kit barked, 'For God's sake, get a move on,' and it was too cold to argue. She pressed the starter until at last the engine coughed into life, got into the driver's seat and manoeuvred the car carefully back and forth till it faced the way she had come.

They drove in silence. It was nearly dark now: Portia had the sensation of falling into a bottomless tunnel, drifting this way and that, like Alice in Wonderland . . . Dead leaves swirled and skittered across the road like small animals, making her stomach tighten and her foot hover tensely over the brake pedal. How hard it was to tell what was alive and what was not! But slowly, as the road took them further and further from Haltington, it was as though an inward claw loosened its grip on her: and Kit, too, sat up, gradually taking more notice of the world that rushed by. Night fell and the darkness closed around them; then the wind blew a ragged hole in the clouds, and the moon came out. At last they went through a little village and round a corner, past the lychgate of a church, and Kit said, 'Do you think you could stop for a moment? Sorry. I need a piss.'

Portia braked and steered the motorcar to the side of the road, almost scraping the running board on the flint wall of the churchyard. Before the car had come to a halt, Kit had opened her door and scrambled out. She squatted at the base of the wall and Portia heard the hiss of liquid splashing into the grass. It took a long time.

'Better?' Portia ventured, at last, when Kit returned to the car. She did not start the engine; she was warmer now, and there was no great rush to go anywhere.

'Yes. I'm drunk, though. My head's spinning like anything.' Kit drew her hand over her forehead, and then sat up straight with a sudden inhalation. 'Oh, Christ, I should have checked Phoebe got home. We should have—'

'Don't worry, darling, she was perfectly compos mentis. She threw that stone through your window, didn't she? And she ran away like a young gazelle. No, tomorrow she'll have a sore head and a crushing sense of embarrassment, and that will be that.'

Slowly Kit subsided back into her seat. 'Poor kid.'

'Oh, do stop going on about her!' Portia smiled, to soften her vexation, and patted Kit's thigh with her free hand. Kit did not move away; that was encouraging. It was, Portia thought, rather like trying to tame an animal: an advance, a pause, an advance. Patience. That was the key. She lifted her hand and stroked a stray lock of hair from Kit's forehead, admiring the colour of her skin in the moonlight. Then, when she could wait no longer, she leant over, letting her lips brush against Kit's cheek. 'Darling,' she murmured, 'oh, my darling . . .'

Kit pulled away. At first Portia thought she was only adjusting the angle of her body, and moved with her: then, with a jolt in the pit of her stomach, she felt Kit wrench herself free. All at once they were sitting with six inches of leather cushion between them, staring at each other.

'What is it, darling?'

Kit shook her head. 'Nothing.'

'It must be *something*.'

'I just don't feel like it, that's all.'

'You always feel like it, darling. I know you.'

'Not any more.'

After a moment Portia swung open the car door and got out. She left the door hanging open and leant on the churchyard wall – as if there were anything to look at but the dreary church and dreary graves! – and took out a cigarette. It took so long to light it that she considered giving up; but finally it was lit. She blew out smoke, and said, watching it disperse, 'I should never have persuaded you to come to Paris.'

There was a silence, broken only by the creak and slam of the other car door and rustling footsteps in the grass behind her.

'I did you a great wrong. I see that now. You were never strong enough to endure it. You were too – too human, I suppose.' She leant over the wall to tap her ash onto hallowed ground. 'You were so young, my dear. I should have protected you. It was like the boys who went into battle, without knowing . . . But I didn't know it would do *this* to you! I didn't know that a *gueule cassée* could be contagious.' There was a silence, but she knew that Kit was just beside her, listening. 'You used to be perfect.'

'And now?' Kit said, her voice unnaturally steady.

'Now you're all gone, aren't you? You're just as fucked up as the boys' faces.' She had not particularly meant to make Kit catch her breath as though she had been struck; but neither did she feel particularly sorry.

'That's – I don't think that's fair. Just because I don't care for you any more—'

That would have hurt, if she had let it. But she did not give herself time to feel the pain. 'No,' she said, 'not just that! I'm not an idiot. Don't you see it in the mirror? Make a self-portrait one day, and you'll know what I mean.' She took another drag of her cigarette, and blew out the smoke in a plume before she trusted herself to go on. 'I'm not angry, Kit. I'm to blame for it. I should have told you to stay in London, and paint your pretty pictures and write me cheerful letters. Then when the studio closed I could have come home to you, and we would have been happy.'

For a long time Kit did not answer. Then she said, 'I expect you're right.'

There was no pleasure in the victory. 'But instead,' Portia said, 'you came here, and hid away from me. Was it because you were ashamed?'

'Ashamed?'

'Of – not being yourself any more.'

Kit turned. Portia straightened, tensing, still – in spite of everything – longing for her touch; but Kit only leant against the wall and folded her arms, her head bowed.

'And to that place, darling!' Portia said; it was like jabbing a needle into someone you had already shot, but she could not help herself. 'That grim, grisly place! Why on earth didn't you go to Cornwall? Or Oxfordshire? Or anywhere, but *there*?'

'It's beautiful in sunlight.'

'I don't believe you. I've never been anywhere that made my skin crawl like that. Driving down the road to your cottage gave me the cold creeps.' The words seemed to summon a chill breeze; she felt it brush her cheek, ruffling her hair with unfriendly fingers. Icy air was beginning to seep in through the seams of her coat. She took a final drag of her cigarette and crushed it out on the wall. 'These horrid little villages . . . I don't think you'll be happy till you're back in London.'

'London,' Kit echoed. Portia could not tell whether her voice held longing or revulsion.

'Well,' Portia said, 'let's get back in the car.'

'Just a moment. I feel sick.'

'Go and puke then,' she said, through gritted teeth. She lit another cigarette, flicked the spent match over the wall and strode away. She was not going to stand beside Kit waiting for her to vomit, like a solicitous VAD.

She went back along the verge, past the lychgate to the corner, and then stopped. Ugh, the *cold*! She had been thawing out in the car, but now . . . it seemed to come in waves, flowing around her like water, pushing her backwards. It could not all be coming from one direction, but it felt as if it were – as if there were an invisible flood rising, overflowing from a source somewhere behind them on the road, back the way they had come . . . She pulled her coat around her as tightly as she could, but it made no difference.

There was the noise of Kit retching, followed by a groan. She took a few steps further away, casting a disgusted glance over her shoulder; then she stumbled to a halt, her heart jumping in her mouth. A man loomed in front of her – a huge, hulking man—

But the figure silhouetted against the stars did not move, and when she had caught her breath she saw that it was too enormous, and too still, to be a man at all. When she took a step towards it she made out the sheen of bronze. A man in uniform – a soldier, generalised, masculine, vacuous – with bayonet and helmet and puttees, facing up to the heavens in a typical attitude of determined valour. Beneath it was a plaque, the names illegible in the darkness, and a few clumps and smears of dying flowers, as if in the wake of a recent ceremony.

She stared at the thing, repressing a childish impulse to spit at it. Not for the soldiers, but for the villagers, who had thought – *this!* – a suitable memorial for their murdered sons . . . Even a cross would have been better. This was obscene – this was *heroic* . . . How dared they? She knew, of course, that she was being unreasonable, of course they wanted to believe their lost sons had not died in vain – but to believe such a lie, to set it up in the churchyard cast in bronze! No one would ever look at the names at all, and the names were the only thing that mattered. She clenched her fists in the pockets of her coat, and drew back her foot to kick futilely at the plinth.

But something stopped her. She looked up at its face again, with its blank eyes and unsliding gleam of moonlight on the square jaw. A memory came into her head: Septimus's friend – Robert, or Rodney? – who had been convinced that his flesh was rotting off his bones. He had visited one weekend and refused to shave or chew or wash, because it might hasten the process . . . Why was she thinking of that now? Because *that* was what the War had done, even to the men who survived, she thought. But it was not only that. It was because she had been afraid then, afraid of nothing she could name; and that was how she felt now.

She spun round decisively to make her way back to the car. But after a few steps she could not resist glancing back, as if the statue might have changed position. As she did her foot caught in a tangle of grass and she steadied herself on the wall. *Had* it changed—? Oh, for Christ's sake! She was getting as loony as Robert, or Rodney, or whatever his name was, of course the fucking statue hadn't—

Not its position. The stance was the same, the chin lifted to the sky, the bayonet brandished. But there was – there *was* – something different—

It was, she thought, with a strange detachment, like watching Kit surface from sleep, before she opened her eyes. Nothing you could exactly see, but some change in the atmosphere, some jump of energy, an unseen inbreath . . . Somehow she knew that the thing was awake, and any moment it would move.

Impossible. She was crazy. The countryside had sent her off her nut, even faster than it had done the same to Kit—

But her senses were stronger than her disbelief. And now she saw, she *saw* the bronze soften into something else: something that was, if not alive, then at least animated, and moving. The angle of the bayonet changed; stars appeared between the arm and torso, where before there had only been shadow. She heard a dry creaking, like stone pulling apart, and knew that it was only a matter of time before the thing wrenched itself free.

She opened her mouth, but her breath was stuck in her throat, and screaming would do no good anyway. She must get away. Somehow, on numb, unstrung legs, she covered the few yards to the car. 'Kit,' she managed to say, 'Kit – we have to go—'

Kit was on her knees on the verge. She raised her head. For a moment she was motionless, staring at the war memorial. She murmured something, some foreign word that Portia did not recognise.

'Come on! I don't know what it is, but we have to go—'

'They shouldn't be here,' Kit said, her voice rising, 'not here . . .'

'Come *on*!'

It shook itself. Or rather – she did not have the words for this – it shifted, with the awful impersonality of earth settling after an explosion. Then, with the same inhuman bearing, it lurched forward. It did not walk, exactly. It moved in a whole jerking judder, like a lead soldier nudged forward by a child's finger; it was as if it did not have hips or ankles or knees – as if its legs were not legs – as if its body was an undifferentiated mass, man-shaped but not a man. Like a golem – and suddenly she remembered the stories Muckle's landlady had told. *Little kiddies havin' accidents all over the place, only their mums don't believe they was accidents* – and then, *it's like he ain't got no feeling inside his flesh* . . . Portia had shut her up as politely as she could, repulsed and afraid. *No feeling inside the flesh*, she thought now; but she did not have time to think it through, to follow the connecting thread.

The thing paused. The head turned, looking: but whatever was going on inside it, there was no brain, only some appalling, inconceivable vitality – *soul*, she thought, but as the hairs rose on the back of her neck she knew it was the very opposite of a soul. Hunger, that was all: enough awareness to want to fill the void where a soul should have been, and nothing more . . .

Come on, come *on*, she tried to say, and failed. She took a step, reaching out for the car, hardly knowing which direction she needed to go. Escape. That was all.

Kit staggered to her feet. She said, choking, 'I – must go back . . .'

The words were so far from what Portia expected to

hear that a second passed before she understood. The shock unlocked her lungs and throat enough for her to gasp, 'What?'

'Florence – Phoebe – oh Christ . . .'

They had no time to argue. The thing was getting closer. She did not know whether it knew they were there, and she did not want to find out. Her hands flailed and clutched behind her, desperate for the touch of friendly metal. Her palms met something hard, and the back of her legs came into contact with a ridge that she knew was the running-board. Oh thank God, thank God. If she could have turned to look where she was going it would have been easier; but she could not tear her gaze from the thing's sluggish, horrifying approach. She navigated blindly around the car to get to the driver's side. 'Get *in*!'

Kit swayed, but she did not obey. Portia could not leave her; but neither could she stay here, frozen, watching and waiting—

And then, from far away – or was it close by, closer than the sound of the sea in a seashell, in the very hollows of her ears? – there came other sounds: the tinkling of glass, the scrape of wood, the crash of something heavy overturned in an echoing building. A squeak of hinges that for a split second made her think of the door of the old haybarn at home: a happy noise, the noise of summer days, and waiting to be found at hide and seek . . . For that single, disorientated second, her fear lessened. Like Septimus, she thought, hearing a skylark at Loos. She looked around, searching for the source of the sound.

There were men coming out of the church. For the duration of a heartbeat she thought they had come to help, they had seen the thing and come to rescue them. Then she saw that she was wrong.

They were not men. And there would be no help, no rescue.

She might have known, logically, that there could not have been anyone in the locked, dark church; and, cynically, that no strangers seeing the memorial lurch to life would have been so valiant as to come to their aid. But her eyes knew before her brain did – before she had time for logic or cynicism. It was the way they moved that extinguished the spark of hope: as if their bodies were homogenous clay squashed into a mould, and there was no difference between bone and muscle, hands and eyes, feet and the ground beneath them.

But they were not clay, any more than they were men. As they moved out of the shadow of the tower she saw them more clearly. The first glittered, as though it wore a shell or a suit of armour, banded at every joint with dull grey; the next was strangely elongated, its face as blurred and mutilated as the plaster *gueules cassées* in the studio, a long stiff tunic reaching almost to its knees. And behind them came another, a low, crawling thing that she could not make sense of at all. They moved closer, jerking in that senseless shamble towards the lychgate. The nearest one turned its head, and moonlight slid across its face. She saw the finely scratched lines of eyes and eyebrows and mouth, neat and effeminate, under yellow-tinged curls; and there was something around the hair, a stiff flat patterned circle, so instantly familiar that she could not understand why she did not recognise it. Then, with a shudder, she understood. It was a saint, a stained-glass saint, and that thing around its head was a halo. The one behind was a crusader from a tomb, so old its face had almost worn away: now that it was on its feet, the medieval proportions were not quaint but horrible, like a deformity. And behind *that*—

The last one came out from behind a tomb. She made a terrible strangled sound.

It was a Christ, crucified; only – oh God – it had not

come down from its cross. Whatever inhabited it could not know, or did not care, that the wooden planks to which it was nailed were not part of the human likeness. The cross had come to life with the rest of it; and the cross moved just as the rest of it did, with the same blundering inefficiency, the naked shape of a man's body hanging underneath like a vulnerable belly. The blunt wooden ends dragged and scraped on the stone path.

Portia heard Kit give a single sob of terror. But she had no room left to care – no space to think of Kit at all, or anything, anything but getting away. She flung herself at the car, almost falling into it; and through some merciful magic she felt the starter button beneath her foot, and stamped on it as hard as she could. The engine – she whimpered with relief – started. She dropped into the driver's seat, and found the accelerator pedal. The door was still open, but she did not stop to close it. As she careered away, swerving across the road in panic and elation, she gave a final glance over her shoulder; and she saw Kit was still where she had been, standing upright, facing down the figures as they advanced towards her.

XX

Girl, With Shadows, oil on board, 1921

When the stone left Phoebe's hand she had felt as if it were her heart flying through the air: a kind of queasy exultation, a sensation of momentum and vertigo. Then she heard the smash and saw the split-second shimmer of breaking glass. The two women's voices fell silent, and she clenched her fists in triumph. They had been laughing – *laughing!* Well, not any more. She stood holding her breath, savouring the moment, until the curtain twitched; and then, with a sudden twinge of fear, spun round and ran. She did not stop until she reached the clump of trees where the road curved. Her heart was back in her chest, drumming.

But then nothing happened. She wanted Kit to come outside and shout at her. And the other woman, too – Portia, with her drawl and her painted fingernails, her black bobbed hair cut as straight as a razor, eyes rimmed with kohl like an ancient Egyptian – yes, she would enjoy being shouted at by Portia. She would keep her face very still, as if she were being ticked off at school, and they would grow angrier and angrier. That would make up for what she had done, the stupid *stupid* thing she had done . . . But they did not come outside, and after a long time the lamplight shrank behind the curtains, leaving the sitting room dim. They had not stoked the fire. But it wasn't possible, she thought, how dare they? Didn't they care? Didn't Kit care? She had been so sure that Kit cared a little – but then, she had thought that Kit wanted her, too.

Long minutes went by, and no one appeared, nothing changed except the darkness that seemed to seep up from the ground and the trees and the roof of the house, as if exuded by anything solid. The world spun to her left, gently at first, then gathering speed. She clenched her jaw and concentrated until it stopped. But as soon as she relaxed, it began again: sliding faster and faster, until at last it whirled greasily, bringing a taste of pungent bile on to the back of her tongue. It was only after a long bewildered minute that she realised she was drunk.

Yes. Of course. Why hadn't she realised sooner . . . ? Because she was not thinking clearly, because – yes – she *was* drunk, too drunk to think clearly . . . Ah, drunk, what a word, how it would shock the girls at school! She had not had alcohol since she made herself sick stealing from Papa's tantalus when she was seven or eight. Tonight she had sipped the measure that Kit had poured for her, savouring each mouthful like a connoisseur; but after a while she'd begun to think it had no effect on her, so she had stolen a few long gulps from the bottle when she was alone in the kitchen, gasping in silence at the burn of it as it went down. Maybe that had not been wise . . . She swallowed, and the top of her stomach gave a nasty little India-rubber bounce.

She had not realised it could come on suddenly like this, long after the last drop of alcohol had been swallowed. It seemed so unjust. Now, when all she wanted was to go home and— but she could not go home, not like this, she was not entirely sure she could walk straight, or speak. Her hands and feet had gone numb; it was as if all the blood in her body had been sucked into the vortex of her belly. She inhaled the cold air as if it were smelling salts, breath after breath, trying to quell her nausea. But it was no good.

She spun round and stumbled towards the Bone cottage. Every step was a little fall, and the only way not to plunge to the ground was to fling herself forward. She pushed ankle-deep through the long grass, to the smell of the outhouse and the midden behind it. Her eyes could not focus, it was all a mess of scribbled black trees and grey sky, with the dark mass of the wooden shack in front. She reached out with one hand – the other was over her mouth – and wrenched the door open. Then she dropped to her knees, and as the stench of excrement hit the back of her throat she vomited. In the immediate aftermath she felt a little better, but as she raised her head her guts began to complain again, and another wave of sickness took hold of her – and then another, until she began to wonder if she would ever feel better. Distantly she heard voices, and the cough of a car starting, but she could not bring herself to care.

At last she raised her head, and found that the world no longer rocked from side to side when she moved. She got to her feet as stiltedly as a puppet being lifted into position, and tottered out of the outhouse. It was getting dark. The air smelt metallic, like blood.

The back door of the Bone cottage was open – not simply unlocked, but swinging on its hinges. Inside, the kitchen was empty, and a ribbon of black smoke rose from the untrimmed lamp on the table. The motorcar had driven away.

Now Kit and Portia had left, she could go inside, she thought. It would be warm – warmer, anyway. She could lie down in Kit's bed and shut her eyes. She would feel better in the morning. Would anyone notice, if she did not go home?

She glanced sideways. For an instant she did not know what had caught her attention. It might have been a movement in the colourless dusk, or a sound just at the edge of audibility. Or, perhaps, the absence of something, like Mama's bedroom in the days after she died, when Phoebe had caught herself looking in through the doorway, surprised that there was no one there . . . She found herself looking up, past the garden wall, at the broad slope of the down. The grass was flat and dead, without even a ripple to show where the bare chalk lines of the Face had been. The Face had been invisible for months, there was nothing remarkable about that . . . But this was different, somehow; now there was no longer anything to look for.

She shivered. With a soft, sudden jolt, it was no longer dusk but dark: as if night had been falling, slowly, gently as a feather, and now it had reached the ground.

And then, quietly, completely, she was afraid. She turned her head, straining her ears, every inch of skin prickling. The back door was a deep patch of black, and guttering lamplight spilt over the grass, dipping lower and lower. Whatever she was afraid of, it was through that doorway. Or rather, it would be. All at once she had the conviction that it was not there yet: that what she felt was only the prologue to something else, like electricity in the air before a storm. It was a warning that soon, *soon* . . . Something was near, and getting nearer.

The lamplight sizzled and jumped, so that for a second she saw nothing but the jaundiced flare of it through the doorway; then it was gone, and she blinked away the after-image, suddenly blind. Beyond the thudding of her heart, the world was unnaturally silent, as though it were a diorama under glass; and as her eyes adjusted again to the darkness, she had the vertiginous sense that something was wrong with what she could see, there was some appalling treachery of scale or perspective, and reality was somewhere else. Her heartbeat grew louder, faster, like something approaching, coming to ride her down. Oh, if only someone would catch her up and swing her out of the way, breathless with relief and reassurance, *oh darling, you scared me half to death, you're all right now...*! She opened her mouth to scream – for Mama, for Papa, for anyone at all – but no sound emerged. And then with a tremor her body told her that she had run out of time, that even if someone came it would be too late.

She heard it, first: a dry, distant rustle, faint but clear in the stagnant air. She could not tell what made it. It was not, in itself, a terrible noise. Perhaps it was something sharp and soft, brushing over flagstones – a broom, she thought, or feathers, like a fledgling in a cat's mouth. But that was not quite right. It paused, then began again, irregular as a gust of wind. As something moved in the darkness of the kitchen it grew louder, and suddenly she recognised the sound of paper: a page turning, a torn wrapper being swept across the floor, a stray corner of newsprint in the grate flapping in the hot draught . . .

Whatever was there, in the shadows, came towards the door. It seemed to flutter and drift, hardly touching the ground. She caught a glimpse of white – a little crumpled, a little smudged – and the door swung wide, as if nudged by an unseen hand.

Then, for the first time, she saw it clearly. The hairs stood up on the back of her neck. She wanted to close her eyes, but she could not.

She was staring, helpless, at her own face.

It stood in the doorway like her reflection: except it was not quite solid. There was still, she thought, a hint of paper in its cheeks, the dullness of graphite in its gaze; but the angle of the head, the wisps of hair, the lines of forehead and jaw – yes, she knew those were like her. But only one eye had an iris and a pupil; the other was blank, unfinished, halfway between blind and lidless. Kit's drawing had come to life, and now it was going to step forwards and reach out, seeking flesh and blood, seeking—

She could not breathe. She had met the thurlath before – she had felt them approaching, gathering around the doll and Mama's picture – but not like this. Not face to face – not *there*, embodied . . . It was the difference between one single wasp, and the dreadful droning tower of a wasps' nest; the difference between a stinking puddle and a ravenous flood. Before, she had felt brave: now she was icy cold, frozen by the knowledge that this was too big to fight, this was no longer the kind of battle she could win. Now it was too late . . .

Why had she let Kit draw her? She should have known, she *had* known, but she had been reckless, flattered, drunk . . . She had thought she could destroy it before there was any danger. But that wasn't important. Nothing was important, except this. She looked into her own expressionless eye, and could not breathe. Her own face . . .

But no, it was *not* her face, because there was nothing – no thought, no humanity – behind it. It was not her. It was not human. It was a parasite, a disease – and how dare it steal her likeness – *hers*? And the jolt of anger was enough to break the ice that had formed inside her. She glanced desperately to either side. If she ran . . . What else could she do? The better part of valour. Get to safety, run and run until she could slam a door and— but what door? The vicarage was not safe. It had not been safe, ever. Nor the church, even devoid as it was of effigies and stained glass, as if the villagers had always known that the Christian God could not keep the oldest evils at bay. There was no door, no wall, no shield except the Face – and the Face had failed, it was gone, she had felt it in that brief shudder just before darkness fell. Now there was no protection. Even if, somehow, she managed to escape this one, there would be more. They would come and come, forever and everywhere.

No. She must not let them.

The resolution came so suddenly that it was as if she heard it spoken aloud, by a voice that was not hers. It was like a hand taking hold of her, shaking her shoulder, refusing to let her sink into defeat. It made her think of Rosamund Jenks, putting her hand up in Scripture Class and asking in a clear little monotone whether it was always wrong to kill; she had been bullied and miserable ever since, but once Phoebe had seen that steely glint of bravery it was hard to forget it. Rosamund had not *wanted* to be brave. No one ever did.

All right, then. She would fight, even if it was futile. But how? *Think.*

She did not have time. The figure in front of her stretched out its white hand, fine as her own, pale as the underbelly of a fish. Think – there was an answer, there must be an answer—

She threw herself sideways and ran, floundering, at the mercy of giddiness and gravity. There was the garden wall, and the down, and the glimmer of the night sky above. She stumbled to the garden gate, and looked up at the slope of the hill, which lay black against the sky, featureless and absolute. Was the thing coming after her, its face blank with that inhuman greed? She could not look back to find out.

She threw the gate open and began to climb. It was uneven underfoot, and every step jarred her to her backbone; she wanted to run, but the best she could manage was a clumsy out-of-breath jog, ducking her head as if she might blunder into a low arch. As she went, the driving cold intensified. That sensation – as if she were drawing closer to a glacier – was a thread that held tight through the panic: it told her she was still alive. And she had a destination. The Face, of course; it could only, ever, have been the Face . . . The first face she had ever known, she thought, remembering Mrs Bone cackling as she told the story of Phoebe's birth: *saw it before you saw your Ma, you did!* She imagined Papa's voice, too, in counterpoint to Mrs Bone's, *I will lift up mine eyes unto the hills, from whence cometh my help* . . .

But she did not have any kind of plan, beyond getting to the place where the Face had been. She concentrated on putting one foot in front of the other, and did not wonder what she would do once she reached it. Once she fell, tripping and scrabbling back to her feet in one movement, her chin stinging where she had scraped it on the ground. The back of her throat was raw, and her eyes stung. Did the thurlath have a physical presence, a chemical signature like a trace of mustard gas in the air? Or was it only her fear? Climb, keep climbing. Was this what it was like to go over the top? But there were no whistles or screams, no guns: only the blaring cacophony in her head, her panting breath and footsteps.

And then, at last, her foot met a hard flat place, and she knew she had found it.

She stopped. Her knees gave way, and she toppled slowly forward. Her hands met thin grass where the ground was closer to the surface. She raised her head, staring through the starlit dark, and thought she could make out the other lines on the slope above: the vertical nose, the horizontal eyes. They were hardly there, mere traces, like lines in velvet where unknown fingers had brushed the nap the wrong way; but she was certain that she had come to the right spot. This was where the Face had been.

But she had hoped for help; and there was nothing. No answer. She pressed her hands harder into the ground, searching for the thrum of the chalk, the sense of the earth turning. Nothing. She tugged at the grass, ripping until she felt the roots peel up and away. But when she threw the clumps to one side and replaced her hands on the bare chalk, there was no more life than she had felt before. Anyone would think that this particular patch of ground was like any other; anyone would think that there was no power, had never been any kind of power—

She fought the rise of panic. For a moment she concentrated on slowing her breath, trying to forget about the thing— the thing with her own face, which might be following— *no*. It was no use being afraid. She had to think. She counted in her head, slow as the ticks of a clock, until her great gasps of exhalation came softer, and slower, and she could hear the world beyond them and feel more than the trembling of her own limbs. Then, as delicately as a surgeon, she laid her hands back down, every nerve alert.

Was she imagining it? It was as insubstantial as a cobweb, fragile from long neglect: but perhaps there *was* a different kind of tension in the earth under her fingers, as though, woven through it, ran threads of something alive. She held her breath for a moment, listening as hard as she could, and found stillness, like the space at the centre of a whirlpool. After the wrenching fear of the ascent, it was like an eddy in the torrent, a space where she could stop. And at the centre of that silence – faint, distant, buried as it was – was the thing she had been seeking. A spark, a mystery. Unknowable, terrifying, made of the same stuff as the thurlath but also, somehow, their opposite . . . She thought that at last she understood Papa's sermons about the dread and horror of the Divine. It was not safe; it was not a refuge; but the peril was impersonal, not malevolent, as clean as fire or frost. *Thank you*, she thought, to no one.

But it was not enough. It would not protect her. It was

like Mama on the last day, eyes closed, too far away to hear her . . . She bowed her head, and the graze on her chin prickled and oozed. She could see the paleness of the chalk where she had torn the grass up; it reminded her of something, some memory that slipped away before she could grasp it.

Was there a way to repair the Face? That was the only thing she could think of. If she recut the lines . . . She might do it with her bare hands, scrabbling at the grass. But the lines did not matter if the power was gone; and the power was so weak it would be like trying to sew rotten lace. She could not bring it back. She was not a Bone. She had no right. And she was too small, too singular. It would be like calling out to the distant shimmering bulge of an airship, asking it to stop – or like walking into a hail of bullets, as if bravery was what mattered. Impossible. She felt her throat close with fear and fury. And it came to her now that it was all mixed up together: the War and the thurlath and the glorious dead, the wounds and the nightmares, the telegrams and the agony and the stupid mourning wreaths on white marble crosses . . . The faceless ones came, drawn by the horrors; they were hungry for the humanity and the inhumanity, they fed on the wrongness of it all, and multiplied. The Face had worn thin when no one was left to repair it, but maybe the killing of the Bone brothers had weakened it already; maybe all the killing ate away at it like acid, seeping down through the chalk and increasing the darkness that lay underneath it. Maybe for every man who had been destroyed – dead, wounded, disfigured – there was one more thurlath, mindlessly seeking what had been taken away. She opened her mouth, baring her teeth silently in a grimace. If it was true, if it was all part of the same pattern . . . She could no more stand against the thurlath than the War. She should lie down and wait quietly to be consumed – just as the soldiers had gone obediently off to France, with docile, bovine courage. Water rose in her eyes and slid down into her mouth, tasting of salt. It might not be so awful. Surely when a thurlath took you, all you felt was oblivion? Then at least there would be no more horror, no more fear.

She rolled onto her back and let her head rest against the bare chalk. She was so cold that she hardly felt it any more. Blood crept down the line of her jaw. And now that she was not searching for it, the elusive memory sprang into the forefront of her mind: being here with George Bone, just before he left for the Front. He had recut the Face; then he had held her down with his body, and scrabbled at her skirt . . . She had hated him, she had told him he would die. And then, not long afterwards, he *had* died – died of a wound gone septic, Mrs Bone said, delirious in a hospital in France. Phoebe had tried not to be glad, and failed. Either it was right to kill, or it was not; and if it was, then George deserved to die as much as anyone else.

She was tired. If she went to sleep, she might simply never wake again. It would be over. She wiped the tickling drop of blood away from her chin with her fingers, then let her bloody hand fall limply to the ground.

There was a faint – very faint – tremble in the chalk. It was as if it rose to meet her hand, deliberately seeking her touch.

She froze, her heart thumping. Then, with shaking fingers, she repeated what she had done: touching her bleeding chin, touching the dry cold stone. She did not think it would happen again. She must have imagined it. But there it was. Why . . . ? She felt a quiver, not of hope but of something that might become hope, if she let it. Blood. Her blood.

She heard George's voice as clearly as if he were there, now. He had said, *Suppose I should be grateful she doesn't want me to do it the way her granddad did, in the dead of night with the blood of a virgin.*

She pushed herself to her knees, her head spinning as the darkness swept past her. She could not repair it. But she might remake it.

Was it possible? She was not a Bone. But it could not always have been Bones, all the way back; it would have been others, all of them singular and small, like her. And she had been born here, her first sight of the world had been the Face on its slope, she was part of this place. And – it was the dead of night, and she was a virgin. She knew what that word meant, now; and for the first time she was glad Kit had not touched her.

But even old Mrs Bone would have quailed at trying to remake it from scratch, as though it had never been. Even though she knew now that the Face wanted to obey her – that the fraying seams of it wanted to knit together, stronger . . . She did not have enough blood. She did not have enough time. Enough life. Her whole being would not be enough—

She pressed her palm down, a thrill of terror going through her. A different kind of terror, the kind that came from standing on a cliff edge. It wanted her. It was thirsty. If she could . . . *would* she, if she could . . . ?

The trick of it was not to think. Lettice Brown's cousin had said that, one day when Phoebe went to tea. He had glared at them as if he hated them more than he hated the Germans, and when Lettice's mother had asked how on earth he had managed to be so brave, he had barked that it was best if you were mad or stupid, and he was lucky to be both. Then he had got out his cigarette lighter and set fire, very deliberately, to a napkin, and for a second they had all sat frozen before Lettice leapt up and upended the milk jug over him. *Don't think, that's all.* He had been a mental case,

Lettice said; but perhaps, Phoebe thought now, he had been right. If she could manage not to think . . .

And after all there was a kind of simplicity in it, as though she had remembered a ritual from long ago, a series of instructions that had once been as familiar as her own flesh. She did not need to think any longer. It was not determination, or even courage, that moved her: it was merely that she must.

She began to take off her clothes. How little time had passed since she had been drunk in Kit's sitting room, giggling at her own daring, stepping hopefully out of her underclothes: and how like and unlike this was to that! She recalled her mortification distantly, as if her past self were a character in a story. The air felt sacred and eager on her skin. Her body tingled. She had laid herself out for Kit like an offering, and been refused. But that had been right, that had been exactly right: *this* was the altar, this was the right place. Alone and not alone, human and not human, here on the chalk in the dark.

She turned, casting one last glance down into the valley. The lights were on in the vicarage. Were they waiting for her? Well, they must wait. She was protecting them. She was protecting everyone. *Greater love*, she thought, *hath no man than this*. But it did not feel like love. It did not feel like anything she could name.

She tested the ground with her bare feet, shifting until she felt a tide of darkness break over her, as though something deep below was rising to the surface, coming to claim its prey. Then she reached out with her hands to touch the chalk, and lay down.

She felt nothing, and everything. The stars put down dazzling roots, the earth spread its wings and lifted her into the high night sky, the Face moved underneath her, knitting itself together, drawing her downwards as though her bones were the chalk, and the chalk her own body. There was no room for thought: her flesh seemed to peel away, taking love and anger and hope and vanity with it, stripping her to nothing but breath and blood. She was being torn apart, she was wounded, dying, she was spinning through space like a meteor. She felt a roiling, sickening judder, a roar at the edge of audibility, vibrating through her – as if some ancient seam of rock had buckled and wrenched itself out of the ground, or some changeless blind river had turned back on itself and burst its banks, overwhelmed by a fury of fighting water.

Then, as if she had come out of the other side of a storm, she was flying, riding on the wind, starlight breaking on her raw skin like sea spray, every breath her first and last. The eddying darkness was far below, left behind, inconsequential, with her thin naked body and the small brief lines of the Face. She did not look at them again, she kept her gaze on the shimmering distance, the galaxy unfurling like a flag. At school when they talked about glory she had always wanted to laugh; but now, at last, she understood.

XXI

The Bone House, Haltington, oil on board, 1921

Kit could never remember walking back to Haltington that night. It was as though her memory jumped, like a scratched record, from one moment of clarity to another, erasing everything that must have passed in between: so that she seemed suddenly to be standing in the road outside the Bone house, and it was morning. She knew, of course, that she *had* walked, and that hours had elapsed, and the sun had risen; but when she cast her mind back there was nothing but a vague impression of weariness and growing daylight, and the jagged pain of a blister on her heel. She did not know how she had found her way. She did not even know – and never would know, since later when she saw headlines in the paper she flicked past the page quickly, not wanting to read beyond VANDALISM TO CHURCH AND MEMORIAL SHOCKS SUSSEX VILLAGE – the name of the place where Portia had stopped the car. Her mind was as blank as the overcast sky, and she stood in front of her garden gate as if she had never been there before, feeling nothing, expecting nothing, fearing nothing.

She lifted the latch of the gate and walked up the garden path, past the broken window and around the side of the house to the back door. It was open, swinging on its hinges. She went inside without closing it behind her. Nothing was exactly out of place, and yet it felt subtly unfamiliar, as if everything had been replaced with a perfect replica of itself. There was a strange smell in the air: brandy, from the last dregs in the cup on the table, but something else too, something more mineral, slightly acrid, unchanging.

The sitting room door was ajar. She pushed it with her fingertips, hanging back as if there might be a booby trap; but of course it only swung on its hinges, showing the room beyond. The smell was stronger. It was unpleasant, she thought, but in a clean, finished way, as though something rotten had burnt to ash.

The room was just as she had left it. She did not know why she was surprised. There was the sofa on which Phoebe had lain naked; there was the broken window; there, no doubt knocked from the mantelpiece and kicked aside as she and Portia left, was the drawing she had made, squeezed into the blank space on the back of the pamphlet. Automatically she stooped to pick it up; but before her hand reached the paper she drew back, her breath catching in her throat.

The drawing was gone. But below the querulous line of print asking who ate all the biscuits – where Phoebe's face had been – the space was not exactly blank. Kit lifted the corner of the pamphlet between her finger and thumb, holding it up to the light. The page was smeared, greyish, and oddly translucent: almost as if the drawing had been erased with an India rubber, too enthusiastically, so that the surface of the paper had started to come away. But it was greasy, too – and there was the smell again, sour as a dying man's breath. Around the margins ran a wavering line of darker grey. For a moment Kit could not think what it reminded her of; then she remembered the ashen tidemark that had edged the bathtub in Paris. It had made her skin crawl to hunch in the tepid water, watching the soap suds lap at the line of grime, tense with the effort not to touch it. Now she imagined something – something with Phoebe's face – lurching out of the page as if from a bath of pale, scummy water . . .

She dug in her pocket, drew out Hannah Smith's locket, and opened it. The empty photograph lay in her hand. The blotch had been dark and sticky, like crude oil; not like the waxen discoloration on the paper where her drawing had been. But then, heavy white paper was not the same as photographic paper. The lead of a pencil was not the same as silver salts. She held the two pictures – the two things that had been pictures – side by side. She thought of a lecture she had been to at art school: *Every mark you make is dictated by your medium. Everything, including art, is subject to the inescapable reality of the world. Nothing exists in a vacuum.* She dropped the page in the cold hearth and wiped her hands on her trousers.

She turned away, went to the stairs, began to climb. *The inescapable reality of the world.* A photograph, a smeared piece of paper – they meant nothing, nothing real . . . But her knees were trembling, and she had to pause before she reached the top; and then, sweeping over her, impossible to outrun, came a sickening flood of memory. She saw again that Christ on its cross, limping towards her in the moonlight; and felt the blank, undoing terror of it. She had been afraid of the others, of course, but that one, the Christ, the thing that was both Christ and cross, a sentient mass that had not differentiated between tortured flesh and instrument of torture . . . Had she truly seen it? Surely . . .

But she had. She had seen the war memorial, the stained glass window, the Crusader – oh Lord, it should almost have been funny, if she put it into words it was like a joke – the statue, the window and the tomb – all walking towards her – Septimus would snort with laughter if ever she tried to describe it – but they had been real. They *had* been real. And then behind them had come the shambling crucified one-legged thing, and that would stay in her brain for ever, ready to lurch into her nightmares. During the War there had been nonsense in the papers about calvaries at the sides of French roads, left miraculously untouched while shells fell all around. The thing she had seen was the opposite of that, the triumph of meaninglessness, and despair . . .

Distantly she had heard Portia's gasp, and then, a little later, the motorcar's engine, and the sound of it accelerating away. She had not cared very much: that small desertion was like a single hair being plucked when you were mortally wounded. It did not matter. Everything was simple now. She waited.

And then . . . then, for no reason, with no warning, they had gone. She could not remember – did not especially want to remember – whether they had dissolved on an unearthly breeze or merely . . . retreated. There had been no climax. It was, she thought, like the coming of peace must have been in the trenches: the guns falling silent, a cessation of the unbearable, nothing more. Had there been some invisible victory, some righting of a wrong? Something must have happened – surely she should have sensed *something*, even if it were only the subtle eddy of a flood reaching its highest point, then beginning its slow sinking away. But all she knew was that she blinked, and they were not there any more. Slowly her ears began to let in other sounds: an owl, the twiggy rustle of an animal in the hedge, the far-away wail of a baby waking from sleep in the nearest cottage. Gradually, too, she became aware of her body, and the racing of her heart. She had forgotten that she had legs; now they were threatening to pitch her over the graveyard wall, wobbling and treacherous as a newborn foal's. And the graveyard was empty and perfectly still, the sort of moonlit pastoral night-piece that might have hung in any Victorian parlour. Only the bare plinth where the memorial had been told her that she had not been dreaming. There must have been broken glass inside the church, a missing crucifix, and a stone tomb left empty as an unmade bed; but she did not think of that then, or care.

She remembered thinking that she had escaped. And then her memory was a blank, until she found herself in the road outside the Bone house, staring at the star-shaped hole in the smashed window.

She glanced through the open door to the studio. There was nothing to see there. In her bedroom, the bed was rumpled and there was a dirty shirt on the floor; but it was her own, familiar untidiness. Nothing had been touched. She crossed to the window, and looked out, tilting her head up to look at the slope of the down.

There was the Face. The four lines shone, clear and white, the brightest thing in the landscape. It had changed, she thought; she could not have pointed out how it was different, but it did not trouble the eye in the same way it had done. Now it was like a wall, where before it had been a closed door. It was simply there, complete, sufficient.

She should have been glad. She *was* glad. The gap in the world had gone. It was neatly plugged, the horrors trapped where they should be, the chalk and the grass and the uncaring sky all in their proper places. A treaty, that held, for now.

Four lines. And they did not really make a face, she thought. Yesterday it had been absent, broken: today it was whole. A real face could not be healed like that. Nothing real – nothing human, anyway – could be healed like that.

She laid her hand against the glass of the window,

blocking out the lines, so that for a moment the down seemed a sweep of uninterrupted green. For a moment she thought she saw someone moving at the base of the slope, where the path went past the garden of the vicarage, but when she looked again she was not sure. It did not matter. Everyone was safe now, everyone: Florence and Phoebe, Dr Manning and Mrs Reed and the others whose names she did not know. Everyone. There was no reason to be afraid any more. The nightmare had passed. Now there was only the naked grey afterlight of morning, and a day to be lived through before they could sleep again.

She let her hand fall; and then, wearily, she sank onto the bed, put her hands over her eyes, and cried.

Florence drew the church door shut behind her, and trudged along the path between the graves to the lychgate. In spite of her coat she was shivering, and she ached all over with cold and exhaustion. Soon she would turn back; but the thought of Horace's accusing stare when he saw her come in made her huddle under the archway, delaying the moment.

Last night, when Phoebe had not come home . . . She had never known such a long, cold vigil, not even when Mother was dying. There was something in the darkness, as the clock ticked on towards midnight, which seemed to whisper and crawl on her skin. She had felt as if the blooms on the wallpaper would open like mouths and swallow her; she had been afraid to look at Horace in case he had died silently between breaths, and she would find herself meeting his fixed, congealing stare . . . She told herself over and over not to be silly. But then – just when she thought she might go mad – she felt her limbs unclench and her heartbeat slow, so swiftly it was as if some external pressure had been removed. She took a deep breath, congratulating herself on her sudden calm. Keeping your nerve, that was the key . . . And at last, instead of glaring accusingly at the door, Horace let his head slump on to his chest with a sigh, and his breaths turned to slow rasps.

She had shifted in her seat, imagining his confusion, followed by his incredulous outrage, if he woke to find her gone – and he would wake, soon enough, as soon as the coals slipped in the grate or a window rattled . . . Only a foolish, unkind fiancée would leave now, taking advantage of his brief unconsciousness. Naturally Florence should not go out alone at night to look for Phoebe. That would be sheer pig-headedness. Mother would be shocked at the mere idea: a woman's job was to wait for bad news, and endure. She had hesitated, thinking of Mother, and Imogen, and then of Phoebe when she was a little girl: the Phoebe who had sometimes come to Florence with a toy to show her or a book that made her laugh uproariously – the Phoebe who had once, unsolicited, slipped her hot, chubby hand into Florence's own, and said, 'I made a present for Mama, do you want to see?' It was only now, in the real Phoebe's absence, that Florence could visualise the child she had been. She remembered that small, six-year-old Phoebe, dazed and docile in black, asking when Mama would be coming home for the picnic; then she got up and hurried out on light feet, determined and brazen as a thief.

She had gone first to the Bone house, of course – oddly compelled, even though Mrs Reed's son had seen Kit driving away in a motorcar yesterday afternoon, so her first, shameful suspicion had been set aside . . . She had seen from the road that there were no lights burning; but all the same she crept round the side into the garden. The kitchen door hung open. She had brought a torch, and she took a few steps inside, swinging the beam of light back and forth. There was a funny kind of smell, although nothing was out of place. She called, 'Phoebe? Kit?' No one answered, and instinct told her there was no one to hear her. For a guilty second she was relieved, in spite of what Mrs Reed had said about the motorcar; but after all, spending the night with Kit would not have been the worst thing that could happen to Phoebe . . . She winced, trying not to think about the Levett girl who fell down a well, or the little boy who choked on a sweet and wasn't found for days. *'Phoebe,'* she repeated, her voice already weak.

She went upstairs, just in case Phoebe was too ill or hurt to answer: but as the torch beam swept back and forth she saw that both studio and bedroom were empty. For a horrid second she thought she caught a glimpse of a face pressed against the glass – blank-eyed, impossible – but as she stumbled back she understood that it was only the Face on the down outside, the chalk lines pale and distinct, standing out against the black hill as if they were suspended in mid-air. She had not seen it so clearly for years.

No one was here. She turned, resisting the urge to run, and retreated down the stairs and outside. If she were honest, perhaps she had known then that it would be no good; but her pride would not let her give up so soon. She walked along the Litlington Road, the torch beam zig-zagging in front of her, calling, 'Phoebe?' At the end of the village she turned aside, to explore the farther reaches, the last few cottages and gardens that gave way on one side to the flat river-fields and on the other to the down . . . At last, hours later, as the darkness thinned, she found herself doubling back. She climbed the hill towards the church, because she could not think of anywhere else to go – and then, out of her numb misery came a final flash of hope, because of course the church was left unlocked, and perhaps . . . ? But the church door had scraped open to reveal emptiness: rows of heavy unpeopled pews, the plain windows grey, nothing moving but a single dry leaf that darted across the floor in the draught.

And now it was light, and the beam of her torch was only just visible, a pale oval on the stone-speckled mud at her feet. She clicked it off. The sound had a stiff finality, as if to signal that the night was over, the morning had come, and it was time to admit defeat. Phoebe would not be found – or, at least, would not be found by her . . .

She sighed, picked her way through the mud to the end of the track, where it joined the path down to the vicarage, and stopped.

Below her, on the path, was a slight, shadowy figure. Her heart jumped, so that for a second she could not see clearly: was it only that she had been looking for so long— ? But it was, it *was* Phoebe, dishevelled, without a hat or coat, her hair loose, her feet bare.

Florence flung herself down the path, plummeting down the steepest section so that she almost crashed to her knees. She struggled out of her coat as she went, almost tripping over the hem. '*Phoebe!* Are you hurt? Where are your *shoes*?'

Phoebe stopped. She glanced at Florence with a faint air of surprise, as if she were not the one who had been out all night. Her shirt was buttoned up wrong.

Florence threw her coat over Phoebe's shoulders and dragged it tight as if it were a net. 'What's happened? Where have you been?'

'Everywhere,' Phoebe said, as if it were obvious.

'Are you hurt? Did someone— ?'

'I was on my own, Aunt Florence. No one did anything.'

'For heaven's sake!' Florence said, not quite knowing if the quaver in her voice was relief or fury. Phoebe looked different, she thought. A bit like the transparent glow that consumptives got, except that her cheeks were pale, not red . . . 'You must be frozen. Are you ill?'

'I don't think so.'

'Then— what on earth— ?' But she knew she would not get a proper answer now, if ever. 'Let's get you home. Come on.' She tugged at Phoebe's arm, manhandling her down the path towards the vicarage. 'Your father has been frantic. And so have I,' she added, realising in that moment that she meant it. 'Come *on*.' She expected Phoebe to give her a long, hostile stare, as she generally did when Florence told her what to do; but instead she allowed herself to be piloted along the path, and went obediently through the gate into the vicarage garden when Florence held it open.

Mrs Reed was in the kitchen. She said, 'Oh!' when she saw Florence, and '*Oh!*' when she saw Phoebe; but Florence hurried Phoebe past without pausing.

There were voices coming from the drawing room. Horace said, 'Well, *I* don't know, you're the policeman! Don't you have procedures of some kind? For goodness' sake, Ezekiel, surely you have *some* idea – perhaps a search party, or something similar—'

Another voice said, with dignity, 'With all due respect, sir, there are no indications that your daughter is in any danger. If you take my advice as an enforcer of the law—'

'Don't take that tone with me,' Horace said, 'you have hardly been in long trousers five minutes—'

Florence hissed to Phoebe, 'Stay there.' Then she opened the drawing room door. 'I found her,' she said. 'She's all right. She got lost on the down, that's all.'

Horace got up from his chair as the policeman looked round. 'Where have you *been*, Florence?' he said, stretching out a hand as if he were claiming something at a Lost Property office. 'When I wanted you—'

'She needs to go straight to bed,' Florence said. 'I'm taking her up to her room. You may talk to her later, when she is recovered.'

Horace blinked. 'But I thought you said she was all right—'

She pushed Phoebe towards the stairs. As the door swung shut, the policeman chuckled. 'Be ruling the nursery with an iron rod, that one, won't she, sir?'

Florence followed Phoebe to the door of her bedroom, and there they paused, face to face, as if there were something else to be said. She searched for words, but none came.

'Thank you,' Phoebe said, with curious formality. That exalted expression had come back into her eyes, as if she could hear music Florence could not.

'That's – all right.'

There was a silence. Phoebe said, 'What is it, Aunt Florence?'

She had not realised she was staring. She stammered, 'I don't know,' as if she were a schoolgirl taking her end of year viva. 'Only . . .' But as she said it she *did* know. She had looked like that herself, the evening of the first time she and Kit— that first evening. As if she had walked through a mirror into a world that was not quite the same: a marvellous, treacherous, extraordinary world. But no, the thought was shocking. Surely Phoebe could not have . . . ? Bare feet and a hastily buttoned shirt did not mean— *no*. She was a child, a mere child – and who, if she had— ? Kit had left – there were no young men – *who* . . . ?

Phoebe gave her a faint, preoccupied smile, went into her bedroom, and shut the door.

Florence dragged her hands across her forehead. It had been a long night, so long a night . . . She was imagining things. Now that Phoebe was at home, as collected and self-assured as ever, there was no reason to fear at all; what did it matter where Phoebe had been, really? The triumph of finding her had passed, if it had ever meant anything at all. She was so exhausted she could hardly stand up. Life could go on exactly as it had.

She wanted to sleep. She wanted to go upstairs and sleep, and never wake—

There was a knock at the door. Automatically she went to answer it, ready to explain that Phoebe had come home, thank you, but the vicar would be very touched to hear of everyone's concern. But some instinct stopped her before she descended the last flight of stairs. She paused on the landing, and looked out of the window above the front door.

It was Kit. She looked exhausted too, red-eyed and gaunt-cheeked. She was as white as Phoebe had been, but her pallor was more like the overcast sky than Phoebe's starry blaze. What was she doing here? She knocked again, and Florence tensed in case someone else decided to answer; but the men were still arguing in the parlour, and Mrs Reed was singing 'Lord of All Hopefulness', beating time with her rolling pin. Florence reached out and held on to the window sill so tightly her fingernails went the colour of the cliffs at the Haven – the colour of the Sisters, she thought, looking down at them – and told herself that she must not go down and open the door. She was so tired, she was worn thin by fatigue, her resolve was as fragile as tissue paper . . . If she looked Kit in the face, she might change her mind. She might stumble out into the road, pulling the vicarage door shut behind her, grab Kit's hand and demand to go away, anywhere, she did not care where. She might say that of course she was not going to marry Horace, it was a terrible mistake, and please would Kit take her back, please . . . It would be so easy; but she must not. She lifted one hand away from the sill, and laid it over the flat softness of her belly, just below the waistband of her skirt.

Kit glanced up. They looked at each other across the yards of distance with a long pure stare, free of judgement or emotion, as they had sometimes looked at each other after the act of love. Then, with a wry little shrug, Kit raised her hand; and Florence, stupidly, mirrored the gesture, as if there were invisible strings that linked Kit's wrist to her own. Kit gave a jerky nod of her head, still holding Florence's gaze. Then she turned, and went down the garden steps to the road.

Too late – in an irrational flash – Florence understood that it had been a goodbye. *That* was why Kit had come. She raised her hand to knock on the glass – if only Kit would turn back— !

But another counter-impulse stopped her: an iron bolt in the joint of her elbow, stopping her fist before it touched the pane. She could not. She must not. She stayed rigid, pain spreading down from her forehead and up from her heart, until it met in the middle, tight around her throat. Kit walked away, without glancing back. Then the road was empty. Nothing moved under the grey sky except a few leaves blowing across the road.

Florence shut her eyes. She thought that perhaps she had never felt so alone.

After a while the parlour door opened again. She heard Horace murmur something unintelligible, and Sergeant Cripps answer, 'Let's hope so, sir,' and march along the passage.

As he went into the kitchen – and then, with a distant clunk, out of the back door – Mrs Reed's voice drifted out again, raised with uncharacteristic vigour. She was supposed to start the wedding cake today; if she had weighed the fruit out to soak, perhaps she had been at the brandy.

'God moves in a mysterious way,' she sang, 'his marvels to perform . . .' Wonders, Florence thought. For God's sake, get the words right. His *wonders*.

She heaved a deep, bracing breath, and went downstairs, ready to be kind to Horace. Things were not so bad. The bad things, whatever they had been, were over. Everything would be all right now. And when she heard Mrs Reed still singing in the kitchen she made herself join in, determined to raise her own spirits: because, after all, there *were* reasons to be cheerful.

XXII

High and Over, oil on board, 1925

The train slowed and the guard shouted, 'Haltington Halt,' from further down the train. The words made it sound as though he had a stutter, like Septimus after he came home on leave after Passchendaele. He called again, '*Halt* – ington – *Halt* . . .'

Kit looked out of the window at the approaching sign on its single bare platform, and considered staying where she was. She might sit in her seat, quite calm, her hands linked in her lap, until she arrived at the terminus; then she would wait, unmoving, unthinking, until the whole train rattled back towards London.

'*Halt* – *ington* – *HALT*,' the guard bawled. If Kit did not stand up now, it would be too late. She swung her haversack on to her shoulder, opened the door and stepped out; but she judged it badly, landing before the train had come to a stop, and as she stumbled sideways, fighting to keep her balance, she wrenched her ankle. She hobbled to the sign and clung on to it until the pain had died down, gritting her teeth, ignoring the slam of doors and the guard's whistle.

When her vision had cleared, the train had gone, and the last shreds of steam were dispersing into the air. A man was sauntering away on the road towards Berwick, his hat just visible above the hedge. Apart from that, she was alone. With a strange flash of hope and disappointment she thought that Florence must have forgotten, or thought better of it after all.

'Kit?'

She swung round. Coming towards her was a stout woman in a flapping coat, her hair hidden under a black cloche. For a moment it was impossible. The woman's gait was a stiff waddle, her face podgy: she was too old and too fat to be the Florence that Kit remembered. Then, like some kind of optical trick, the veil of unfamiliarity lifted, and Kit's heart gave an uncomfortable jerk. 'Florence,' she said. 'I – forgive me, I was in a brown study.'

Florence smiled at her. She held out a hand as if she were a dignitary attending a vernissage, and Kit shook it. 'Is that all your luggage?'

'Yes. I wanted to travel light.'

'Very sensible.' There was a silence that seemed to go on longer than the years since they had seen each other. This, of course, was the moment for Kit to say that she had been sorry to hear of Horace's death; but it was so gross and obvious a lie that she could not bring the words into her mouth. She tried to think of something else to say, and failed. Finally Florence swung her arms like a gym mistress, and said, 'Well, come on, then.'

Kit followed her to the road. It was just as well she had not brought more baggage, since there was no pony and trap waiting for them. She thought of her aching ankle and said, with too much jollity, 'Well, it's a lovely day for a walk . . .' Then she stopped. Just round the corner, half hidden by the hedge, was an open-topped motor car. Florence picked up a pair of driving gauntlets from the back seat, and began to put them on.

'My God.' The car was scarlet and shining. 'Is that— ? It's flashier than Portia's Rolls.'

'I got it cheap, actually,' Florence said, 'the Archbishop's sister-in-law thought it wasn't quite the thing. Dashing, isn't it?'

'It's – surprising,' Kit said, more honestly than she meant to.

'You're not scared? I promise I won't go very fast.'

'No, that's . . . it's all right.' She opened the door and settled herself into the passenger seat. It was like sitting in a leather bucket. She put her haversack between her feet.

'Oof,' Florence said, lowering herself into the driver's seat. 'Thank goodness it has an electric starter. I couldn't manage a crank in this state.'

Kit slipped her a sidelong glance. Of course there was no reason why Florence should not be sanguine about her new-found plumpness – maybe these days, having no husband to please, she was quite happy to neglect her appearance – but her tone of voice had been positively complacent. The old Florence, Kit thought, would have cared . . .

Florence caught her eye. 'Oh, Kit,' she said, 'I didn't think *you* would be so stuffy about it. You should hear Mrs Reed going on! Anyone would think that I should be confined to a nunnery until the baby's born.' She pressed the starter button, and the car coughed into life. Checking the mirror ostentatiously, as if to reassure Kit that she was a competent driver, she manoeuvred the car into the road, and accelerated away.

Kit was glad of the sudden roar in her ears, and the wind cooling her cheeks. She stared at the glass in front of her face, frowning as if she were intent on some intellectual problem. After a long time, when they had gone over a crossroads, she said, casually, 'You didn't mention that you were expecting a child.'

'No. I thought it was easier just to – to let you see. It seemed silly to worry about the right words, when you were coming to visit.'

But she hadn't seen. Or rather, she had seen, but not understood. Now, with an effort, she turned back to Florence. Yes, her cheeks and neck were fuller, fleshier, and her breasts larger; under her dress, a thinnish spring frock in dark purple satin, there was the curve – unmistakable now! – of a swelling belly. So Florence was not old, or fat, but pregnant. It should have been a relief, but Kit felt a pang of something else. 'Congratulations,' she said.

'Thank you.'

There was a silence. So Dr Manning had done his duty, just in time. No wonder Florence was smiling. Kit sank down lower in her seat, wishing she had stayed on the train.

They flashed past a row of flint-walled cottages. 'No, that isn't true,' Florence said brusquely, as if there had not been a pause. 'I was afraid that if I told you, it might – make a difference.'

'Why would it make a difference?'

'I mean, I thought you might not come.'

'Why wouldn't I come?'

'I thought you might be angry.'

'Why would I be angry?'

'Stop it! You know why.' She eased them round a corner, biting her lip; then, with a sigh, she braked hard and pulled the car into a gap beside a gate. In the new silence, the breeze was full of birdsong and the rustle of grass. She took her hands from the steering wheel and plucked her gloves off, finger by finger. Then she turned to look at Kit.

Kit stared back, deliberately keeping her face as blank as possible.

'I'm sorry, Kit.'

Kit shrugged. 'No need—'

'I am. I am sorry. I treated you very badly. Will you forgive me?'

'It's a long time ago.'

'That's not what I asked,' Florence said, with a faint smile.

'I know,' Kit said, and could not help smiling back. And with a strange shimmer the world seemed to become real again: even if years had passed, she and Florence were the same people they had been then. The hand that lay close to hers, with its simple gold band on the third finger, was the same hand that had— well, it was Florence's hand. The eyes that met hers were the same sea-sky blue, the hair the same rich ripe-corn gold—

'Oh! Florence,' Kit said, before she could stop herself, 'you cut your hair—'

'Yes.' Florence laughed, and took off her hat. Her hair curled just below her ears, catching the sunlight and blowing across her mouth. 'I was too cowardly to have it shingled.'

'It suits you.' It did; but even so Kit was not sure she liked it. Florence had never made her feel boring, or old, before. 'Goodness, the car, the baby, the hair . . . I was afraid you'd be the picture of a sorrowing widow, but you seem happier than ever.'

She had said it lightly – or as lightly as she could – but Florence flushed. She lowered her eyes and laid a hand over the bulge in her dress. She said at last, 'That isn't fair. I know I'm not wearing black, but that's because I'm superstitious – you know, about the baby – and these days people don't seem to mind so much as they did. I didn't think *you* would think less of me for it.'

'I never said I thought less of you.'

She did not answer at once, but held Kit's gaze with a new steadiness. Kit was the first to look away. 'He's dead,' Florence said at last, 'and I don't regret marrying him. I grieved for him, you know. He was kind to me . . . We had a very quiet wedding. The Bishop officiated, but there were only a few people there, apart from the parishioners. I wore green silk, with a posy of lily of the valley. Mother would have approved.'

'And were you happy together?'

Florence hesitated. 'We weren't unhappy.'

'And then,' Kit said, resisting the temptation to linger on Florence's answer, to weigh it for every speck of meaning, 'then he died.'

'Yes. In March. He'd had a cough for ages . . . I liked looking after him. He said to me once that he always thought he was doing me a kindness by marrying me, but he'd been wrong. He grew weaker and weaker, but it was peaceful, really. I think in the end we loved each other. And . . .' She ran her hand down over her belly, smoothing the fabric. 'It's funny. All that time, nothing happened. I mean, he did – did *it*, but I didn't catch. And then, just before he died, when he could hardly lift himself up . . .'

'It is his, then?'

Kit had meant it – oh, unforgivably! – to wound; but Florence did not flinch. 'It was,' she said, simply, 'although now it's only mine.'

The wind whispered gently around Kit's collar, wafting the smell of blossom from the hedge. Kit pressed her thumbs together and looked at them. 'You're lucky.'

'I know. Do you remember the census? Two million women without men . . . I do miss him, in a way. But I'll have the baby.' She leant back, running her hands through her hair, ruffling it into a cherubic halo. 'And the diocese have been awfully kind. They're letting me stay for as long as I need to. The vicarage is too big for me, though, I'm going to look for somewhere smaller. Just for me and the baby, and a nursemaid.'

'Not Phoebe?'

She shot Kit a glance, but instead of answering she reached for her hat and gloves, and put them back on. 'Shall we drive up to Hindover Hill?' she said. 'It's such a beautiful day. I made sandwiches.'

'All right.'

'Or there's a little tea room near Alfriston—'

'Hindover Hill sounds perfect.'

Florence adjusted her hat, and started the motor. The acceleration pressed Kit back into her seat. She did not resist. Insects flew into the windscreen, pattering, leaving smears on the glass. They drove through a village and then up and up, until at last they came to the top of the hill and saw fields stretching down on both sides. Florence swung the car sideways onto a flat portion of grass, and put on the handbrake.

'Here,' she said. 'Let's walk down a little. There's a good spot below the trees.' She bent over the back seat and lifted an ancient rucksack. It was the same one that she had brought with her the day they cycled to the coast; and the sight of it did something strange to Kit's insides, as if her gut remembered that day as vividly as her mind.

'Give me that,' she said roughly, taking it. 'You can't carry things in your condition.' She heard Florence laugh and protest, but she had already marched away, making her way through the band of trees and scrub in the direction that Florence had indicated. It was good to be out of sight, however briefly: she could think, without worrying that her thoughts might show on her face. Christ, Florence . . . *In the end we loved each other.* Could that be true? And did it matter? Why should she care, when it had been over four years since . . . ?

She came out into the open. In front of her a gate gave on to a field; beyond the field the land dropped sharply, and Cuckmere Valley lay spread out beneath, a trail of silver looping back and forth until it reached the sea. It was warm, and the breeze had lessened. The sky was pale, the sun obscured by a soft bank of cloud that lay in silky ruffles over the horizon.

She looked over her shoulder. Florence was coming down the path, with the waddling gait that Kit had mistaken for infirmity. Now it only seemed undignified and touching. She leant on the gate next to Kit, so close that the scent of clean skin and violet water mingled with the smell of grass and distant sheep. 'There?' she said, pointing. 'We can sit on my coat.'

Kit opened the gate and beckoned her through. They picked their way through the grass to the place Florence had chosen; then with a laughing groan Florence lowered herself to the ground, grasping Kit's arm to stop herself dropping the final few inches. 'Oh – my coat – I should have taken it off. Bother.'

'Don't be silly. These trousers have seen much worse.'

'When the baby's born I'm going to wear trousers too. I can't at the moment, because of my waist, of course.' She stretched her legs out, showing her black-stockinged ankles. They had not changed, Kit thought, and in spite of herself she remembered Florence's plump, rosy feet, the down on her calves, the generous flesh of her thighs and hips. The place where those thighs met . . .

She dug in the haversack and drew out a packet of sandwiches and a flask. There was a bar of chocolate too, and two hard-boiled eggs. 'May I?'

'Tuck in.' But Florence did not take the rest of the sandwiches when Kit held them out. She lay back, her eyes closed, her hands clasped above the curve of her belly. Like this, the bulge of her pregnancy was statuesque, magnificent, as if her body and the hills were part of the same landscape.

'It's beautiful,' Kit said.

'It is now. During the War they did exercises down there, when there was a training camp at Seaford. It got horribly churned up.'

Kit ate her sandwich. It was good, with real butter and a thick slice of meat; good enough to force her to pay attention, in spite of her whirling thoughts. When she had finished she folded the rest of the paper neatly over the round that was left, and put the packet back in the rucksack. There was such quietness up here, such stillness: even though the breeze murmured in her ears, she had a sense of underlying peace, the bones of the earth deeply asleep, the sky like glass. It was a long way from London.

Florence yawned, and opened her eyes. 'It's funny,' she said, 'so much has changed, but I feel the same.'

'The same as what?'

'As if we could begin again, from the beginning.' She sat up, arching her back to ease the muscles. For a moment Kit thought she would ask, point blank, if Kit felt it too; but instead she smiled and reached for the bar of chocolate that lay on the grass. 'Mmm. Lovely.'

Kit crossed her legs and leant back on her elbows. 'How is Phoebe?' she said, and Florence paused mid-mouthful, with a glinting look at her as if to say that they had both known that the question was coming.

Florence swallowed, wiping her mouth with the back of her hand like a scullery maid. 'She's all right,' she said. 'She's living at the Bone house now, did you know that?'

'How would I know?'

'She's . . . I suppose you didn't write to her, either.'

'I didn't think she would want me to.'

'No, perhaps not.' Florence kneaded her back, grimacing. 'The night before you left, something happened,' she said, without looking at Kit. 'She didn't come home. In the morning I found her on the hill, without any shoes on. We never found her hat and coat. She wasn't hurt, though. I still don't know what happened. She never told us. All I know is that afterwards she was . . . different.'

Kit bit her lip. Was it a question? But she was not sure she could explain; or if she did, whether Florence would believe her. She said, 'It wasn't what you think—'

But Florence went on speaking as if she had not heard the interruption. 'She was like – oh, I don't know. Like a maiden from a Greek myth. She was always odd, you know. There was something cold about her. I used to believe it was because Imogen died when she was so little. She hated me, I think. But now . . . when I found her that morning, she had changed. There was a – oh, how idiotic it sounds! – there was a kind of power, about her. As though she had come home from distant lands, and could forgive us all for being so little and silly.'

Kit said carefully, 'That sounds like Phoebe.'

'But it *wasn't*. It was . . .' She grimaced. 'The villagers say she's a witch. They say it very quietly, when they think I can't hear, because I'm the vicar's widow and she's the vicar's daughter. They don't mean it unkindly. But sometimes I think they're right.'

There was a silence. Then, without haste, Florence turned to look at her, as if the silence itself had been a question. 'You weren't there, that night,' she said. 'Billy Reed saw you driving away in a motorcar with a friend – the car made a great impression on him, actually, he said it was racing green, with a lovely shine on it . . . So it can't have been anything to do with you. Can it?'

Kit sat up, to look straight into Florence's eyes. 'I didn't touch her,' she said. 'I promise, Florence. I didn't touch her.'

Florence held her gaze for what seemed an eternity. Then she took a deep breath, and although she did not change position Kit felt the tension leave her. 'Good,' she said, on a long exhalation, and turned to stare at the gleaming sea. After a minute she said, 'Why did you leave, then?'

Kit pulled up a blade of grass and wound it through her fingers. She did not know, even now, why exactly she had decided to leave that day. There had been no decision: only a realisation that she had nothing left to keep her there.

'All right,' Florence said, smiling. It was a real smile, warm and amused, as if the answer did not matter, really. 'Then tell me why you knocked at the door. What would you have said, if I had opened it?'

Kit drew the grass tight, until it snapped. Then she flicked the halves away, tiny fragments of green flying on the breeze, and plucked another handful. What *would* she have said? She had gone there to make sure Phoebe was safe – or at least that was what she had told herself, in spite of Portia murmuring in her head, *I say, is Phoebe here, because I plied her with brandy and let her take all her clothes off . . .* But perhaps, if she was truthful, it might have been to see Florence. And if Florence had answered the door, and said, 'Hullo, Kit,' then would she have— ?

But she would never know what she would have done. She had not been thinking at all. She had waited, listening, until she realised that no one was coming to the door; then she had looked up at the window above, and seen Florence there. They had gazed at each other, unmoving. Florence had not smiled, or gestured, or done anything that might have meant she cared; and in that moment Kit had felt something inside her disintegrate quietly, like a long-cold ember finally crumbling into ash. She had raised her hand, and Florence did the same, like her reflection, and then Kit had turned away. It had been easy, as if something that had anchored her had come loose; and for the first time in years she felt a kind of lightness, the bleak bare sensation of a burden lifted, a heavy treasure left by the side of the road.

Then, when she arrived at the cottage she had found Portia there, who said, 'Well then, time to pack, methinks. Shall we fall aboard?' and sprang into action, never giving Kit the chance to demur. She had followed Portia's lead, glad not to have to think. Trust Portia, to come back like that, without a word of explanation or apology! She had never mentioned the churchyard or the war memorial, then or later, and Kit had never brought it up either; it would have meant admitting that Portia had driven away, leaving Kit to face the danger alone – and that would have been too much trouble, when it was easier to drift apart, amicably, without fuss. And, perhaps, Kit was afraid that if she did say something, Portia would blink and wrinkle her nose and tell her to see a head-doctor, because it wasn't normal to hallucinate, darling . . . A few times she came close; but every time she was too cowardly, and as the months passed, it was harder and harder to be sure she believed it herself. After Muckle's body was dragged from the Thames, and had a sober, sorrowful funeral as befitted a war hero, and then a few weeks later Septimus announced he was getting married, and the lease ran out on the house in Oxfordshire, Kit had been grateful not to see Portia much any more, not to have to wonder. She still had nightmares about the thurlath; but she had begun to doubt, a little, that they had really existed. *Something* had existed: but after the War it was impossible to trust what you saw, or thought you saw. It would have been so apt, after the studio in Paris, for her to imagine hollow men, faceless men, hungry men . . .

She opened her palm and let the crushed stems of grass and clover fall. Florence was still waiting for her to reply. 'I don't know,' she said. But as she said it the answer came to her: if Florence had opened the door, she would have said,

I love you. How simple it was, really. But there was no point saying that now, just as there would have been no point saying it then.

Florence nodded, although Kit could not tell whether she was satisfied or resigned. Apropos of nothing she said, 'You can see the Haltington Face from here. Look – just there, to the left of the church tower.'

'Yes, I see it.'

'Phoebe keeps it white. I offered to help once, but she said she wanted to do it alone.'

'I dream about it,' Kit said, 'quite a lot.'

'Me too.' They shared a glance, and looked away, smiling at the same time. The shared smile was like an open door; but a door in an old house, where age and subsidence had dragged the foundations out of true, and after a moment it swung shut of its own accord.

Kit said, 'Why did you ask me here, Florence?'

'I wanted you to paint the Haltington Face from my old bedroom window.'

'That's what you said in your letter.'

'And it's true.' Kit did not answer immediately; and as if her silence were an accusation, Florence shifted uncomfortably on the grass. 'You're a successful artist now, aren't you?'

Kit bit back the retort that she had been successful before she came to Haltington. What did Florence know about art, or success, come to that? 'Yes.'

'Well then. I'll pay you properly, of course.'

'Of course,' Kit echoed.

Suddenly Florence knelt up, shuffling on her knees to look Kit full in the face. She held her hands over her belly, as if to protect it from missiles, and said, 'Do you hate me?'

Kit almost said, *Don't be an idiot*. But the automatic impulse to comfort did not quite reach her lips. Instead she let her eyes go past Florence, to the pale glittering valley and the distant, bleached-out lines of the Face. No doubt if she looked carefully she would be able to make out the church, and the vicarage, and the Bone cottage. How long ago it had been, and how it felt like yesterday!

'Do you remember,' she said, 'how you killed that squirrel, for me?'

'Oh! Yes. The poor thing, I wanted to put it out of its misery—'

'It's strange,' Kit went on, without pausing. 'When I met you – for a long time after I met you, in fact – I thought you were weak. I don't mean that I despised you. Just that – you were alone, dependent, desperate to be loved . . . You'd settle for me, because you knew you wouldn't get anyone better— no, I haven't finished, listen. I thought I was the strong one, the one who knew who she was, the one who could fuck a beautiful woman and not fall in love. You were the one who said *I love you*, and I never said it back.'

Florence sat still, attentive, self-possessed. But of course, Kit thought, she was not alone any more; she could not be alone until after the baby was born, and even then she would know herself beloved.

'I was wrong,' Kit said. 'I didn't recognise strength when I saw it. I believe that you felt what you said you felt. But you didn't let it get in the way. You were ruthless. You pitied that squirrel, but you killed it. You loved me, but you put me to one side. Out of all of us, I thought *you* were the feeble, the feminine one – but out of all of us, you're the one who's ended up with everything you wanted.'

There was a silence. It was impossible that Kit could hear the sea on such a calm day, from so far away; but she thought she did, a faint, unearthly susurrus.

'Not everything,' Florence said. She took her hands away from her belly, spreading her arms: it was as if she were nude, letting fall the last concealing cloth. She said again, very softly, 'No, not everything.'

Kit stared at her. Her heart gave a treacherous leap, filling and emptying itself of blood with nauseating swiftness. She had come here to make her peace, she thought, not to destroy it again, not to put it into Florence's hands to be destroyed. She should not have come.

Florence got to her feet, levering herself awkwardly off the ground without asking for help. When finally she was standing upright, she walked down the slope a little way, shading her eyes with her hand as she looked towards the Haven.

Kit waited for a long time, expecting Florence to call to her, or come back. She did not. Finally Kit raised herself into a crouch to gather the remnants of the picnic and pack them into the haversack. She could leave now; everything that needed to be said had been said. She would drop the haversack onto the back seat of the Vauxhall, and walk down the hill; there might be somewhere to stay in Alfriston, or she could keep on walking, all the way to Berwick or Haltington. But as she tightened the drawstring of the bag, she felt a shadow fall over her. She looked up. Florence's face was outlined against the sky, the soft brightness of the clouds making her features dissolve into shadow, extraordinarily lovely.

'I was going through Horace's things,' Florence said, as if there had been no pause in the conversation. 'He went on studying the Face, you know. He'd written a new draft of *Sussex Folklore.*'

Kit stood up, clutching the haversack.

'It was sacred, the Face. It kept the village safe from the – oh, I can't remember the name, the—'

'The thurlath.'

'Yes, that's it. He used to think that was all it was for. But recently he came across a Victorian monograph which said that the Face was more than that. It was a sort of – threshold. Hallowed ground. The villagers used it as we use the church, for ceremonies and rituals and things. Apparently there was a wedding rite, with blood, by the full moon . . . Like Irish peasants jumping through fires together.'

'Really?' Kit said. 'Would you like to get married in front of the Face, at midnight? In green silk, with lily of the valley?'

There was a silence. Then Florence laughed, and took Kit's arm, and swung her round to look at the sinking sun and the largesse of space and air and freedom. As they spun, Kit felt the mass of Florence's belly against her own waist, the warm hardness of it as miraculous as the earth beneath her feet. She had never painted a pregnant woman; probably no gallery would ever exhibit it, if she did, and yet she thought it might be the best picture she would ever paint.

'Tomorrow let's go up to the Face,' Florence said. 'You'll want to sketch it, for your painting.'

Kit heard her own voice say, 'Yes, tomorrow,' and fall silent.

They stood holding on to each other, like survivors after a storm; and the light was as soft as gauze, with the improbable dazzle of an allegorical painting of heaven, so that they could hardly believe it would ever get dark.

Acknowledgements

I am extraordinarily lucky to work with so many amazing people, and most of the time I am very grateful; the only time that I'm not is when it comes to writing acknowledgements, when I start to worry that I can't possibly remember everyone. To make matters worse, I'm writing this sitting in the middle of a sea of boxes full of stuff to move to a new house, balancing my laptop on my knees, and with a raging cold – so if I have forgotten you, please take it as evidence of oversight rather than ingratitude, and let me know so I can apologise and buy you a drink.

Every novel I write seems to go through a different process, with different pitfalls and crises—ahem, I mean challenges. But one constant throughout all of them is my reliance on my brilliant agent, Sarah Ballard, and her endless tact, sensitivity, intelligence and humour. In addition, for this novel I was lucky enough to benefit from the input of Liv Bignold – together you kept me sane and rescued the book from being, frankly, more than a bit of a mess. I will never forget our marathon meeting, and the relief I felt when I asked how long we had, and you said you had both blocked out the whole day . . . Thank you.

Equal thanks should go to my equally brilliant editor, Suzie Dooré, who provided her usual (and inimitable) brand of incisive, wise, rigorous and occasionally hilarious feedback and suggestions, under circumstances that were not usual at all. I hope *The Naked Light* feels as much your baby as our other books together do – it certainly does to me. (And to anyone else reading this, if she taps you on the shoulder and says, 'I edited that!', she is not a random madwoman, she is telling the truth. Blame her if you haven't enjoyed it.)

I am also extremely grateful for everyone else at The Borough Press, who are all consistently talented, passionate, committed and generally a joy to work with. Particular thanks should go to Beth Coates, whose intelligence, generosity and drive made such a difference to the book and its progress; to Jo Thompson, who was a fresh and perceptive pair of eyes at exactly the right moment (and who made me laugh inordinately with the clitoris comments); and to Jabin Ali, who has been a pillar and a rock (and many other metaphors, all of them good). Thanks are due too to Edward Wall, whose sharp-eyed and thoughtful copyediting was exemplary, and everyone else who has contributed to the book or helped it on its way – including, of course, everyone at C&W and Dunow, Carlson and Lerner, especially Eleanor Jackson.

I can never quite believe that I am lucky enough to get covers designed by Micaela Alcaino, who is officially a genius.

Finally, thanks, as always, go to my friends and family. I will never forget how Kris Robertson asked about the progress of my first draft the last time I saw him, and nodded and smiled with characteristic generosity of spirit while I burbled about lesbian sex in the 1920s. I wish I could tell him how much that means to me. But I am very, very lucky to know so many other wonderful, warm, delightful people who support and believe in me; in fact, I'm often overwhelmed simply by how *nice* you all are. All I can say is thank you.

Finally (really finally), a special mention goes to Nick. I love you.